To So Few

Overlord

Books by Cap Parlier:

—

Anod series
The Phoenix Seduction (1995)
Anod's Seduction (2004) [reprint of The Phoenix Seduction]
Anod's Redemption (2004)

—

Sacrifice (2000)
Apocalypse Endeavor (2019)
Indulgence (2021)

—

To So Few series
To So Few – In the Beginning (2014)
To So Few – The Prelude (2014)
To So Few – Explosion (2015)
To So Few – The Trial (2016)
To So Few – The Verdict (2017)
To So Few – Frustration (2018)
To So Few – Deflection (2019)
To So Few – Hunter (2020)
To So Few – Struggle (2021)
To So Few – Overlord (2022)

—

Non-fiction
The Clarity of Hindsight (2016)
and with **Kevin E. Ready**:
TWA 800 - Accident or Incident? (1998)

—

Coming soon from Cap Parlier, To So Few – Victory, the eleventh book of the series novel of flight and a warrior's life is anticipated in 2023.

—

These and other great books available from Saint Gaudens Press
Post Office Box 405
Solvang, CA 93463-0405
URL: http://www.saintgaudenspress.com
Visit Cap Parlier's Web Site at: http://www.parlier.com

To So Few
Overlord

by
Cap Parlier

SAINT GAUDENS PRESS
Phoenix, Arizona & Santa Barbara, California

Saint Gaudens Press
Post Office Box 405
Solvang, CA 93464-0405

Http://www.SaintGaudensPress.com

Saint Gaudens, Saint Gaudens Press
and the Winged Liberty colophon
are trademarks of Saint Gaudens Press

Print edition ISBN: 978-0-943039-65-7
Ebook edition ISBN: 978-0-943039-66-4
Library of Congress Catalog Number - 2022946120

Printed in the United States of America

Dedication

—

This volume of the To So Few series is dedicated
to all of the patriots from the various Allied nations
who served in combat during World War II in defense of freedom.
May God bless the immortal souls of all those who served
and sacrificed.

—

Acknowledgement

—

John Richard continues his valiant efforts to challenge me to do better and to tell a more compelling story. His interest in history always stimulates me to dig deeper into the extraordinary details I have tried to capture in this series of historical fiction stories. I owe John a debt of profound gratitude that can never be repaid for his critical and constructive review of the manuscript. Thank you so very much, John.

The author offers his deepest and sincerest gratitude to former colleagues Barbara McEvoy-Fullmer and Dr. John W 'Jack' Rutherford, PhD (Aeronautical Engineering) for their support, contributions, and permission in sharing the service of their family members in the tapestry of this historical story.

Jeanne remains my steadfast and irreplaceable partner in life. Her support and care sustain my writing. I cannot imagine life without her.

The editors and staff at Saint Gaudens Press continue to amaze me, offering invaluable support and assistance along with incomparable skill and attention to detail.

—

List of Terms

As a consequence of complex, evolving, military operations, a consolidated list of operational code names and abbreviations is provided for the reader's benefit. These are terms used throughout this story, and this is not a comprehensive list for the era.

AEF	Allied Expeditionary Force
AFHQ	Allied Forces Headquarters
AGO	*Apparatebau GmbH Oschersleben Flugzeugwerke* (Machine-making Aircraft Works Company in Oschersleben)
ANGEL	TS-SCI compartment for all classified material associated with listening to German POWs (fictitious code name)
ANVIL	original code name for the Allied Forces amphibious landing at St. Tropez, France [15.August.1944] – later known as Operation DRAGOON
ATA	Air Transport Auxiliary – British aircraft ferry service
ATS	Auxiliary Territorial Service –women's branch of the British Army
AUTUMN MIST	Operation AUTUMN MIST (*Unternehmen Herbstnebel*) – code name for the German winter counter-offensive in the Ardennes Forest region of Belgium and Luxembourg (16.Deember.1944); began known as the Battle of the Bulge; originally known as *Unternehmen Wacht am Rhein* (Operation Watch on the Rhine); name changed in early December, two weeks before execution
AVALANCHE	Allied Forces amphibious landing at Salerno, Italy [9.September.1943]
BAGRATION	Soviet spring offensive of 1944, named for Russian General of the Infantry Prince Pyotr Ivanovich Bagration
BARREL	TS-SCI compartment for all classified material associated with the Operation SHINGLE—Anzio landing (fictitious code name)
BAS	Bainbridge Air Services, Inc. – Drummond's airline company (fictional)
BC	Bomber Command, Royal Air Force

BDST	British Double Summer Time, time shift two hours ahead of astronomical time from 25.February.1940 to 7.October.1945
BIGOT	TS-SCI compartment for Operation OVERLORD planning, documents, photographs, surveys, research, intelligence, and support materials
BODYGUARD	Allied umbrella deception operations plan to coordinate all of the related sub-element deception plans
FORTITUDE	Allied deception operation in support of Operation OVERLORD
QUICKSILVER	Allied deception operation to convince the Germans the fictional First U.S. Army Group (FUSAG) poised for a cross-Channel invasion centered at the Pas de Calais
BOLERO	Allied operation to move, collect, train and prepare the combat forces for the OVERLORD invasion
Boniface	code word used predominantly by the British to refer to ULTRA Enigma decrypted messages
BREAKERS	TS-SCI compartment for all classified material associated with the Soviet post-war intentions and actions (fictitious code name)
CBS	Columbia Broadcasting System –American radio broadcasting network
CEC	Civil Engineering Corps – one of numerous U.S. Army specialty branches of service
CIGS	British Chief of the Imperial General Staff (Army)
CinC or CINC	Commander in Chief, pronounced 'sink'
CINCPAC	Commander-in-Chief Pacific, pronounced 'sink pack'
CINCPOA	Commander-in-Chief Pacific Ocean Areas
CINCSWPA	Commander-in-Chief Southwest Pacific Area
CIRCUS	daytime bomber attacks with fighter escorts against short range targets, to occupy enemy fighters and keep them in the area concerned
CO	Commanding Officer
COBRA	American offensive to breakout of the hedgerow country of Normandy (25.July.1944); also known as the Breakout at Saint-Lô

COI	Coordinator of Information -- the precursor strategic intelligence service of the Office of Strategic Services (OSS)
COSSAC	Chief of Staff, Supreme Allied Command – early OVERLORD planning staff, absorbed by SHAEF
CNO	Chief of Naval Operations
CROSSBOW	Anglo-American effort to counteract German retaliation weapons
D-Day	designated launch day for a military operation; also known as L-Day, and other designators; D-Day is not unique to the Normandy landings
DFC	Distinguished Flying Cross
DNI	Director, Naval Intelligence
DRAGOON	Allied Forces amphibious landing at St. Tropez, France [15.August.1944]
DSC	Distinguished Service Cross
DUC	Distinguished Unit Citation
ETH	*Eidgenössische Technische Hochschule* (Swiss Federal Institute of Technology) in Zürich
ETO	European Theater of Operations
EUREKA	Allied summit conference in Tehran, Iran (Roosevelt, Churchill & Stalin for the first time; immediately after the SEXTANT conference) [28.November – 1.December.1943]
FRANTIC	series of seven shuttle bombing operations conducted by American aircraft based in Great Britain and southern Italy that landed at three Soviet airfields in liberated Ukraine
FUSAG	First United States Army Group – a façade paper unit, part of the Operation FORTITUDE deception campaign in support of Operation OVERLORD
GC&CS	Government Code and Cypher School (AKA Bletchley Park, Station X) [predecessor of British Government Communications Headquarters (GCHQ)]
Gestapo	*Geheime Staatspolizei* (Secret State Police, AKA Gestapo) under the SD and SS
GRIEF	Operation GRIEF (*Unternehmen Greif*) – code name for the German special operations

	campaign in support of the Battle of the Bulge (16. Deember.1944); Germans disguised as American soldiers, using captured and disguised equipment
GUMPS	**G**as-**U**ndercarriage-**M**ixture-**P**rop-**S**peed – pilot's quick landing readiness acronym
Hg	mercury –inches of mercury used to measure air pressure
HMG	His Majesty's Government
HMS	His Majesty's Ship
HUNTER	TS-SCI compartment for OSS air support information and Bainbridge Air Services operations
JONAS	joint Jedburgh team (fictious)
LCVP	Landing Craft, Vehicle, Personnel – an amphibious assault craft designed to beach and offload soldiers and light vehicles via a bow ramp; also known as a Higgins Boat, for the designer/builder
LST	Landing Ship Tank – an amphibious assault ship designed to beach and open bow doors to offload heavy armor vehicles and other heavy equipment
MAGIC	TS-SCI compartment for decrypted messages from the Japanese Purple encryption device
Manhattan Project	Allied nuclear weapons development program
MAP	Manifold Air Pressure – a measure of power for a reciprocating engine
MARKET GARDEN	Allied operation to cross the Rhine River at Nijmegen and Arnhem
MI5	Security Service – British internal security service, roughly equivalent to the American FBI
MI6	Intelligence Service – British Secret Intelligence Service, responsible to collection, analysis, and distribution of foreign intelligence information
MI19	British interrogation service of German POWs
MPH	Miles Per Hour
NKGB	*Narodny Komissariat Gosudarstvennoi Bezopasnosti* ([Soviet] People's Commissariat for State Security) responsible for foreign intelligence operations
NKVD	*Narodny Komissariat Vnutrennikh Del* ([Soviet] People's Commissariat for Internal Affairs) responsible for internal security

NSDAP	*NationalSozialistische Deutsche ArbeiterPartei* – National Socialist German Workers Party (AKA Nazi Party)
OCTAGON	Allied Summit Conference in Quebec City, Canada (12/16.September.1944)
OSS	Office of Strategic Service [predecessor of the Central Intelligence Agency (CIA)]
OVERLORD	Allied Expeditionary Forces (AEF) amphibious, airborne and glider landings in Normandy, France (6.June.1944)
PAC or Pac	-- Pilotless Aircraft -- Pacific
PACCOM or PacCom	Pacific Command
PARAMOUNT	TS-SCI compartment for all classified material associated with the Manhattan Project (fictitious code name)
PhD	Doctor of Philosophy – a high level education degree
POINTBLANK	Allied strategic air forces operations to diminish Nazi German fighter operations
POW	Prisoner of War
PTO	Pacific Theater of Operations
PURPLE	TS-SCI compartment for decrypted messages from the Japanese naval code from the JN-25 device
QF	Quick Firing
RADAR or radar	RAdio Detection And Ranging
RAE	Royal Aeronautical Establishment – British aviation research organization, roughly equivalent to the aviation segment of NASA
RAF	Royal Air Force
RAAF	Royal Australian Air Force
RaLa	contraction of radioactive lanthanum (^{140}La) and a broad, general descriptor for implosion technique experiments within the Manhattan Project
RHUBARB	fighter or fighter-bomber sections, at times of low cloud and poor visibility
RN	Royal Navy
RODEO	fighter sweeps over enemy territory
ROVER	armed reconnaissance flights with attacks on opportunity targets
RPM	Revolutions Per Minute

SA	*SturmAbteilung* (Storm Division) – Nazi Party paramilitary unit (AKA storm troops, storm troopers, or Brown Shirts)
SAS	Special Air Service – British special operations service
SCR	Set, Complete, Radio – a general U.S. designation for a variety of radio frequency units
SD	*SicherheitsDienst* (Security Service) – Nazi Party organization granted state police powers under Hitler regime and the umbrella of the SS; also served as the intelligence service for the SS
SHAEF	Supreme Headquarters Allied Expeditionary Force
SIGSALY	sophisticated secure voice encryption telephone system (AKA X System, Project X, Ciphony I, and the Green Hornet)
SIS	Secret Intelligence Service (also known as MI6 and the Intelligence Service)
SHINGLE	Allied Forces (AF) amphibious landings at Anzio, Italy (22.January.1944)
SOE	Special Operations Executive – secret espionage agency of the Economic Warfare Ministry
SS	*SchutzStaffeln* (AKA Black Shirts) – Nazi Party paramilitary organization under Himmler.
STALEMATE II	amphibious landings at Peleliu, Palau archipelago, Micronesia (15.September.1944) in support of Operation KING TWO
SWPA	Southwest Pacific Area
THUNDERCLAP	staff tabletop simulation exercise to assess the readiness of the Operation OVERLORD amphibious assault plan
TIGER	OVERLORD amphibious rehearsal exercise at Slapton Sands
TS-SCI	Top Secret – Sensitive Compartmented Information
TUBE ALLOYS	British nuclear weapons development program collateral to the Manhattan Project
TWA	Transcontinental & Western Airlines (predecessor to Trans World Airlines)
ULTRA	TS-SCI compartment for decrypted messages from the German Enigma device
U.S.A.	United States of America
USA	United States Army

USAAF	United States Army Air Forces (predecessor of the U.S. Air Force)
USAFFE	United States Army Forces Far East
USAR	United States Army Reserve
USMA	United States Military Academy, West Point, New York
USMC	United States Marine Corps
USN	United States Navy
USNA	United States Naval Academy, Annapolis, Maryland
USO	United Service Organizations Inc. – American nonprofit-charitable corporation provides live entertainment to members of the U.S. Armed Forces and their families
USS	United States Ship
VHF	Very High Frequency radio band
VHF-AM	Very High Frequency – Amplitude Modulation – a type of radio commonly used by aviation units
VHF-FM	Very High Frequency – Frequency Modulation – a type of radio commonly used by ground units
VIP	Very Important Person
VMI	Virginia Military Institute

British honors:

bar	second and subsequent award
CB	Companion, Most Honourable Order of the Bath
CH	Order of the Companions of Honour
CIE	Companion, Most Eminent Order of the Indian Empire
CSI	Companion, Most Exalted Order of the Star of India
DFC	Distinguished Flying Cross
DSO	Distinguished Service Order
FRS	Fellowship of the Royal Society
GC	George Cross

Most Excellent Order of the British Empire

GBE	**Knight** Grand Cross, Most Excellent Order of the British Empire

KBE	**Knight** Commander, Most Excellent Order of the British Empire
CBE	Commander, Most Excellent Order of the British Empire
OBE	Officer, Most Excellent Order of the British Empire

Most Honourable Order of the Bath

GCB	**Knight** Grand Cross, Most Honourable Order of the Bath
KCB	**Knight** Commander, Most Honourable Order of the Bath
CB	Companion, Most Honourable Order of the Bath

Most Distinguished Order of Saint Michael and Saint George

GCMG	**Knight** Grand Cross, Most Distinguished Order of Saint Michael and Saint George
KCMG	**Knight** Commander, Most Distinguished Order of Saint Michael and Saint George
CMG	Companion, Most Distinguished Order of Saint Michael and Saint George

Royal Victorian Order

GCVO	**Knight** Grand Cross, Royal Victorian Order
CVO	Commander, Royal Victorian Order
MVO	Member, Royal Victorian Order

KPM	King's Police Medal
LM	Legion of Merit
MC	Military Cross
MP	Member of Parliament (an elected member of the House of Commons)
OM	Order of Merit
PC	Privy Council – selected advisors to the King/Queen
TD	Territorial Decoration
VC	Victoria Cross

—

Prologue

The year 1943 proved to be a pivotal time for the Allies—the Soviet Union, the United Kingdom, and the United States—as they gained the upper hand against the Axis dictatorships in both the European and Pacific Theaters. The Soviet Red Army stopped the German advance at Stalingrad and began a series of offensives that led to the fall of Berlin two years later. The U.S. Navy handed the Imperial Japanese Navy a terrible defeat during the Battle of Midway in June 1942, marking the end of the Japanese hegemonic expansion. The Western Allies—the United Kingdom and the United States—secured North Africa and Sicily, and began the offensive north on Mainland Italy. They also turned the Italians to the Allied side against the Germans.

More critical to the eventual liberation of Europe and defeat of Nazi Germany, the Western Allies approved Operation BOLERO—the build-up of U.S. forces and material throughout the United Kingdom. President Roosevelt and Prime Minister Churchill selected General Dwight David 'Ike' Eisenhower, USA [USMA 1915] to be Supreme Commander of the Allied Expeditionary Force and to lead the long-awaited invasion of Continental Europe. Operation OVERLORD was in the final stages of planning. To support OVERLORD and other Allied strategic objectives, the leadership approved Operation POINTBLANK—the day and night bombing of German industrial and support facilities, principally the fighter production and operations infrastructure. The daylight heavy bomber raids were taking a terrible toll on the crews in part due to the limited range of the P-47 Thunderbolt and the Spitfire fighters that left the daylight bombers without fighter escort and vulnerable to German day fighters.

President Franklin Delano Roosevelt was serving in his unprecedented third consecutive term. The 1942 mid-term elections reduced his party's share of seats in Congress, but they still held a commanding majority in both chambers. The burden of the nation's economic welfare during the Great Depression and the intensity of war readiness, and the war itself produced a marked effect on the handicapped president's health, which was carefully concealed from everyone. The Lend-Lease Program approved by the president in March 1941 was in full flow, realizing the president's proclamation that the United States would be the great arsenal of democracy. Lend-Lease had been extended to China and the Soviet Union as well. The personal relationship between Roosevelt and Churchill proved vital to the developing war effort.

Prime Minister Winston Leonard Spencer Churchill, CH, TD, FRS, MP for Epping, was approaching his fourth year as King George VI's first minister, the leader of Great Britain, and the nation's coalition wartime government. The two leaders met in August 1941 and signed the Atlantic Charter that committed the two countries to defeat fascism and to the independence of all people; the agreement signaled the end of the British Empire. While Churchill remained deeply involved in military affairs, he spent progressively more time and energy influencing President Roosevelt and ensuring the two nations were coordinated and in synch. Churchill de facto served as the go-between for the Western Allies and Soviet dictator Josef Stalin. He also worked hard to maintain the joint development effort for the highly secret nuclear fission program known as the Manhattan Project or Tube Alloys to the British—the extraordinary physics and engineering program to develop the atomic bomb.

Brigadier General William Joseph 'Bill' Donovan, USA, a Columbia Law School classmate of the president and a Great War Medal of Honor recipient, formed and led the United States' first national intelligence apparatus—the Office of Strategic Services (OSS). In cooperation with the British Secret Intelligence Service (MI6) and the Special Operations Executive (SOE), the OSS began joint training with the British and Canadians. They initiated deployment of agents behind enemy lines in both the European and Pacific Theaters. Donovan utilized his extensive international contacts to recruit agents with special skills and abilities, and to develop the strategic intelligence President Roosevelt needed.

Captain Brian Arthur Drummond, USAAF, elected to waive the 50-combat sortie rotation threshold for U.S. Army aviators and continue his combat service with the 334th Fighter Squadron, 4th Fighter Group, 8th Fighter Command, 8th Air Force. He continued to accumulate combat sorties and time as he approached the fifth year of his service in both the Royal Air Force (RAF) and the U.S. Army Air Forces (USAAF). Brian acquired the callsign 'Hunter' for demonstrable reasons and became a decorated ace fighter pilot during the epic Battle of Britain. Brian was also known as one of The Few, who had served in RAF Fighter Command and survived the Battle of Britain during the summer of 1940, the largest aerial combat event in history. The Battle of Britain also proved to be the decisive battle that handed Hitler's Nazi Germany its first defeat and stopped the imminent invasion of England.

In the spring of 1939, Brian had departed from his childhood home in Kansas when he turned 18 years of age with the assistance of his mentor and flight instructor, Malcolm Bainbridge, who perished in a tragic 1940 winter aircraft accident. Brian crossed the border into Canada and joined the RAF before the war in Europe began. Brian inherited from Malcolm a menagerie of small aircraft known as Bainbridge Air Services (BAS). Two years later, he also inherited a small empire his parents had quietly accumulated with no sign of pretense or privilege. His newly acquired wealth was not sufficient to convince him to leave his fighter cockpit, but the money provided the resources for the Drummonds to expand Standing Oak Farm and begin growing crops to support the war effort. In addition, a hybrid government contract helped to significantly expand BAS. The fledgling airline began operating as a public commercial transportation company but surreptitiously moved OSS personnel around North and South America, Europe and Asia.

The widow Charlotte Grace Palmer, née Tamerlin, had been in the right place at the right time during the summer of 1940 when an unconscious RAF pilot descended under a parachute into the large pond on her farm in Hampshire—Standing Oak Farm. She risked her life and nearly drowned, but she saved the pilot. As she would learn, the pilot was an American volunteer fighter pilot stationed at RAF Middle Wallop, just north of her farm. For her courage and heroic, selfless rescue, King George VI awarded her the George Cross. The pilot was Brian Drummond. Brian felt the connection before Charlotte, but they married two days after Christmas 1940, and their first child, a son Ian Malcolm, came into the world the following June.

Before Malcolm's passing, he had engaged his Great War Royal Flying Corps comrade to assist Brian in reaching the cockpit of the premier British fighter aircraft, the Supermarine Spitfire. Malcolm's war buddy was now Air Vice Marshal Sir John Henry Randolph Spencer, KCMG, DFC, who left England to serve as Air Officer Commanding in Chief No.37 Group, a new RAF fighter group assigned to the Mediterranean Theater. John was also a nephew of Winston Churchill. John's wife, Mary Elizabeth Ann Spencer née Armstrong, gave birth to their first child, a son named Malcolm Brian, who was two months older than Ian. The Spencers and Drummonds held considerable common ground, including a strong and growing friendship that transcended their service.

Squadron Leader Jonathan Andrew Xavier 'Harness' Kensington, CVO, had been best friends and mates with Brian since they were together in flight training before the war began. They served together in the same fighter squadron, No.609 Squadron, during the Battle of Britain. After his latest promotion, Jonathan took command of No.266 Squadron, flying Hawker Typhoon Mk IB fighter-bombers. Jonathan was also an ace fighter pilot and held the distinction of being one of the RAF's designated operational exploitation pilots, having flown all of the British array of captured German aircraft. In addition, the Spencers and Drummonds had been Jonathan's guests at his wedding to Linda Kensington, née Mason, a friend Brian had known almost as long as the American had known Jonathan.

The third member of the trio of RAF fighter pilots, well, at least one former RAF fighter pilot, was Wing Commander Lord Jeremy Robert Kenneth 'Mud' Morrison, Esq., who had served as their flight instructor during the operational training of the two younger pilots. He remained a close friend of both younger pilots. Jeremy's older brother, 'Bobby' Morrison, was the 8th

Duke of Cottingstone. Mud also served a full tour as the commanding officer of No.32 Squadron before being promoted and assigned as the base commander at RAF Hamble, where he met Air Transport Auxiliary (ATA) Third Officer Marilyn Powell. Marilyn served as an American volunteer pilot with the ATA as part of famed aviator 'Jackie' Cochran's contingent of 30 American female pilots preparing to establish an ATA equivalent in the United States.

Trevor Thomas 'Diamond' Andersen served as a special agent in the Special Operations Executive (SOE). He had been serving in the Royal Navy's Intelligence Directorate since he graduated from Cambridge University in 1933 and transferred to SOE in October 1940. Trevor had numerous key intelligence successes, including the successful capture of a vaunted German Enigma encryption device, reconnection with an undercover French Army intelligence officer, participation in a Special Air Service (SAS) attempt to capture or assassinate German general Rommel, and he witnessed the Gestapo capture of the Scholl siblings, leaders of The White Rose—*die Weiße Rose*—with whom he had been working to undermine the Nazi German war effort. As a consequence, Trevor narrowly escaped capture in March 1943, when the Gestapo rolled up the student dissent network.

And so, here begins our story.

—

Chapter 1

You were too fast to live,
too young to die, bye-bye
-- Eagles "James Dean"
Songwriters:
Jackson Browne / Glenn Frey /
Donald Henley / John Souther

Wednesday, 5. January. 1944
USAAF Station 356 (formerly RAF Debden)
Saffron Walden, Essex, England
United Kingdom
08:05 hours

"**P**lease be seated, gentlemen," commanded Lieutenant Colonel Donald James Matthew 'Don' Blakeslee, USAAF, gesturing with both hands, after his introduction by the commanding officer of the 334th Fighter Squadron, Lieutenant Colonel James Averell 'Arnie' Clark Jr., USAAF.

Blakeslee and Clark possessed exceptional records as fighter pilots. Both were double aces, highly decorated for combat, and veteran Eagle Squadron fighter pilots with No.121 Squadron, although neither was a member of The Few. Blakeslee's previous assignment had been as commanding officer of 335th Fighter Squadron.

The colonel waited for the shuffling to vanish. "As I'm sure you're aware, I became the commanding officer of the 4th Fighter Group four days ago. Most of you were part of the Eagles when the group formed up. Two of your number are members of The Few. Thank you, Hunter and Dusty."

Brian nodded in acknowledgment from the back of the squadron operations shack. Dusty simply raised his right hand. Brian knew both leaders, liked them, and witnessed their exploits in the air.

"Winter weather in England has given us a small respite from the rigors of combat, so I want to talk with each squadron individually to make this a little more personal. I have three specific topics I want to discuss, and I am open for questions if you have any." Blakeslee paused as if to allow for questions. None came. "First, events are going to happen fast over the next few months. We must be prepared for to show flexibility for unusual engagements. I'm not at liberty to discuss future operations, but I think all of you have been around long enough to figure out what lies ahead of us. We must play our part. To that end, leadership changes should facilitate a more aggressive fighter stance. General Doolittle has been selected to replace

General Eaker as commanding general of the 8th Air Force, which brings me to my second information item."

Major General James Harold 'Jimmy' Doolittle, USAAF, had been personally selected by the supreme commander to replace Lieutenant General Ira Eaker, who in turn was transferred to the Mediterranean Theater to become commander-in-chief Allied Air Forces. Doolittle had led the famous raid on Tokyo in April 1942 and had risen swiftly to command the 8th Air Force. Eisenhower had recognized Doolittle as a renowned and accomplished aviator, and more importantly, as an aggressive combat leader.

"Last month," Blakeslee continued, "I enjoyed the pleasure of flying a P-51 'B' model. Since that flight and my selection to lead this group, I have been pushing very hard to transition as soon as possible from the Thunderbolt to the Mustang. While the orders have not yet been finalized, I am assured that we will transition in roughly a month. The biggest improvement from the perspective of our primary work is the integral incorporation of an auxiliary fuel system with jettisonable fuel tanks mounted under the wings. Those tanks will enable us to stay with the bombers throughout their operational range. That fact alone will significantly reduce our bomber losses and increase their effectiveness on targets throughout Germany. As with all changes, there are pluses and minuses. We'll have the time to discuss those changes in due course. Oh, one more item on this topic, we should transition into the 'D' model rather than the 'B' model, which means we'll get a bigger engine and a bubble canopy rather than the cage on the 'B.'

"Lastly, on a personal level, Hunter Drummond, front and center."

Brian glanced around rapidly as if the others might have detected some practical joke. *I've got no idea what this is all about.* As Brian approached, Blakeslee gestured for him to stand between the two leaders. Blakeslee continued, "Now, I must confess to my selfishness, but that is the prerogative of a new group commander. These orders were effective on the first of January, but I wanted to do the honors myself. Therefore, on behalf of the president, the chief of staff, the chief of the Army Air Forces, and the commanding general of the 8th Air Force, it is my distinct honor to announce the promotion of Brian Arthur 'Hunter' Drummond to the rank of major." Blakeslee and Clark replaced his epaulet 'railroad tracks' with brand new, shiny, oak leaves of his new rank. Both men shook hands with Brian.

"Drinks are on Hunter tonight," shouted Captain Paul James 'Dusty' Langford, 'Green' Flight leader.

Everyone laughed and cheered. Blakeslee allowed the cheers, congratulations, and light-hearted jabs to go on for several minutes before he nodded his head to Clark, who raised both arms. Brian returned to his seat at the back of the room with lots of back slaps along the way.

"Take your seats, gentlemen," Clark commanded.

Blakeslee waited for quiet to return. "I'm done. What questions do you have for me?"

"We've heard rumors about the P-51, Sir, but none of us have flown it. You have. Can you tell us a little more about the machine?" asked Second Lieutenant Billy Bob 'Boy' Williams, USAAF, from Birmingham, Alabama, the second section wingman in 'Yellow' Flight and 'tail-end Charlie' of Brian's 'B' Division. Boy was the next to youngest squadron pilot, just five months older than Brian.

"I'm not prepared to provide a thorough, detailed briefing, Boy, but I say there are a few notable differences with the Thud. First, it has six instead of eight 50-caliber guns and less armor protection. I've not flown the P-51 in combat, so I can't say for sure, but just those facts alone suggest it has less punch than the Thud. The 51 feels more agile with better turning and comparable altitude performance to the Thud. As with the Spitfires we flew, the Mustang has a liquid coolant system, which adds a vulnerability the Thud does not have. Yet, as I already mentioned, the biggest improvement over the Thud is the drop tanks. The days of leaving the bombers by themselves to deal with German fighters will soon be over."

"Yeah." "'Bout time." "Yea dawgie," came a set of colloquial affirmative comments from the gathered pilots.

"I think we all feel the same about having to bingo at the German border with the Thud. However, I will also say in confidence that we can expect more aggressive instructions and guidance from General Doolittle."

"Why can't they just add drop tanks to the Jugs?" asked Second Lieutenant Jackson 'Horn' Lee of Richmond, Virginia, and the second section wingman in Brian's Red Flight.

"Well, Horn, the best I can say is that option has become a political question. I can't expand on that answer. I suspect the Thud will eventually get drop tanks, but the timing is way off now. The Mustang comes ready-made for the work we have before us." Blakeslee waited for the next question. None came. He swung his arm around the room as if to ask if there were any more questions. Again, none came. "Very well. This weather is forecast to be with us for another day or two, so I shall leave you to your games, magazines, or whatever you do when we don't fly. Good day, gentlemen." The squadron came to attention. Clark left the squadron operations building with Blakeslee.

The rumble of muffled conservations filled the room. Brian leaned his chair back against the wall and closed his eyes as he so often did. *Not much to discuss. Too much missing information. I need to call Charlotte and give her the news before I get distracted by other stuff.* The jumbled conversations served as white noise for Brian as he dozed off.

—

Friday, 7.January.1944
Flower Villa
Route d'Ourika
Marrakech
Protectorat Français du Maroc
16:45 hours

Major General Walter Bedell 'Beetle' Smith, USA, chief of staff of the newly forming Supreme Headquarters Allied Expeditionary Force (SHAEF), was the first to arrive.

"Welcome to my home away from home, Beetle," greeted Prime Minister Churchill.

"Thank you, Sir."

Smith followed the prime minister to the living room of the luxurious villa. Winston gestured for him to sit.

"When does Ike arrive?" Churchill asked straight away.

"The inbound message states that he should arrive on Sunday the 16th."

"Everything ready for him to hit the ground running?"

"Yes Sir . . . at least as a functional staff, but we still have a lot of fleshing out to do."

"Quite so, and not much time to do it. We must jump into finalizing the operations plan promptly. We do not have much time left if we are to execute a spring invasion."

"General Morgan has done a magnificent job with minimal staff, but I can assure you that General Eisenhower fully appreciates the validity of your words."

Lieutenant General Frederick Edgworth Morgan, CB, had been appointed as Chief of Staff to the Supreme Allied Commander (COSSAC) in the spring of 1943. His assigned deputy was Major General Ray Wehnes Barker, USA. The COSSAC staff had been charged with planning Operation OVERLORD—the invasion of Continental Europe.

Churchill smiled at Beetle. "I shall take this quiet moment to say thank you very much for your sacrifice, Beetle. I know Ike invited you to return home for a quick visit with your family. Your contributions to the war effort do not go unnoticed."

"Thank you so much, Prime Minister. That means a lot."

"We are going to have a hectic few months until we get roots down on the Continent. I know you are busy in London, but I am most grateful that you could take a break to represent Ike at this conference. Jumbo and Harold should be here shortly."

General Sir Henry Maitland 'Jumbo' Wilson, KCB, GBE, DSO relieved General Eisenhower as Supreme Allied Commander Mediterranean when the latter was selected to lead the pending OVERLORD invasion forces.

General Sir Harold Rupert Leofric George Alexander, GCB, CSI, DSO, MC, served as General Officer Commanding 15th Army Group, which was comprised of the 5th Army under the command of General Mark Wayne Clark, USA [USMA 1917] and the 8th Army under the command of General Sir Bernard Law 'Monty' Montgomery, KCB, DSO. The entire 15th AG was engaged with German forces on mainland Italy and blocked by the German redoubt at Monte Cassino.

"How are you feeling? How is your recovery?"

"Doing well. Thank you for asking. This dry air works wonders for my health."

"Would I get the same assessment from Lord Moran?"

They both laughed hard, causing Churchill to cough a few times. "I suspect the good doctor may have a slightly different opinion."

"Slightly?"

They both laughed hard again, inducing more coughing by the prime minister. Then, finally, the metallic sound of the door knocker broke the spell.

"It appears the remainder of our foursome have arrived," Churchill said and stood to greet the new arrivals. The four men exchanged familiar greetings and moved directly to the secure map room established by Captain Richard Pike Pim, RN—the prime minister's supervisor of the Defence Map Room.

"Let's get down to business," the prime minister declared as soon as the door closed and before everyone had taken a seat.

Alexander opened the small conference. "The situation at Cassino remains unchanged. Our attempts to dislodge the Germans from the heights have failed, and our casualties mount. The 15th Army Group has insufficient forces to perpetuate a direct assault. However, the pressure to bomb the Abbey is growing. Several commanders are convinced the Germans are using the Abbey for precise artillery spotting, and their artillery has been very effective against our armor and infantry."

"Why am I feeling the butchery of the Western Front?" Churchill mused aloud.

"Because that is what we are facing. This situation is degenerating into a battle of attrition."

"So, you're proposing an end run," Churchill queried.

"Yes," Wilson responded. "We want to land the VI Corps 10 miles behind the Gustav Line at Anzio, which is 35 miles south of Rome."

"Operation SHINGLE."

"Yes Sir. The plan calls for the rapid advance across the coastal plain to cut the German lines of communication that sustain the Gustav Line. We can choke them and divert forces from the Cassino area to amplify the assault forces to breach their defensive line."

Alexander stood, went to the wall map of Italy. He summarized the amphibious assault plan on both sides of the Anzio promontory and coastal village. The objective was to hold the beachhead and reach the Alban Hills southeast of Rome to dominate both primary lines of communication sustaining the German X and XIV Armies. Accordingly, the VI Corps was withdrawn from the 5th Army's combat forces and reinforced with the British 1st Infantry Division. The 8th Army shifted to the west to support the 5th Army.

"Who is the ground force commander?" Churchill asked.

"Major General Lucas, John Lucas."

"Is he up to the task?"

"General Lucas is a capable combat commander, although a bit cautious on occasion," Smith added.

"This plan is audacious. It will work. But, we need bold, not cautious," Churchill proclaimed. Silence blanketed the room for several long seconds.

"Are you suggesting we relieve the corps commander two weeks before we execute the operations plan?" General Wilson asked, looking directly at the prime minister.

Churchill held Wilson's eyes with a scowl and glare. "I don't know the man. I have no history on him. A reinforced corps is going in behind the German XIV Army. They are not untested novice troops we're facing, and they will fight like hell to protect their rear and lines of communication."

"Yes, they will, Prime Minister," responded Alexander. "That is the plan. The Anzio landing will diminish the forces defending Cassino and the Gustav Line, diverting them to deal with the SHINGLE force."

"You will have warships for bombardment support," observed the prime minister, almost musing.

"Thin, but yes," interjected Wilson.

Churchill ignored the comment. "I presume the plan includes coordinated attacks elsewhere to occupy the Germans."

"Yes," Wilson answered. "There will be coordinated attacks by land, sea, and air forces along the Gustav Line and against *Luftwaffe* airfields in central Italy." Wilson pointed at multiple sites of the combined attacks.

"What about air superiority and air support over the beachhead?" he asked.

"We have committed a substantial portion of both the strategic and tactical air forces to the protection of the SHINGLE beachhead," Wilson answered. "I must say the new guided weapons like the Fritz-X and Hs293 make the air defense task more difficult."

"None of this is easy, General. We're taking a helluva risk with precious troops we need everywhere and a cautious commander. That makes me uneasy and nervous. Yes, we must break Cassino and advance." Churchill turned his gaze to the wall map. None of the generals interrupted his contemplation. "Very well. I've spoken my peace. You've your plan and your commander. I shall be on pins and needles that Saturday. I know you'll keep me properly informed of your progress."

The four men adjourned for an extended cocktail hour before dinner. All three generals would spend the night at Flower Villa and return to their duty stations in the morning. Wilson and Alexander would fly back to Italy. Beetle Smith would board a waiting B-17 for the flight back to London. The die was cast.

———

Tuesday, 11.January.1944
USAAF Station F-356
Saffron Walden, Essex, England
United Kingdom
05:25 hours

The nearly full but waning moon offered no illumination due to the heavy, low overcast that darkened the early morning hour. The 334FS pilots gathered in the light and warmth of their operations building. Clark waited for the pilots to situate themselves and quiet down. Finally, after several seconds of silence, he began his briefing.

"Today's mission is another POINTBLANK escort. We are assigned the forward, left flank, top cover position for the 1st Bombardment Wing. One of the wing's bomber groups is assigned to the AGO aircraft factory in Oschersleben, roughly 100 miles west-southwest of Berlin."

The *Apparatebau GmbH Oschersleben Flugzeugwerke* (AGO) had been a German aircraft manufacturing company since 1911. The mainstay of AGO's production since 1941 was the Focke-Wulf Fw190 frontline fighter aircraft.

"What the heck is at this AGO factory that warrants an entire bomber group?" asked First Lieutenant Arnold Samuel 'Salt' Morton, USAAF, from Oakland, California, the second section leader of Brian's Red Flight.

"Focke-Wulf 190s." The statement caused a demonstrative stir among the pilots, but no further questions. "Now, if you misfits would allow me to continue." Arnie chuckled, but no one else did. "As has been our operating plan, we will take off after the bombers and rendezvous with them at altitude prior to them crossing the Dutch coast. We expect them to be at Angels 18 for penetration, although the weather may alter that. We will provide the necessary protection to our fuel limit bingo at roughly the German border. The weather over the target remains good for the bombers. However, the weather here is marginal, and we have marginal weather along the ingress and egress routes, so we need to be prepared for difficulties with the bomber rendezvous. As with other such missions, we are cued up to take off an hour after the bombers to allow them to form up and climb to their penetration altitude. The opening to their launch window is 07:00. We can launch as early as 08:00."

"It's still twilight at that time," observed First Lieutenant Robert Charles 'Sweet' Sweeny, Jr., USAAF, leader of 'Yellow' Flight and an ex-patriot resident of London. Great Britain had been on Double Summer Time (BDST) that shifted time two hours ahead of astronomical time during the duration of the war.

"Does your aircraft not fly without sunlight, Sweet?"

"She flies just fine."

"Then, we'll be ready to launch by seven." Arnie stared at Sweet, and then he scanned the other pilots. "With this weather, we may have some blind flying, so flight leaders make sure your crews follow the penetration procedures. We don't need any mistakes or accidents. Let's be on our toes. Any questions?" None came. "Now, we wait," he concluded and returned to his office.

"The aviator's curse," Salt muttered, and Arnie ignored.

The pilots quickly settled into the waiting routines as they were constrained by winter weather outside. The telephones remained silent, which meant the mission plan would proceed as briefed. Finally, at 07:50, Arnie emerged from his office with his flight gear.

"OK, gents. No calls. Let's mount up."

The sounds of the squadron pilots standing and donning their flight equipment filled the room. They walked calmly to their assigned aircraft, conferred with their crew chiefs, and climbed into their comparatively spacious cockpits of the hulky Republic P-47D Thunderbolt fighters, often referred to as Thud or Jugs.

Brian strapped into his parachute and seat harnesses, connected his oxygen and radio fittings, and completed his pre-start procedures. His eyes remained on Arnie's QP-A Thunderbolt. When the start hand signal came, Brian signaled his division in the same manner.

The 334FS taxied first of the three 4FG squadrons. By the time they completed their pre-takeoff checks and taxied to the runway hold-short line, the entire group's 48 fighter aircraft were lined up with Arnie at the vanguard. Their engines had been at fast idle, consuming precious fuel for nearly 15 minutes. *Something's not right here. They rarely leave us out here like this when fuel and range are so bloody important. What the hell?* Brian took his eyes off Arnie to glance at the tower. *Nothing.* As he returned his sight to Arnie, a red flash in his peripheral vision attracted his attention in time to see the red flare arc high over the field. *Well, that does that.*

Arnie signaled the mission abort. Unfortunately, he had to taxi down the runway to the next taxiway because the taxiway behind him was chockablock full of 13-foot spinning propellers.

By the time they returned to the ops shack, Squadron Operations Clerk Sergeant Julius Roman 'Juli' Ellison had heard from group that headquarters had canceled the mission due to deteriorating weather on the ingress route. The bombers had been recalled. They were done for the day.

Three bomber wings had briefed Mission 59, the day's task to attack numerous primary POINTBLANK targets deep inside Germany. The 1ˢᵗ Bombardment Wing under the command of Brigadier General Robert Falligant Travis, USAAF [USMA 1928], had been assigned to a subset of those targets in Central Germany. The 381ˢᵗ Bombardment Group, one of the wing's assigned bomber groups, was specifically assigned to the Oschersleben factory. One of the heavy bombers in the 381BG formation was the B-17F, serial number: 42-29999, AKA 'Fertile Myrtle' with a triangle 'L' fin symbol and VP-Z tail designator, assigned to the 533ʳᵈ Bombardment Squadron, 381ˢᵗ Bombardment Group. The 'Fertile Myrtle' pilot was First Lieutenant Matthew Joseph 'Matt' McEvoy, USAAF.

Travis missed the recall radio message and led his wing to their targets without fighter escort. The other two bomber wings received the recall and aborted their missions, returning to their bases. Fortunately, the *Luftwaffe* fighter force had chosen not to challenge the ingress, so the missing Allied fighters did not alter the outcome. The Germans were waiting for the American bombers at the border and beyond.

German fighters jumped the bombers en route to the target. The 8ᵗʰ Air Force lost 60 bombers on that Tuesday mission. Of the 60 bombers lost, 34 of those were on the attack on Oschersleben that failed to return, and one of the 34 B-17s was Fertile Myrtle.

The entire crew bailed out successfully. The aircraft crashed near the village of Eicholz, three miles south of Melle and 14 miles southeast of Osnabruck, Germany. German soldiers eventually captured each member of the Fertile Myrtle crew. They were interrogated and transported to *Stalag Luft*

I near Barth, Western Pomerania, Germany, on the Baltic Sea coast. *Stalag* is a contraction of *Stammlager*, which itself is a contraction of *Kriegsgefangenen-Mannschaftsstammlager*, meaning prisoner of war main camp. The *Luftwaffe* operated and controlled a subset of camps referred to as a *Stalag Luft*, or air POW camps for captured air force personnel.

The Red Army reached *Stalag Luft I* on 1.May.1945, after the camp's Senior Allied Officer Colonel Hubert 'Hub' Zemke, USAAF, an 18-victory fighter ace, refused the German commandant's order to evacuate the camp the day before. The Germans abandoned the camp as the Red Army advanced. The Soviets treated the Allied aviators with respect but refused to release them from confinement. It was not until two weeks later that the repatriation process began.

Zemke had been the commanding officer of the 56th Fighter Group since the 8th Air Force arrived in England. He was transferred to command the 479th Fighter Group in August '44 to lead the least experienced fighter group in the 8th Air Force until he was forced to bail out over enemy territory from his damaged P-51 on 30.October.1944.

The men of the 381st Bombardment Group were awarded the Distinguished Unit Citation (DUC) for the Oschersleben raid—the second DUC for the men of the 381BG.

Lieutenant Matt McEvoy was also and more importantly the father of Barbara McEvoy-Fullmer, a colleague of the author at McDonnell Douglas Helicopter Company, now part of The Boeing Company.

———

Friday, 14.January.1944
North Front Airfield
British Overseas Territory Gibraltar
14:15 hours

The twin-engine RAF Dakota standard troop transport aircraft landed with Prime Minister Churchill and his immediate staff aboard. As they taxied to a stop in front of the small terminal building, Winston glanced out the window to see the familiar figure of Governor-General of Gibraltar General Noel Mason 'Mac' MacFarlane waiting for him.

Churchill, dressed in his RAF air commodore uniform, debarked first. He usually traveled under the alias and persona of Air Commodore Frankland. Churchill returned MacFarlane's salute to him as prime minister rather than his persona as a junior flag officer. "Thank you for accommodating our last-minute change, Mac. I'm still not fully recovered from my bout of pneumonia. I could not tolerate the altitude, which made the transit along Occupied France simply problematic."

"We were lucky, Sir. *King George the Fifth* made port yesterday for refueling and resupply. The captain has informed me she is ready to depart immediately once you are aboard."

His Majesty's Ship *King George V* was one of the premier battleships operated by the Royal Navy. Her 14-inch naval rifles were not the largest on the seven seas, but they were still formidable. Churchill was quite familiar with the battleship, having been aboard her numerous times during the war.

"Excellent. Thank you. Have you received any messages for me?"

"No Sir. Not a one."

Winston had not expected any, but the pace of events was increasing. They watched as the baggage was swiftly transferred from the aircraft to a waiting truck. The signal that the transfer was complete caused the prime minister to say, "Looks like they're ready. Let's get me aboard *King George* so that we can be on our way."

"Very well, Sir," MacFarlane replied and gestured to the waiting limousine.

Within two hours, HMS *King George V* was underway behind a fan of her escorting destroyers. They had a two-day, high-speed transit back to Portsmouth ahead of them.

———

Saturday, 15.January.1944
Oval Office
The White House
Washington, District of Columbia
United States of America
16:30 hours

"**G**ood afternoon, Bill. Thank you for your quick reaction. I had an unexpected opening, and your message this morning seemed rather urgent."

"Good afternoon, Mister President. I remain at your service."

The president nodded impatiently for Donovan to sit across the Hoover Desk from him.

"What have you?"

"Bern Station received two German emissaries of a group plotting to execute a *coup d'état*." Roosevelt did not react and stared at his intelligence chief. "They reached out seeking Allied support for their operation. The two army general officers were in civilian attire and indicated they were in the final planning stages."

"What are they asking for from us?"

"They seek immediate recognition when they depose Hitler so that they can sue for peace."

"The Nazis are far thicker than one demented man," the president stated.

"Yes, they are."

"They have Göring, Himmler, Bormann, and all the others, not least of which are the S-S to deal with before they can claim success." Roosevelt lapsed into contemplation that Donovan did not disturb. "Those are the facts. What is your assessment of this . . . this approach?"

"I think the offer is sincere and genuine. It took a lot for those two generals to reach Zürich and the Bern station chief."

"Allen Dulles?"

"Yes Sir."

Roosevelt nodded his head. "I'm sure it did, but the policy of the Allied powers has been and remains unconditional surrender and no separate peace arrangements."

"Dulles made sure they understood that. They accepted that fact. They also suggested an arrangement as we did with the Italians."

"We turned the Italians against the Germans. Who are the Germans going to flip upon against in turn? The Japanese? They would be the only Axis power left."

"The talks did not progress to that stage. Dulles feels the door would be open. The Germans he met with are convinced the war is lost, and they are terrified of the Soviets, who are the real enemy . . . the genuine threat."

"Of course, they do. They poked the bear, and the bear bit back. We must tread very lightly and carefully, Bill. As you well know, the Soviets have accused us of duplicity in our armistice with the Italians. While I heed Winston's apprehensions, I disagree with his assessment of Stalin or Soviet intentions, at least so far. Nonetheless, this gesture is not materially different from that made by Brigadier Castellano on behalf of Marshal Badoglio in August of last year. This brings me to a question I should have asked you a year ago, or at least since the EUREKA Conference in Tehran. How do you feel, or rather what is the O-S-S position on Winston's suspicions of Stalin's motives in post-war Eastern Europe?"

"Mister President, with the deepest respect, I have tried to confine the work of the O-S-S to the facts as best we can gather them and strive to avoid the political arena. But, unfortunately, the O-S-S has very little hard, factual information regarding Soviet intentions, although I must say, we are working very hard to collect those facts."

Roosevelt smiled mischievously and waved his hand dismissively. "I do not have that luxury. I have and still do trust your judgment, Bill. I appreciate your caution, and I don't want to compromise your wise position. But at this moment, I am asking you as a friend and fellow traveler, not as the O-S-S director. I want your personal opinion."

This time Donovan smiled. "You're a wily leader, Mister President. As I've stated many times, I'm at your service. I've known Winston since the Great War. I studied his words during his wilderness years and tested his views during those years. He has an uncanny instinct for the assessment of world events and leaders. He was the first to raise the clarion call of Hitler's intentions before he became chancellor, and he was precisely correct. I think he is doing exactly the same alerting for us now. Stalin has craftily tried to say the correct things to placate our western sensitivities, but he does not share any of our values. He is our ally but as a convenience of war. We need the Red Army to maintain their relentless pressure on the Germans. But we should hold no illusions of any beneficence. He has always been and will always be a street thug. He has personally directed the killing of more Russians than Hitler will ever achieve. Stalin may be our ally, Mister President, and we need him, but he is emphatically not our friend. Thus, to be blunt, I think Winston is quite likely spot on correct, as the Brits like to say."

"That is rather stark, Bill."

"Yes Sir, it is. You asked for my personal opinion."

"Yes, I did, and I thank you for that. Your words give me plenty to consider as we move to victory." Again, the president lapsed into contemplation. Roosevelt turned his chair and stared out the window for several minutes. When he turned back around to face Donovan, he said, "I assume you have created a sensitive compartment."

"Yes Sir. I have opened BREAKERS plural for this matter. At present, only you, Allen Dulles, my deputy Ned Buxton, and myself are on the access list."

Colonel Gonzalo Edward 'Ned' Buxton, Jr., had been Donovan's principal deputy since the Coordinator of Information (COI) days before the U.S. entry into the war. Donovan brought Ned along and kept him as his chief assistant when COI transitioned into the OSS. Buxton and Donovan had known each other since the early creation days of the American Legion in 1919.

"OK. Keep a close eye on this, Bill. Let's keep it very close hold for the time being. I need to confer with Winston, but on this one, it must be eye-to-eye in secure surroundings."

"So it shall be."

"Anything else?"

"Yes Sir, one last item." Roosevelt nodded his head. "As you may recall, Mister President, Ambassador Winant's firstborn son, John Jr., was shot down during a raid on Munster and reported missing last October."

"I remember. A B-17 bomber pilot, as I recall."

"Yes. Correct. We received confirmation this morning, well actually late last night, that he was captured and is incarcerated at Colditz Castle, Colditz, Saxony, about 30 miles southeast of Leipzig."

"How do I know that name?"

"It was the seat of Saxon kings. At the start of the war, the Nazis commandeered the castle to use it as a P-O-W camp. By 1940, they had too many pesky officers who persisted in escaping from other camps. The castle is designated *Oflag IV-C*, which is a contraction for *Offizierslager*, or Officer Camp. They converted the castle to a special officer's camp for escape-prone officers. We do not yet have the details of his capture or why he was sent to Colditz. We have some evidence that Himmler has designated part of the camp under his direct control for special handling of officers. My guess is they know who his father is, and he is one of Himmler's special prisoners."

"I need to remember that detail. I presume Gil has been notified."

John Gilbert 'Gil' Winant was a three-term, Republican, former governor of New Hampshire, who has been U.S. ambassador to Great Britain since the president terminated his predecessor's tenure in late 1940.

"Yes Sir. Our London Station chief informed the ambassador himself."

"I'll write a personal letter to Gil and Constance."

Donovan thought for a second about informing President Roosevelt of Winant's estrangement from his wife and his continuing affair with Winston Churchill's second daughter, Sarah Millicent Hermione Churchill, but the urge passed quickly. The president did not need the complication.

"That's it for me, Mister President," Donovan pronounced.

"Before I let you go, I have a question for you." Donovan waited for the president to continue. "Are you aware of the Paul memorandum?"

"No Sir."

Roosevelt handed Donovan a stapled, 9-page document marked SECRET and titled "*Report to the Secretary on the Acquiescence of This Government in the Murder of the Jews.*" The report was written by Josiah Ellis DuBois, Jr., a Treasury Department attorney who served as special assistant to Treasury Secretary Morgenthau. The document was initialed and released by Treasury General Counsel Randolph Evernghim Paul. "I'd like your opinion of this advance copy of the document." The president turned to other paperwork as Donovan read. Bill re-read several parts before he looked up to the president's waiting gaze.

"This is a most unusual document," Donovan stated.

"A tad of an understatement, I should think. Again, I want your opinion. I want to tap your knowledge of these facts and your view of the situation described in the memo."

"Some facts are beyond my reach and knowledge, but I can corroborate many others. The memo certainly does not paint the State Department in a favorable light. The die was cast in 1939 with the SS *St. Louis* fiasco."

"Yes, but in contrast, Bill, we can't take in all of the world's refugees. Cordell's threshold of tolerance is much lower than mine, but he has been and remains the Secretary of State."

"This memo," Donovan said, holding up the document, "is not just an indictment of Secretary Hull but a goodly portion of his whole department. Nonetheless, at this stage, I think the decision you and the prime minister took in 1942 remains the best course."

"Defeat the Germans as soon as possible?" Various military and special operations options had been repeatedly discussed at the summit level including breeching the camp perimeters enabling escape, to bombing railroad tracks and junctions near the camps to make transfers more difficult. All of the interceding options were deemed to not likely achieve the desired results and could cause unintended significant collateral damage. Winning the war quickly was the best choice.

"Yes Sir. Any other course would require the expenditure of inordinate precious resources on a very low probability of success. From my perspective, I can't see a path that would help the Jews and shorten the war. Therefore, I think the government's policy remains the best course."

"What do you think I should do with that?" Franklin said, pointing to the document still in Donovan's hand.

"Thank him for his exceptional work and diligence. There is no point in debating this matter. We must defeat the Nazis to end their suffering. The Jews are beyond rescue."

"Thank you for your time and opinions, Bill. Keep me current on BREAKERS as it evolves."

"You know I will, Mister President. Have a good rest of the day."

"And to you, Bill."

Donovan departed. President Roosevelt returned to his paperwork.

—

Sunday, 16. January. 1944
Supreme Headquarters, Allied Expeditionary Force (SHAEF)
Norfolk House
No.31 St James's Square
St. James's, London, England
United Kingdom
14:20 hours

"Welcome back, Ike."

"Thanks, Beetle. You've done a magnificent job getting the headquarters up and running. I truly appreciate your sacrifice, and I made sure the president knew about your extraordinary work, Beetle."

"You arrived this morning?"

"Actually, we were four hours late to plan due to weather south of Greenland, but Kay was waiting for me. We landed at Northolt," Eisenhower checked his wristwatch, "a little over an hour ago. She insisted on taking me to the Cottage for a rest after the long flight, but I had to come to see you and Norfolk House."

Kathleen Helen Mary 'Kay' Summersby, née MacCarthy-Morrogh, joined the British Mechanised Transport Corps at the war's outset. She had been assigned as General Eisenhower's driver since he first arrived in England in 1942. Kay had grown to be more than just the general's driver. She had begun to serve as hostess for social events at the Cottage.

Eisenhower retained Telegraph Cottage in Coombe Hill, Kingston upon Thames, London, as his residence while he was in command in the European Theater.

"I've arranged the schedule for tomorrow. You will meet with General Morgan first thing in the morning. He's eager to show you the plan. I've allotted two hours for him to bring you up to speed on the OVERLORD plan as it stands today. After that, you will meet with the staff, such as it is at the moment, at nine. After that, we should have a long chat over lunch on changes and additions you would like us to get in place."

"We don't have much time, Beetle . . . just five months to the landings."

"How were your meetings in Washington, if I may ask?"

"Surprisingly well, I must say, Beetle. I thought I would take some heat for AVALANCHE and ANVIL, but there was not a word from the president, Stimson, or Marshall. Besides the usual social stuff, all of our talks were focused on OVERLORD."

"Understandable."

"They are quite apprehensive about Churchill's fear of stalemate at the beachhead. I've seen that fear many times. It is genuine. We've got to get overwhelming force across those beaches before the Germans can move those armor divisions from Calais to Normandy. My job is to keep the prime minister from freezing with uncertainty. We cannot ignore his fears."

"He won't let us," interjected Smith, causing both of them to laugh.

"And, rightly so. He knows the risks we are taking, and no matter what we do, we will be very vulnerable for the first few hours, days, and weeks. Fortunately, the Navy and Air Force have done their part. It will be show time for the Army in a few months. How is BOLERO?"

Operation BOLERO was envisioned at the TRIDENT Conference in Washington after the U.S. declared war and was planned to build up U.S. forces in anticipation of the approaching moment in history.

"We are ahead of plan, Ike. The assault forces, at least to the current plan, have been in place and training well. The follow-on forces through D+30 are either here or en route."

"We may need to shift the plan depending upon how the first few reviews go."

"I believe the staff knows that, and the Home Office has some capacity to adapt . . . within reason. We are butting up against the hard logistic constraint of assembly and transit across the Atlantic. Our demands are in direct conflict with the Pacific. No matter what MacArthur gets, he wants more."

"As do we." Eisenhower smiled. "But, we have an ace in the hole." His chief of staff's puzzled expression made him chuckle. "Churchill. If we run into obstacles at the War Department, we have but to plant the seed in the prime minister's ear. He will take the argument directly to President Roosevelt . . . with success more likely than not. How is George doing in his assignment?"

Lieutenant General George Smith Patton, Jr., USA [USMA 1909] had been relieved of his command of the II Corps in Sicily for two incidents of him slapping soldiers hospitalized for "shell shock," which the general did not approve of in his command. Trying to make lemonade out of the lemons Patton handed him, Eisenhower assigned him to be the commander of the fictitious First U.S. Army Group in Southeast England, across the Dover Strait from Calais in German-occupied France. Patton was an important, if not essential, player in Operation FORTITUDE, the Allied deception program intended to freeze a dozen German armor and infantry divisions in the Pas de Calais region and away from the Normandy landing beaches.

"I would say he is playing his part perfectly. But, the intel guys will have to validate that he is holding the Germans in place. From the last report I've seen, those divisions continue to train in areas around Calais. So far, so good."

"Excellent. I intend to leave him alone and stay out of his way as long as he does what he is supposed to do and keeps his nose clean."

"We'll keep a close eye on him for you."

"Thanks, Beetle. Now, I think Kay was correct. So I'm going to cut this one short and try to get a good night's sleep."

"We'll hold down the fort for you. See you in the morning."

"Bright and early."

The Cadillac with olive-drab Army marking stood outside the London mansion right where he had left it. Summersby jumped out of the front passenger's seat door and opened the rear door for her charge. Eisenhower stepped into the passenger compartment, and Summersby closed the door behind him.

Once the driver's door closed, the general said, "The Cottage, Kay." He could see her grin in the rearview mirror.

"Yes Sir."

Friday, 21. January. 1944
Office of the Director, Office of Strategic Services
National Institutes of Health Building
2430 E Street Northwest (AKA E Street Complex)
Washington, District of Columbia
United States of America
08:45 hours

One knock on the director's closed door announced the opening and stopped his reading. Ned Buxton stepped in and closed the door behind him. "This was just deciphered," Ned announced as he approached Bill's desk. Buxton handed the single pink paper to Donovan.

TOP SECRET - BARREL

```
NO
OSS INT NR 027
TS 212223Z JAN 44 URGENT
FM 769
TO 939
INFO 109
T O P   S E C R E T   B A R R E L
BT
RELIABLE SENSITIVE SOURCES INDICATE
ENEMY FORCES ASSEMBLING ALBAN HILLS STOP
COUNTERATTACK SHINGLE LIKELY ALBANO RATHER
THAN CISTERNA STOP ADVISE CINC END
BT
NO COPIES
NNNN
```

TOP SECRET - BARREL

"They haven't even landed yet, Ned," Donovan protested.

"We don't have any more information, Bill."

"This went directly to John Croze with the amphibious task force," Bill continued his protest. "What on earth is Tompkins thinking? Does he have evidence the Germans know in advance about the SHINGLE landings at Anzio?"

"You're jumping to a whole bunch of conclusions there, Chief. He only notes the assembly of German forces in the Alban Hills area. Those forces could be gathering to reinforce the Gustav Line. We don't know his sources, but I suspect he has good contacts with the Italian Resistance. We can ping

Peter to ask those questions, but I think he is doing exactly what we put him in Rome to do. There is nothing in his message that even remotely suggests the compromise of operational security for the SHINGLE landings. I read the message differently. Thompkins is providing what he believes is reliable, accurate, source intelligence. When the landings occur tomorrow morning, the Germans will be looking for reinforcements to counterattack the beachhead. Peter only suggests those reinforcements are close by in the Alban Hills and can be rapidly diverted from their intended purpose to an Anzio counterattack."

"I see your point, Ned. The timing surprised me." Donovan thought for a few seconds. "If we query Tompkins, it might cause him to doubt his action. For operational information like this, we do not want to be the clearance and dissemination conduit . . . too slow."

"Exactly."

"Alexander is taking a helluva risk landing a reinforced corps behind enemy lines, but that is the nature of war. Make sure the Italian desk sees this and then file it."

"Do you need to inform the leadership?" asked Buxton.

"This is tactical intelligence applicable to General Lucas. I don't see a strategic dimension. I think not. It's good for the file. I think we can assume that John Croze has informed General Lucas and the corps intelligence chief in an appropriate manner. I'm far more concerned about what Croze does when the landing force pressures him for more information. The O-S-S has done what it was designed to do. It is up to VI Corps intelligence to develop the battlefield situation for the commander."

"Makes sense," Buxton responded.

"Anything else?"

"No Sir. This was the only urgent we've received since last night. The normal traffic should arrive shortly. Do you have anything for me?"

"Nope. We're good, Ned. Thanks."

Buxton departed and closed the door behind him. Donovan returned to his perpetual reading.

—

Friday, 21.January.1944
USAAF Station 356
Saffron Walden, Essex, England
United Kingdom
19:45 hours

It had been a long day of stop & start and waiting until they finally launched in the late afternoon to escort a squadron of B-25 medium bombers on a raid against a railroad marshaling yard at West Ghent, Belgium. The bombers encountered some serious flak, but the fighters stayed well above the bombers. Surprisingly, the attack force saw no enemy fighters going into, at, or leaving the target area. The 334FS stayed with the bombers the whole way and had to make a cloud penetration along with a night landing back at Debden. It appeared the bombers hit their target precisely, but only the bomb damage assessment by post-mission aerial photograph could confirm the result. Several bombers were hit and damaged by the flak, with several wounded, but they all made it home safely. None of the fighters were hit, and all of them landed safely.

As each of them finished their debriefings, they hung up their flight gear on their assigned wall pegs. Then, they loaded on the truck, taking them to the Officer's Mess. The 334FS pilots had barely 15 minutes to make evening meal at the Officer's Mess.

Brian glanced at the message corkboard as he entered the lobby. A folded white paper with his family name prominently lettered on the outside had been tacked to the board along with several others. He stopped to read the message quickly.

January 21, 1944,

Linda K just called. She is heading to Royal London Hospital and the Maternity Ward, seems her baby is on the way. She asked me to attend her. I'm leaving SOF for the hospital. Ian staying here with Edith. Jonathan on the way. Get to the hospital when you can.

C

I can't get there tonight, and I can't reach her. I'll try to make it tomorrow. Brian refolded the message and placed it in his trouser pocket.

The time left them with the odds & ends of what was left in the kitchen. It was not the best of a barely adequate mess, but it was edible and filling. Most of the pilots joined many 4th Group pilots in the bar for a beer with their compatriots. The bar was always loud, smokey, and raucous, usually dominated by laughter, as it was this night.

"Everything OK, Brian?" asked Dusty behind him.

Brian turned to face Langford. "Sure. Why?"

"Messages on the damn board always seem more negative than positive."

Brian chuckled softly. "S'pose so huh, but not this time." Brian retrieved the note and handed it to Dusty, who read it and handed it back to Brian.

"Linda K?"

"Linda Kensington, wife of Squadron Leader Jonathan Kensington, who is the C-O of Two-Six-Six Squadron at Duxford."

"Ah yes, I remember him. He's the bloke who got to fly the bunch of captured German aircraft. He briefed us last March on the Fw190."

"That's him. We've been mates since '39. We served in Six-Oh-Nine Squadron during the Battle."

"Are you going down to see 'em?"

"Charlotte asked me to, and I always do what I'm told."

"Not always." Both men laughed hard, and then they took a good swig from their pints.

"Yeah. I'll talk to the skipper in the morning. Maybe he can let me knock off a little early. She doesn't ask me for stuff like that unless she feels it's important. Shoot, just seeing her would be great. I've not been able to get to the farm since Christmas, and the last I've seen her was New Year's."

"Good luck. Nice to have a cakewalk for a change today, huh?"

"Yeah. Not quite the intensity we faced during the Battle, but hey, flight time is flight time."

"What do you think about the upcoming transition to the Mustang?"

"I think Blakeslee gave it to us straight. Of course, there will be pluses and minuses, but it's a good lookin' bird more like the Spit than the Jug." Pilots and mechanics referred to the P-47 Thunderbolt by a variety of nicknames, one of which was 'Jug." The name was often attributed to a contraction of juggernaut, or the aircraft's appearance if stood on its nose, or acknowledgement of the twin banks of nine air cooled cylinders the mechanics called jugs.

"But, one less gun per side and less armor. The Thud's armor has saved both of us more than once."

"True. Perhaps the better performance will keep us from needing that armor. I certainly look forward to flying it, to getting a good feel for the machine."

"Yeah, me too. The 'D' model has a better look than the 'B,' and that bubble canopy should give us better eyes."

"Agreed." Brian finished his beer. "I'm going to call it a night. This damn smoke burns my eyes. I can only take so much."

Dusty drained his glass. "I'm with you."

Both pilots left the bar and climbed the stairs to their rooms. They said good night and split. Brian decided to take a shower to wash off the dried sweat from the day's mission and especially the stench of cigarette smoke that saturated everything.

—

Saturday, 22. January. 1944
Anzio beachhead
Italy
03:25 hours

Operation SHINGLE began in the dark with H-Hour met on time at 02:00. The initial landings had been carried out in two major segments. Task Force X-Ray comprised of the U.S. 3rd Infantry Division assaulting across Red and Green Beaches to the south of Nettuno and the 6615th Ranger Force assaulting Yellow Beach between Anzio and Nettuno. The other segment, Task Force Peter comprised of the British 1st Infantry Division assaulting across Red, Yellow, and Green Beaches north of Anzio.

Morning nautical twilight had not lightened the eastern horizon, and the assault forces had encountered very light resistance. The Rangers quickly secured the coastal villages of Anzio and Nettuno. Even in the dark, they found most of the defense works not manned, and the resistance they did meet was neutralized in short order. They still had more than two hours until dawn, and the landings were progressing faster than planned. The early results suggested they caught the Germans completely by surprise.

With the alert from the OSS field agent in Rome, II Corps Intelligence was keeping a very close watch on the approaches to the beachhead, especially from the Alban Hills area to the northeast of the Anzio beachhead. The interrogation of the captured German infantrymen indicated a single infantry company had been assigned to defend the entire beachhead area. Everyone from General Lucas on down knew that the beneficial situation would not last long.

The plan and early results offered such great expectations.

—

Saturday, 22. January. 1944
Royal London Hospital
Whitechapel Road
Whitechapel, London
United Kingdom
17:15 hours

Colonel Clark had been surprisingly generous. The squadron had been on alert standby all day for a backup mission that never materialized. Brian had been released in mid-afternoon and allowed him to return by noon tomorrow. Sweet Sweeney's Yellow Flight would lead 'B' Division with Salt Morton leading Red Flight behind Sweeney if they were scrambled for any reason. The potential was low, but there was always the possibility.

The train ride into London's Liverpool Station had been on time, smooth, and uneventful. A short two-stop ride east on the London Underground's Hammersmith & City Lines from Liverpool Station took him to Whitechapel Station. The hospital stood just across Whitechapel Road from the Underground exit.

An elderly man with longish all white hair and disheveled attire sat behind a desk in the virtually empty lobby with some bomb damage from The Blitz three years ago still not fully repaired and restored. "Welcome, Sir. May I help you?"

"Yes Sir, you may. I have been informed that Mrs. Linda Kensington has delivered a baby girl into this troubled world."

The receptionist held up his right index finger and then consulted a binder full of pages. "Kensington, you say?"

"Yes Sir."

He leafed through the pages to presumably the 'K' pages. "Here we go, Sir. Kensington, Linda, yes Sir. She was admitted to the Maternity Ward yesterday and delivered a baby girl, name unknown at present." The man stepped gingerly from behind his desk to a long wide hallway to the left. "The Maternity Ward is on the ground floor at the end of this corridor," he said, gesturing with his right arm. "A nurse inside the double doors will assist you from there."

"Thank you kindly, Sir."

"Thank you so very much for your service, Major."

Brian nodded his head in recognition and walked down the hallway. Inside the swinging double doors, he needed no guidance, hearing laughter from a small group gathered around the fourth bed on the right. Brian pointed to the group. The nurse nodded her head. He had taken only four steps when Charlotte burst from the group and ran toward him. Brian spread his arms, and she leaped into his waiting arms. Holding her off the floor, Charlotte displayed no modesty as she kissed her husband passionately in the middle of the 20-bed ward that was only a quarter in use. They exchanged whispers of affection and yearning as they remained joined.

"We're going to need another bed in here in nine months with the way you two are carrying on," Jonathan said loudly enough for the whole ward to hear. He was halfway to his compatriot. Charlotte did not let go and held Brian tightly.

Holding her with his left arm, Brian extended his right hand to Jonathan. They shook hands. "Sorry, mate. I seem to have this woman attached to me." They all laughed, including Charlotte, who eventually loosened her grip on him. He lowered her to the floor. "Congratulations, Daddy."

"Thanks, mate. She's a gorgeous baby girl like her Mum. Would you like to see her?"

"Sure."

They walked to Linda's assigned bed. Jonathan's younger sister, Doctor Rosemary Alice Kensington, MD, turned to Brian. He started to kiss her cheek when she swiftly turned her head to kiss him on the lips.

"It is so good to see you again, Brian."

"And you, Doctor Kensington."

"Oh stop. You know better."

Brian turned to see Linda, who appeared no worse for the wear, holding her swaddled infant. "Oh my, Linda, you are gorgeous as ever."

"Why are all of you flyboys such fibbers?' Linda protested with a giggle.

"It's the God's honest truth, my dear," he said as he leaned over and kissed her cheek. "My goodness, she is such a beauty." Brian leaned down to smell and kiss the sleeping baby's forehead. "Um, um, um, the sweet smell of youth." He looked up to Linda's admiring eyes. "Julia Carly, I hear?" Brian whispered.

"Correct."

"You two have done well."

"Thank you, Brian. Now, my challenge is getting everything back in place with an absentee husband."

"I know your pain, sister," Charlotte added, causing laughter from everyone, although young Julia remained soundly asleep.

"What sort of frivolity do we have here," stated George Kensington, Jonathan's and Rosemary's father, with his wife Theona beside him. Greetings passed between everyone. No introductions were necessary. Theona gently lifted Julia from Linda's arms. Grandmother rocked her granddaughter gently and doted on her. It had been over two years since Brian and Charlotte had seen George and Theona at the marriage of their son & daughter-in-law.

George, Jonathan, and Brian chatted, bringing George up to date on a summary of changes in Brian's life since Jonathan's wedding in July 1941. The Kensington businesses were doing quite well.

Holding and rocking Julia, Theona returned to the bedside and asked Linda, "Are your parents coming, dear?"

"Yes, tomorrow. My Da had to work today. They should be here tomorrow morning."

"Excellent. I look forward to seeing them again. How are you feeling, dear?"

"I'm still quite sore, but things seem to be settling down more swiftly than I anticipated."

"Excellent. Are you letting down for Julia?"

"Yes, Mum. It was a little tortuous yesterday, but the little bugger seems to be voracious and drawing nicely now."

"Excellent, yet again. You are so much ahead of me with either of the children."

"And ahead of me as well," Charlotte added.

"What no good are you reprobates up to?" came the familiar voice of Mud Morrison before he appeared from behind the drawn side curtain with Marilyn on his arm.

Brian and Jonathan greeted their new arrivals and their former flight instructor in the mandatory RAF flight training unit. Introductions were completed since Theona and George had not met Jeremy and Marilyn before this evening. Once complete, the ladies gathered around Linda to chat and fawn on the new mother.

"My God," Brian proclaimed, lifting the right sleeve of Jeremy's uniform tunic displaying the four stripes of a group captain on his sleeve. "Congratulations, Sir. When did the promotion come through?"

"Before I answer that query," Mud said, "congratulations to you, Major." Brian nodded his head as he waited for his answer. "Ten days ago."

"New assignment?" Jonathan asked.

"Yes, indeed. I am now the deputy controller at Fighter Command in Stanmore."

"Back into the thick of things," Jonathan commented.

"So it seems, gentlemen, and I use that term loosely. It is not quite the intensity of 1940, but operations keep us busy directing the complex air traffic over England."

"Did you move from Hamble to Stanmore?" Jonathan asked.

"We retained the house and property in Hamble," answered Jeremy. "The property is just too good to let go. We have a magnificent view of The Solent—the estuary between the Isle of Wight and the mainland south of Southampton. Marilyn is still flying, probably until production begins to taper off toward the war's end. I'm at Bentley Priory for days and weeks, and I leased a small flat not far from the Priory. We try to see each other at one place or the other whenever one of us gets a break."

"Like all the rest of us," Jonathan added.

"Yeah," contributed Brian. "This evening is the first I've seen Charlotte since New Year's."

"These are the times in which we live."

"Won't last forever."

"Indeed. The Allies landed a substantial force behind enemy lines early this morning," Mud announced softly, "to break the Gustav Line in Italy. Hopefully, that will be the breakthrough we need to secure Rome and Italy."

"That's news," George offered.

"Yes, it is, Mister Kensington, but the facts have been released to the press, so you should see it in the newspaper or on the wireless tomorrow."

"What about France?" asked George.

"I can't . . . none of us can . . . talk about that one. But, I think that eventuality it will be easy enough to deduce."

The ward's head nurse interrupted the reunion surrounding the Kensington birth. "Excuse me, Group Captain, but I'm afraid we are well past visiting hours. I must ask everyone to leave. Our new mother needs her rest, and Baby Julia will need feeding soon."

The group said good night to Linda and waited for Jonathan to give his wife a good night's kiss. Then, they all walked out together. All of them were spending the night at Hawley House, just a block away from the hospital. An evening pint or two at the corner pub kept the entire group together for another hour or so. Theona was the first to break, and the rest of them followed suit. Charlotte already had their room. Once the door was closed on their room, they tended to their conjugal needs and talked between sessions into the wee hours of the morning. Before they gave into sleep, they agreed to visit Linda after breakfast to wish her well before heading to the Underground. Brian would head back to Liverpool Station and Debden, while Charlotte would head to Waterloo Station and Winchester. Brian had not seen Ian, but a father's reunion with their son would come soon enough. *But Momma sure did feel good.*

———

Chapter 2

No man can be ignorant that he must die,
nor be sure that he may not this very day.

-- Cicero

Thursday, 27.January.1944
No.10 Downing Street
Whitehall, London, England
United Kingdom
15:15 hours

Lieutenant General Sir Hastings Lionel 'Pug' Ismay, KCB, DSO, held many positions that ultimately boiled down to military liaison to the prime minister. Among his official assignments were Principal Assistant to the Minister of Defence (Churchill), Secretary of the Imperial Defence Chiefs of Staff Committee, and Deputy Secretary of the War Cabinet.

"Yes, Pug. What have you?" Churchill said, looking up from his reading material.

"Communications just heard a general public wireless broadcast by the Red Army declaring that they have broken the German siege of Leningrad after 880 days, according to the broadcast. The Soviets claim the Germans have withdrawn in part, but not yet in toto."

"Three cheers for the Red Army," the prime minister said, pumping his right fist in the air three times. "Hopefully, the Red Army has brought medical treatment teams and plenty of supplies. The inhabitants of Leningrad have been desperate for a very long time. Some died of starvation during the siege."

"I will make appropriate, discreet inquiries to Broadway House," Ismay said, referring to the headquarters of the Secret Intelligence Service (MI6) at No.54 Broadway in Westminster.

"Yes, please do, Pug. Ask what you wish. I would like to know the condition of the people and the efforts to bring them back to health. I would also like to know their estimate for the siege to be completely broken, and the Germans pushed back beyond the suburbs and the surrounding villages."

"I will see to it first thing in the morning."

"That should do nicely. There is no rush. The Red Army has had the upper hand since Stalingrad. I can feel the end, Pug . . . finally. Leningrad is a long way from Berlin, but I am gaining confidence by the day of our inevitable victory. But, I must confess, Pug, these days, I worry much less about our ultimate victory than I do about what post-war Europe will look like. It is my biggest worry, if I must say."

"Quite understandable, Sir."

"And, to make matters worse, I sense that Franklin listens . . . but he does not believe. He has not told me so yet, but I sense that he believes he can connect with Uncle Joe and turn him away from his hegemonic plans. I have to tread lightly, or I fear he will turn me off. He certainly does not see the Soviets in the same terms I do. As you recall, I was particularly perturbed by the president belittling me, the Kingdom, and our empire to ingratiate himself with Stalin at Tehran. He apologized but not sincerely from my perspective. We must work with Uncle Joe. We need the Red Army to pound away on the *Wehrmacht*. The Germans, from *der Führer* on down to the common citizen, are far more fearful of the Russians and specifically the Communists. Consequently, they have no choice but to focus the majority of their field resources on the Soviets to our benefit."

"Yes Sir, but they still have several full-strength *Waffen-SS Panzer* divisions at Calais. They are fully equipped, rested, well-trained, disciplined troops. Worse yet, they all have that damnable Tiger tank with its terrible 88 main gun."

"The Sherman is no match."

"Exactly . . . by any metric."

"Then, we must ensure we freeze those tanks at Calais until we can get sufficient forces ashore to deal with them."

"COSSAC has done their part with the deception units. General Eisenhower's assignment of General Patton to the task has been a godsend to that end."

"Yes, it has. General Patton is playing his part to perfection . . . so far."

"I know General Smith is exceptionally sensitive to that aspect, and I presume General Eisenhower is as well."

"I've not talked with Ike about that particular topic as yet, but I must. From prior discussions with our new supreme commander, I believe he is as well. Do you have anything else for me, Pug?"

"No Sir."

"Very well. Would you be so kind to ask Mister Peck to send in Mister Kinna? I need to dictate a letter of congratulations to Uncle Joe for their success at Leningrad."

John Peck had been and remained one of four private secretaries assigned to the prime minister's office. Peck had the duty this day.

Patrick Kinna served Winston Churchill as his chief stenographer and typist. The prime minister had come to rely upon his demonstrated and accomplished skills.

"Yes Sir, straight away," Ismay responded and departed.

Thursday, 3.February.1944
Oval Office
The White House
Washington, District of Columbia
United States of America
10:55 hours

President Roosevelt had dispensed with the first two appointments and used the resultant free time to work on his inbox. A single knock on the curved office door usually announced the arrival of his chief of staff. The president looked to the door in time to see Admiral William Daniel Leahy, USN [USNA 1897], enter and close the door behind him.

Leahy held an illustrious history. He had served a full career in the Navy that culminated with his service as Chief of Naval Operations (CNO) from '37 to '39. After retirement, President Roosevelt appointed him to be governor of Puerto Rico until the president asked him to be U.S. ambassador to Vichy France. The United States tried to maintain diplomatic relations with the Vichy government, but those tenuous relations broke down when fascist sympathizer Pierre Laval became prime minister. The U.S. government recalled Leahy in protest. Upon return to the United States, President Roosevelt appointed Leahy to be his chief of staff and recalled him to active duty.

"I needed to catch you before your 11:00 appointment," Leahy announced.

"Something serious?"

"Yes Sir, I'm afraid so. We just received a message from PacCom. This morning's casualty report listed Private First Class Stephen Peter 'Hoppy' Hopkins, USMC, as killed in action on Roi-Namur—an island in the north part of the Kwajalein Atoll in the Marshall Islands. He served with Able Company, First Battalion, 24th Marines. Young Hopkins was just 18 years old."

"Dear God above. Does Harry know?"

"Yes Sir. I told him to take as much time as he needs to grieve and make the arrangements the family wishes. It will likely take a few weeks for his remains to make it back here."

"I need to send a personal note of condolence to Harry and Diana. I must also send a note to Ethel Gross, his mother. Hoppy was the youngest of their three children. He was just four years old when they divorced in '29, but they've remained close. I think she is living in Scarsdale. I'll ask Grace to confirm her current address."

"I'll take care of it, Mister President."

"It's every parent's worst nightmare...losing a child," Roosevelt muttered.

"Yes Sir, and we all have children serving in these troubled times. Fortunately for me, my son William is serving in the Bureau of Ships here in Washington."

"And doing a smashing job as head of the Landing Craft Section."

Leahy nodded his head in acknowledgment. "We know the risks, and yet, the silent fears persist."

"Indeed."

"One more item, Mister President. The anticipated German counterattack on the Anzio beachhead began this morning. So far, they are holding the line."

"It was a gamble, a serious gamble."

"Yes, it was, just as Normandy is another more serious gamble ahead of us."

"Quite so. Winston sent me a personal two days ago. The first full-up review of the OVERLORD plan with the British chiefs didn't go well. His most serious objection was the woefully inadequate assault forces—his words. According to Winston, Eisenhower agreed. They are looking for more landing craft and shipping. Winston wants to double the initial landing force at least."

"I don't know Mister Churchill as well as you do."

"He has uncanny instincts. My inclination is to trust his judgment," the president responded.

"With your permission, Mister President, my instincts would be to ask our new commandant for his review and counsel as the plan exists today."

"Vandegrift?"

Lieutenant General Alexander Archer 'Archie' Vandegrift, USMC, had become the 18th Commandant of the Marine Corps a month earlier. The president had awarded him the Medal of Honor for his leadership of the 1st Marine Division during the Guadalcanal campaign.

"Yes Sir. If there is anyone who knows amphibious assault operations, it is Archie and his Marines."

"That's a good idea, but you must ask him to do so with the utmost discretion. The last thing we need at this stage is for the Army and, more importantly, Ike, to think we are second-guessing him. But, I think you're correct. He'll give us a good metric."

"Very well. I'll go talk to Archie privately and personally. He'll give you a good reading."

"Thank you, Bill."

Leahy left the Oval Office and the president returned to his reading. Bill stopped at the desk of Grace Tully, private secretary to President Roosevelt.

"Grace, would you please confirm Ethel Gross's current postal address for the president."

"Yes Sir."

"He wants to send his condolences to Hoppy's mother."

"Of course, Sir. Right away."

Leahy returned to his office to tend to his work.

Wednesday, 9.February.1944
USAAF Station F-356
Saffron Walden, Essex, England
United Kingdom
08:10 hours

All the 334FS pilots had been outside in the light rain yesterday afternoon, as the ferry pilots brought three squadrons worth of brand new North American P-51D Mustang fighters to Debden. The last bunch had been designated for the 334FS. The maintenance crews worked through the night to perform their acceptance checks, paint the required markings, and validate the precise convergence of the wing-mounted machine guns for each pilot. Brian liked his guns set to 500 yards, the middle of the range, giving him the best convergence and the best spread when he needed it.

Each crew chief called to report when his aircraft was ready for the assigned pilot. Six of the pilots had already gone when Brian's current crew chief, Sergeant Larson Tomlinson from Wichita, Kansas, notified him. Brian had been with Tomlinson for nearly a year. Larson had worked for Clyde Cessna before the war, and they continued to trade stories about Clyde Cessna and Walter Beech when they found a free moment. Brian stood outside in the cold air dressed in his full winter flight gear and watched Tomlinson tow the shiny silver aluminum fighter with the squadron's 'QP' designator and his 'G' assigned letter painted on the empennage. The spinner and rudder had been painted bright signal red. *She's a beauty.*

Pilot and crew chief slowly walked around the new machine. Brian did not need to see under the cowling but knew from the flight manual that a Packard V-1650-7 Merlin powerplant was bolted to the airframe under the sheet metal. The engine was based on the Rolls-Royce Merlin engine drawings given to the United States during the Tizard Mission in 1940 and subsequently updated to the Merlin 66 configuration. All 1,490 horsepower drove a Hamilton-Standard, four-bladed, 11-foot diameter, hydraulically operated, constant speed propeller.

"I like the red spinner," Brian observed.

"Yes Sir, group directive. 3-3-5 has white, and blue for 3-3-6," Larson offered.

Brian listened as Larson conveyed what he knew about the new machine. He understood virtually all of it from his flight manual, but Brian did not want to interrupt or disturb the pride Larson took for the new airplane in his charge.

Before they stepped onto the left wing root, Tomlinson asked, "How long will you be out?"

"Depends on what I find. I suspect an hour or so, but I'll give her a good wring out. We were lucky to get one check flight. The skipper had told us we would likely have to learn on our first mission, so all of us are grateful for a non-combat flight."

"From my perspective, she's in great shape. I'm confident she'll meet your expectations, Major."

"Thanks, Larson," Brian responded as he climbed up on the left wing.

Tomlinson followed Brian and assisted him with strapping into his parachute and seat harnesses, and then he held his radio and oxygen fittings for him to ensure they were correctly engaged.

"Thanks, Larson. I'm going to take my time since it is my first opportunity in one of these, so relax. I'll give you a whistle when I'm ready to fire her up."

"Sure thing, Major. I'll be ready when you are."

Brian touched every switch, knob, handle, and control in the cockpit. He stepped through the pre-start procedures a couple of times slowly to imprint each step and his actions. At the first start of the day, the procedures called for the propellor to be turned by hand through four blades prior to start. Brian signaled by hand for Tomlinson to pull the propeller through as required. When complete, Larson stood in front of the left wing with the large fire extinguisher hand cart and gave Brian a thumb's up.

Brian held the primer switch down for four seconds since the engine was cold. He shouted, "Clear!" to warn anyone near the big propeller that he was going to start the engine. Again, Larson gave him a thumb's up. Brian pushed and held the starter switch. The whirr of the starter motor accompanied the turning of the propeller. He moved the Mixture Control lever to RUN. The engine sputtered a couple of times and fired off, producing a blue-gray cloud of unburnt fuel that was swiftly blown away by the propwash. Brian quickly checked the oil pressure. *Coming up nicely. In the green.* The engine was running smoothly, purring comfortably. Brian adjusted the RPM to about 1,200 to allow the oil temperature to reach 40°C. While he waited for the oil to warm up, Brian switched on his radio and pipsqueak (the British designation for the identification transponder). *Suction gauge? In the green.* Brian checked remainder of his gauges. *I'm ready.* He gave Larson the chocks out hand signal. Larson held up both wheel chocks to confirm the aircraft was free, and then saluted. Brian returned the salute, depressed the toe brakes, and released the parking brake.

"Carmen, Pectin Red, taxi to runup."

"Pectin Red, Carmen, you are cleared to taxi to the runup area for runway one seven."

Brian dropped his heels to the deck, releasing brake pressure, and gently advanced the throttle to move forward. As he moved away from his parking spot, he unlocked the tail wheel and tapped the right brake to turn down the taxiway. With the engine oil temperature and pressure in the normal range, Brian checked his propeller control and magnetos, and then configured the aircraft for takeoff. Trim. *Set. Rudder five right. Aileron zero. Elevator two up.* Altimeter. *Set, three zero zero two.* Controls. *Free and clear.* Flaps. *Set Ten degrees.* Prop. *Full increase.* Mixture. *Run.* Supercharger. *Auto.* Radiator control. *Auto. Ready.*

"Carmen, Pectin Red, ready for takeoff."

"Pectin Red, Carmen, winds one nine five at seven. Cleared for takeoff runway one seven."

"Pectin Red, cleared for takeoff one seven."

Brian checked the approach for the runway in both directions. *Clear.* He taxied into position on the centerline, and then checked his controls and gauges one more time. *Let's do this.* Brian released the brakes, dropped his heels to the deck, and smoothly pushed the throttle forward about halfway—35 inches Hg. The aircraft accelerated nicely. The tail rose gracefully. As the rudder became effective, Brian applied rudder to keep the plane on the centerline as he advanced the throttle smoothly to takeoff power—61 inches Hg at 3000 RPM. *Airspeed's alive. 80 MPH.* The aircraft bounced once and jumped into the air, accelerating well. Brian held the aircraft just above the runway, raised the landing gear and flaps. He glanced at his gear light. Green. At the upwind end of the runway, Brian pulled back on the stick. The nose came up to 30°. He held the angle to 1,000 feet, rolled inverted, pulled the nose down to level, rolled upright wings level, pulled the throttle back to 48 inches Hg, pulled the prop handle back to 2,700 RPM, and then pulled the nose up to 10° to continue his climb.

"Pectin Red, Carmen, nicely done. Switch to Sector."

"Switching." Brian pushed his number two button on the radio. He checked into Sector Control and was assigned an area and altitude band for his check flight.

Brian exercised the aircraft through the full speed range, progressively harder turns, various aerobatic maneuvers, and then spent some time with stalls. He executed several spins to feel the aircraft and the recovery process. While no fighter pilot wanted to stall or spin his aircraft, that was always a potential during aggressive maneuvering in aerial combat. Brian also requested and received clearance to the aircraft's service ceiling of 36,900 feet. The aircraft controls became a bit mushy at high altitude, but he still had reasonable control and still had some performance margin. He performed a series of dives to maximum speed with rolling pull-outs left and right. Back in his assigned airspace, Brian lowered and raised the landing gear and flaps. He completed basic maneuvering to feel the aircraft in the landing configuration. Satisfied with his foundational feel for the airplane, he requested a return to Carmen. The scattered clouds made the return easy. Once he was in sight of the tower and cleared to land,

Brian slowed to 170 MPH, lowered the landing gear, and checked the green light on to indicate his wheels were down and locked. The airspeed indicator told him he was already below 165 MPH. Brian lowered the flaps to full down. He lined up on runway 17 and slowed to 115 MPH.

Brian remembered the last safety check Malcolm Bainbridge had taught him from his very first flight at the controls—GUMPS. Gas. *Fuel balanced. Selector on right-wing tank.* Undercarriage. *Down, green light on.* Mixture. *Run, full rich.* Prop. *Full increase.* Speed. *115 and steady. Ready to land.* Brian pulled the throttle back to idle as he crossed the threshold and gently arrested his descent rate. He held the fighter just off the runway as the aircraft slowed and let the machine settle onto all three wheels simultaneously.

Once clear of the runway and with clearance to taxi back to parking, Brian opened the canopy to the cold air, moved both radiator switches to Open, raised the flaps, dialed the trim wheels to zero, and switched the fuel boost pump Off.

Tomlinson directed him with hand signals into his parking spot. With the parking brake set, Brian switched off his electrical equipment, his oxygen, unsnapped his oxygen mask, secured the generator, and moved the Mixture lever to Cutoff. The engine slowed smoothly to stop. Brian switched the battery off, and then he began unbuckling from his seat and parachute harnesses.

Sergeant Tomlinson waited for Brian on the ground behind the left wing. "She was perfect, Larson. Feed her, brush her, and put her to bed."

Tomlinson chuckled softly. "Yes Sir."

A couple of the squadron pilots were still waiting for their check flights. Of those who had flown, Brian joined the unanimous opinion that the Mustang was a sweet machine with superior combat qualities. Many wanted some target practice, but Arnie told them they were lucky to get an acceptance check.

———

Wednesday, 9.February.1944
Supreme Headquarters, Allied Expeditionary Force (SHAEF)
Norfolk House
No.31 St James's Square
St. James's, London, England
United Kingdom
16:30 hours

The staff planning review had been completed and adjourned. The prime minister and the British chiefs of staff had attended and participated vigorously. At least, they had an executable plan, although the opinions were unanimous that while executable, they were not ready. Unit training was progressing well, but they were behind schedule on amphibious landing practice. The airborne jump training still needed some work, and they had not yet advanced to nighttime jumps, which they had to master to support the plan.

As the meeting broke up, Chief of the Imperial General Staff Field Marshal Sir Alan Francis 'Brookie' Brooke, GCB, DSO & bar, had asked for a private word with General Eisenhower. The two senior Army generals retired to the supreme commander's corner office and closed the door. Ike gestured to the facing couches for a more informal discussion.

"I must say, Ike, I do believe you summarized the plan quite well," Brooke began.

"Thank you. The fellows have done exceptionally well since our last review."

"I do agree."

"But, there is more on your mind," Ike interjected.

"Yes, there is." Brooke paused. Eisenhower chose not to speak, allowing the British Army chief of staff time to frame his thoughts. "Two items that are private and personal between us only." Brooke paused and received a consenting head nod from Eisenhower. "First, I think we all recognize the difficulties of an ocean between our two countries, and as with all of us in leadership positions, we have many demands upon our time and attention. I have talked about this issue with George," which Eisenhower understood to mean the U.S. Army chief of staff, "last year when we dealt with North Africa and Italy. This latest review has heightened my apprehension. I must ask you directly and bluntly, are the American chiefs being kept current with the evolving plan?"

"Fair question, Alan. I cannot claim General Marshall and the other American chiefs are as current as you and the British chiefs. However, we work hard to keep them current within the limits of our communications means. One of my active open questions with General Marshall is an appropriate date for the American chiefs to attend our final review before entering the execution phase."

"I will confess to my serious worry that the opportunity for us to diverge with our American counterparts nags me continuously."

"We fully intended to do our best to ensure minimal if any divergence in these last few months."

"Extra or extraordinary effort to that end is warranted."

"Understood," Eisenhower responded.

"My second item is the prime minister's remarks this afternoon." Again, Eisenhower simply nodded his consent. Brooke continued, "The King's chiefs share his concerns. The worse outcome of the endeavor short of annihilation is stagnation. The prime minister has persisted in referring to the genuine tragedy of Passchendaele remains all too real and burning in our history 27 years hence.

I sense resistance among the American staff that to us seems rather cavalier with a matter of such vital importance."

The Great War Battle of Passchendaele, also known as the Third Battle of Ypres, was fought from 31.July.1917 to 10.November.1917, near the Belgian village of Passchendaele. During those three plus months of bloody, grinding, trench warfare, the British suffered 240,000 to 450,000 casualties, while the Germans added 217,000 to 400,000 casualties. Of those, 76,000 British Commonwealth soldiers died. Passchendaele was arguably the most devastating battle of gruesome combat on the Western Front and became the legend of Flanders Fields.

"I cannot and should not discount your observations here, Alan. I recognize that same . . . the same frustration. I think many of us feel the pressure being applied by the Soviets to get on with it."

"But, that resistance is becoming a distraction at a critical time, as we struggle with finalizing the plan."

"Beyond the obvious constraints of weather, geography, and such, we have variable constraints like enemy dispositions, naval and aerial bombardment effectiveness, and the like. We've dealt with most variables and issues, but the one item that has become the most problematic is two aspects of the same issue—landing craft . . . in all forms. We can get only so many landing craft of each wave onto the beach at the same time. We have not been able to, and I respectfully submit, we do not have sufficient time to clear the mines and surf line defenses the Germans have laid out. We are placing extraordinary pressure on the coxswains of those craft to remain in the cleared lanes and meet the other approach and egress constraints. Expanding the assault beaches is not an option, and I do believe we all accept that reality."

"Agreed."

"The assault plan endeavors to move as many divisions as possible across those beaches in the shortest amount of time. If you, or anyone, can see a path to achieve the prime minister's desire for 12 to 15 divisions in the initial assault force, I am all ears. Today, we have seven divisions, including two airborne divisions. The air and naval elements are in better shape than others, but we keep coming back to our ability to move divisions across those beaches swiftly. All it will take is one of the German defense points, like Pointe du Hoc, to hold and jam up the initial assault, and we could face a cascading, domino effect."

"I think we stand a good shot at adding a Canadian division, although that is not yet agreed. As you know, we are in negotiation to extract another American division from Italy."

"I have asked General Morgan to independently analyze the calculated maximum number of divisions we can move across the beaches during daylight hours of D-Day."

"I eagerly await the answer."

"Likewise. Nonetheless, our present number one constraint is landing craft of all types, from L-C-V-Ps to L-S-Ts. Even if we had unlimited landing craft, there is only so much space and time on the cleared portions of the beaches. We can't flood the beaches and expect to maintain control."

"No argument, Ike. The beaches and landing craft may be our chokepoint until we can expand the beachhead sufficiently to open other harbors. Perhaps, we can find other ways."

"FORTITUDE?"

"That's one. I was thinking airpower."

"How so?" Eisenhower asked.

"Well, thinking out loud, what if we stationed aircraft over every bridge, road junction, river crossing, or any channelization we can find . . . seal off the approaches to the beachhead. The Air Force likes to have defined targets rather than loiter for something that may or may not come along."

"That's a lot of airpower."

"Yes, it is. We might have to suspend POINTBLANK for a few weeks or maybe a month or two."

"That would bear its own adverse consequences. Nonetheless, I'll ask Arthur to take another look at the air plan. We might buy some time."

Brooke smiled as he held Eisenhower's eyes. "While I share many of the prime minister's worries, I wanted to privately tell you that, in this question, I doubt anything will satisfy him. We shall help as best we can to support the plan but coaxing the prime minister along is going to rest on your shoulders alone . . . as the supreme commander. This is not going to be an easy sell. Passchendaele had a lasting and profound impact on him . . . on all of us. Nevertheless, you are going to have to deal with his doubts, questions, uncertainties, and misgivings until we are established ashore on the Continent with a substantial, if not overwhelming, force. That won't be until at least D + 30."

"I've worked with him, dealt with his doubts, for nearly two years. I'm fully prepared to see this through. I appreciate your counsel, Alan. I always have. I thank you for your initiative. I suspect we are all a little nervous on this one. We are planning and will soon execute the largest amphibious invasion in history. We are blazing a new trail. While we have some precedent to follow, most of this is new. We are writing the book as we go."

"A grand endeavor, Ike . . . a noble crusade."

"Perhaps, Alan, but you know as well as anyone that no matter how many divisions we place on the ground in France, our forces will be quite vulnerable until we can get a fully developed fighting force established—artillery, armor, engineers, and all the other support units to sustain the fighters. The initial combat units must be able to defend the ground and quickly expand the beachhead far enough to preclude German artillery from striking the landing beaches, but it is the logistics of fleshing out our force that will determine the outcome. The Mulberry Harbor components must be able to operate day and night without obstruction or interference."

"Agreed."

"While we must fight the inevitable fight on the Continent, I am more convinced by the day that we shall win or lose on our logistics. We must overwhelm the Germans with food, water, ammunition, and other war supplies. Our soldiers will do the work, but we must do everything else to keep them in the fight."

"You stated that reality very well, Ike. We have a couple of months remaining to deliver against that expectation."

"Yes, we do, Alan. May God help us all."

—

Saturday, 12.February.1944
Standing Oak Farm
Winchester, Hampshire, England
United Kingdom
11:20 hours

Charlotte sat at her desk by the window in her small study/office. The paperwork and especially the farm's accounts ledger consumed more and more of her time. The irritation of the business burden grew with each passing day. The urge to hire an accountant to manage the books mounted with her annoyance. Brian had several trusted and educated people to handle his businesses . . . their businesses, in America. Charlotte put her pen in its holder and stared out the window at the pond and the hills beyond the water. After perhaps ten minutes of peaceful contemplation, Charlotte watched Mabel ride up smartly and secured her horse to the new hitching rail they had installed.

Mabel Jane Bloodworth had been an employee of the farm since the spring of '43. She managed the horticulture portion of the farm's rapidly growing business. Mabel's gardening skills had translated well to farming on a larger scale. Her preserving knowledge and abilities, including pickling, canning, drying, and salting, had impressed everyone. Her productivity required them to build a small storeroom adjacent to the kitchen, complete with floor-to-ceiling shelves around the available walls. The pantry was not quite full. Another growing season would fill the room. Mabel had been pregnant with their first child when her husband was killed in action near Dunkirk in 1940, just a few days before Charlotte's husband Ian had been killed in the sinking of HMS *Glorious*. Her son, Todd, was born fatherless and had taken to Charlotte and Brian's son Ian, who was seven months younger.

Shortly after Ian's birth, Charlotte hired Edith Hanscom to serve as Ian's nanny. The now 22-year-old young woman had become an essential household member, tending the children, the endless farm chores and duties.

The farmhouse had become the farm's headquarters as it had grown over the years and was now the residence of Edith, Mabel, and Todd. Charlotte had arrived in life and grown up in the house that had been a Crown grant to her father's great-grandfather. She inherited the farm at just 19 years of age when her mother committed suicide, succumbing to her despondency over the loss of her husband and Charlotte's father, Sergeant Stanley Tamerlin, who had died as a casualty of the Great War in France in 1917. With Brian's help, they doubled the size of the farm in November 1941 with the acquisition of the adjoining Harris and Brownfield farms.

Charlotte moved from her desk and met Mabel at the front door. Mabel went directly to the fire to warm herself.

"I bring good news, Charlotte," Mabel began with a broad smile brightening her face.

"Do tell."

"The American Army completed their construction of the greenhouses, six of them covering nearly five acres of Brownfield. They are magnificent structures, quite substantial. The glass is perfect. I just completed the acceptance with the captain of the engineer company. They are built to last. They're not temporary structures. We have electrical power for the lights and heaters in each building, along with ducting and fans for heat distribution. The engineers also laid a small diversion intake in the stream and an aqueduct. As a result, we have plenty of water for all six buildings." Mabel paused presumably to choose her next words. "I still have to figure out something productive to do with the excess water. They are like nothing I have ever seen before. We were able to prepare the soil and beds in anticipation of our planting. With the Army's assistance, we have seeds to plant lettuce, tomatoes, carrots, celery, potatoes, cucumbers, and onions in our first crops. The heaters are on and should take several days to a week to warm the soil inside each greenhouse to a sufficient temperature for planting."

"Impressive indeed. It's been several weeks since I was over that way. When do you anticipate your first harvest?"

"I expect to achieve perfect or near-perfect growing conditions. I hope we'll see our first yield in roughly two months, likely tomatoes, cucumbers, and perhaps carrots. Lettuce should take roughly 30 days. The longest will be the onions. By the way, I should say, we will plant several varieties of potatoes and onions, as each variety offers different purposes in cooking."

"Excellent."

"Oh, I almost forgot, to my amazement, the engineers also installed a wood gas generator for backup electricity for each building. It seems like too much, but the captain told me his orders where better to have too much than not enough. The Army was incredibly generous."

"They must really want vegetables."

"Yes, they do."

"I don't recall. What does the contract require in return? Do we get any of the yield?"

"Yes, ten percent outright and all that might be excess to their needs."

"We'll have to feel our way through the first couple of pickings. After that, you're going to need more help, especially when the picking time comes."

"Exactly. I needed to brief you on the acceptance inspection, but more importantly, I wanted to offer a proposal."

"I am all ears," Charlotte responded.

Mabel presented her argument for six new employees, one to manage each greenhouse building and another six as picking time neared. She believed she could find women who had the skills for the preservation process and a few older men beyond conscription age for manual labor. Her concept involved the pickers working full time. They would preserve the vegetables they could not consume in between crop harvests. In addition, she wanted to convert the Brownfield house into a dormitory for those that needed housing.

"Agreed. Do you need my help for hiring?"

"I think I can handle it. I'll start searching for greenhouse managers right away. I'll bring my recommendations to you as I get them."

"What about deliveries? The Bedford stake-side can barely handle the dairy deliveries."

"The U.S. Army's 9th Division supply battalion has agreed they will send their trucks to pick up their produce, and they'll take care of distribution to their companion units. We simply notify the division at Winchester Barracks two days before delivery. They take it from there."

"That should work. I'm sure we can refine our processes as we gain experience."

"Yes, Ma'am."

"Exemplary work, Mabel. You are a godsend."

"Thank you, Charlotte. Todd and I are blessed to have connected with you. This is a better paradise than I have or could have ever imagined. I am so happy to have you as a boss in this idyllic place."

"I am so glad you are happy. I am blessed to have you as such an important member of the team."

"It's nearly time for dinner. The lads will be hungry."

Mabel set to the task of preparing dinner. Before she could rise to help, Charlotte heard Edith coming down the stairs, supervising the descent of Todd and Ian, who were managing the stairs quite well. When they reached the ground floor, Ian ran to his mother's outstretched arms for a warm, motherly embrace. Todd ran to and latched onto Mabel's left leg as she chopped vegetables.

As dinner started to go on the large dining table, Charlotte's long-time farm hands were Lionel Bridges, soon to be 65 years of age, and Horace Morgan, who was four years younger than Lionel. The youngest member of the crew, Jacob Holden, now 15 years old, worked with Lionel and Horace, and for Charlotte since March 1941. Today, Jacob was in school for his last year of compulsory school and a little over two years from conscription age.

"The morning delivery went well, Ma'am," Lionel announced. "The American Army is very demanding. We need more cows."

"More cows means expanding the milking shed, and you know how hard it has been finding supplies of all kinds—wood, nails, paint, everything."

"The American Army built those magnificent greenhouses," Horace added. "Perhaps we can make another arrangement with them."

"They have tried," offered Lionel, "to buy everything we produce—milk, cheeses, butter, yogurt, anything, and everything. They pay more, but as we agreed we can't cut off our local customers."

"Good point. As my parents and grandparents used to say," Charlotte explained, "we never know unless we try. Mabel and I will go over to Winchester Barracks on Monday."

"Dinner is served," announced Mabel.

They all sat down at the long table. The conversation was vigorous and wide-ranging. Laughter percolated throughout lunch. They all helped with clean-up, and then they dispersed to attend their afternoon chores.

———

Monday, 14.February.1944
Headquarters, 82ⁿᵈ Airborne Division
Braunstone Park
Leicester, Leicestershire, England
United Kingdom
11:20 hours

The division began settling into their new bivouac sites in the Leicester area while the division staff established the headquarters. Division Commanding General Major General Matthew Bunker Ridgway, USA [USMA 1917], stopped by the quickly coalescing headquarters unit before heading to London for consultations with the SHAEF staff.

The division had been known as the All-American Division since the Great War because it had soldiers from all 48 states unlike other divisions. The division retained its "AA" patch reflecting its origins and had been re-designated as the first American parachute division in February 1942. Many traditionalist generals considered parachute infantry experimental and not worth the risk in combat. General Eisenhower had bucked the traditionalists and utilized the division in the initial assaults of both Sicily and Salerno. As the SHAEF commander in chief, General Eisenhower favored the employment of both airborne divisions—the 82ⁿᵈ and the newly formed 101ˢᵗ Airborne Division.

One of the 82ⁿᵈ Division's regiments, the 504ᵗʰ Parachute Infantry Regiment (504PIR), had been detached and remained engaged in the Anzio beachhead as part of VI Corps. The 501ˢᵗ and 502ⁿᵈ Parachute Regiments were transferred to form the 101ˢᵗ Airborne Division.

The 505ᵗʰ Parachute Infantry Regiment (505PIR) remained the veteran core of the division's assault units. The 505PIR's former commander, Brigadier General James Maurice Gavin, USA [USMA 1929], had just been promoted and reassigned as the deputy division commander.

General Ridgway had a monumental task ahead of him. The division had to train two new regiments—the 507ᵗʰ and 508ᵗʰ Parachute Regiments. The general knew what lay ahead, and they had only a few months to prepare for what many in command believed would be the largest airborne assault in history. They also had just a few months to train and integrate the 325ᵗʰ Glider Infantry Regiment as the division reserve for the assault. Other glider units would move the division's artillery and support equipment.

So much to be done, so little time to prepare.

———

Tuesday, 15.February.1944
No.10 Downing Street
Whitehall, London, England
United Kingdom
16:25 hours

Director-General of the Secret Intelligence Service (SIS, AKA MI6) Major General Sir Stewart Graham 'C' Menzies, KCMG, CB, DSO, MC, arrived unannounced and without an appointment in hopes of seeing the prime minister at his earliest convenience. He acquired the moniker 'C' when he was promoted on the passing of his predecessor, Admiral Sir Hugh Sinclair, KCB, in November 1939. The director-general retained the 'C' designation since the first director—Captain Sir George Smith-Cumming, KCMG, CB. Menzies waited patiently in a chair outside the prime minister's office. Only a few knowledgeable people could recognize and understand the manacle that attached a metallic case to Sir Stewart's left wrist.

Roughly ten minutes later, the door opened, and Deputy Prime Minister Clement Richard Attlee, PC, MP for Limehouse and Leader of the Labor Party, walked swiftly out of the building without acknowledging anyone. His expression suggested a less than desired outcome to his private conservation with the prime minister.

Principal Private Secretary John Miller Martin, CVO, entered the prime minister's office and came back out less than a minute later. "The Prime Minister can see you now, Sir Stewart."

"Thank you, Mister Miller." Menzies entered the prime minister's office and closed the door behind him. He went to Churchill's desk and placed the case on the desk. "Thank you for seeing me on such short notice, Sir. I have a Boniface," Menzies said, using the double codename for an Enigma decrypt, "I simply had to bring it over myself."

Churchill retrieved his personal key. "Must be important."

"Yes Sir."

Churchill removed the single sheet of paper.

MOST SECRET - ULTRA

```
MOST SECRET ULTRA
DATE 0647 15 FEB 1944
TO PM UK FM FO
FROM STATION X
SUBJECT MOST URGENT ULTRA
```

```
SECRET
DATE 1713 14 FEB 1944
TO ARMED FORCES HIGH COMMAND
FROM THE LEADER
COPY RSHA
BREAK
EFFECTIVE IMMEDIATELY MILITARY INTELLIGENCE
BRANCH IS HEREBY DISSOLVED BREAK PERSONNEL
AND DUTIES WILL BE ABSORBED AND PERFORMED
HENCEFORTH BY EMPIRE SECURITY MAIN OFFICE
FOREIGN SECURITY SERVICE BREAK WILHELM CANARIS
HAS RETIRED BREAK VICTORY AWAITS BREAK BY
ORDER OF THE LEADER END
SECRET
DECYPHERED 0456 15 FEB 1944
MOST SECRET ULTRA
```

MOST SECRET - ULTRA

"Himmler."

"Yes Sir."

"The bloody S-S and Himmler are going to be military intelligence, now?"

"That is the way we read it."

"What of Canaris?"

"The message indicates he retired. We don't know, and we may not gain confirmation for some time. With an event like this, Canaris may have been arrested or under some form of house arrest at a minimum, and likely under close surveillance by the Gestapo. Our folks and the Americans inside Germany will listen and watch carefully for any signs. The situation is probably too fluid and volatile to make an approach."

"And Himmler has acquired even more power."

"So it would appear."

"What does it mean to us?" Churchill asked.

"The answer is most likely far more complicated than the query."

"I'm on pins and needles waiting for the answer."

Menzies nodded. "First, as we have discussed previously, Admiral Canaris has been our most likely candidate for our anonymous source of the Oslo Report in November of '39. He was probably the most approachable of the senior German leadership. The *Abwehr* under Canaris was top rung. More than a few times, my analysts suggested their suspicion that their bad intelligence might be intentional as if they were purposefully but subtly trying to mislead one or a combination of the combat branches. Second, the S-S and S-D are political units with teeth, fully committed to protecting the party before the nation. Our assessment is, this change is not positive for our intelligence collection associated with their military's prospects. This change may be worse for them than for us."

"We can only hope. Anything else, Sir Stewart? I've got another meeting I am late for now."

"No Sir. My apologies for intruding. I thought this was important enough," said Menzies softly.

"Yes, yes, I will always make time for you, Sir Stewart. I was merely stating fact."

Churchill returned the highly classified message to the case and locked it. "I presume I will see this one again in the normal routing."

"Yes Sir. Thank you for your time, Prime Minister."

They walked out of the office together. Menzies turned right to leave the building. Churchill turned left to the Cabinet Conference Room.

———

Wednesday, 23.February.1944
No.10 Downing Street
Whitehall, London, England
United Kingdom
19:15 hours

"Excuse me, Prime Minister," Pug Ismay said as Churchill came down the stairs from the residence dressed in his black tie tuxedo. "This message just arrived." He handed the folder to Churchill.

"I am late for cocktails, and I have an important supper, Pug."

"Yes Sir. I know, but I think you would want to see this one."

Churchill opened the folder with a single message and read.

SECRET

```
DATE 22 JAN 44 1445 HOURS
FROM GOC 15AG
TO PM WC WM MED US5A
SUBJECT OP SHINGLE
BREAK
```

EFFECTIVE IMMEDIATELY MAJGEN LUCAS RELIEVED OF
COMMAND BREAK MAJGEN TRUSCOTT ASSUMED COMMAND
OF US VI CORPS END

SECRET

"This was yesterday afternoon. A bit late on the message, but long overdue on the action. I had my doubts, but I trusted Alexander's judgment. Truscott? The commanding general of the American 3rd Infantry Division."

"Yes Sir, precisely. They finally stopped the German counterattack and regained some of the lost ground."

"But, it has been more than a month, and the Highway 1 and Highway 7 lines of communication remain open. The VI Corps has not accomplished its mission, and Cassino remains the essential roadblock to our advance on Rome."

"At least they have stabilized the beachhead."

"Finally. Good luck to General Truscott."

"Do you wish to send a reply?"

Churchill thought for several seconds. "No," he said sharply and turned to walk away.

—

Monday, 28.February.1944
USAAF Station F-356
Saffron Walden, Essex, England
United Kingdom
08:05 hours

The 334FS completed their mission briefing early. The weather was worse over Southern England—800-foot ceiling solid overcast with tops at 3,600 feet. The clouds were broken over their targets. If they launched, it would be the squadron's 1st combat mission in their new P-51D Mustang fighters. They had missed Big Week (19/25.February.1944)—the concerted, massive, day and night bombing of German industrial centers by the 8th and 15th Air Forces in coordination with RAF Bomber Command.

Today's mission was an escort mission. A squadron of B-25 Mitchell medium bombers would hit a known V1 assembly and launch installation on the north side of Grand Parc, France—8th Bomber Command Mission 63. What made the day's mission different was not just their new aircraft, but also a split mission. The first portion was the designated CIRCUS 83 escort of the bombers. If they met minimal resistance and the bombers were over the

Channel safely headed back to England, then the squadron would execute its RODEO 292 fighter sweep into Southern Belgium. They would hit the railroad switching yards at Charleroi, and if possible, Namur.

The blue telephone rang, and Sergeant Ellison answered. "Yes Sir. Skipper," he shouted.

Arnie Clark walked from his office to the ops desk and took the proffered handset. "Clark." "Yes Sir." Arnie listened. "Very well. Thank you." He turned to the pilots. "OK, fellas. Group says the latest weather reading and forecast look acceptable over the Continent. Don't forget, use your drop tanks first. We'll jettison them prior to the French coast. Whatever is left in the tanks will be lost. Let's mount up."

Brian had his flight gear on since the briefing was complete. He stood and watched as his pilots donned their flight gear, and then Brian let them out into the cold winter air.

As was their practice in winter, the crew chiefs had the engines running at fast idle to warm the oil. Brian received a thumb's up and smile from Sergeant Tomlinson, meaning his aircraft was ready to go. Larson jumped up on the left-wing root after Brian and assisted his pilot with his parachute and seat harness straps. Brian connected his oxygen and radio connectors. As expected, his engine oil temperature and pressure were both in the green. His coolant temperature was also in the green. He was ready. Brian looked to his right. About half of his flight still had their heads inside their cockpits. The squadron was fully ready within a couple of minutes.

They took off by sections. With his fighter cleaned up and in climb configuration, Brian glanced over his wingman. Second Lieutenant Henry Carl 'Buddy' Courtland from Bridgeport, Connecticut, was a former Eagle squadron pilot. Buddy maintained a perfect position in tight behind and beneath Brian's right wing. He smoothly initiated his left climbing rendezvous turn before he and Buddy entered the clouds. Brian concentrated on his instruments to maintain his state and make Buddy's task a little easier. Once they broke out on top of the cloud deck into the bright morning sun, Brian first checked on Buddy—*perfect*. He next spotted Able Division. They were nearly formed up. Next, Brian checked over his left shoulder to see three of four sections out of the clouds with good pursuit position and closing nicely. He switched from his main tanks to his drop tanks to burn those off. Brian joined up in his trail position with his second section in position and the Yellow Flight closing. Arnie rolled the squadron out on their rendezvous heading, still climbing. The squadron of bombers was easily spotted ahead and above them, just as expected and briefed. The fighters joined the bombers on course at not quite mid-Channel. Able Division had the left flank with Blue Flight at the front left corner 500 feet above the bombers, and Green Flight at the left rear corner. Brian's Baker Division had the right flank with the flights deployed in the same fashion.

As the formation approached the French coastline, the fighters pickled their drop tanks to clean up for potential combat. Arnie and Brian crept their divisions up to gain a little more separation in case the bombers encountered flak en route. They fully expected flak in the vicinity of the target. Brian spread his flight to get more eyes scanning the sky around them. *Where are the Germans? This is just weird compared to what we faced in the summer of '40. The lack of German fighters over France is probably a measure of how bad things are for the Germans in Russia.*

The ugly gray-black blossoms of flak bursts around the bombers forced Brian to check his map, clipped to his left thigh. *Yep, the bombers are on the run-in to the target.* Brian could not see the target on the ground, but the map said they were close. Their bomb bay doors are open. Brian scanned the sky around them. *Still nothing.* By the time he looked back at the bombers, a stick of 500-pound bombs fell from all 12 bombers nearly simultaneously. Their bomb bay doors slapped shut, and the whole formation banked left to a north-northeasterly egress course. Baker Division was on the outside of the turn. Brian advanced his throttle to nearly full power to hold position and give his flight some power margin to maintain their formation positions. *There is something reassuring about the sound of that engine.*

"Pectin. We're done with the circus. We'll break off for the rodeo." Arnie did not wait for an acknowledgment. Able Division passed beneath and behind Baker Division. Brian rolled smoothly to the right and his division easily followed. Baker Division took up its trail position in the descent. Arnie turned to the south for a dogleg to allow the squadron to reach its treetop approach altitude before turning toward their initial point. The Charleroi marshaling yard came in two parts. Per the mission plan, Able Division took the east side, while Baker Division had the west side.

They were dead on the railway, and the first marshaling yard was in sight. "Pectin Baker, combat spread, echelon right," Brian radioed. He saw several Mustangs in the rearview mirror move to the right. Brian scanned the sky around them quickly. *Clear.* His division's fighters smoothly took their positions. They were skimming the tops of buildings. *The sound of these machines at high power so low has to be awesome on the ground.* Their instructions were to shoot up anything in German grey. Per the mission plan, Arnie and Brian were on either side of the primary track line. Brian grinned inside his oxygen mask. An engine with its coal tender was pulling a train of about two dozen mostly gray railcars with only two green cars mixed in. *Target.* Brian jinked to the right and then the left to line up on the long axis of the train. *Perfect!* He took a quick scan around him. *Nothing.*

Tracers from his division sprayed the city streets. Tracers also rose from unseen weapons in the city. Several explosions in his peripheral vision confirmed their success. As the pipper of his gunsight tracked toward the locomotive, Brian squeezed and held his trigger down. The guns burst with streams of red tracers. Dust kicked up short of the locomotive. Impacts flashed all along the length of the machine. A billowing eruption of steam rose from and obscured the sight of the locomotive. Brian kept the streams of bullets on the train. Impacts flashed along every railcar. The fourth one exploded in a giant yellow, red and black fireball. Brian rolled onto his left wing, releasing the trigger, and pulled hard to avoid the fireball. He could feel the heat and barely missed the edge of it. Brian rolled hard back to the right and returned to his lineup. He squeezed his trigger. Dust, wood fragments, and other nondescript debris burst from his bullet impacts on several more railcars. Toward the end of the train, another huge fireball exploded. This time, Brian rolled hard right, but he was not quick enough. The heat surrounded him and was very intense. His big Packard coughed. Fortunately, his momentum carried him through the periphery of the fireball. The Mustang sank toward the ground. Brian rolled wings level as the aircraft decelerated. He pulled the throttle back to the idle stop. The engine protested, burped, and pulsed alive. Brian smoothly advanced the throttle to full power as he pulled smoothly back on the stick. The powerful Packard roared to full power just in time to miss the ground and tracks below him. A static, red railcar loomed ahead of him in the rapidly decreasing distance. *Damn!* Brian pushed the throttle hard through the gate wire and against the war emergency power stop. The engine delivered 67 inches Hg and 1,720 horsepower. He pulled back on the stick as hard as he dared to avoid a stall. A hard bump kicked his tail up. *Damn! I must've hit the railcar.* But, he held the back stick pressure, and the elevator brought his nose up. *I'm still flying.*

As he rose away from the ground, Brian kept the engine at emergency power. He sucked in a deep breath of oxygen and dropped his nose to regain his lost speed. He was behind his division. His task now was recovery from his very close call. Skimming the rooftops, Brian minimized his exposure to ground fire and gave himself the best power margin.

"Pectin, Pectin Six, bingo," came the command from Arnie.

Thank God for that. I'm low on ammo, and I've got to save some for the flight home.

Racing along the rooftops, Brian could only catch quick glances of a few Mustangs, but they were all turning left and staying low. Brian rolled left, setting up a good pursuit turn. Arnie took up a beeline heading back to Debden, which also served to miss the large Belgian cities of Brussels, Antwerp, and Ghent. Once clear of Charleroi city and over farmland, the skipper initiated a good cruise climb. 'A' Division was already formed up in their combat spread. Brian's 'B' Division held what could best be described as a loose combat spread formation led by Sweet Sweeney. Buddy Courtland must have just noticed Brian closing. He executed a smooth barrel roll over the top of Brian, leveling out below and behind his leader. Buddy quickly adjusted to take up his proper wing position off Brian's right wing. Sweet throttled back the rest of the division, and 'B' Division soon reformed as they closed. They were a complete squadron by the time they reached the Belgian coastline. Arnie leveled the squadron out at 8,000 feet for their return.

As they approached the English coast, Buddy radioed, "Pectin Baker, Pectin Red Two, you've got some tail damage."

"How bad?" Brian asked.

"Your horizontal and vertical look good, but you may not have a tail wheel."

"Thanks, Two."

As long as I can get the mains down, I should be able to minimize any more damage on landing. I'll take the grass and land last, so I don't interfere with anyone else landing. Should I shut down the engine to avoid any damage to the powerplant?

Arnie reported the squadron to sector control before crossing the coastline. The clouds had broken up but remained broken to overcast. Arnie ordered the squadron to penetrate the clouds by sections.

"Pectin Red, Pectin, you're the damaged one. What do you want to do?"

"I need to land last, and I'll take the grass."

"Might be too wet."

Damn! I didn't think of that. He's right. "OK. It's the runway, but even more of a reason to land last."

"Very well. Good luck. We'll be watching."

"Pectin Yellow, Pectin Red, you have the division lead. Pectin Red Two, Pectin Blue, switch Button Four." Brian pushed the second frequency selector button on his radio.

"Two," Buddy checked in.

"We'll orbit while the rest of the squadron lands. Before we penetrate, we'll configure for landing. Give me a good look-see to make sure I know the state of my landing gear, and then I want you to penetrate and land. Let me know on Tower when you're clear of the runway."

"Wilco."

"Switch Button One."

"Two."

They listened as the squadron went through the landing procedures and watched them disappear into the clouds. Yellow Three was next with his section. Brian hand-signaled Buddy to reconfigure for landing. He moved the landing gear handle to down. Sounds normal. What's that vibration? Brian rechecked his airspeed and lowered his flaps for landing.

"Looks like the mains are down and locked. The tailwheel did not extend."

The red unsafe gear light shined brightly. "Thanks, Buddy. Now, get on the ground so that I can get this machine to the hangar."

"Wilco. Carmen, Pectin Red Two, for penetration and landing. I'll need the crash trucks."

Debden Tower gave Buddy his vectors for penetration and landing. Brian watched his wingman disappear into the clouds.

A couple of minutes later, Brian heard, "Pectin Red Two, Carmen, in sight. Winds light and variable. Clear to land runway two eight."

"Cleared to land."

A few minutes later, "Pectin Red, Carmen, the runway is clear. From your present position, turn to heading three six zero, vectors for penetration."

"Roger, Carmen, heading three six zero." Brian turned smoothly to 360° magnetic and held that heading for about a minute.

"Pectin Red, Carmen, turn left to two eight zero, cleared to penetrate."

"Roger, Carmen, turning to two eight zero, cleared to penetrate." Brian pulled his throttle back to set up a 500 foot per minute descent rate, heading 280° magnetic. He scanned his instruments and kept the scan of his primary instruments to maintain a stable approach. Brian broke out below the clouds at 1,400 feet. He turned his landing light on to make it easier for the tower to spot him. The runway was about two miles ahead on his nose. Brian adjusted his heading to line up on runway 2-8 and opened his canopy. The cold air sent a heavy shiver through his body. *Better chilly than trapped.*

"Pectin Red, Carmen, in sight. Winds light and variable. Cleared to land. Crash trucks in position on standby."

"Cleared to land."

The flashing red lights on the yellow crash trucks confirmed the tower had prepared the airfield for his partial gear-up landing if something went wrong. *Nice and steady. Good flight path. Good descent rate, on speed. I'm going to keep the motor running. Here we go.* Brian brought the throttle back to the idle stop, heard the engine spit and sputter in protest, and gently slowed the machine while he held it inches off the runway surface. The aircraft settled softly onto the runway. Shortly after the main wheels touched down, a heavy scraping sound and higher nose attitude confirmed the missing tailwheel. He applied the brakes harder than normal up to the point of feeling the aircraft lurch forward slightly and held the brake pressure. The nose was pitched up more than normal. The combination brought the aircraft to a stop quickly. Brian switched off his electrical equipment and shut down the engine. By the time he disconnected and unstrapped from the Mustang, the crash trucks were all around the aircraft and prepared to dowse any flames. None burst to life. Brian jumped out and went immediately to the tail, where several firefighters joined him. The wrinkled aluminum had been ground down. The railcar impact damaged the tail wheel extension system, but surprisingly, it had not broken open the hydraulic retraction line.

"Right down the centerline," one of the firefighters pronounced. "Good job, Major."

Brian nodded his head.

"Could've been much worse," another said.

Again, Brian just nodded his head.

Just then, Sergeant Tomlinson drove up in a small tug, tow bar, and dolly to support the damaged tail. "You just couldn't fly one mission without goobbering up my beautiful new airplane, huh, Major."

They all laughed.

"I almost didn't come back at all," Brian added with quiet solemnity that instantly stifled the joviality. No one asked him about what happened to cause the damage.

An unknown private first class drove up in a 1/4-ton, 4×4, light utility vehicle, more popularly known as a Jeep, to retrieve Brian and take him to the 334FS operations building.

Some of the pilots besieged Brian before he could make it to the intelligence shed for his debriefing. After the official debriefings were completed, they spent the rest of the day and into the evening talking about the day's events. Brian knew and expressed the reality that he had been extraordinarily lucky and close to a far worse outcome. *Better lucky than good, as Malcolm always told me.*

—

Chapter 3

The universal brotherhood of man
is our most precious possession.
                        -- Mark Twain

Saturday, 4.March.1944
USAAF Station F-356
Saffron Walden, Essex, England
United Kingdom
05:25 hours

The damage to his "QP-G" Mustang on the Charleroi mission proved more severe than initially thought. A structural repair team had decided several bent frames and stringers had to be replaced to make the aircraft flightworthy. Fortunately, Colonel Blakeslee approved the release of one of the group's new, spare aircraft to replace Brian's aircraft while it was being repaired.

Brian elected to forego a maintenance check flight to participate in the day's mission. They would be performing many firsts. Today would be the first long-range bomber escort for the fighters. There would be no more turning back at the western border and leaving the bombers to face German fighters and flak. It was also the first daylight raid on the German capital. The British Bomber Command hit Berlin for several months at night and suffered terrible losses. That fact was not lost on the American aircrews.

Arnie Clark returned to the squadron operations building from his group briefing. The room fell silent immediately. They were all keyed up for this mission. "Before I begin the mission brief, Group asked me to make an important announcement." No one so much as whispered. "The War Department has decided and ordered that we comply with the 50-mission limit. Most of us are well past that number with our RAF credit."

I already have my waiver, Brian thought. *This should not apply to me, but I had better check with the Skipper to be sure.*

"What about a waiver, Skipper?" asked Dusty.

"Well . . ."

"Yeah, Skipper, we want to stay," Sweet added.

Arnie held both hands up. "Look, fellas, I'm just the messenger here. I appreciate the sentiment. The best I can say is, I'll ask Colonel Blakeslee. I will also say the rule is intended to prevent burnout and prevent mistakes that will kill you. This is not some test of your manhood. We all need a break from this fight."

"That may be, Skipper," Dusty replied, "but some of us want . . . no, we need to see this to the end . . . to finish this fight."

"I will pass along the sentiment. Now, if you reprobates will get off your sanctimonious high horse, we've got a mission to brief." Clark paused to allow for any rebuttal. None came. "Today's mission brief is the same as yesterday's aborted mission." Clark provided the essential mission data but did not repeat the whole briefing. He covered the current forecast weather en route and over the target, which was decidedly better than yesterday's forecast. They were headed to Berlin on their first and the U.S. Army Air Force's first long-range bomber escort mission—a maximum effort raid.

The 4ᵗʰ Fighter Group was one of 15 P-51B & D fighter groups assigned to protect 504 B-17 and 226 B-24 heavy bombers. Their targets included airfields in and around Berlin. The 4FG would be part of four fighter groups assigned to three B-17 groups with a target of the Berlin-Gatow airfield site west-southwest of Berlin Center. The aerodrome was strategically noteworthy as the location of *Luftkriegsschule 2 Berlin-Gatow*, an imitation of the Royal Air Force College at RAF Cranwell, and *Luftkriegsakademie der Deutschen Luftwaffe*, an air war college for advanced training and thinking.

Brian thought, *It's odd that we're sending 150 heavy bombers, each with 4,000 pounds of high explosive bombs, against schools. There must be more about Gatow than we are being told. Then again, Gatow appears to be the incubator for German pilots. We hit manufacturing and supply sites. Why not pilot training sites as well. This really is total warfare.*

Colonel Clark completed the mission briefing. There were no questions. Arnie returned to his office. The pilots, to a man, retreated to their thoughts. There were no games, no magazines, no newspapers—only the individual mental rehearsal of the first of what would be many long-range escort missions.

Blessedly, they did not have to wait long. Twenty minutes later, at 06:35, the red phone rang on Sergeant Ellison's desk. Sergeant Julius Roman 'Juli' Ellison had been the squadron's operations clerk since the squadron formed in September 1942.

Clark did not wait to be called. He took the handset. "Clark." "Yes Sir." "Very well, Sir. Good luck." Arnie turned to face his pilots. "The bombers are in the air. Let's mount up. Show's on."

Sounds of chairs scraping along the wooden floor and the rustling of flight equipment filled the room as the pilots filed out of the operations building without speaking a syllable, not even a grunt, from anyone. The scattered to broken clouds meant they would not need extra time to join up and reach their rendezvous with the bombers.

"So, you fellas are going to Berlin, ay, Major," Sergeant Tomlinson said as Brian approached.

"Yep." Brian did not feel particularly talkative.

"The bird's ready to go."

"Thanks, Larson. Are the drop tanks full?"

"Yes Sir, as ordered."

"The bombers are in the air, so let's get your baby spun up."

Within a few minutes, the engine was purring nicely. All the gauges were in the green. This time, the 334FS would be the last squadron to takeoff. Brian chose to burn fuel from the right drop tank while idling on the ground. *I'm not too keen on my first opportunity to use the gunsight in air-to-air combat. Arnie meant exactly what he said, and we'll learn how to fight this machine with Germans all around us.* While they waited for takeoff, Brian noted the gunsight gyro switch ON, and FIXED & GYRO selected. The adjustable target wingspan scale covered 30 to 120 feet, and the scale display sat just below the sight optics. He set the span knob for 33 since they would most likely face Bf109 (32 feet) and Fw190 (34 feet) fighters. The fixed reticle '+' along with the gyro-stabilized dot and the diamond ring for ranging were illuminated. He twisted the throttle grip clockwise and counterclockwise several times. The diamond ring expanded and contracted, and the range dial displayed the selected range from 600 to 2,400 feet. Brian rolled the grip full clockwise to 600 feet.

The Sperry K-14A gyro-stabilized gunsight was designed to provide the pilot with lead computation based on normal acceleration—the 'g's the aircraft was pulling in a turn.

Arnie took the runway. Sections took off in rapid succession since no separation for cloud penetration was necessary. Brian and Buddy were up next. Brian switched his fuel selector to LEFT MAIN tank before he positioned to the center of the far half of the runway. As soon as he saw Buddy in position behind his left wing, Brian nodded his head forward, signaling take off. With the aircraft cleaned up and climb configuration set, Brian switched to the right drop tank earlier than the recommended 2,000 feet above ground level. He knew the right tank worked and wanted to use as much of his drop tank fuel before he would have to jettison the tanks.

As briefed, Arnie set up his climb, creating a long trail of fighters climbing to the east. Brian led his 'B' Division airplanes in the same line. They would maintain the loose cruise climb to the rendezvous since they did not expect opposition across the North Sea.

As Arnie reached their join-up altitude of 20,000 feet, 2,000 feet above the top bombers, the bomber formation was in sight ahead of them. With a positive power margin, the 334FS was the last escort squadron to form up in position at the left rear and above the bombers. The mission plan called for the bombers to penetrate the German frontier just south of the border with Denmark and turn to the southeast for the run to the west side of Berlin and Gatow airfield. As the amassed formation approached their feet-dry crossing point, the fighters began jettisoning their wing drop tanks. Brian switched his fuel selector to the fuselage tank, which he wanted to empty next to avoid a tail-heavy condition before they entered combat. As soon as he saw the tanks drop off Arnie's wings, Brian depressed his release button and felt the tanks jettison. He quickly checked both wings. *Clean.* Nobody radioed that they could not drop their tanks.

After the planned right turn to the southeast, their route split the distance between Hamburg and Kiel to avoid as much anti-aircraft fire as possible. They could expect German fighters at any time. Brian kept his head and eyes constantly moving with an occasional glance at his cockpit instruments to confirm what the hum of the big engine told him in sound.

The bomber formation leader increased their altitude to 27,000 feet, with each engine exhaust producing a condensation trail (contrail) as if they wanted the Germans to see the mass of heavy bombers heading into the heartland of their country. More pragmatically, the increased altitude gave them a little help with the flak. The escort leader shifted the forward two fighter groups to the low cover position.

"Hunter, Arnie. We're going up to Angels Three Three. You hang back. I'm moving forward about halfway. Sharp eye."

"Wilco, Arnie."

Their contrails seemed minuscule compared to the bombers. Brian scanned the skies. 'B' Division held an excellent combat spread. *We're ready.* They could see Hamburg on the right and Kiel on the left from their altitude. *Where are the Germans?* Just as Brian had asked himself that question, the lower group maneuvered to deal with climbing enemy squadrons. It was tempting to watch the action below them, but such self-indulgence would distract them from their part of the mission. The radio chatter would have to suffice. Brian saw them first—thin contrails to the east.

"Pectin, bandits 10 o'clock level and climbing."

"Pectin Able, tally-ho. Able, we're going up. Let's stay ahead of 'em. Baker, stay with the big iron." Arnie executed a climbing left turn with the rest of 'A' Division.

"Pectin Yellow, Red, stay put. I'm going to shift forward."

"Yellow, wilco."

Brian continuously scanned the sky around them. The bombers appeared unperturbed. The lower fighters were becoming busier. The only incoming contrails were those on the left so far. *There's something not right here. Damn, it's cold up here. I sense some kind of bait & switch tactic. Where are the others?* Arnie's 'A' Division eight Mustangs soon became a ball of spaghetti as they mixed it up with the 12 incoming Germans. *Looks like Fw190s.* There was surprisingly little radio chatter from the 'A' Division engagement. The furball migrated forward but not as fast as the bombers on their relentless approach to their target. Brian caught a quick glance of what he thought was Berlin ahead of them. They had to be about 20 minutes out. A few dark grey blooms began to appear among the bomber formation. The Germans abruptly disengaged from 'A' Division. Arnie turned to return to the bombers. 'A' Division was halfway back when the sky seemed to erupt with inbound contrails arcing toward them from every direction. *Looks like the fight's on.* 'A' Division did not make it back to their escort position and turned swiftly to face an incoming enemy squadron. Brian watched another squadron inbound from the eight o'clock direction. 'B' Division remained in position with the bombers and well above the approaching raiders. As they waited for the proper time to engage, Brian noticed three, maybe four, incoming enemy fighter squadrons from the south and west. As the Germans advanced, more of the escort fighters engaged. Brian began a level left turn to meet the enemy.

"Pectin Baker, Upper," radioed 'Horseback' Blakeslee, "position over the bombers to take any bleed through from either side. Shirtblue Baker, take the eight o'clock raid."

"Wilco," Brian radioed and reversed course. "Wilco," responded Brian's 336FS counterpart.

Brian watched their comrade division turn to intercept the eight o'clock adversaries. The 334FS 'B' Division settled into a position 6,000 feet above the bombers. Flak burst blooms began to burst ahead of and through the bomber formation. Fighter engagements the pilots liked to call furballs boiled all around the bombers, but Pectin Baker watched from their perch. The myriad contrails had become a mass of twisted, knotted, white lines in the sky all around straight contrails of the inexorably advancing bomber formation. Several of the fighter tangles inched closer to the bombers.

"Pectin Yellow, take the right. Red will take the left."

"Wilco."

As the two flights shifted their position to meet the potential threat, the flak bursts began to thicken. Before the enemy closed for engagement, they turned and dove away. On cue, the flak thickened even more and began to take its toll. Five bombers had to deal with engine fires, shutdown those affected engines, feathered the propellers, and inevitably began to fall out of formation. The fighter standing orders told them they had to stay with the main formation.

The fighters began to reform on the flanks above the bombers. Another bomber lost most of its right horizontal stabilizer and part of its left wing, causing the large aircraft to pitch down and roll left. Other aircraft had to maneuver to avoid the mortally wounded machine. Small dots began to drift away from the airplane as it slowly spiraled down. The crew was bailing out. Brian's attention was on the join up with Arnie's Able Division, which still had all eight fighters. He could not count the number of crewmembers making it out of the bomber. Perhaps they would find out later. *The flak is taking a helluva toll that the enemy fighters had been prevented from taking on the bomber formation. I've no idea how those bomber guys endure that punishment?*

The entire bomber formation wheeled to the right before 'B' Division completed their join up with 'A' Division. They must've dropped. Too many things were going on even to check the bomb impacts. Flak shells continued to explode among the bombers. The only damage the escort fighters could see came from an aircraft dropping out of formation. They completed the 180° turn and took a beeline back to England. The contrails of enemy fighters appeared all around them and were converging. *They might be after the other wings hitting Berlin. Hopefully . . . Stay focused on the mission*, Brian reminded himself.

The egress proved more difficult. The escort got behind the Germans. They were all chasing German fighters among the bombers. On the positive side, the Germans appeared to be more intent upon hitting the bombers than defending themselves against the American fighters. However, they had significant negatives to consider. What was behind their target that might be affected by their bullet stream? Mid-air collisions? Getting back to their escort position? Brian had impacts on German fighters—two Fw190s and one Bf109, but no confirmed kills. They fought hard against continuous German fighters from Berlin until past the Ruhr Valley. Despite their best efforts, they lost several more bombers to enemy fighters.

From the German border to the coastline west of Amsterdam, they encountered no adversarial fighters and only a few flak shells over Amsterdam. As the bombers when feet wet over the North Sea, the fighter groups peeled off and dove for the deck. All the pilots appreciated General Doolittle's more aggressive directives allowing the fighters to seek out targets of opportunity once the bombers were safe. Today, the 4FG was assigned to hit the German E-boat base at the mouth of the Rotterdam estuary.

The sight of 12 fighter squadrons diving away from the bomber formation toward the ground was impressive in itself. Each squadron had a different objective for their ground attack. The 334FS reached the low-level altitude above the beach and surf line just past Katwijk aan Zee. Arnie formed them in a left echelon of finger-four flights. Brian put Buddy off his right wing and

Salt's 2nd Section off his left wing. They strafed several coastal defense bunkers and structures short of The Hague and a number of Army vehicles on the streets of The Hague.

"Pectin Baker, shift right, follow Able."

Damn! Brian immediately jinked right to shift his division. *Notice much? He probably wants double the impact on the E-boat docks.* They were racing at the docks at high speed. Tracers rose from the anti-aircraft guns on the enemy torpedo patrol boats at the mouth of the Rhine River flowing into the North Sea. Seconds later, clear tracer streams from the fighters converged on all six visible E-boats. Brian shifted his position slightly to allow Buddy a shot as well. Fires broke out on two of the patrol boats. Able Division pulled up sharply to avoid any ricochets that might kick up from the 'B' Division attack.

Brian selected a boat on the far side of the yard. Tracers came directly at him. He walked the fixed reticle and squeezed the trigger. Brian gently pushed forward to keep the reticle on the target. The tracers coming at him stopped. A torpedo in a starboard side tube exploded. Brian pulled back hard, rolling left to avoid the growing cloud. Loud metal-against-metal bangs told him shrapnel had hit his airplane from the explosion. *I'm still flying.* Brian continued his climb, noticed bright flashes in his rearview mirror, rolled back to the right, and then leveled his wings, climbing toward Arnie's Able Division. He throttled back to cruise climb power, and then he looked over both shoulders and counted seven Mustangs climbing with him. Looking back again over his right shoulder, Brian gave a hand signal for Buddy to check his aircraft. His wingman came in closer to check the underside of Brian's fighter. *He's taking longer than usual. Not good.* Buddy returned to his wing position and gave Brian a thumb's up. *The engine gauges are still normal. So far, so good.*

After the join-up, the rest of the transit was smooth and uneventful. Arnie signaled for flight echelons in trail for the break and landing singly. Once Brian was downwind and configured to land, he decided to open his canopy for quick egress should the need arise and felt the refreshing chill of the air. The landing gear green light indicated the wheels were down and locked. The machine landed smoothly.

Back in his spot with the engine shutdown, Brian unstrapped, disconnected, and hopped out. "I took some hits," he declared to Sergeant Tomlinson. Brian thought he would see perhaps a half dozen jagged shrapnel impacts. They counted more than a dozen, some larger than others. No fluid leaks were detected.

"We'll give her a good look-see for any internal damage," Tomlinson said. "If there is nothing else, we should have these holes patched up good as new tonight."

"Thanks, Larson. Please let me know if you find anything inside or more serious."

"Will do, Major."

The other guys of his division gathered around him.

"Damn, Hunter," Sweet shouted, "I thought you were a goner. You must've hit a torpedo."

"Yeah. I think so."

"Is your bird OK?" asked Salt.

"I took a lot of shrapnel hits, but my chief thinks they should have her patched up by tomorrow."

The debriefings took longer than usual. Arnie wanted a private chat about what Brian had observed during the mission, especially the E-boat docks attack. By the time they left Arnie's office, only Sergeant Ellison had remained. Arnie drove Brian to the Officer's Mess, just in time for dinner. The squadron, less Arnie, celebrated the day's mission despite the fatiguing seven and a quarter-hour combat operation. More laughter and joking filled the bar as they enjoyed a few drinks and camaraderie. No one mentioned the serious topics from the day's experience.

The American Eighth Air Force suffered 37 losses on the day's mission, including 11 fighters. Fortunately, the 4FG lost none of their aircraft, although many were damaged, but all the 4FG aircraft made it back to Debden. No one was wounded. The losses on the day's Berlin raid were not as bad as the Schweinfurt–Regensburg missions last year, but they were still terrible losses.

———

Monday, 6.March.1944
No.10 Downing Street
Whitehall, London, England
United Kingdom
12:30 hours

Generals Eisenhower and Smith arrived at the famous residence and office of the British prime minister in a single Cadillac Army staff car with a four-start flag flying on the right front fender. The driver, MTC chauffeur Kay Summersby, jumped out to open the passenger door for the generals. Usually, as was his practice, Eisenhower would have brought Summersby inside with him, but in this instance, he knew the 'private luncheon' invitation from Churchill meant sensitive topics would be discussed. Accordingly, Summersby was asked to remain with the limousine.

The door to No.10 magically opened as the two American generals stepped toward the black oak door with the polished brass numeral '10' affixed.

"Welcome back to Number Ten, General Eisenhower," the receptionist announced. "The prime minister . . ." His salutation was interrupted when Prime Minister Churchill appeared.

"Greetings, Ike, Beetle. Welcome back to Number Ten. Let's get down to business." Churchill led the two American generals to the dining room. The prime minister gestured to the chair on his right for Eisenhower while he took the seat at the head of the long table. "As a good host, I offer, although I'm certain I know the answer, champagne for either of you?"

"No, thank you, Sir," they answered in unison.

"Suit yourselves." A full flute of chilled Pol Rogers champagne was poured for the prime minister.

"Coffee for me, please," Ike said.

"Me as well," added Smith.

They were served their lunch of roasted pork chops, roasted potatoes, and mushy peas. They ate a few bites while the servers vacated the room.

"Before we delve into the heart of the matter, what do I need to be apprised of?" Churchill asked.

"We're in the process of moving the SHAEF headquarters staff from Norfolk House to Bushy Park."

"Are you joining the 8th Air Force?" Churchill asked.

"No Sir," Ike responded. "We've moved them to High Wycombe. We're moving the SHAEF staff into their buildings."

"Bushy Park is a beautiful place, second largest of the royal parks and site of Hampton Court Palace, one of King Henry the Eighth's favorite residences. It has quite the history."

"And, we're making more history," Smith added.

In 1942, the U.S. Army Air Forces swiftly began their build-up of combat air units in England. Those units became the Eighth Air Force. Temporary wooden buildings were constructed on the north edge of Bushy Park and a separate, controlled gate for access to the area. The site had been named for Lieutenant Colonel Townsend Edwin 'Tim' Griffiss, USAAF [USMA 1922], who had been shot down over the English Channel while riding as a passenger in a U.S. B-24 Liberator returning from a special mission to Moscow. RAF Spitfires flown by Polish pilots had mistakenly identified the Liberator as a German Fw200 Condor. Camp Griffiss was also known by the code name Widewing and USAAF Station 586, the designators were not changed when SHAEF moved in. Camp Griffiss offered much less grandeur than Norfolk House but substantially more space.

"Yes, we are," mused Churchill. "But, the history we are making is not so good at Anzio. I acknowledge that it is not your sphere anymore, but what is the latest from that dreary endeavor, pray tell?"

"Beetle is probably more current on Anzio than me," Ike answered.

"The VI Corps is still tied up in a back and forth with the Germans," Smith added.

"An opportunity lost," Churchill mumbled. "And the 15th Army Group remains stalled at Monte Cassino."

"Yes Sir."

"Most regrettable! This is precisely what I fear most . . . stagnation. Back and forth, as you say. I would rather postpone OVERLORD than risk stalemate. That damn corporal will apply a lot more attention to an invasion of France than he has for Italy, which is precisely why I fret about the initial assault force and our capacity to expand the beachhead swiftly."

"We certainly understand and appreciate that issue, Prime Minister," Eisenhower responded.

"They hit the abbey hard," Smith continued, "and destroyed the whole structure, but it appears the rubble just made more hiding places for the enemy. The 15th Army Group, both at the Gustav Line and at Anzio, are working to sustain pressure on the Germans while they rest and refit the assault units for a coordinated breakthrough."

"I appreciate the explanation, Beetle, but to be frank and blunt, that is exactly what I heard during my service on the Western Front with the 6th Royal Scots Fusiliers. It was always just 'one more push, lads.' I cannot tolerate that happening again."

"We share your intolerance, Prime Minister. We're planning to cram two field armies through a comparatively narrow portal of five suitable beaches with no port facilities and with one of those beaches being nearly problematic and marginally acceptable. The cliffs of Omaha Beach and the narrow, steep ravines breaking those cliffs leave all of us quite apprehensive."

"Your apprehension is good, Ike. Use it."

"We are re-evaluating our air plan to see how we can use our resources to advantage in delaying the inevitable movement of German forces to counter our landing. I have a small team working with the FORTITUDE folks to see what we can do to reinforce and prolong the enemy preconception that Calais is our primary landing site. We recognize that we will be in a race to move troops and supplies across those beaches faster than the Germans can reinforce. The reality is a double-edged sword. We must gain a sufficient beachhead to protect the Mulberry port facilities while we hold and slow the Germans."

"Now, my dear Ike, I've kept you from your lunch. I shall take the floor, so you can consume at least part of your meal before it is entirely cold." The three men chuckled. "First and foremost, I acknowledge the enormous complexity of this pending operation. I also concede that my fretting over the plan is not making your task easier, but in my defense, Ike, I know of no other way. I doubt I will ever be comfortable with this endeavor, no matter how well this thing is thought out. We all know that the plan is only the plan until the first bullet is fired, and then it is up to the sergeants." Both generals nodded their heads in agreement. "I have a few thoughts that now is perhaps the appropriate time to convey. We are teetering dreadfully close to the threshold 20 to 25 German mobile combat divisions within seven days movement of Normandy for OVERLORD to proceed. I eagerly await your revised air plan.

"Then, after the EUREKA Conference in Tehran last November, I am convinced with little remaining doubt that Stalin has no intention of liberating Eastern Europe but rather to occupy and perhaps even conquer those lands. They will offer myriad excuses for dominating those nations taken back from the Germans. They likely will make gestures of compliance, but we will not be fooled by any pretty façade constructed to mask the cages. The president and I will continue to press Premier Stalin for the concessions we need to return Europe to tranquility, democracy, and peace. You will hear me reiterate my guidance many times. We must meet the Soviets as far east as possible."

"I've heard you offer that guidance, Prime Minister, and I cannot argue with its wisdom. I can assure you that advice will not be far from my consideration every single day. We don't have an approved plan yet. And, we have an invasion to win, set aside a long march into Germany against a likely determined resistance."

"I understand you and Monty have a related wager," Churchill observed with a mischievous twinkle in his eyes.

"Yes, we do . . . five quid this nastiness will be over by Christmas."

"This year or next?" They all laughed. "And which side of that wager are you on?"

"For."

"Well, my dear Ike, I shall pray you win that wager. Now, with our meals complete, may I entertain you in a snifter of brandy?"

"No, thank you, Prime Minister. I beg your forgiveness. I have a full schedule this afternoon."

"Yes, yes, quite understandable. Thank you for coming, Ike and Beetle. I look forward to great things from both of you."

"We shall strive to exceed your expectations, Prime Minister," Ike responded as both generals stood, followed by the prime minister.

Churchill walked his guests to the front door, and upon seeing their driver, he continued on. "A delight to see you again, Miss Summersby."

Kay nodded her head to the prime minister and said, "The honor is mine, Prime Minister."

Churchill shook hands with Eisenhower and Smith and then returned to his office.

———

Wednesday, 15.March.1944
American Eagle Club
No.28 Charing Cross Road
Covent Garden, London, England
United Kingdom
18:25 hours

They spent the day on standby as back-up for the RAF No.266 Squadron Typhoons that had been sent across the Channel to attack a V-1 launch site north of Saint-Omer. Brian thought of Jonathan and hoped they would not be scrambled to scrub off any assailants. He smiled to himself when the call came releasing the squadron for the rest of day.

A half dozen of the lads decided to make a run into London. Brian did not have enough time to make it down to and back from Standing Oak Farm. He desperately missed Charlotte and Ian, but he feared missing morning muster more.

They had barely walked halfway from Leicester Square Underground Station when they saw that things had changed. "Wow! We might have a struggle gettin' a burger tonight," Salt observed as they all saw the mass of American servicemen gathered outside the Eagle Club.

"Yeah, it's been more than a year since I've been here," Dusty added.

"Been more than two years for me," Hunter contributed.

"What is this place?" asked Second Lieutenant Jackson 'Horn' Lee, USAAF from Richmond, Virginia, Salt's wingman.

"The club was opened in April 1941 by the American Red Cross," Dusty explained. "The Queen actually came down here to dedicate the place. They wanted to offer a little touch of home for us Yanks while we're over here."

"Not all of us are Yankees," quipped Horn.

"In the eyes of the Brits, we're all under the Stars & Stripes and thus Yanks." Horn offered no argument.

"Are we going to be able to get inside?" asked Second Lieutenant Stephen 'Stove' Sarron, USAAF from Pueblo, Colorado—the Green Flight, 2nd Section wingman.

"We never know unless we try," Brian said.

With that, the 334FS pilots walked to the entrance and made their way through the throng of rowdy soldiers and sailors. All seven of them signed the register at the reception desk, and then they ascended the stairs to the grill and dining room on the second floor. To their surprise, the dining room was only about half full, and the order line was only three deep and moving nicely. A quick scan of the room detected a handful of officers, with the remainder being enlisted personnel. A good hamburger was more important than the separation of officers and enlisted. None of them saw anyone even remotely familiar.

The group ordered and picked up their hamburgers, French fries, and ice-cold Coca-Colas. Each of them stopped at the condiments buffet to plus up their sandwiches.

"Wow!" exclaimed First Lieutenant Joshua David 'Frog' Forcier, USAAF from Durham, North Carolina—the Green Flight, 2nd Section leader. "Fresh tomatoes and lettuce. Where do they get this stuff?"

"Must be someplace close. Perishables would never make it across the Atlantic," suggested Dusty, "and everything else is German."

"At least for now," said Frog, inducing chuckles all around.

Brian took advantage of the fresh condiments—lettuce, tomato, sliced onion, pickles, and catsup. *I wonder if any of these veggies, or are they fruits, came from Standing Oak Farm? Damn, I miss Charlotte and Ian. I need to ask her about the greenhouses. I don't know much about what she's doing.*

As each of the pilots loaded up their burgers, they shuffled to an open table at the back of the dining room. The moans and groans of their simple pleasure in eating the best . . . well, the only . . . hamburgers with all the fixin's in England complimented the simple meal. Frog enjoyed his sandwich so much he went back and ordered another one. Brian chose to remain with him and have another Coca-Cola. The new guys, Stove and Horn, wanted to see what else was available in the building. Frog and Hunter finished before the tour group. Brian and Joshua found a spot, out of the flow of people traffic at the stairs. Muffled laughter came down the stairwell.

"They must be showing some kind of comedy in the theater," Frog said.

"Seems so, huh."

More laughter was heard as Dusty led the others down the stairs.

"I'm going over to Shepherd's for a beer," Brian announced. "Anyone want to join me." The pilots were unanimous. Horn and Stove had never visited the renowned London pub favored by in-country fighter pilots.

"Hey, what was the movie?" asked Frog.

"Some Abbott and Costello comedy," Dusty answered.

The pilots signed out in the register and walked back to the Leicester Square Station, took the Piccadilly Line two stops west, and walked the last few blocks from Green Park Station to the public house. They were all amazed at how many American servicemen and women of many ranks filled the Underground and the streets.

Wednesday, 15.March.1944
Shepherds Tavern
No.50 Hertford Street
Mayfair, London, England
United Kingdom
19:40 hours

Just as the pilots had witnessed at the American Eagle Club, Shepherd's clientele were predominately American aviators, and virtually all of those were Army Air Forces. None of them recognized faces. They were content to stick together. Each of them ordered and received a pint of their desired brew.

"I don't think I've seen this many Americans since I arrived in Europe in the spring of '40," Dusty noted. "Somethin's up."

"Yeah, kinda hard to hide this many Americans," Frog added.

"We're now going all the way to Berlin," Buddy chimed in, "so I suspect the long-anticipated invasion is getting closer."

"Safe bet," Hunter replied and took a good swallow of his beer. Brian noticed a handful of American Army lieutenants getting more rowdy than usual, so much so that the RAF pilots either left or went to the dining area. *I don't like this at all. We are guests in this country. This is not our house.* Brian finished his first pint, considered leaving to avoid the induced ruckus, but decided one more pint would be appropriate.

"Are we going to be part of the invasion?" Stove asked innocently.

"The reason we are here, Stove, is for that invasion," Brian responded patiently. "I've no idea, none of us does, how we will be involved, but I am fairly certain the answer is inevitably yes. While the *Luftwaffe* remains in the occupied countries and a threat, they are a mere shell of what they were in the summer of 1940. So, I imagine our first task will be air superiority over the beachhead, wherever that may be, and then our task will be interdiction. We do not carry the punch of a B-17 or even a B-25, but we can move fast."

"That we can," interjected Salt Morton.

"I suspect we are going to get very busy in the spring," Brian added.

"Spring comes in five days," Frog said. Everyone chuckled.

"Does it feel like spring outside?" Horn contributed.

"This is England," observed Dusty with a hearty laugh. The others joined in.

Brian finished his beer, placed the glass on the bar, and announced, "OK, lads. I'm not risking the last train back to Newport just for another beer."

Newport Station was the closest railway station to Debden and the airbase. The station was served by the West Anglia Main Line of the London and North Eastern Railway. The last train leaving Liverpool Street Station London and stopping at Newport departed at 23:05.

Brian took several steps toward the door through the mass of boisterous aviators. "I'm not letting my leader go without his wingman," he heard Buddy pronounce behind him. Brian smiled but did not look back or miss a step. Buddy did not catch up to him until they were outside the pub and headed toward Green Park Underground Station.

"Hunter!"

I know that voice, but it was too distant and mixed with so many other rowdy voices to identify positively. Brian and Henry turned together. Jonathan trotted across Market Mews toward them. Brian and Henry walked toward him.

"What?" Jonathan shouted. "Were you running off without saying hello?"

"A little rowdier than I care for in there," Brian said. "By the way, this is my wingman, Buddy Courtland. Buddy, this is the famous and renowned Squadron Leader Jonathan 'Harness' Kensington, Commanding Officer of Number 2-6-6 Squadron."

"Isn't that the squadron we were back-up for today?"

"Yep, one and the same." Brian looked to Jonathan. "I imagine your raid went well today."

"Yes, it did, but before all that detail, let's go inside."

"No, thanks, Harness. I've got to get back to Debden. How are Linda and young Julia?"

"Mum and daughter are doing well," Jonathan answered. "I just had dinner with them, but she wanted to get Julia to bed. I've got to head back to Duxford tonight."

"We were on standby to cover your mission today."

"Helluva mission. We hit a new V-1 assembly and launch site north of Saint-Omer. RP-3 3-inch rockets made splinters of the place. By the way, how are your new Mustangs?"

"I can sum it up with one fact. We stayed with the bombers all the way to Berlin a couple of weeks ago."

"My, that is most impressive. More fighters, I suspect."

"Quite so . . . a lot more. Based on one mission to Berlin, I'd say Gerry has pulled most of his fighters from France to protect the Fatherland. What's left over gets shipped off to the Eastern Front."

"We saw some of that today—no fighter opposition. We faced plenty of anti-aircraft fire. I lost one pilot, and another handful shot up rather badly but managed to make it home."

"I'm so glad you're OK, my friend. Now, we really must be going. Give Linda and Julia a hug and a kiss from Brother Brian."

"Wilco. Oh hell, I don't need another beer. I'll walk with you lads to the Tube. We both leave from Liverpool Street Station."

The three pilots walked the several blocks to the Green Park Underground Station, took the Piccadilly Line to Holborn Station, and then they transferred to the Central Line to Liverpool Street Station. During the Tube ride, Jonathan interrogated Buddy, trading stories about the third-highest scoring ace in either air force. Brian took the jabs as he usually did in a calm, light-hearted manner. Jonathan's train departed first. They exchanged their goodbyes and embraced as close friends.

Brian wanted to doze on the hour train ride north to Newport Station, but Buddy was intensely curious about Jonathan's experience with the exploitation flights of captured German aircraft and especially about their experience during the great air battle of summer 1940. Brian understood and tolerated his wingman's curiosity until they reached Debden and their quarters.

———

Monday, 20.March.1944
OSS field office
Allied Forces Headquarters
Reggia di Caserta
Viale Douhet
Caserta, Campania, Liberated Italy
17:40 hours

"**W**elcome back, General," Major Alfredo Stephano 'Al' Morelli greeted OSS Director Brigadier General Donovan as he entered the secure office space next to the Special Communications secure spaces.

Morelli had been the chief of Amalfi Station since the liberation of the Sorrento Peninsula last year. He became the OSS-5ᵗʰ Army liaison two months ago.

"Thank you, Al," responded Bill Donovan as he shook hands with the senior OSS agent in Italy. "I was not sure I was going to make it with the eruption."

"We've not been affected up here, but it sure is impressive to watch."

"When did it start?"

"The volcano seriously started belching steam and smoke on the 13ᵗʰ about the same time as we felt more than a few significant earthquakes. Vesuvius erupted big time on the 17ᵗʰ. Fortunately, the winds have kept the ash cloud south and east of the mountain. *Monte Vesuvio* subsequently exploded on the 18ᵗʰ, and the caldera overflowed spewing lava flows down into surrounding villages."

"The pilots of the Dakota made a serious detour to avoid the rain of rocks. They were probably overly cautious, but I was grateful for their prudence. Has the eruption affected operations?"

"Not yet, but it will. While the eruption has our attention, we are well north of the zone of effects so far. The Gustav Line is 45 miles north of us.

We brief General Clark every morning, and the eruption has been top of page since the big eruptions began on the 17th, especially now. The roads south of the mountain have been closed. The port facilities at Naples have not been seriously damaged yet, but the supply ships are standing off. The 5th Army staff are looking for alternate means of getting the required supplies to the combat units."

"How long will it last, or at least, how long will it affect logistics operations?"

"General Clark has repeatedly asked the exact same question. The best volcanologists we have been able to find all say the same thing, we don't know. The best they can give us is a few weeks based on past eruptions."

"Well, that throws quite the clot in the churn, doesn't it? I suppose there is nothing we can do but adapt."

"Exactly. We strive to give the 5th Army staff the best information we can find."

"Let us know if there is anything we can do to help." Morelli nodded his head. "Now, what of Cassino?"

"As you know, a month ago, the 12th and 15th Air Forces bombed the abbey into rubble. Unfortunately, that bombing didn't shake the Germans loose. The Air Force hit it again five days ago. But the 15th A-G still haven't taken the redoubt."

"And, they keep pounding away at that hill."

"Yes, they do."

"That is exactly what Churchill seems to fear the most—stalemate."

"They will break it."

"Did I hear correctly that they are pulling the 504th Parachute Regiment from the Anzio beachhead?"

"Correct, Sir. Against Clark's strenuous objections, I must add."

"The 82nd needs them more than the VI Corps. OVERLORD is a few months away at best. That is one of the reasons I need to chat with you now." Morelli nodded his head. "We had hoped that relieving Lucas and replacing him with Truscott would have broken the stalemate at Anzio, cut the lines of communication to the German 14th Army, and broken the Gustav Line."

"Lucas was a good man."

"Yes, he was, but he was the wrong man for that job. Too cautious. *Fortis Fortuna Adiuvat* . . . fortune favors the bold, as the old saying goes. But, Clark and Alexander waited too long to do what had to be done. We also hoped that the 15th Army Group would have been to Rome and beyond by now. They are not, and it falls to us to make up the difference."

"I don't follow," Al said.

"We need to redouble our guerrilla plan to mobilize the resistance more than we have to date. We must give the Germans more to worry about. We need them to commit more forces to Italy."

"Easily said, not so easily done."

"I trust you are up to the task."

"We'll find a way, General."

"I know you will. I'm leaving for London tomorrow morning. I'll be there for a few weeks. I eagerly anticipate your plan when I get back to Washington."

"You'll have it."

"Now, if I am informed correctly, General Clark is up at the front, and General Alexander is with Montgomery."

"Correct, Sir."

"No need to pay my respects. How about I take you to dinner at your favorite restaurant?"

"Works for me," Morelli answered. He checked out with the duty agent. "We'll be at Boriano's for dinner and then at the officer's quarters for the night in case you need either of us."

"Roger that, Major. See you in the morning."

———

Wednesday, 29.March.1944
No.10 Downing Street
Whitehall, London, England
United Kingdom
16:10 hours

Lord Selborne had been the last of the three intelligence professionals to arrive for their private meeting with the prime minister. Sir Stewart Menzies had requested the meeting, and Bill Donovan happened to be in London. They all knew each other and had worked together for several years, so introductions were unnecessary. They simply shook hands.

The Minister of Economic Warfare came into this world as Roundell Cecil Palmer 57 years ago. He had been elevated and became the 3rd Earl of Selborne on the passing of his father in 1942, four days after being selected for his ministerial position, which included the Special Operations Executive (SOE).

"Follow me, gentlemen," the prime minister commanded and marched off smartly to the secure conference room. Once inside the small, protected, conference room with the door closed and four men seated at the table, Churchill said, "You requested this meeting, Sir Stewart. You have the floor."

"Yes Sir. We have been picking up bits and pieces from field agents that something significant happened in Germany four days ago. But, first, we needed to inform you of what we know so far and put our heads together on what we can do. Four days ago, our information suggests whatever happened took place during the night at Sagan. The only entity we know of significance at Sagan is a prisoner of war camp administered by the German Air Force--*Stammlager Luft III* or *Stalag Luft III.*"

"An escape?" Churchill asked.

"We aren't sure."

"Our field agents in that region indicated the Germans are looking for something," contributed Wild Bill Donovan. "We queried him about what they were looking for, but he did not know."

"What about Boniface?" queried the prime minister, referring to a façade code name meaning ULTRA and the British decoding of the German Enigma encryption device.

"Nothing we have been able to discern so far," Menzies answered. "We have heightened their attention to any traffic from there or the surrounding area."

"If there was an escape, our lads would be trying to make their way to Switzerland, Sweden, or even to the Soviet lines," mused Churchill.

"We do not know if there was an escape," Sir Stewart said, "but if there was, I think we can agree, we will do what we can to assist. We had no foreknowledge of an escape attempt. We can only alert our field agents to keep an eye out and help as they are able."

"Agreed," interjected Lord Selborne.

"I'll add my commitment as well," said Donovan. "If it was an escape, those boys would need all the help we can give them, and they deserve the best we can bring to bear for them."

"I caution," interjected Menzies, "we do not know for certain that it was an escape. So, our first task is to confirm whatever it was that happened in Sagan."

"I will urge each of you," Churchill said, "should you gain even a sliver of information associated with whatever this event was, to let the other three of us know immediately. I shall put the joint chiefs on alert as well that they made be called upon to render assistance at a moment's notice." The three intelligence chiefs nodded their heads in agreement. "Now, Wild Bill just arrived from his visit to the Italian front, so it is perhaps apropos to hear his observations, and I am most intrigued by the eruption. Pray tell us what you saw, Bill."

Donovan smiled. "Fortuitous is the best single-word description. I arrived by air and a rather circuitous route to avoid the rain of ash and rocks during the peak of the eruption. I have never seen anything like it. My liaison officer with the 5th Army arranged a briefing by an Italian volcanologist who studies Mount Vesuvius. He indicated it was not the volcano's largest eruption, but it was likely in the top five as far back as records exist. The eruption disrupted land movement from the south and affected logistics operations at the Naples port facilities. However, most of the serious damage and destruction was confined to the proximate villages. This eruption appears to have ceased on the 23rd, although the volcano was still smoking when I departed yesterday. The 5th Army planned and began to execute resupply operations across the beaches in the vicinity of Mondragone, but the Naples port recovered quickly, and the beach plan never had to be carried out."

"What is the latest of the Cassino obstacle?" Churchill asked.

"The 5th Army is finally making headway against the redoubt, but it still has not been neutralized. I witnessed the devastating precision of German artillery using the spotting on the heights of *Monte Cassino*. Neither General Clark nor his staff offered any forecast. The rubble of the abbey has made the clearing of the mountain a foul, nasty process."

"And Anzio?" further pressed the prime minister.

"They are also making slow progress. However, they have not reached or cut the German 14th Army lines of communication."

"And therein lies the rub, gentlemen. If Normandy becomes another Anzio, the Red Army will not stop, and we shall consume another generation of precious men at the altar of war and destruction." None of the intelligence chiefs chose to speak. "Very well then," the prime minister nearly growled. "I believe we are done here. Thank you for making me aware of the Sagan situation. I anxiously await more information. Good day, gentlemen." Churchill rose and departed the room.

The three intelligence chiefs looked at each other and shrugged their shoulders. Then, they rose, shook hands, and left No.10 in different directions.

As history would eventually record, 76 Allied pilots and aircrewmen escaped from *Stalag Luft III* during the night of 24/25.March.1944. Of those escapees, 73 were recaptured, and of that lot, the Gestapo summarily executed 50 on orders from Hitler and Himmler. At the war's conclusion, a special squad of RAF investigators searched for, tracked down, and captured the surviving executioners who were, in turn, tried, convicted, and punished; 13 of them were hung. The Great Escape was popularly depicted in the movie by the same title (1963).

—

Mortimer 'Morty' Jurdy, the Winchester taxi driver who was becoming a regular for Brian, stopped at the crest of the hill as he had done the last three times he had transported Brian from the railway station to the farm. Brian got out despite the light mist partially obscuring the view of the farm. "Damn, I just love that sight," he said aloud to no one other than himself, although Morty heard the pronouncement.

"It is gorgeous, Major. Every time I come out here, I truly enjoy the scenery. How long has it been this time?" asked Morty.

"Since Christmas."

"Far too long, Sir." Brian felt odd since Morty was probably as old as his father would have been. "This war won't last forever. Let's get you home before you get soaked out there."

Brian chuckled, nodded his head, and got back inside the 1938 Austin 12/4 'Low Loader' taxicab. Morty drove down the hill. Brian saw no activity outside, which was understandable given the hour and the dreary weather. Brian paid the fare and added a generous gratuity. As he reached for the house door handle, the large oak door burst open, and Charlotte leaped into his arms.

"I didn't see you drive up and only saw the cab drive away." Charlotte kissed her husband with vigor and feeling. "I knew that cab had to be my sugar bun."

"Morty and I stopped at the crest to appreciate the view. I think he appreciates the scene as much as I do."

"Morty, you say?"

"Yeah, Mortimer Jurdy. He prefers Morty and owns the taxicab. He's driven me out here several times and knows me now."

"Apparently, he takes good care of you," Charlotte observed.

"Yes, he does. We should call him when we need a taxi. This is his telephone number," Brian said and handed a slip of paper to Charlotte.

"I'll put it in the book. Now, what is the plan?"

"As I said last night on the phone, I expect General Donovan to arrive this afternoon. As I said last night, I had a short conversation with him just before I called you. He asked to spend a couple of days with us, partly as a break for him, partly to talk to us and me. I'm sorry I volunteered you without talking to you first, but it sounded important. I told Colonel Clark and asked him for three days. He gave me a little more. I have to catch the early train Monday morning."

"Well, then, we shall make the most of your time, and I really need to get out of these dungarees, wash up, and make myself presentable for our guest. Should we dismiss the crew for a more respectable evening?"

"No, absolutely not. First, we have a farm to run. They are a vital part of the farm. Second, General Donovan was quite insistent upon experiencing the farm as it is."

"Very well, then."

"Where is everyone?" Brian asked as Charlotte turned to leave.

"Edith is upstairs with Ian and Todd. Mabel is at Brownfield supervising our new greenhouses and growing staff. Lionel, Horace, and Jacob are expanding our milking shed with many thanks to our American Army friends, who manage to find things to help us. They gave us a dozen new milking machines and some excess lumber. We had to scavenge other lumber from one of the outbuildings on the Harris property. The building addition is a bit of a hodge-podge, but it will work."

"Do we have the capacity?"

"We've had to make some inventive adaptations, but yes, we can handle the additional milkers. It is the cheese-making that is proving more difficult."

"I'd like to see these changes. Perhaps, we can take a ride with the general if he is willing. By the way, I should tell you that I don't know what the general will want to talk about, so I would urge you to expect anything. While we do not know at the squadron, there are signs that the invasion of Europe is getting closer. Most of us suspect it is coming in late spring or early summer."

"That will be a challenging time for you," Charlotte observed with solemnity in her voice.

"Yes, it will mostly be a very busy, an all-hands-on-deck affair, I'm afraid. Sooner or later, we'll not be allowed to take leave until some degree of stability is achieved across the Channel."

"I shall brace myself for losing contact with you for a few months."

"Wise, I should think."

"Now, I really must go if I'm to be presentable for our guest." Charlotte kissed Brian and went to the bedroom suite.

Brian hesitated at the stairs but decided not to disturb Edith. He removed his uniform tunic and donned his overcoat and rain hat. Brian went outside to the barn that was more than a barn now. It had become a complex of multiple additions over the years. The mist had stopped and cleared. Signs of the cloud overcast breaking up could be seen to the west.

Changing into his muck boots in the barn's workshop/anteroom, Brian found the lads assembling makeshift milking stalls inside a claptrap assortment of multicolored and multisized boards that made the walls and roof of the expansion that was indeed a hodge-podge.

Jacob was the first to notice Brian's presence, "Good afternoon, Major. Welcome home, Sir."

All three of them stopped their work. They all shook Brian's hand and gave him a quick laughing tour of the makeshift milking shed. Lionel also showed him the changes to the plumbing and their processes to make the collection tanks handle three times the number of milking machines than they were originally designed to serve.

"I'm impressed, gentlemen. You've done a magnificent job making all this work." Brian looked around the shed again. "I'll make this promise to you all. Once this war is over and we can obtain proper materials, we will build a good permanent structure with all the correct equipment."

The three men and one nearly grown teenager laughed and celebrated the recent achievements in their own way.

"If I may say, Major, Mrs. Drummond informed us of your guest coming to the farm," Lionel said. "Are you certain you want us to attend?"

"Yes, absolutely. The general insisted."

"General?"

"Yes."

"What should we know, if I may ask?"

I'm not going to discuss his job or how vital his organization is to the war effort. "Our guest will be Brigadier General Donovan of the American Army. He is passing through England on his way back to Washington from a field visit to Italy. He is spending a few days with us to take a break from his war duties. Just be yourselves. He wants no special treatment and doesn't want to disrupt the farm's operations. I'll only ask that we do not ask him or talk about the war. He wants to enjoy our little oasis." They all nodded their heads in agreement. "We expect him this afternoon around milking time. We also expect you to have dinner with us in our usual manner. Because it's around dinner time, we will probably save the farm tour for tomorrow morning. I think that about covers it. Any questions?"

Horace and Jacob shook their heads. Lionel answered, "So, it is business as usual, except we shall have a guest at the table with us."

"Exactly."

"Very well, Sir. We shall do our part."

Brian thanked them and returned to the main house. As he entered, he heard the distinct sounds of two toddler boys playing. Brian waved to Edith and dropped to his knees, extending his arms. Ian hesitated for a few seconds and then ran into his father's embracing arms. To his surprise, Todd joined Ian and

Brian held both boys. Both boys began babbling in their own language. In short order, they squirmed out of Brian's embrace.

"Great to see you again, Edith. How have the boys been?"

"Welcome home, Major. Rambunctious in one word. They are full of energy after their nap."

Charlotte appeared dressed in beige slacks and a simple white long-sleeve blouse. Brian smiled broadly at his wife's appearance, and then he hung up his overcoat and hat. Charlotte and Brian set about preparing the evening meal for the crew and their guest—Shepherd's Pie with a few embellishments from their newly productive greenhouses. Edith helped as she was able amid her task of herding the boys. Brian tended to the manual labor of grinding up beef and pork acquired in trade with the Selborne's estate. Charlotte covered the large casserole dish until it was time to bake the concoction.

General Bill Donovan arrived by taxicab, not with Morty Jurdy, toward the end of milking time. Introductions were made as the farmhands arrived at the main house. Donovan fit right in as each of them reported on their accomplishments for the day. Laughter and joviality generously sprinkled the table talk.

As was the farm's routine, Lionel, Horace, and Jacob departed first. They would deliver the day's dairy products to the distributor in Winchester and then drop off Jacob at his family home. Mabel helped Edith clear the table, store the leftovers and clean up the dishes. Charlotte, Brian, and Bill collected a brandy and moved to the plush chairs by the fire, while the boys played with their toys at the center of the semicircle.

Each of them took turns excusing themselves from the conversation to say goodnight to their son at his usual bedtime.

The evening's conversation focused on the farm's operations and products. Donovan displayed considerable knowledge of farm operations and appreciation of what the Drummonds had accomplished expanding and growing the farm during a world war. They did not disband and retire until nearly midnight, well after the Drummond's normal bedtime. Charlotte and Brian showed General Donovan to his room and private bath.

Charlotte and Brian were so tired by the time they fell into bed that they confined their intimacy to a simple kiss goodnight.

Saturday, 1.April.1944

As was their practice, the Drummonds rose first, got the fire going, and brewed a large pot of tea for the crew before the morning milking. They would arrive just after dawn. Charlotte also prepared to make fried eggs and toast for breakfast.

Bill was the next to rise and accepted a proffered mug of tea. He sat by the fire with Brian, who mapped out an agenda for the day. First, they would feed the crew breakfast and then participate in the morning milking. The process had become somewhat of a tradition for guests. Then, in mid-morning, they would take a ride around the farm. Mabel would provide a briefing on the greenhouses and their operation.

The house quickly picked up the cacophony of many voices as the farm's working day began. The breakfast table displayed the same light-hearted-ness seen at dinner last night. Bill conveyed his thorough enjoyment of the crew's interaction and attention to the farm's operations.

Breakfast and the morning's activities went smoothly. General Donovan showed genuine engaged interest in all of the farm's operations. He remained affable and complimentary to the workers he encountered. Bill very easily won friends and supporters, not that he needed their support.

After lunch, Donovan looked to Charlotte. "If you will excuse me, I would like to borrow your husband for a conversation that I must insist on being conducted in private."

Brian shrugged his shoulders behind Donovan. Charlotte replied, "Yes, of course, General. Would you like us to leave the house?"

"No! Absolutely not! Your oak tree bench you showed me this morning would suffice nicely." Charlotte nodded her head in agreement. Bill turned to Brian and gestured to the door. "Shall we?"

They walked in silence to the oak tree bench. Donovan sat on the far end of the large bench. "Would you like a fire, Sir?"

"Not necessary. It's nice, a little cool, but comfortable. If you would like a fire, by all means, please do. I shall not object."

"I'm good."

"I wanted to talk privately about the future," Bill began.

"Do you mean after the war?"

"Yes." Brian nodded his head in recognition. "Let it suffice to say we are finally over the hump. I'm not at liberty to discuss pending plans, but the Germans are on the run in the East, and I am confident they soon shall be in the West as well. Now, from this moment, the rest of this conversation should be considered top secret. Further, I must ask you not to discuss the contents with anyone, including Charlotte. Do you understand and accept?"

"Yes Sir, and I accept."

"Very well. Several realities are essential to this conversation. One, the burden of rebuilding after the destruction of war will fall upon our shoulders. The United Kingdom has been virtually bankrupt for four years and will need our support for years to come. The war has applied its own burden, but the recovery and rebuilding process will apply another load on us. Complicating that process will be the Soviet Union. As he forecast the scourge of Hitler and his Nazism in the 1930s, Prime Minister Churchill is forecasting the consequences of the uncaged Russian bear. The Soviets will not help and will likely add significant additional demands upon us. I say this not to be dire or morose . . . only realistic."

"If I may interrupt, General, are you suggesting the Soviet Union will transform from ally to adversary at war's end?"

"Good question. I don't think it will be that simple or clear. I believe their interests are not the same as Great Britain and the United States."

"How so?"

"We have insisted upon democratic elections and hopefully governance for all countries. That principle stemmed from the Atlantic Charter in August 1941. I agree with Prime Minister Churchill. Unfortunately, the Soviets are likely to occupy the lands the Red Army liberates and install governments loyal to Moscow. While you may not have heard his guidance, he insisted we meet the Red Army as far east as possible, which places even more pressure on General Eisenhower. He thinks the only thing that will stop the Red Army advance is with strong armies of the Western Allies in front of them."

"That is rather stark and discouraging," Brian mused.

"Yes, it is. Welcome to the realities of today's geopolitics. Nonetheless, as a consequence of this assessment, President Roosevelt has requested me to produce a proposal for a future strategic intelligence operations organization. It is that proposal that is the subject of this chat." Brian nodded without responding. "The C-O-I/O-S-S experience with intelligence collection, analysis, and clandestine operations has given me a very clear vision. To come directly to the point, the O-S-S, or whatever its successor may be, needs a robust, dedicated, air element to support clandestine operations. The argument for this clandestine air element is quite similar to the argument the Marine Corps has presented for dedicated air assets that specialize in their type of operations."

I think I know where this is going.

"Do you recall our conversation in New York on the 1st of October 1942?"

"Yes Sir, I do," Brian responded.

"What are your plans for the post-war time?"

"I've not spent a lot of time thinking about that. I have my hands full doing my current job, just surviving the next fight. What I've considered to date is, I've got businesses to run, a farm to operate."

"Which brings me to the salient question in this conversation," Bill paused perhaps for effect. Brian held Donovan's eyes and did not react—not even a blink. "If I may, what are your holdings?"

Brian smiled. "First, none of our holdings are publicly traded companies. They are private and shall remain private. I will answer your query, but first, I must ask you to keep this information to yourself."

Donovan smiled. "Fair enough. So be it."

"The farm is now 385 acres here in Hampshire. Charlotte is doing a magnificent job growing this business. You've seen some of the elements. We can show you the rest if you wish." Brian paused. Donovan shook his head. "On the passing of my mentor, teacher, and friend, Malcolm Bainbridge, I inherited six vintage aircraft that became the seeds of Bainbridge Air Services, which I believe you are well aware." Donovan nodded his head. "When my parents passed on New Year's Day 1941, I inherited a mind-boggling estate that includes ten sections of land, an oil company, a land-use company, a small bakery, and a house in Wichita."

"How many oil wells?"

"Thirty-seven and several in the drilling process."

"So, if my math is even close, several million dollars a year just from the wells alone."

"Roughly speaking, yes."

"You could live quite comfortably on just that income."

"Yes."

"But here you are, an Army Air Forces fighter pilot who passed the mission threshold long ago and who is entitled to a training or staff job, and who does not need to serve as employment."

"Correct."

"If I'm properly informed, you were offered a non-combat assignment at the end of the 1st War Bonds Drive in December of '42."

"Yes Sir."

"And yet, you specifically requested a waiver from the War Department to remain in your fighter cockpit."

"Yes Sir. I love flying these machines. I've been blessed to fly many of the best airplanes in the UK or the U.S. I don't particularly appreciate being shot at, and I've had some very close calls. One of which was in that lake," Brian said, pointing at the water in front of them. "I know I'm risking my wife, my family, and the wealth that was given to me. But that must be. I guess we could say I'm addicted to flying these aircraft."

"Thank you for being honest and frank with me, Brian. Offering you a job after the war is rather moot. You don't need a job. Perhaps I can convince you to help us with what we will call O-S-S Air for now."

Brian stood, walked toward the lake's edge, picked up a smooth rock, and skipped it several times across the water. He stood contemplating Donovan's proposal until the stone's ripples dissipated. Finally, Brian turned back to face the general but did not return to the bench. "Are you suggesting Bainbridge Air become the O-S-S aviation arm?"

"That is one option," Donovan replied.

"You bought the aircraft we operate."

"You own them now, and they will be written off during the downsizing after the war." Brian waved his hand dismissively. "Another option is you help us form up O-S-S Air. Perhaps, if you are interested in continuing your service, you could serve as the director or even fly if you wish."

Brian chuckled softly. "Excuse me, General. I'm not laughing at the offer or proposal, only at the vision in my head. My limited knowledge of clandestine aviation is a very long way from a single-seat fighter cockpit. I am not a transport pilot. I believe I can fly anything put in my hands, but transport pilots have a different mindset, and rightly so."

"Brian, allow me to be direct and frank." He did not wait for a response or reaction. "You've impressed me from our very first meeting during my familiarization tour in the summer of 1940, before the great air battle. I'm frankly in awe of your commitment and sacrifice. You don't have to do what you do, but you do it nonetheless out of a greater sense of obligation to the nation. That is exactly the attitude we need in the O-S-S, to do what we are asked to do."

"Thank you for your confidence, General Donovan. I'm humbled by that confidence. How much time do I have to think about it? I really need to talk to Charlotte in a general non-specific sense because we are talking about the future."

"By all means, please confer with your wife in a general sense. Please protect the details we've discussed. Take what time you need. I am obligated to the president to provide a proposal for a post-war O-S-S by the end of this year. Regardless of your specific choice, I'd truly appreciate your contributions to what O-S-S Air should look like."

"I'll see how Charlotte feels. I'll try to give you an answer in a few days or weeks."

"That should work. If I'm no longer in the U-K by the time you decide, I'd ask you to see the chief of London Station. His name is Bruce, David Bruce, at 70 Grosvenor Street, Mayfair."

"I met Colonel Bruce at the station last year."

"Ah yes, I forgot."

Donovan stood, extended his right hand to Brian, and shook hands. He remained at Standing Oak Farm until after breakfast Sunday. Brian was not able to discuss the general's proposal until bedtime, but their conversations began. Her initial reaction was not positive.

—

Chapter 4

There is nothing so likely to produce peace
as to be well prepared to meet an enemy.
-- George Washington

Wednesday, 5.April.1944
USAAF Station F-356
Saffron Walden, Essex, England
United Kingdom
04:05 hours

The entire group had been warned yesterday afternoon that they had an early morning call, and here it was. The pilots grumbled about the dark, but the nearly full moon was less than an hour from the western horizon. The pilots were all present and ready when Arnie stepped out of his office.

"OK, gentlemen, and I use that term loosely, settle down and listen up. We've got a big day ahead of us. We'll fly another RODEO mission; this one is 2-9-4." RODEO was a code name for a fighter mission type, in this case a fighter sweep over enemy territory. "Today's event will entail a repeat of the Berlin bombing mission we flew a month ago. Although we are not part of the escort, the bombers will have a full escort. The entire 4th Group will launch just after sunrise in precise timing with the bombers. The intention is to fixate the enemy air defense network on the advancing mass heavy bomber formation, while we penetrate at high speed, low-level, under the bombers. The objective is to hit five German fighter bases in Eastern Germany in advance of the planned heavy bomber mission on targets in and around Berlin. The 335th has two bases, Friedersdorf and Plaue. The 336th has a fighter base at Stendal, and the additional task of covering our egress. We are assigned to two bases west of Berlin – Brandenburg and Potsdam. The 335th has the farthest to go, so they will launch first. We will be second. The squadrons will take off in 15-minute intervals. We are trying to catch the enemy as they prepare to launch in opposition to the bombers."

"Wooo hoo!" exclaimed Second Lieutenant Billy Bob 'Boy' Williams of Birmingham, Alabama, the Yellow Flight, 2nd Section wingman, and the newest of the squadron pilots. His callsign struck Brian as odd since he was older than himself. Several of the other pilots chuckled nervously.

Clark ignored the interjection. Arnie continued the briefing. Their first target was the Brandenburg-Briest airfield that served a wide range of operational aircraft squadrons, including two Bf109 squadrons, a Fw190 squadron, a new He177 heavy bomber squadron, and various fighters and bombers at the airfield for repair or refit. They divided the base into quarters. Brian's Red Flight was assigned to hit the sizeable main repair hangar and one of the dispersal areas for one of the Bf109 fighter squadrons.

From Brandenburg, the squadron would press on at high speed and low level to the east to the Werder/Havel airfield just west of Potsdam. Red Flight's assignment was the Air Cadet College and the fuel storage facility next to a motor pool parking area on the south boundary. Brian was not too keen on shooting up a school, but it was another pilot training organization.

They would fly the same route as the bombers at treetop level. They would retain their wing tanks until they were empty or unless they were jumped by fighter aircraft. The route would minimize their exposure to anti-aircraft fire. Clark informed the pilots that they had been authorized to engage any military targets of opportunity with their remaining ammunition once they completed their primary mission objectives.

Arnie covered the weather forecast and communications procedures. They would egress on a slight dog-leg route to avoid known air defense sites. They would remain at low level for the entire seven-hour flight.

This is going to be a taxing mission for the coolant system, Brian thought.

The map occupied the focus and attention of Brian and most of the other pilots. Brian carefully memorized the checkpoints on the ingress as well as the egress routes. Low-level flying required special attention. Reading a map so close to the ground at high speed was never a good idea.

The sky began to lighten, and they still waited for their launch command. Brian went through the mission on his map for the umpteenth time, rehearsing what was planned, what was likely to happen, and most importantly, what could happen. There were more than a few ways this mission could go sideways. *I'm as ready as I will ever be.*

The launch window opened in the middle of morning twilight at 05:10. They had already passed that threshold. Brian had gotten used to waiting long ago, but *it is never easy, especially with a mission like this one.* As was Brian's practice at such times, Brian leaned his chair back against the wall in the far corner from the skipper's office and closed his eyes to doze if and as much as he could. Although they did not notice, the first sunbeams reached the squadron operations shack at 05:27. They still waited. The call finally came at 05:43.

"Show's on. Let's mount up," Arnie declared.

The pilots did not run to their planes and did not rush their pre-takeoff checks. As briefed, the 334FS was the second of three group squadrons to launch. Arnie kept his throttle back to enable a quick join-up. Once everyone was in position, the skipper throttled up to a maximum range cruise power setting of 36 inches Hg Manifold Air Pressure (MAP) at 2,400 RPM. He also kept the squadron low at 1,000 feet pressure altitude. Brian closed his radiator and cooler flap about halfway to keep his engine temperature in the middle of the green arc. Brian could not see the other 4FG squadrons, but the bomber formation was easily and readily located well above and ahead of them. He had switched to his right wing fuel drop tank just after takeoff. When the lateral balance added right stick pressure, Brian switched to the left wing tank until he felt the opposite roll trim pressure.

The bombers almost directly above them began turning to Berlin over the German coast. Arnie descended to a mere 50 feet over the water, pushed his throttle up to maximum continuous power of 46" MAP at 2,700 RPM, and increased their speed to 350 MPH. They crossed the coastline over farmland just south of Husum, Germany, and turned southeast toward their target. Brian opened his radiator and cooler flaps full open.

Over the flat country of Schleswig-Holstein, Brian scanned the sky. *No fighters.* The only detected aircraft were the mass bomber formation and escorting fighters now falling behind them rapidly. Scanning the sky would become more difficult over the hills ahead of them. *Still no fighters; so far, so good.* Arnie jinked the squadron into the Elbe River Valley southeast of Hamburg to give them a little more radar defilade.

As the squadron swiftly approached Brandenburg, the four flights spread out on their attack lines. Cresting the last shallow ridgeline, the Brandenburg-Briest airfield was clearly identifiable, and the Red Flight initial objective of the large repair hangar was unmistakable. Brian lined up nicely, not quite square on the open hangar doors. *The concrete and low angle should allow me to skip early shots into the hangar.* Brian settled his fixed reticle short of the hangar and squeezed the trigger. All six 50-caliber machine guns fired a stream of high-velocity bullets. The sparks and concrete dust confirmed his aim. He allowed the reticle to rise into the hangar—several aircraft inside burst into flames. Brian released the trigger, saw a large He177 bomber on the far side. He adjusted slightly to put the reticle on the wing-fuselage junction and squeezed the trigger. The flashes of many impacts kicked up smoke. A fire erupted, and then the left wing fell hard to the concrete. Brian did not have time to do more. The Bf109 dispersal area was just to the left of his flight line. Three fighters had propellers spinning. One was taxiing. Brian quickly adjusted to hit the closest turning aircraft. More impacts demonstrated hits. He kept the trigger down and walked the reticle to the other live fighters. Releasing the trigger just an instant, Brian moved the reticle to the taxiing German fighter. Trigger down. Bullet impact walked up the fuselage from the tail to the nose. The aircraft burst into a giant fireball and veered hard right.

Brian quickly adjusted to his inbound track to Potsdam. A minute later, he spotted the western suburb southwest of Berlin. Tracers arced over them—not close. His map study told him where the Werder/Havel airfield was relative to Potsdam, but he could not identify any of his next target features. Brian glanced left and right. A zagged line of P-51Ds skimming the tree and building tops was an awesome sight.

A mile short of the airfield, the distinct structure of the Air Cadet College appeared beyond the trees. More tracer streams shot out just above them—*closer but not close enough*. Brian tweaked the track of his fixed reticle short of the center of the building and depressed his trigger. Six lines of high-velocity 50-caliber projectiles chewed up the building. Similar impacts had similar results to his left and right. Finally, he saw the motor pool beyond the school, adjusted to where he knew the fuel farm was located, and squeezed the trigger. A massive fireball exploded in front of him, confirming his success. Brian pulled up slightly, rolled right, and pulled back hard to avoid the expanding bloom of black, red, and yellow. Clear. Brian continued his turn over the top of Yellow Flight, who began their turns below him. When he rolled out, a large gray column appeared in front of him. Damn! The column appeared to be concrete.

On top was a single 88mm flak gun, and a bevy of uniformed German soldiers were scrambling to swing their cannon toward him. *That's not like the photographs the intel guys have shown us.* Brian instinctively bunted the aircraft to put his fixed reticle on the tower's base and allowed the reticle to rise. As his aim point neared the top, he squeezed the trigger and held the reticle on the gun. Metal-on-metal molten flashes mixed in with the concrete clouds and the destruction of the men around the gun. Brian flew just over the top of the tower.

"You got 'em, Hunter," radioed Buddy.

Brian drifted down and throttled back to allow the 'B' Division to reposition and the 'A' Division to reform in the lead. The process took just under ten minutes, and then they throttled up to maximum continuous power to make their egress. Their route took them north of the Ruhr Valley industrial complex, between Amsterdam and Rotterdam, and directly to Debden. Again, they encountered no fighters and no more anti-aircraft fire, landing without incident.

Brian and Larson gave the aircraft a quick look—nothing obvious. A few of the others had some shrapnel damage. He knew Tomlinson would give the bird a thorough, detailed inspection and servicing. Brian waited for his turn with the intelligence debriefer. A new, rather large staff sergeant, Brian had not seen before, would take his debriefing.

"I've not seen you before."

"Name's Bradford, Sir. I'm assigned to the 8th Air Force headquarters at High Wycombe, but I requested some field experience. So, here I am."

"Well, then, welcome to the party, Staff Sergeant Bradford. Let's hop to it."

They methodically stepped through each mission phase, including hitting his assigned portion of each target airfield. "Please tell me more about the tower you hit after Potsdam," Bradford asked.

Brian recounted his confrontation and spur-of-the-moment decision to engage the tower. "The tower had a single 88 and looked smaller than the photographs you guys showed us."

"Your description suggests you may have encountered a new version. We'll study your gun camera film to get more details like specific dimensions. According to your wingman, you dealt with the gun quite well. The gun camera film should confirm it. We preliminarily marked the location by your estimate, and we'll task a photo recon mission to locate it precisely. After all, those things don't move."

"We certainly did not know it was there, or we would've avoided it. It sure surprised me."

"It was unknown to Force Intel. When we collect the data, we'll compare notes with the British. Until your discovery, we knew there were three types of flak towers. The German word is *Flaktürme* (Flak tower). We all seem to have adopted the term flak, which is also derived from the German word *Fliegerabwehrkanonen*, or air defense cannons, otherwise known as anti-aircraft guns. Flak towers are located in three cities: Berlin, Hamburg, and Vienna. Potsdam is considered a suburb of Berlin, although we did not know any towers were that far away from the city center. There were three generations of flak towers: a massive eight-story quad, a mid-sized dual, and a still large single tower. Their primary armament is a twin mount of 128mm anti-aircraft cannons. Army Intelligence has long believed the towers became smaller as resources grew scarcer. Perhaps they are downsizing again. Did you happen to notice a radar tower close by?"

"No. I was pretty busy and rather focused."

"Quite understandable. Anyway, Major, that should do it for me. Eighth Fighter Command or 8th Air Force may want to interview you personally."

"No problem. They have but to ask. Thank you for the education, Staff Sergeant Bradford. I hope my gun camera film and information will prove useful."

"They will, Sir. Good day to you, Major."

"Thank you, Sergeant, and good day to you."

Only Buddy Courtland and Sergeant Ellison remained by the time Brian made it back to the squadron's operations building.

"The Skipper released the squadron," Buddy announced. "I wasn't going to leave you alone."

"Thanks mate," Brian answered.

Brian and Buddy walked back to the Officer's Mess. Juli would remain and secure the building for the night. Hunter conveyed what he had learned from Staff Sergeant Bradford. They had another hour before dinner. A pint was thrust into Brian's hand when he walked into the bar. The other pilots interrogated Brian about the tower. The story got embellished as the listeners added observations. The beer did not help the telling. Once finished with dinner, Brian tried to call Charlotte without success due to some unspecified problem. He was done for the night.

———

Friday, 7. April. 1944
Headquarters, XXI Army Group
St. Paul's School
Lonsdale Road
Barnes, London, England
13:30 hours

The Allied Expeditionary Force general and command staffs gathered to review the findings of Exercise THUNDERCLAP—the tabletop simulation of the Operation OVERLORD plan. Major elements of the plan had been declared stable and ready. The afternoon's review was the latest evaluation exercise and arguably the most problematic of the overall plan—the ground forces element.

Among the general staff were Major General Kenneth William Dobson Strong, OBE, LM, Assistant Chief of Staff for Intelligence (G-2), who had served under Eisenhower at Allied Forces and now SHAEF, and Major General Harold Roe 'Pink' Bull, USA [USMA 1914], Assistant Chief of Staff for Operations (G-3). The leaders of the command staff were all present: naval forces commander, soon to be promoted, Vice Admiral Sir Bertram Home Ramsay, KCB, KBE, MVO; ground forces commander and General Officer Commanding-in-Chief XXI Army Group General Sir Bernard Montgomery; and air forces commander Air Marshal Sir Trafford Leigh-Mallory, KCB, DSO. In addition, of course, the British joint chiefs of staff attended, Admiral Cunningham, General Brooke, and Marshal of the Royal Air Force Sir Charles Frederick Algernon Portal, GCB, DSO & Bar, MC.

Although the day's review was considered a routine assessment of the plan, Prime Minister Churchill invited himself to observe and listen to the tabletop findings. The prime minister had assured the supreme commander that he would strive mightily to listen and not speak. They both knew that position was a virtual impossibility.

First up was Sir Bertram. "The naval element portion of the master plan remains stable. Naval forces are focused on training and general rehearsal exercises with better-than-expected progress. We have a major full-dress rehearsal with associated ground forces scheduled in three weeks at Slapton Sands, just west of Plymouth. The tabletop exercise demonstrated that movement timing from the south coast to the landing beaches is critical in meeting our initial objectives.

"The simulation demonstrates that we can maintain the delivery schedule to the Normandy beaches with a 5% loss rate of landing craft. However, if we exceed 6.7%, we will begin to suffer delays and fall short of the plan. We do not have much room for combat losses. We examined several loss combinations like L-S-Ts or God-forbid a troop transport. We believe we are ready to support the ground plan and protect the invasion fleet from attack. We are very near our capacity to cycle landing craft from the shipping to the beach until the Mulberrys are in place and functional. Our request for more landing craft to stage as spares will give us flexibility and the ability to make up losses swiftly. All that said, the combined naval forces are ready to execute OVERLORD. Are there any questions?"

The questions dealt with traffic control on D-Day and after. They also recognized there was no way to hide the gathering of so many ships of various sizes. Numerous derelict or non-operational ships were moved to eastern ports in association with Operation FORTITUDE—the broad deception campaign of which General Patton was a vital part. Sir Bertram also answered a couple of specific questions about sealing off both ends of the Channel. Ramsey sat down.

Sir Trafford stood as the next to present his command findings. "The combined air forces have more surge capacity than the other branches. The current plan calls for the air force to divert mostly tactical assets and a portion of strategic units to directly support the preparation, execution, and sustainment of the OVERLORD plan. In addition, we will continue to prosecute the strategic bombing campaign over Germany. OVERLORD will have priority over POINTBLANK.

"The tabletop simulation evaluated a series of scenarios including a maximum effort in and around the beachhead. The air plan meets all of the OVERLORD requirements with a surge capability should the need arise. We met all of the contingency scenarios with margin. I am compelled to report that some of our participants noted the potential for communications difficulties between air and ground units, especially when close air support is called for. The ground uses lower frequency V-H-F-F-M radios, while the aircraft use V-H-F radios. The tabletop exercise did not find a solution that would be available in time to support the Normandy action. We have refined the communication procedures to mitigate the potential problem, and both air and ground units have been training with the new procedures. We urge caution."

"That seems like a very important finding," Eisenhower interjected. "Do the ground and naval forces commanders agree?"

"Yes Sir," responded Sir Bertram and Sir Bernard in unison.

"I will also add," Ramsay continued, "that we have all agreed on procedures to avoid anti-aircraft fire over the fleet, should it become necessary. I do believe all our forces have been briefed and trained on the procedures."

"Agreed," Monty added.

"Very well, then. We do not need any friendly fire incidents. We have enough on our plate already."

Sir Trafford summarized the air defense portion of the plan to protect the fleet and beachhead. Several questions addressed the interdiction campaign by the air forces before and during the landings to isolate the beachhead to slow the enemy's reinforcement efforts. When he had addressed the questions, Sir Trafford returned to his chair.

"Last but not least," Eisenhower said, "General Montgomery, the ground forces findings."

Sir Bernard took the podium. "To summarize, as we agreed on the assault plan last month, we are landing on D-Day seven, line infantry divisions, an armored division along with three armored brigades, three airborne divisions, and various special-purpose units. We have quite a few moving parts. We have examined a number of potential failures, for example, the inability of the 6th Airborne to secure the Pegasus Bridge at Bénouville to the failure of FORTITUDE and the release of a portion or all of Panzer Group West units to counterattack our landing force. Before I cover our findings, I must commend the FORTITUDE team. To date, the deception appears to be working, but we consider the release of all or part of the armored force held in reserve by Hitler our greatest threat.

"As a consequence of the early findings, we decided we needed more armor on the left flanks since the 21st Panzer Division will likely take a direct shot at the beachhead. Therefore, we traded two infantry divisions in the initial assault force for two additional armor brigades, both equipped with Sherman Firefly tanks."

Sherman Firefly tanks have a standard M4 Sherman chassis with their short-barreled, low-velocity, 75-mm gun standard main armament retrofitted with a QF 17-pounder (76.2 mm), long-barrel, high-velocity main gun. Firefly was the only effective Allied tank against the formidable German Tiger and Panther tanks.

"The landing plan meets our ground objectives through D+5. However, the uncertainty of the German reaction makes D+30 objectives more problematic. Our greatest vulnerability is the swift deployment of the 21st *Panzer* Division, which is currently deployed 20 miles southeast of Caen.

"Early in the planning, we decided to leave the three bridges over the River Orne and the Caen Canal off our preparation target list, since we believed the preservation of the bridges would be more advantageous to our offensive than to the German counterattack. The tabletop evaluation considered all three bridges intact to all of them destroyed and the combinations in between. As we have known since our earliest assessments, we are in a race against time. If we can get our armor, especially our Firefly tanks ashore and across the Pegasus Bridge and the associated lower Orne River Bridge, in sufficient force to meet the inevitable 21st *Panzer* counterattack, then we expect to meet and defeat the counterattack. Without the bridges, the importance of Caen becomes even greater and beachhead expansion more difficult. While the 21st *Panzer* remains our greatest threat, the most difficult landing beach is Omaha because of those imposing cliffs and narrow ravines.

"The beach is defended at present by the 352nd Infantry Division, the best equipped and manned enemy infantry division in the Normandy region, and the terrain is demonstrably to their advantage. The Pointe du Hoc coastal defense battery has the potential of seriously slowing the landing process by engaging the fleet and diverting the attention of the warship from assault support to neutralizing the threat. We witnessed a dress rehearsal by the 2nd Ranger Battalion on a beach cliff in Cornwall. The Rangers have a workable plan and the skills to execute the plan, not without considerable risk, I must say."

General Montgomery covered the remainder of the ground tabletop findings and handled the myriad questions calmly, methodically, and professionally. With that, Monty sat down.

General Eisenhower asked for other observations, questions, concerns, statements, or opinions. No one had anything more to add. The answers to their questions had been sufficient.

"Prime Minister, would you care to comment?" Eisenhower asked.

"I must say," began Churchill, "my sincerest compliments to the planning, command, and general staffs of the Allied Expeditionary Force. While I still have my concerns, I am now convinced we have the best plan given terrain, time, and resource limitations. Well done, I must say. I shall message President Roosevelt forthwith that I am warming to the plan. Well done to all."

"Thank you, Prime Minister. With that, I do believe we have a plan. Our task is to ensure the assault units have completed their training and preparations to execute the plan. With that, gentlemen, we have a long road ahead. Let us set ourselves to the task of ensuring our troops are ready for the grand crusade ahead."

The various chiefs offered Eisenhower their congratulations. Then, out of his peripheral vision, Ike noted that Prime Minister Churchill had not budged. He knew what that meant.

Eisenhower started to sit down next to Churchill for the chat he knew was inevitable. Churchill promptly stood facing the general. "No, for this, I want to be eye-to-eye, man-to-man. Since I first met you all those years ago, I have known that you were destined for greatness. And, here we are on the verge of the grand crusade, as you say. I wanted to convey my respect for what you have done to make a combined staff work so well. We cannot lose. Lastly, I meant what I said to the staff. I am warming to this plan and the pending affair. That is a tribute to you, Ike . . . your skill in making a disparate staff work like a well-oiled machine. Thank you, Ike. You made it easy to convey my observations to the president."

"Thank you, Prime Minister. I appreciate your words of encouragement. The easy part is done. The hard part lies just ahead of us."

"Indeed! We shall go forth together, my dear Ike." Churchill shook Eisenhower's hand, turned, and departed without another word.

Eisenhower waited until the door closed behind the prime minister.

As if on cue, Beetle entered. "I thought it went rather well, if you ask me, Sir."

"Agreed, Beetle. It will soon be up to the sergeants."

Both generals set to their work for the rest of the day and into the night.

—

Tuesday, 11.April.1944
USAAF Station F-356
Saffron Walden, Essex, England
United Kingdom
09:00 hours

The group had no missions and only a group parade formation scheduled for the day. All three squadrons stood at parade rest with the officers in front of the enlisted ranks, and the group staff officers formed up in front of the 335th Fighter Squadron officers. The day's formation served two purposes—an inspection by the supreme commander and an award ceremony. I've never been a fan of these formations. The colonel saw the limousines approaching before Brian did. General Eisenhower arrived with Lieutenant General Carl Andrew 'Tooey' Spaatz, USAAF [USMA 1914], Commanding General, Strategic Air Forces Europe, and Commanding General, 8th Air Force, Lieutenant General Doolittle, who had been promoted just a month ago. Colonel Blakeslee called the group to attention and presented the group to the supreme commander.

Brian heard the other squadron commanders order their squadrons to return to parade rest, while the generals and colonel followed the supreme commander on his inspection tour. Eisenhower walked through the ranks, occasionally stopping to have a short chat with a few pilots and enlisted men. As General Eisenhower completed his inspection of the 334FS and moved to 335FS, Colonel Clark commanded the squadron to parade rest, and then he heard the 335FS come to attention. A similar sequence took place when it was the 336FS's turn.

Eisenhower and his entourage proceeded to the position 15 paces in front of Colonel Blakeslee, who resumed his command position. A voice over unseen loudspeakers ordered Lieutenant Colonel Blakeslee and Major Drummond to front and center. The voice announced attention to orders and read Colonel Blakeslee's Distinguished Service Cross (DSC) citation to the group. General Eisenhower pinned the DSC on his uniform tunic. Then, the voice read Brian's DSC citation, which recognized the consequences of the torpedo detonation that nearly destroyed Hunter's Mustang. The important enemy E Boat base was obliterated and removed from service. The citation used the phrase "who displayed extraordinary heroism in combat with an armed enemy force" *What? I was only doing my job, just like all the other pilots. I don't see the rationale for a DSC—the second highest award in the Army. But I'm not going to argue with the recognition.*

General Eisenhower pinned the award on Brian's tunic below his wings. Brian saluted. The general returned the salute and then shook Brian's hand. "I understand we have one important fact in common, Brian," Eisenhower said softly, not a whisper but firmly. The instant puzzled expression on Brian's face induced a quiet but noticeable chuckle and a broad smile by the general.

What on earth is he talking about?

"We're both Kansans," Ike offered with another chuckle.

Brian smiled. "Yes Sir. That we are."

"You have developed quite the reputation as a fighter pilot. This award," Ike said, lifting the DSC on Brian's tunic, "is a direct tribute to that fact. And, if I am informed properly, you have substantial holdings in Kansas."

"I suppose that is a matter of perspective, Sir."

Eisenhower chuckled softly again. "As with all things. Perhaps we can have dinner sometime, in a more informal setting. I would love to hear more about our Kansas connection."

"I am humbled, Sir. I am at your service."

The general smiled, nodded his head, and returned to his position.

Blakeslee whispered, "Post."

Brian executed a crisp military about-face in unison with Blakeslee. The awardees returned to their positions in the formation. Eisenhower and Blakeslee traded salutes, and then the generals departed. The colonel waited until the limousines passed from view, and then he ordered the squadron commanders to dismiss their squadrons. Each commander complied in order.

Congratulations came from those Brian worked with, including pilots from the other squadrons who knew Brian. They gradually moved toward their respective operations buildings. Blakeslee was talking to Clark, and then Arnie left and presumably returned to his office.

Blakeslee pointed to Brian as he approached and gestured for Hunter to join him, which Brian did. He saluted the senior officer.

"Walk with me," Horseback said and gestured to his right.

"Yes Sir."

"First, congratulations to you for your D-S-C."

"Thank you, Sir, and the same to you for your D-S-C."

"Thanks. Second, you seemed rather chummy with the supreme commander. Is there something I should know?"

"It is just chit-chat, Sir. We're both from Kansas."

"Not every swingin' Richard gets a dinner invitation from a general officer, set aside the supreme commander."

"Sir, he wanted to know more about my holdings in Kansas."

Blakeslee stopped and faced Brian. "Holdings?"

"My parents were killed in an automobile accident New Year's night in 1942, and I inherited several businesses from them." *I don't see any reason to go into the details unless he specifically asks. I am what I do, not what I own.*

"Good. You just seemed more familiar."

"I never met the man, and we still have not been formally introduced. I think it was simply friendly banter, Sir."

"Perhaps so. I'll leave it there and only ask you to inform Colonel Clark and myself if you do, in fact, eventually have dinner with the supreme commander."

"No problem, Sir . . . well, unless he asks me to keep whatever conversation occurs private."

"Understood. Thank you, Hunter." Blakeslee shook Brian's hand. "Keep doing what you do so well."

"Yes Sir."

"Your life is like a good book, Brian. More unfolds with the turn of each page." Blakeslee held Brian's eyes without words. "I have followed your exploits since I arrived in England in May of '41."

Do I ask him to sustain my mission limit waiver? I'd love to settle the uncertainty but now is not the time.

"Well, anyway, Hunter, I just wanted to mention my sensitivity to General Eisenhower . . . or any general for that matter. Are there any others I should be aware of?"

"Yes Sir. Air Marshal Sir John Spencer is a friend and mentor of mine, and he has been since 1938. Our families are close." *Probably a serious understatement.* "He was recently relieved as commander Number 3-7 Group in the Med, and he is now the chief of air operations for the Mediterranean Theater. One of his uncles is Prime Minister Churchill, whom I've met several times. I probably should add that Lord Selborne, Minister of Economic Warfare and chief of the Special Operations Executive is a neighbor of ours in Hampshire."

"Hampshire?"

"Yes Sir. My wife Charlotte inherited, owns, and operates Standing Oak Farm, northeast of Winchester, Hampshire."

"And we turn a few more pages."

"Have I done something wrong, Sir?"

"No, no, of course not. I'm just surprised you know so many important men."

"I've not sought these contacts, other than Sir John. He was a squadron mate of my flight instructor in Kansas. Together, they helped me join the RAF in June 1939."

"Before the war began?" Blakeslee asked with a hint of incredulity.

"Yes Sir."

"Damn, man! My curiosity has reached obsessive levels, but I've taken too much of your free time already. The group was released from duty after the formation. I've already cut into your free time, which you should enjoy while we can. Changes are afoot."

"Thank you, Sir." Brian saluted. Blakeslee returned the salute. They both turned and went opposite ways.

Sergeant Ellison informed him that the squadron had indeed been released for the day. Brian walked to the Officer's Mess. Most of the pilots had already departed. Brian tried to call Charlotte, but the telephone connections remained troubled. He was seriously tempted to make the run to Standing Oak Farm just for a few hours with Charlotte and Ian, but without knowing they would be there, he decided against the effort. Brian had started reading Charles Dickens' *A Tale of Two Cities*, which somehow seemed appropriate given rumored events ahead of them. He began reading the classic book several months ago. *That will be my day.* Brian removed his uniform tunic, loosened his tie, and then removed the DSC medal and placed it in a drawer with his other decorations. He still chose to wear only his RAF wings above his right pocket and his Army wings above the left pocket. Brian settled into his comfortable, cushioned chair and resumed his reading.

———

Tuesday, 11.April.1944
No.10 Downing Street
Whitehall, London, England
United Kingdom
17:10 hours

Prime Minister Churchill had taken an extra day to enjoy a rare early spring day at Chequers, although the burdens of wartime leadership were never very far away. The limousine ride back into London this morning had been smooth, quiet, and without incident or delay. The late morning's meeting had gone smoothly—no surprises. Lunch and his afternoon nap proved refreshing as usual.

The prime minister was tending to his daily reading workload when the knock on the door interrupted him. Peck stepped inside and closed the door. "A Mister Goodman, Herbert Goodman, is here to see you."

"I don't know a Goodman. Who is he, and where is he from?"

"He would not say, but he has a case chained to his left wrist."

"I think we know what that means. Please show him in."

Peck opened the door and said, "The prime minister will see you, Mister Goodman."

The middle-aged man with balding hair and a rather scholarly appearance waited until the door closed behind him. "Excuse me, Prime Minister, 'C' asked me to bring this," he held up the case, "to you myself immediately. He thought I might be useful in answering any questions you might have."

"Pardon me for not knowing the answer, but what is your job, Mister Goodman?"

"I'm the chief of the German Desk at M-I-6."

Churchill nodded his head and gestured for Goodman to place the case on the desk. Winston retrieved his personal access key and opened the case. There was only a single sheet of paper with red-striped margins.

MOST SECRET - ULTRA

```
MOST SECRET ULTRA
SECRET
DATE 1539 10 APR 1944
TO EMPIRE LEADER PROTECTIVE ECHELON
FROM THE LEADER
BREAK
```

```
IT HAS BECOME CLEAR TO ME THAT OUR RECENT
SETBACKS IN SOUTH RUSSIA ARE DIRECTLY DUE TO
THAT TREACHEROUS BADOGLIO AND COLLAPSE OF
ITALY BREAK THEY HAVE SIPHONED OFF THIRTY
FIVE PRECIOUS COMBAT DIVISIONS BREAK BADOGLIO
DESERVES TO BE SEVERELY PUNISHED FOR HIS
BETRAYAL BREAK AS A CONSEQUENCE YOU MUST
REDOUBLE YOUR EFFORTS TO RAISE MORE OF YOUR
VAUNTED COMBAT PROTECTIVE ECHELON DIVISIONS
BREAK VICTORY WILL BE OURS END
SECRET
DECYPHERED 0837 11 APR 1944
MOST SECRET ULTRA
```

MOST SECRET - ULTRA

"This is a personal from Hitler to Himmler?"

"Yes Sir."

"Do we agree with the 35 divisions?"

"No Sir. Our number in Italy is 29, so we are apparently missing half a dozen divisions. We're looking for them."

"Please let us all know if you find them. This message implies that our strategy of taking on Italy before Normandy was the correct one. I would like to believe we have drawn off 35 combat divisions from Russia and France. More significantly in my reading, the foul corporal is ordering his loyal minion to create more *Waffen-SS* divisions for the Eastern Front."

"Yes Sir. Himmler set aside the all-Aryan requirement for the *Waffen-SS* several years ago. They have formed numerous S-S combat divisions from nearly all of the occupied countries. They also have the 12th *SS-Panzer Hitlerjugend Division* – Hitler Youth. The majority of troopers in the heavy division are teenagers, most not even conscription age. The division is in Northern France and assigned to Rommel's mobile reserve."

"Thank you, Mister Goodman. Is there anything else?"

"Yes Sir. 'C' asked me to inform you that two of the escapees from *Stalag Luft III* have arrived safely in Gothenburg, Sweden. Two of our field agents carried out a quick preliminary interview. Both are Norwegian airmen who had been flying with the RAF. They were numbers 43 and 44 who escaped. They are being returned to England, where they will be thoroughly debriefed once they arrive. We should eventually obtain a listing from the Red Cross. The Gestapo has kept a very tight lid on the escape. They know at least 44 escaped from the Sagan camp, and they believe many more were after them, but they did not wait around to see how many."

"Quite understandable. Please convey to 'C' to keep me informed as we learn more."

"By your command, Sir." Goodman started to retrieve the ULTRA message.

"No, no, Mister Goodman. I have a scheduled appointment with the supreme commander in ten minutes. I want to discuss this message with him before you secure it."

"Do you need me to assist?"

"That will not be necessary. However, I would like you to remain for a few minutes. I will address this decrypt," Churchill said, holding up the ULTRA message, "first thing, then return it to you for safekeeping."

"Very well, Sir."

Goodman stepped outside the office to wait. Peck stepped in. "Do you need anything, Sir?"

"Just Eisenhower. I've asked Mister Goodman to wait to retrieve a missive for safekeeping. Please show the general in as soon as he arrives." Peck nodded and closed the door.

Churchill began his review of the latest shipping report, including losses and deliveries. Although the losses due to U-boats remained at essentially zero, weather and mechanical failure still claimed far too many ships.

Peck appeared. "General Eisenhower has arrived, Sir."

"Please show him in." Churchill moved from his desk with the ULTRA message to the small conference table in his office. They greeted each other and sat.

"I just received this Boniface," Churchill said, handing the paper to the general.

Eisenhower looked up. "Confirms our Italy decision."

"My thoughts precisely. I wanted you to be aware of that corporal's order to form more *Waffen-SS* divisions."

"Quite understandable given their circumstances." Eisenhower passed the intercept back to the prime minister.

"Excuse me for a moment. I must return this to the courier." Churchill stepped out of the office for a minute and returned, closing the door behind him. "Before I step to the next item, I wanted to ask you if the troops are prepared to deal with German youth—teenagers—in the coming battle."

"You're referring to the 12th *Panzer*." Churchill nodded. "Yes. Every combat unit, infantry to artillery, has been briefed on the presence of very young enemy soldiers. They know the potential and know that an enemy soldier is still a soldier regardless of age. They will do their duty."

"As it should be. Thank you, general. Now, I received yesterday a message from Marshal Stalin confirming their coordinated attack – Operation BAGRATION by their reference, after the legendary Russian prince/general in the Napoleonic Wars – will occur within weeks of OVERLORD."

"Thank you for that. Good news indeed. As you know, Prime Minister, we have a major dress rehearsal scheduled in two weeks, which will be our last major milestone in advance. Our next biggest concern is the weather. Group Captain Stagg is watching the weather in the U.S. and Canada, and of course, in the North Atlantic. We don't have enough data to give us a forecast six weeks out. I'm convinced the troops are ready, and we continue to receive landing craft that will help the transport. But, it is the weather that might upset the apple cart."

"We shall all pray for decent weather. FORTITUDE appears to be working so far. From my perspective, General Patton is doing exactly what we wanted and expected him to do—keep the Germans' attention on the Pas de Calais."

"That is our opinion as well. At some point, based on any one or combination of criteria, Patton will be released quietly from FUSAG duties to establish the 3rd Army headquarters element. We expect the 3rd Army to enter combat around D+45 depending upon the enemy's reaction and our progress. That point will be when our ruse no longer has value."

"At least, for now, FORTITUDE is working."

"Agreed. May I ask, Prime Minister, do we know the axis of advance for BAGRATION?"

"No. I have asked for more detailed information without success. However, it is my understanding that the primary axis is directly west into Poland and Germany."

"That's more advantageous for our battle plan, but not so much for your dictum of meeting the Red Army as far east as possible. They will be closer to Berlin than we will be."

Churchill chuckled more visibly than audibly. "I appreciate the recognition, Ike, but I think dictum may be a smidgen too strict of a word choice." They both laughed.

"Our first task is to land sufficient forces to hold the beachhead against the inevitable counterattack. The next objective is to sink sufficiently deep roots to withstand the full weight of the German Army. It most likely will not be until George can bring the full force of the 3rd Army to bear that we will be able to make our run to Berlin."

The two leaders turned the conversation to more social than professional topics until the prime minister ran out of time. Eisenhower departed to his waiting limousine and Kay Summersby. "We're done for the day," Ike declared. "Let's go to the Cottage."

—

Wednesday, 19.April.1944
RAF Hamble
Hamble-le-Rice, Hampshire, England
United Kingdom
14:20 hours

The morning's mission had involved each flight of the 334FS shooting up anti-aircraft installations around Cherbourg's port and then hitting the Cherbourg-Querqueville Aerodrome.

Hunter never made it to the enemy airfield. A previously unknown German quad 20 mm *Flakvierling 38* caught him on the run-in to his assigned 88 mm *Fliegerabwehrkanone 36* installation. His aircraft took at least four hits that Brian could count, forcing him to abort the remainder of the mission and try to make it home.

Buddy stuck with Hunter. Sweet took over the lead of 'B' Division. The engine was already running rough. *Keeping the engine running just enough to make it across the Channel is going to be a challenge.* The damage to his left wing meant at least one and probably two of his guns had been rendered inoperable. *I'm in no shape for a fight. Thank God Buddy is with me for some protection.* Brian throttled back to 36 inches MAP, stayed low until they were five miles out over the Channel, and then he began a gradual climb. *I need some altitude in case I must jump.* He leveled off at Angels Five. *I've lost at least one cylinder and probably two, but the engine is still running.* Brian throttled back some more to 30 inches MAP. He looked back behind his right wing to see Buddy's Mustang and hand signaled him to give his underside a good assessment. Brian focused on keeping his machine steady to make Buddy's inspection easier.

By the time Buddy reappeared, he was in a tight formation position making his hand signals easy to understand. Courtland reported a fuel leak, a slight coolant leak, and six impacts. *There's not much I can do about any of that.* He opened up his coolant and radiator flaps to lower the coolant and oil temperatures to the bottom of the green arc for the most margin he could control.

Brian checked his map. RAF Hamble was the closest airfield *if I can make it that far. One step at a time.* Brian switched them both to their emergency radio channel. He checked in with Sector Control and informed the controller of his situation and intentions. The engine remained very rough but not changing . . . *at least for now.* He planned to leave everything as is until he was overhead the landing area and then execute a spiraling precautionary approach at idle just in case the engine quit. Brian signaled Buddy his intentions. His wingman would stay with him until Brian was safely on the ground and then depart for Debden.

The distinct shape of the Isle of Wight at the mouth of The Solent was readily recognizable. Brian adjusted his flight path slightly to place the aircraft over the

Hamble grass landing area. As he reached that position, Brian slowly retarded his throttle and began a left spiral descending turn around Hamble. The engine did not like the change. The spit and sputter did not sound good. Despite the engine being at low power and the coolers wide open, the coolant temperature rose swiftly. The rate of increase was faster than his approach to the ground. *I'd better get the gear and flaps down before the engine quits.* Brian lowered the landing gear handle, expected to get a red unsafe light but was surprised when he saw the green down-and-locked light illuminate. He lowered the flaps to only the 20° position. Brian kept his spiral descent close to the field. *Another turn should do it.* He opened the canopy, again just in case. And then, the terrible, grinding, metallic noise preceded the sudden stoppage of the propeller. Brian quickly adjusted his flight path in a glide to ensure he made the field. The power-out landing occurred without further problem.

Emergency vehicles quickly surrounded the aircraft. Out of habit, Brian moved all of the appropriate levers and switches to complete the shutdown of the aircraft, although it was really moot. Smoke began to waft out of the edges of the engine cowling. The emergency crew opened the cowling as if they knew the aircraft. There was no fire, but the engine was definitely smoking.

After Brian answered the necessary questions, the operations staff helped him call 4FG at Debden. Brian repeated his story and told them he was safely on the ground at RAF Hamble. Unfortunately, the aircraft was not flyable and probably needed an engine change as well as repairs to other battle damage. Brian tried to call Charlotte again without success. *What the hell is going on with the telephone system? Why can't I connect with Standing Oak Farm?*

Brian watched as the ground crew towed the damaged fighter out of the landing area and to one of the repair hangars. They parked his machine on the line as if they were awaiting space. They closed the canopy and reinstalled the engine cowling panels. Satisfied they had put his damaged baby to bed properly, Brian returned to the operations desk and asked the sergeant to contact ATA Third Officer Marilyn Powell Morrison.

"I am informed she is on a mission and is due back this afternoon. The A-T-A operations building is the third hut beyond the last hangar to the left. She will check in there when she returns."

"Thank you, Sergeant."

Brian ambled down the flight line. After all, he had several hours until Marilyn was expected back at Hamble. The airfield was an aircraft modification, repair, and delivery center. Mostly various marks of Spitfires occupied the hangars and flight line. The main Supermarine factory sat just up The Solent in Woolston. They also had many other models in repair and waiting for repair. The senior aircraftman, who served as the ATA operation clerk, confirmed what Brian had been told earlier. He added that they had delivered half a dozen Spitfires and were inbound in a Hudson transport aircraft.

A chair outside in the sun for a little doze seemed like a great idea. Brian removed his flight gear and unzipped his flight suit to mid-chest. The warm sun on a clear day proved more than enough to vanquish the cool air. Brian leaned back in the lounge chair, pulled his hat over his eyes, and swiftly lapsed into sleep.

Rotary engines at idle woke Brian from his slumber. He stood, straightened his tunic, and adjusted his hat properly. Brian recognized Marilyn before she recognized him.

"My goodness, Brian, what are you doing down here."

"Waiting for you."

The Hudson pilot kept the engines running. As soon as the last of their passengers departed and the hatch closed, the aircraft took off presumably to return to its home base or perform another transport mission.

"Why? Has something happened? Mud's not here, but I expect him this evening. You're in a flight suit, not your uniform. You flew down here to see me? What's wrong?"

Brian smiled. "Easy now." He turned slightly to his right and pointed at the distinct shape of the only Mustang visible on the airfield. "I got shot up over Cherbourg and nursed the machine to a dead-stick landing here."

"Are you OK? Are you wounded or injured?"

"Nope. I'm fine . . . not even a nick. I'm just without wings at the moment."

"Are your folks coming to get you?"

"No. I've not asked. I tried to call Charlotte, but the phones have not been working right for weeks now."

"Does she have a travel permit?"

"Permit?"

"Yes, effective on the 1st of April, three weeks ago, the Home Office implemented a 10-mile restricted zone across the entire southern coast of England. Everyone, including you and even Mud, must hold and present a registered permit to enter or leave the restricted zone. Mud got both of us permits."

"I don't have a permit. I'd have to look at a map, but I think Winchester and thus Standing Oak Farm are beyond ten miles inland."

"I suspect you're correct, but this restricted zone may be why you're having problems with the telephones."

Several other ATA pilots came out to tease Marilyn about her male pilot friend. Marilyn introduced Brian to the five women. One of them remembered his family name and connected him to another ATA pilot, Jennifer Brentwood, in August 1941. Several of the women knew some of Brian's aviation accomplishments. When they finished teasing Marilyn, they informed her that they were done for the day.

"Are you going to stay with us?"

"I can't get to the farm, and I apparently can't get Charlotte to meet me here, so yes, if you will have me."

"We'd love to have you. As I said earlier, Mud should be home in a few hours. I presume you need transport in the morning." Brian nodded his head. "I'm sure it can be done, but I need to get you and Debden on the itinerary for tomorrow." Marilyn gestured for them to go inside.

The operations clerk checked several binders and then took down Brian's name, service number, squadron, and destination. He was on the manifest for tomorrow morning at eight. The ATA had a shuttle service of sorts—a truck or lorry, as the British called it. Brian grabbed his flight gear, and they jumped on board. It was not the most comfortable transport, but it was functional.

The Meadows
School Lane
Hamble-le-Rice, Hampshire, England
17:35 hours

Marilyn and Brian were the last two passengers to be dropped off. The well-constructed, stone masonry, modest-sized house sat on the western end of a four-acre property overlooking The Solent.

"What a magnificent house and property," declared Brian.

"Yes, we are both quite pleased."

The house was warm and surprisingly homey for a newlywed couple. Marilyn suggested they call Charlotte first thing. Brian requested Marilyn make the attempt. She got the same response from the operator—the connection is not available. And, the operator was unable or refused to explain why the telephonic connection was not available.

"I've never heard that before. I've no idea why that would be. Once Mud gets here, one of us can drive up to check on her. You won't be able to go because you do not have a permit, and every person must have a permit."

A middle-aged, graying, stocky woman silently appeared at the end of the hallway but did not approach. Marilyn had her back to the woman and did not notice or detect the woman's presence.

"No, Marilyn. Not necessary. I'm certain one of our crew would have contacted me if something was wrong. Thank you for offering. I'm scheduled for a three-day leave pass at the end of the week. I'll figure all this out then." Brian gestured with his eyes over Marilyn's right shoulder.

"Ah, there you are," Marilyn said and waved for the woman to come forward. "Agnes, this is Major Brian 'Hunter' Drummond of the American Army Air Forces. He is a very good friend of ours." She turned to Brian. "Brian, this is Mrs. Agnes Gorman, our housekeeper, cook, and all-around woman Friday," she added in reference to Daniel Defoe's character 'my man Friday' in his 1719 novel *Robinson Crusoe*.

Brian shook hands with Mrs. Gorman and learned she had been widowed in the Great War when her husband of four years had been killed in action during the brutal Battle of Passchendaele during the late summer and early fall of 1917.

"Have you heard from Mister Morrison?" Marilyn asked Agnes.

"No, Ma'am. Dinner is ready and warm in the oven. We can wait if you wish."

Marilyn looked at Brian and received a head nod consent. "Very well. We'll wait for now." Agnes nodded and departed. "Would you care for some wine or spirits?'

"A little wine would be nice."

Marilyn retrieved a bottle of vintage French Cabernet Sauvignon. She opened the bottle easily and poured two glasses. They stood at the windows overlooking the lawn sloping to the water as the sun was a few fingers above the western horizon.

"I've never seen so many ships," Brian observed. He did not recognize the various types of ships, but he guessed they were transports of many forms. Warships appeared to be anchored toward the mouth of the estuary.

"Neither Mud nor I have either. The Solent began to fill with these gray ships several weeks ago. These ships," she said, gesturing to the array of vessels anchored in the estuary, "and the restricted zone suggests the invasion is getting much closer."

"Indeed. We've been warned that all leaves may be canceled soon. They've not told us when . . . just soon."

"Jeremy told me a week ago that this might be the last time he could get home for many months."

"We've been told essentially the same thing, which makes me regret imposing upon you both."

"Nonsense, Brian. You didn't choose to get your motor shot up. I'm just glad one of us was here to give you a good meal and a nice bed for the night."

"I'm most grateful for your generosity."

"Now, you're being silly."

"Perhaps so, but let's not forget I literally dropped out of the sky into your lap." They both laughed, and their cyclic laughter instigated heartier laughter.

"What did I miss?" Marilyn's husband said from the entryway.

The two comrades embraced, and then Jeremy hugged and kissed his wife. Marilyn insisted that her husband skip the cocktail hour and that they sit for dinner since Agnes had been holding the meal. The trio laughed and shared stories from their mutual past as they enjoyed a simple meal of well-prepared lamb chops, mashed potatoes with a savory gravy, and roasted Brussels sprouts. The laughter and sharing continued well after dinner, lubricated by ample brandy. They talked about flying but not about war.

Brian was the first to reach his tolerance limit, as the fatigue of combat took its toll. He begged for forgiveness and took the good-natured ribbing from his hosts. They bade each other a good night's sleep, as least what was left of it, and they retired for the night.

—

Saturday, 22.April.1944
Standing Oak Farm
Winchester, Hampshire, England
United Kingdom
14:25 hours

"So, what has happened to the telephones?" Brian asked after greeting his wife and son.

Charlotte looked puzzled. "Have you been having problems reaching me?"

"Yes . . . for several weeks now." Brian recounted his protracted effort, including Marilyn's attempt last Wednesday. Charlotte had been unaware of any problems, but she also confessed to not depending upon the telephone for much, mostly to speak remotely with Brian. He also told Charlotte about last Wednesday's mission and emergency landing at Hamble. "Someday, I would like you to see The Meadows—the Morrison's residence. They have a modest but beautiful stone masonry house with a gorgeous view of The Solent, which by the way, is filled with Navy transport ships of all kinds. When I spent the night with the Morrisons, Marilyn told me about the travel permit requirement."

"Quite so. The ten-mile boundary is just south of Winchester."

"Yeah. Marilyn offered to come up here to check on you, but I knew I would have heard from Edith or Mabel if something wrong had occurred."

"Why on earth would anything be wrong, my love? Nothing happens around here other than milking and farming."

"Accidents, all manner of accidents could happen. It's wartime. Millions of things can cause injury or worse. I was worried. I would have taken advantage of Marilyn and Jeremy's offer if it weren't for the travel permit restrictions. What of these permits?"

"I was notified by the Constable of Winchester last month that specific, registered permits would be required for every individual traveling into or out of the restricted zone, effective on the 1st of this month. On the constable's advice, I applied for and received permits for all of us."

"Do I need a permit?" Brian asked.

"The constable said everyone. We can go into Winchester on Monday to obtain a permit for you as well. You have to appear in person."

"Better safe than sorry. Monday it is."

"How long do I have you this time?"

"Three days. And, Arnie tells us it will likely be our last leave for several months." Brian noticed someone out the window. "Were you expecting Lord Selborne and his lady?"

Charlotte turned to look out the window to see Lord and Lady Selborne arrive on horseback. "No. I was not. But, we should welcome our guests."

Charlotte and Brian went outside. "Welcome to Standing Oak Farm, Lord and Lady Selborne."

"I apologize for our unannounced visit, but we are neighbors after all. I was hoping to catch you at home," Cecil said, looking directly at Brian.

"You caught me."

"Are you two up for a ride? We'd like to see the farm," Cecil looked again at Brian, "and perhaps we can have a private word as we ride."

I wonder what that is all about? "Of course, Sir." Brian looked at Charlotte, who nodded her consent. "Let me get us saddled up, and we'd be honored to show you around." Brian went to the corral.

The Selbornes dismounted to chat with Charlotte while Brian tended to the horses.

Brian walked the saddled horses back to the courtyard. Charlotte told Edith that they were going for a riding tour of the farm. They mounted up and headed to the Brownfield parcel to see the greenhouses first. Cecil dropped back as they moved to the Harris tract, and Brian stayed with him. Grace kept Charlotte occupied with questions.

"I'm glad I'm able to talk with you. We're going to get very busy quite soon. I, well Grace and I, wanted to thank you and Charlotte for the milk, cream, cheese, and vegetables you have provided."

"In trade for your beef, pork, and mutton. We're most grateful. But, that is not why you wanted a private chat, and Grace has been quite subtle in occupying Charlotte."

"No, and most perceptive of you. My friend, Wild Bill Donovan, and I share a common vision." The horses sauntered as they talked. "Bill and I believe

Winston's assessment of Soviet intentions once the war is won. I can't predict whether S-O-E will survive the war, but I must plan for what I see ahead, just as Bill must plan for the O-S-S. We need a clandestine air service. I have not seen Bainbridge Air Services in operation, but Bill has, and I trust his judgment. To my point, I wanted to add my weight to Bill's proposal. We see B-A-S as ideally suited to serve as a special operations air service."

"A two-pronged attack, ay."

"Only to show the confidence Bill and I have in the capacity of your airline to do what will inevitably need to be done."

The two men simply followed the two women by about 20 yards. Selborne was clearly far more interested in the conversation than the sightseeing. Brian felt no reason to distract Selborne from his purpose.

"Thank you, Cecil. Charlotte and I have discussed the potential since General Donovan presented his proposal last month. I've not answered Bill just yet."

"I most certainly do not want to upstage General Donovan, Brian. I just wanted you to know that I support and agree with Bill's proposal. We both see the same need, and we both agree that a contract service is preferable to an indigenous unit. We also agree that a joint contract in principle has distinct advantages for both of our organizations."

"I haven't been able to get into London to inform Colonel Bruce. My answer to General Donovan through Colonel Bruce will be, I think we can work something out. Are you suggesting that S-O-E would want a similar service?"

"Yes, precisely. I wanted to add my voice to Bill's on this issue. I cannot predict the future, but I'm chartered to think. I clearly see the need for a clandestine air service since I also believe our need for covert operations will not disappear in the euphoria of peace.

"One more thing related to this topic, Brian. Bill indicated that he asked you for an air plan if you agree to meet the need." Brian simply nodded his head as Cecil glanced at him. "He has agreed to share that plan with me as a joint venture. Please confirm with General Donovan or Colonel Bruce, but I would like to see your plan as soon as possible rather than wait."

"I see no problem, but I will need to confirm with Colonel Bruce."

"By all means, Brian. Thank you for your consideration. Now, on a more personal curiosity topic, if I am properly informed, you are friends, or at least acquaintances, with the film actress Marlene Dietrich. Is that correct?"

Brian chuckled audibly. "Well, that is quite the redirection. In the spirit of candor and openness, my succinct answer is yes. I met her in '42 while assigned to the War Bonds Drive. She came out to Wichita with Howard Hughes when he wanted to fly my Sopwith Camel in the dead of winter no less, and she spent the weekend with us here in May of last year."

"You travel in interesting circles, Brian."

"All happenstance, I'm afraid."

"I doubt that, but humility is a noble trait. Wild Bill Donovan has stayed at the farm as well, so I hear."

"Yes, he has . . . just last month."

The quartet arrived back at the main farm and toured the various buildings and corrals on horseback, including the new makeshift milking shed annex. The private conversation apparently concluded, Cecil asked questions about the farm and its operations. Both Cecil and Grace displayed an unusual fascination with their milking machines, collection equipment, and cheese-making processes. At the conclusion of the horseback tour, Charlotte offered the Selbornes tea and cookies, which they eagerly accepted.

They talked only of the land and its bounty. The Selbornes also met Edith and the two boys. Cecil and Grace seemed to be genuinely interested in the farm, its people, and the operations. It proved easy to overlook that they were an earl and countess. Charlotte invited them to a farm dinner, but they respectfully declined, citing a pending prior engagement. Charlotte and Brian stood outside as the Selbornes rode off to the east and their estate.

"Well," Brian mused as their guests disappeared over the eastern ridgeline, "that was an interesting afternoon."

"What can you talk about?" asked Charlotte.

"He added the S-O-E to Bill Donovan's special operations air service proposal."

"That doesn't change anything, does it?"

"No, not from my perspective."

"What are we going to do? It's not like we can just telephone Bobby Joe on this."

Bobby Joe Sales and Brian had known each other since '39 when the former served as a mock aerial combat adversary with then Group Captain Spencer before Brian joined the Royal Air Force. Brian hired him to be the general manager of Bainbridge Air Services in February 1941 and had done a magnificent job expanding the business.

"I've got to get into London, convey our answer to the O-S-S station chief, and arrange for a coded message to be hand delivered to Bobby. We need him to put together the plan requested by Donovan and Selborne." Charlotte nodded her head, and from that, they returned to the daily routine that served Standing Oak Farm and its crewmembers.

Friday, 28.April.1944
Hobcaw House, Hobcaw Barony
Waccamaw Neck, Georgetown County, South Carolina
United States of America
13:30 hours

The expansive, 16,000-acre, coastal estate of Bernard Mannes Baruch occupied a goodly portion of the peninsula across Winyah Bay and the Waccamaw River from Georgetown, South Carolina. Baruch purchased a dozen adjacent plantations on the peninsula between 1905 and 1907 to control the area. The history contained on his property dated back to a 1718 royal grant and long-term rice production. While his land no longer produced rice, Baruch saw the land and its historic buildings as a winter retreat and hunting resort. Baruch built the large, red brick, Hobcaw House mansion in 1930 and often used the house as a peaceful country entertainment venue for his family and friends.

Baruch amassed a considerable fortune as a stockbroker and financier on Wall Street in New York City. He had South Carolina roots from childhood, but the family moved to New York when Bernard was 11 years old. Baruch served President Woodrow Wilson as an advisor on national defense during the Great War and now served President Roosevelt as a special advisor on war mobilization. His experience and success in finance and government service gave him access to an interesting circle of friends, contacts, and acquaintances. His South Carolina estate was a popular destination for his friends. Even Winston Churchill and his daughter Diana had stayed at Hobcaw House in 1932 and availed themselves of the quiet and solitude of the estate during Churchill's wilderness years as the outcast "warmonger" in the House of Commons.

On this particular visit, President Roosevelt had arrived at midday on the 9th for what was publicly stated to be a working vacation planned to be a month or so in duration. Admiral 'Bill' Leahy, Doctor McIntire, and General 'Pa' Watson accompanied the President on the train south, along with his Secret Service detail and traveling support staff. Roosevelt made a point of fishing or crabbing nearly every day when the weather was decent enough for such activities.

A special news conference held that morning had gone quite well and dealt with the sudden passing of Secretary of the Navy 'Frank' Knox, who suffered a fatal series of heart attacks earlier that morning. The small group of reporters assembled in the large living room of Hobcaw House pressed the President on Knox's successor, but Roosevelt deftly deflected their attention. Knox had just died; it was far too early to settle upon a successor.

The Roosevelts' oldest child and only daughter, Anna Eleanor Boettiger née Roosevelt, was 38 years of age and married to Major Clarence John Boettiger, USA, who was serving on active duty as a general staff officer in North Africa.

Anna had moved into the White House during her husband's military absence and had become the president's social hostess, tending to the daunting social interactions of her father, as her mother kept her own agenda and schedule. She also had grown quietly concerned for her father's health, especially after the EUREKA Conference in Tehran, Iran, in November 1943; he seemed more depressed and withdrawn afterward. Consequently, in collaboration with her father, Anna also arranged his more private and personal engagements. On this particular occasion, Anna ensured presidential business would be conducted away from Hobcaw House for an important and private lunch guest.

"Papa," Anna announced, "I need to push you out to the gazebo. Your luncheon has been set up out there." Franklin nodded his consent, and Admiral Leahy ushered out the remaining staff. Anna pushed her father's wheelchair out of the main house, down the specially built wooden ramp, and out the concrete walkway to the large gazebo. A tall hedge nearly surrounded the gazebo, except for the unobstructed view south overlooking Winyah Bay. "I'll get you situated. Lucy should be here shortly. I'll bring her here directly." The duty Secret Service agents had taken up positions at a discreet distance.

"Thank you, Anna," he responded. "You are such a dear."

Anna had gone to considerable effort to coordinate all the arrangements for the first meeting between Franklin and Lucy Page Mercer Rutherfurd since 1918. Anna knew the surface history of her father's intimate affair and her mother's discovery. There was no question Anna was conflicted; however, her concern for her father's well-being overwhelmed her misgivings. With her father's consent, Anna had contacted Lucy several months ago and met with her in New York City to set up this initial encounter.

Mercer arrived precisely on time. Anna escorted Lucy to the gazebo. The expression on her father's face upon his first sight of his former lover confirmed the correctness of her collusion. Franklin extended his arms to Lucy. She kissed him on the lips and then hugged him. Lucy had not seen the consequences of Franklin's poliomyelitis affliction, which occurred in August 1921, and she handled his clear, current disability without a twitch. She then kissed him passionately without the slightest modesty in Anna's presence.

"You have plenty of tea, and your lunch plates are under the covers," Anna announced. "I will leave you two to your luncheon and reunion." Anna departed. She would keep watch over the scene from the house to ensure they were not disturbed.

Franklin gestured to the adjacent chair.

Lucy kissed him again and then sat, turning toward him. "So much has happened since I last saw you," she said. "The day I had prayed for is finally here."

"First, my condolences for the loss of your husband last month."

"Thank you, Franklin, but Winthrop had been in failing health for quite a few years. He was 85 years old – a good man, but I was never really in love with him. His death was not unexpected, but thank you nonetheless."

"It warms me to no end to finally see your gorgeous face, my dear. The years have not been kind to me, but you have become even more beautiful and radiant in that time."

"I am grateful to Anna for all the effort she has gone to in facilitating our meeting. Why did you change your mind if I may ask?"

Franklin smiled. "I am not immortal, Lucy. The war . . . this job," he said, waving his arm as if the surroundings were his domain and the essence of his demise, "has consumed me. I have had three terms. No other president in our history has had three terms, and we have yet another election this fall. I cannot admit this to another living soul, but I sense the end. I could not let my limited time remaining to pass without saying, I truly regret what happened in 1918."

"Don't . . . Franklin," Lucy said. "I just could not have you that way."

"Shall we have our lunch?" Franklin reached for the plate covers. Lucy beat him to removing the plate covers. She stacked the covers on the far side of the table. Baruch's family chef prepared exceptional garlic and basil marinated, grilled sea bass filet on a bed of wild rice with green beans. They ate a few bites in silence. Then, Roosevelt continued his thought. "I understand. I'd be lying if I claimed I wasn't disappointed, but I understood."

"Thank you for that. I am most grateful, for whatever reasons, that you changed your mind. I certainly appreciate the requirement for discretion, and I am immensely thankful for your daughter's progressiveness in support of our reunion."

"Yes, she is a peach. Anna is also caught between a rock and a very hard spot. I don't want her hurt in all this. Yet, you've always brought light, joy, and pleasure to my life. Anna is hoping that you can work your magic for my health."

"I do not want to talk about this dreadful war, but I will ask a quick question, if I may." Lucy paused to receive an accepting head nod. "Will this tragedy be over soon?"

Roosevelt wanted to chuckle but could not do so. "The answer depends upon how you define soon. I can't talk about pending plans. However, let is suffice to say, momentous events are in the offing . . . on a scale unprecedented in human history. So, it's certainly our hope and expectation that those events will bring this terrible affair to a rapid conclusion. How long that is, I don't know, and no one can predict."

"Thank you for that and enough of the war." Lucy Mercer stared into Roosevelt's tired eyes. "To speak frankly between friends . . ."

"I hope we're more than friends, Lucy."

"Yes, of course. I was only going to say that the last time we were together, you were a virile young man . . . before your affliction. I don't know how your disability has affected you, but . . . is there anything I can do for you?" She winked at him with a radiant, mischievous smile.

Franklin smiled broadly, and that characteristic, impish twinkle in his eyes returned. "Thank you so much for thinking of me in that way, my dear. I can't tell you how joyous that question is to me. Yes, that particular appendage still works in fine form, if I do say so myself . . . although I'm no longer able to employ it as I once was able to do. I'd love to say, yes . . ." She leaned toward him as though she was going to move to him, but she stopped when he shook his head and held up his hand. "Not this time. I wanted to see if the spark still existed, and I see that it does, both within me and with you. That said, I'm mindful of my schedule as well as Anna's plan and proximity. I'd like to say goodbye properly, for now, before Anna or anyone else disturbs us."

"May I sit on your lap?"

Roosevelt smiled broadly, again. "I'd love that, but that is probably not a good idea either." Lucy stood, stepped toward him, and leaned over to embrace him. He wrapped his arms around her torso. "I just love the smell of your hair. I always have." She drew back just enough to hold his eyes for a moment and then kissed him very passionately. They kissed several more times.

Lucy knelt beside him. "Will I see you again?" she asked.

"I'd like that very much, but that's up to you."

"Then, so it shall be. I look forward to our next meeting."

"As do I," Roosevelt replied.

"Knock, knock," came Anna's voice from beyond the hedge.

Lucy rose, stepped back, and sat in her chair.

"We're decent," declared Franklin.

"Well, that is good to know," Anna said before appearing at the scenic opening. "I'm afraid it is time. I hope you had an enjoyable visit."

"We did," answered Lucy.

"Excellent." Anna looked to her father. "Let me escort Lucy to her car, Papa, and then I shall return to fetch you."

"Thank you, Anna."

Lucy stood. She grasped his proffered left hand with both of her hands. Lucy leaned over and kissed Roosevelt on the forehead. "Until the next time . . ."

The president kissed the top of her hand and simply replied, "Indeed!"

The two women departed. Franklin stared out to the bay and the far shore as he considered what had just happened in his stressful life. He smiled to himself. *It was a good day . . . the best of days.*

Saturday, 29.April.1944
Supreme Headquarters, Allied Expeditionary Force
Camp Griffiss
Warren Plantation and Sandy Lane
Bushy Park, Teddington, London, England
United Kingdom
08:30 hours

   Beetle Smith entered the supreme commander's modest office at their expanded headquarters site. While most of the accommodations at Camp Griffiss were temporary, the new American tenants built a secure building with guarded buffer ground to ensure that highly classified discussions could be carried out. Eisenhower's office, conference room, and encrypted communications were housed in the secure building.

   "Pink is up first, Ike. I've got George cooling his heels in my office when you're ready."

   "Thanks, Beetle. Neither of these will be good discussions, so let's get on with 'em."

   Major General Harold Roe 'Pink' Bull, USA [USMA 1914] served as Assistant Chief of Staff for Operations (G-3) SHAEF.

   Smith opened the door and gestured. General Bull entered. The three generals sat around the small circular table. Eisenhower nodded to Bull to begin.

   "We completed our assessment of the preliminary data late last night, well actually, early this morning. Exercise TIGER began as planned after evening nautical twilight. The exercise was a full-up dress rehearsal for OVERLORD and involved the Navy's 11th Amphibious Force Convoy T-4 and troops of the 1st Engineer Special Brigade, the 4th Infantry Division, and the VII Corps Headquarters. Weather, sea state, and surf conditions were nominal with a waxing half-moon.

   "The ships were loaded and ready to execute the landing just after dawn yesterday morning. Per the plan, the ships were circling in Lyme Bay to simulate the Channel transit. We believe nine German E-boats from Cherbourg made it past our destroyer and motor torpedo boat screen undetected. They attacked at 02:00, and the attack lasted until 03:30. They sank two L-S-Ts and seriously damaged two other L-S-Ts sufficiently to preclude their participation in OVERLORD. Our preliminary count as of this morning is 705 killed, 205 still missing, and 210 wounded."

   "Has OVERLORD been compromised?" Eisenhower asked.

   "We don't think so, Sir. We're still collecting information. The Navy is conducting a detailed assessment; however, Admiral Moon, the task force commander, suspects they had insufficient radar-equipped destroyers to detect the enemy. The Royal Navy motor torpedo boats in the screen force didn't have radar. Another complication, we apparently discovered another communications disconnect, too many links to alert the task force of the E-boat approach. It looks like a lucky strike."

"That may well be a gross understatement, Pink. Seven hundred plus precious men is a tragedy of epic proportion and even more so five weeks prior to D-Day. I wanted all of this, every shred of information, classified Top Secret – BIGOT. I also specifically direct that everyone associated with or even aware of Exercise TIGER to remain silent on penalty of isolation for the duration of the war." Eisenhower looked directly at Smith. "I want the censors to excise any even remote mention of the exercise, not the Press, not in letters home, not in idle conversation in a bar. As far as the public is concerned, this tragedy did not occur. I will inform the command staff." Looking into the eyes of both generals, Eisenhower said, "I want a final report in a week or two at most. Our final commanders' assessment is scheduled for the 15th of next month. We absolutely must know if OVERLORD has been compromised. I also want a precise assessment of the consequences of the losses of troops and shipping on the OVERLORD assault plan."

"Yes Sir," Smith and Bull responded in unison.

"Let's understand what happened as soon as you possibly can, Pink. Time is the essence. The go-no-go decision is just over two weeks away, and we're risking the lives of 160,000 men in just the first day alone."

"I fully understand the gravity of the moment, Sir. We'll get the best answers we can in the time we have."

"Thanks, Pink. Anything else?"

"Not at the moment."

"Very well."

"By your leave . . ."

Eisenhower nodded his head with his mind occupied in contemplation. Beetle recognized the expression and did not interrupt. Smith waited patiently in silence and stillness for several minutes. Finally, when Ike returned, he looked at Beetle and said, "Let's have George."

Smith nodded his head and left the office. Several minutes passed with Ike considering the potential ramifications of the disaster at Slapton Sands, and then George entered, followed by Beetle. Ike gestured to the chair across from him. Beetle closed the door and sat to the right of Eisenhower.

"You know why you are here?"

"Yes Sir," Patton responded softly.

In his capacity as the troop-less commander of the fictitious first U.S. army group, General Patton had been invited to the opening of the Welcome Club at the Ruskin Rooms on Drury Lane in Knutsford, Cheshire. The founders created the club to welcome the officers of the growing 3rd Army, not quite the Eagle Club in London but certainly dedicated to their American guests. The modest inauguration ceremony took place on the 25th of April 1944. His hosts had assured Patton that his remarks would be off-the-record, but they were unaware that members of the Press were present.

"We've all seen the Press reports . . . including the War Department, the chief of staff, and Washington, DC. What is your side of the story?"

The majority of his brief speech at Knutsford was innocuous. However, one phrase reported in newspapers on both sides of the Atlantic created the diplomatic controversy. Patton had said, "It is the evident destiny of the British and Americans and, of course, the Russians to rule the world." The widely reported statement left off the Russians.

"First, Ike, it was a small, innocent ceremony, and the ladies told me my remarks would be off the record. Second, the Press edited my words incorrectly, so I must say. I included the Russians. The reporters may not have heard the words because of applause but others at the ceremony heard me include the Russians."

"Rule the world, George?" Ike asked calmly.

"I did say that, and I now see that as a poor word choice. I certainly didn't intend to imply an autocratic authority."

"George, damn it all to hell," Eisenhower said with demonstrably more emphasis. "That is exactly what you said, and it's directly contradictory to the Atlantic Charter. I specifically asked you to keep your mouth shut, avoid controversy, and act your part in Operation FORTITUDE. You were literally on probation with the War Department, the president, and me. You have once again placed me in a terribly vulnerable position. I saved your ass last summer and put my reputation on the line. We are five weeks from executing the greatest amphibious operation in human history, and I must deal with your imprudence. You're a high-ranking general officer. So much more is expected of you. There comes the point when your liabilities exceed your potential. You're dreadfully close to that threshold, George."

"Ike, please, they misquoted me. I have witnesses. The Press created this controversy to sell newspapers."

"We're in the business where perception is reality, George. The troops, the government, and the people must believe. Those words corrode the perception."

"What do you want me to do?"

Eisenhower stared intently at Patton as he thought about the question. Neither man blinked nor looked away. "I want you to keep your bloody mouth shut. You'll continue to serve as C-G FUSAG. And I want you focused on spinning up the 3rd Army staff." Eisenhower paused and again stared at George Patton. "Lastly, I want to tell you officially and definitely that if you are again guilty of any indiscretion in speech or action that leads to embarrassment for the War Department, any other part of government, or for this Headquarters, I will relieve you instantly from command and ship your sorry ass back to the States. I have reached the end of my tolerance. I have a war to prosecute, and I shall not brook a rogue general who makes the tasks before us more difficult with his bloody mouth. Do you understand me, George?"

Patton held up his index finger and opened his mouth intending to reply but decided to check his urge. He lowered his hand. "Yes Sir," he responded in a calm, professional manner.

Eisenhower nodded his head once and said, "Dismissed."

George offered no further response and left the supreme commander's office. The door closed.

Ike waited a couple of dozen seconds, and then he looked at Smith. "I'll reply to the chief of staff on my decision. This one is not as blatant as last year's slapping incidents, but I could not give him that quarter. We need him to focus on Rommel and Berlin. General Marshal has not said so, but I suspect the War Department's patience with my handling of Georgie is also approaching their threshold of tolerance." Smith nodded his head. "Stay on Pink. We must know how bad the Slapton Sands disaster really is with respect to the OVERLORD plan."

"I will, Ike."

"By the way, I talked to Churchill. It is interesting to note that he saw nothing wrong with Patton's speech. It was Washington that reacted negatively. As Winston said, 'he was only speaking the truth.'" They both chuckled. "Georgie has his advocates despite his mouth."

"Indeed, Ike. He's good at what he does."

"OK. Let's get back to work." Smith departed. Eisenhower returned to his desk and the drafting of his official, for the record, letters to Patton and Marshall.

———

Chapter 5

There is in most Americans some spark of idealism,
which can be fanned into a flame.
It takes sometimes a divining rod to find what it is, but when found,
and that means often, when disclosed to the owners,
the results are often most extraordinary.

-- Associate Justice Louis Brandeis

Wednesday, 3.May.1944
Oxford University Hospital
Headley Way
Headington, Oxford, Oxfordshire, England
United Kingdom
11:30 hours

Linda and Jonathan Kensington used a precious day's leave for the train ride to Oxford for a requested meeting with his sister, Rosemary Alice 'Rose' Kensington. Rosemary's request had been rather cryptic but sounded urgent. Unfortunately, neither brother nor sister-in-law had a hint of the purpose.

Rosemary met them outside the main entrance on a fine spring day. She embraced Linda, kissing both cheeks. "Thank you for dragging my brother up here."

"You're welcome, Rose. You said it was important."

"It is to me," Rose said. "But, before we get into my problem, let's get some lunch."

"This is our first time visiting your hospital, so we'll follow you."

Rosemary walked with them inside and down a few corridors to a closed room with a sign that said, physicians only. Inside it was a modestly appointed dining room. They ordered their meals. "Where is Julia?" asked Rosemary.

"With my Mum," Linda answered. "She takes care of our daughter, your niece, while I'm at work. We felt it was better to keep Julia in her routine rather than deal with the rigors of this journey."

"Sounds like a wise decision. She is such a sweetie."

Linda giggled softly. "Most of the time." Her giggle transitioned into a hearty laugh that attracted the attention of others in the dining room. "Sorry. She's only four months old, but she is developing quite the personality. You can see the evolution of her sense of self."

"I look forward to seeing her again soon."

"You're always welcome any time, Rose. London is not that far away."

"True. It is just my work schedule. We receive so many war wounded . . . orthopedics, burns, brain injuries. We face a cornucopia of damaged bodies in a never-ending stream, more like a constant flood. And we are only one primary care hospital."

"This war will not last forever," added Jonathan.

"You and your best friend will see to that. Until then, I'll remain constantly exhausted trying to save precious lives."

"Rose," Jonathan interrupted, "you did not ask us up here . . . together . . . to enlighten us on your medical workload."

"No, my brother. If you are one thing, you're consistently a to-the-point bloke. Anyone for dessert?"

"No, thank you," Linda answered. Jonathan just shook his head.

The waiter cleared the dishes. Rosemary asked for a glass of water.

"So, to business it is. I'll come directly to the point. I'd like your help in convincing your best friend to come up here."

"Why?"

"I intend to ask him to do what he did for Mary Spencer."

"Impregnate you," Jonathan exclaimed louder than he intended, which induced Linda to grasp his forearm as Rosemary shhh'ed him.

Rosemary looked around at the sparse patrons. She answered softly, "Yes."

Jonathan leaned forward onto both elbows. He mustered the sternest expression he could create. "He's my best friend. He's married to a great woman and has a growing son. He's practically family, for God's sake."

"All true."

"What about Charlotte?"

"I will talk to her personally and eye-to-eye, but I need to know first that Brian would agree."

"You're not married," Jonathan protested. "You're a gorgeous woman. You could have your pick of any Brit, American, or myriad other foreign nationals in exile. Why Brian for your scheme?"

"You know the answer, Jonathan. You know the answer."

Jonathan looked directly into Linda's eyes. "My sister has been in love with Brian since she first met him when I brought him home for Christmas in 1939."

"That's true," Rose reacted. "And I still do. But I know and recognize that he is happily married. I have absolutely no interest in interfering in their marriage or their family. Likewise, I refuse to become an old maid without a part of him in my life."

"What if you do find someone? What will you tell him about this episode?"

"The truth, of course."

"How do you think most men will feel about that disclosure?"

"Frankly, Jonathan, I don't care. If my story, my reasoning, my objective offends a man, any man, then I know for certain he is not the correct man for me. I don't know why, and perhaps one day I shall learn that it's not true for me, but until that time arrives, Brian Arthur Drummond is my one true love, and I cannot have him. I respect Charlotte most emphatically. She is a grand, generous, glorious woman. I envy her in many ways, but most of all, she has Brian's heart." Rosemary paused and looked at Jonathan and Linda alternately as if expecting some sort of response. None came, not even a twitch or a blink. Rose smiled softly. "I'm not asking for your support or endorsement, Jonathan. This is all on me. I'm only asking for your help. Brian respects and listens to you."

Jonathan stared at his sister without expression.

Linda felt the need to break the silence as Jonathan contemplated whether or how to respond. "It's probably not my place in this . . . this . . . this situation, but I'd say follow your heart, Rose. I must say it is a most unusual request, and yet, it is not without precedent. I think . . . no wait . . . I've said too much already. If you want a vote, I say follow your heart."

"Thank you, Linda." Rosemary looked at her brother and waited patiently.

Jonathan cleared his throat, sat back and straight up in his chair, and then he smiled, although it was more like a smirk. "Rose, you've always been a headstrong, determined, stubborn woman since you were a toddler. For the record, I do not like this. I think it is wrong for a host of reasons. That said, I know my baby sister, who is all grown up. I'm proud of you, Rose. I know Mum and Dad are as well. So what do you need me to do?"

"I just want you to get him up here. It would help if you did not tell him what I want to talk to him about. Do you think you can do that?"

"I can make no guarantees, Rose. He has his own mind. I don't want you hurt, but I know you've set your sails, so hold your course and trim your sails. I don't want your heart broken, but I also recognize that is something you have to do. So be it."

"Thank you, Jonathan. Thank you, Linda, for bringing him along."

Rosemary returned to her work. Linda and Jonathan spent the train ride back to London discussing Rosemary's intentions.

———

Friday, 5.May.1944
OSS London Station
Nos. 70-72 Grosvenor Street
Mayfair, London, England
United Kingdom
18:05 hours

Brian made it through the extraordinary security procedures without a hiccup. He was escorted to the station chief's office and announced.

David Kirkpatrick Este Bruce was a career public servant handpicked by General Donovan to be chief of London Station. He assumed the duties of his current assignment in the fall of last year. Bruce was also given the rank of colonel within the OSS hierarchy.

"Thank you for seeing me so late in the day, Sir," Brian began. "I had a full day in the cockpit."

"Nonsense, Brian . . . and David is sufficient between us. I'm glad you made it home unscathed." Brian nodded his head. "I presume you have an answer for Wild Bill."

"Yes. I must also inform you and Bill that Lord Selborne, Cecil Palmer, a neighbor, stopped by the farm a week ago when I happened to be home, luckily. He added SOE to the OSS proposal and informed me that Bill had agreed to include a separate but similar contract for SOE. Assuming that is acceptable, I believe we can put together good plans for both organizations."

"Excellent."

"Combat operations are picking up for me."

"Understandable."

"I'd like my general manager, Bobby Joe Sales, to prepare and present the plan to the O-S-S for approval. I can probably manage the presentation and approval for S-O-E, although I would prefer that Bobby do the honors."

"I think we can arrange that."

"Now, the hard part. I need a secure means of communication to convey authority and instructions to Bobby Sales. I certainly cannot use the telephone, telegraph, or even letter for this message. I assume we can send an encrypted message to O-S-S Headquarters. I will ask for the B-A-S project officer, Chip Warner, to hand carry the message to Wichita and assist Bobby in framing the O-S-S expectations for the plan."

Major Chester Hugh 'Chip' Warner, USAR, had been the OSS-BAS project officer from the beginning of the contract in October 1942. Chip served as Sales primary contact with the OSS.

The two men discussed what Brian wanted to communicate to Sales. Bruce drafted a message to convey Hunter's thoughts. Brian agreed to the terse text and delegation to Sales. David sent the paper off to the OSS station secure communication center for transmission.

They talked about Brian's status with 334FS and Charlotte's work on the farm. Bruce seemed surprisingly fascinated with the greenhouses and the year-round production process.

Twenty minutes later, a man wearing a captain's railroad tracks returned and delivered the sent message. Bruce read it and pushed it across the table for Brian to read.

TOP SECRET - HUNTER

```
OS
LONSTA OSS NR 193
TS 051627Z MAY 44 ROUTINE
FM 105
TO 109
INFO 106 743
T O P   S E C R E T   H U N T E R
BT
REF 109 PROPOSAL 987 STOP 987 ACCEPTS WITHOUT
CONDITION INFORMED 105 THIS PM STOP 987 REQ
THIS MSG HAND DELIVERED TO GM BAS WICHITA
BY 743 STOP GM TO PREPARE BAS PLAN FOR
CLANDESTINE AIR SERVICE IN SUPPORT OF OSS AND
SOE POST WAR OPERATIONS STOP PLAN MUST INCLUDE
SCOPE OF OPERATIONS AND EQUIPMENT TO EXECUTE
STOP ANY QUESTIONS TO 987 VIA THIS MEDIUM END
BT
NNNN
```

TOP SECRET - HUNTER

"Wow!" Brian exclaimed. "There's a lot of stuff in such a short message. I'm not accustomed to reading these things. You've opened a T-S-S-C-I compartment with my callsign?"

Bruce chuckled. "Yep. That was Bill's idea. All future communications will be within this compartment. Just a word of caution, you should not refer to this compartmented information."

"Understood," responded Brian. "What are all these numbers?"

"Again, one of Bill's notions of an extra layer of security. You've been assigned code number 987. I'm 105. Bill is 109. And Bill's deputy, Ned Buxton, is 106. You can probably surmise from the message that Chip Warner is 743. Do you think B-A-S can handle clandestine air operations?"

"Yes, absolutely. I imagine we will need specialized aircraft, but we can sort that out as we go. I appreciate the general need, but I confess to my lack of direct knowledge of what's involved."

"We can take care of that." They both laughed.

With chuckles in his voice, Brian answered, "I'm sure you can, but I'm doing what I need to be doing."

"It's very dangerous."

"Yes, it is, but so is clandestine air operations in a different way."

"Touché," David said in a refined French accent.

Bruce invited Brian to dinner, but Hunter begged off, professing his need to get back to Debden for an early morning mission.

———

Monday, 8.May.1944
Headquarters, Special Operations Executive
No.64 Baker Street
Marylebone, London, England
United Kingdom
13:15 hours

"Thank you for seeing me privately, Lord Selborne," SOE agent Trevor 'Diamond' Anderson said as he entered the minister's office. The door closed behind him. Selborne gestured to the plush leather chairs arranged around a small round table. Trevor sat across from the minister.

"What seems to be the problem?"

"I'm grateful that you would see me privately. I'm here to seek your counsel as much as to inform you."

"I'm intrigued."

"Admiral pike asked me to support a meeting between D-N-I and M-I-6 regarding a mission I ran in Germany before the war."

Vice Admiral Sir Geoffrey Ian 'Jumper' Pike, KCB, DSC, became the Director of Naval Intelligence (DNI) in 1938, less than a year before the war began. He had an exceptional background in the intelligence community. Pike had also recruited Trevor from Cambridge for intelligence work and had been his mentor ever since.

"After the meeting, I stopped by a pub near Broadway House for lunch and a pint. A former classmate of mine at Cambridge happened by. We had lunch and reminisced about our university days and subsequent work. He's the chief of the counterespionage department within M-I-6. All seemed innocent and innocuous enough. However, after lunch, I started thinking about a few things he said that just did not connect. I may be totally off the mark, but I suspect he may be more than he seems."

"How so?"

"My gut is telling me he may be a double agent."

"For the Germans?"

"No. For the Soviets."

"Our ally?" Selborne said with incredulity

"Yes Sir."

"What do you want me to do with this?"

"Thus the counsel I seek. I can't go to M-I-6. I can't go to M-I-5. I'm afraid they would not take it seriously. You could make a discreet inquiry chief to chief with an anonymous tip. M-I-5 may have a file already, for all I know. My gut is telling me if they don't have a file, they need to open one."

"Who is this person?"

"Philby. His full name is Harold Adrian Russell Philby, but he prefers Kim. We all know him as Kim."

"Such an accusation could go sideways very easily for your classmate."

"I know that. I didn't come to you on caprice. He is hiding in plain sight."

Selborne looked to his left out the window. "What is it that made you so suspicious of your classmate Philby?"

"At Cambridge, we studied and explored the philosophers, including Marx and Engels. We were all intrigued by the concept of community and the common good. What was different was that Kim and several others joined the student group. Most of us saw the reality of Stalin. Now, Kim denies his flirtation ever existed. He sees Stalin as a pragmatist rather than a murderous dictator."

"We all have opinions, Trevor. Is that sufficient to condemn a man?"

"No Sir. Frankly, it was not so much what he said but rather the way he said it." Trevor paused to allow for a question or comment. "Regardless, I came to you because I respect your perspective." Trevor thought for a moment. "Maybe I'm just looking for reassurance that I'm wrong. I desperately want to be wrong."

"I think I can handle this delicately without exposing you or your hunch. I'll make an appointment to see Sir David privately tomorrow morning. I'll see what they know and convey your suspicion in a generalized manner. If you're correct, this fellow Philby is already far too high within M-I-6 and has access to our most sensitive intelligence information. I'll see what Sir David has before talking to Sir Stewart, but M-I-6 must know what they have potentially in their midst. I shudder to think what this would mean to our intelligence security at M-I-6. The Soviets are allies, but if Churchill is correct, they may quickly become adversaries after the war."

Sir David Petrie, KCMG, CIE, CVO, CBE, KPM, became director-general of MI5 in April 1941, replacing the founding director Major General Sir Vernon Kell, KBE, CB. Kell had been director-general since the creation of the service in 1909 and had been dismissed by Churchill the day he became prime minister. The Security Service was responsible for counterintelligence and domestic security.

"That should work, Sir. Something's just not right, but I have no hard evidence . . . just a vague impression."

"Understood, Trevor. Sometimes, it is just such misty suspicions by a professional that turns the corner." Selborne lapsed into thought for a few seconds. "Sir David may want to talk to you directly."

"I trust your judgment. I'll follow your guidance."

"Very well. Thank you for bringing this to me."

Trevor thanked the minister for his advice and assistance, and then he departed.

———

Thursday, 11.May.1944
USAAF Station F-356
Saffron Walden, Essex, England
United Kingdom
09:00 hours

Yet another formation, Brian said to himself. *We've had more of these damn formations in the last month than we had in the previous year.*

On this occasion at least, they did not have a general officer inspection to endure. The group formed up for Generals Spaatz and Doolittle. Commanding General 8th Fighter Command Major General William Ellsworth Kepner, USAAF, attended for the first time. Spaatz would make the presentation. Doolittle stood behind Spaatz on his right, and Kepner was behind on the left.

The unseen announcer read the citation. The 4th Fighter Group had earned the Distinguished Unit Citation (DUC) for their aggressive attacks on enemy aircraft and air bases inside Germany between March 5th and April 24th. The group's flag and guidon were presented to General Spaatz, who attached the appropriate streamer. Every member of 4FG, officer and enlisted alike, got to add another ribbon to their awards.

Once the generals departed, Colonel Blakeslee dismissed the group for the day. A majority of the 334FS pilots decided to make a run into London for an afternoon/evening of letting loose. *I can't make it to the farm and back by tomorrow morning.* Brian chose to remain at Debden to rest and read his book. The telephone system remained far from normal without explanation. *I've gotten so used to talking to Charlotte it makes this telephone problem all the more aggravating. Maybe I should just write a letter.*

———

Friday, 12.May.1944
Headquarters, Special Operations Executive
No.64 Baker Street
Marylebone, London, England
United Kingdom
16:20 hours

Trevor had received the message to meet with Lord Selborne this afternoon. No subject or purpose had been given, but he was fairly certain he knew the subject. He arrived early for the appointment, and the minister's secretary indicated Lord Selborne would see him earlier than the appointed time.

"Good afternoon, Lord Selborne," Trevor said as he entered the minister's office and the door closed behind him.

Cecil came around his desk and gestured to the comfortable chairs. They sat across from each other. "I completed my portion of the bargain, and I wanted to report my findings as soon as possible." Trevor did not react. "I had a private, non-specific discussion with Sir David. As I suspected, M-I-5 has had a file on Philby and several others in the Cambridge cohort. Just an informational item at this juncture, I asked about you since you were in the same class at Cambridge, and you know Philby. You are not in their sights."

"Well, I hadn't thought of asking about that, but thank you for the assurance."

"Certainly. Sir David was very clear and precise. They have more than a few what he referred to as indications, but they are a very long way from arrest or even active surveillance. They are watching, but in a more casual manner at present. Sir David does not know your identity. Nonetheless, he offered some related guidance. Do not initiate contact with Philby, but do not avoid contact either. Philby needs to feel everything is normal, and he is above suspicion. Sir David was also insistent upon you reporting every contact of any sort or form, social or professional. He assured me M-I-5 is attentive to the potential, but they must be very careful not to spook him."

"I understand and accept all of that. However, it had been ten years since I last saw him, so it may well be ten more years before I run into him again."

"I also took the liberty, with Sir David's consent, to have a private chat with Sir Stewart at M-I-6. I would not have been able to forgive myself if I had not alerted him to the potential for a double agent among his principal lieutenants."

"How did he take it, if I may ask?"

"He confessed his own distant misty concerns. He also pointed to the exceptional work he has done in countering German espionage efforts."

"That aspect is way beyond me. I have done my part. I felt something was wrong, and I reported my observations. My instincts were not wrong."

"No, they weren't, Trevor. God bless you for your instincts. They've kept you alive in a risky business."

"Thank you, Sir."

Trevor departed and headed back to his apartment.

———

Monday, 15.May.1944
Headquarters, XXI Army Group
St. Paul's School
Lonsdale Road
Barnes, London, England
United Kingdom
14:00 hours

The generals gathered for the last assessment of the readiness of the OVERLORD plan and the troops assigned to execute the plan. On this auspicious occasion, King George VI, in his uniform of a Royal Navy admiral of the fleet, sat front and center with Prime Minister Churchill just to his right.

General Eisenhower stood at the podium. "Welcome, Your Majesty." The generals applauded. "Welcome, Prime Minister." Again, the generals applauded. "Would either of our guests like to address the supreme headquarters staff?" The King stood. Eisenhower moved aside but remained standing.

"Thank you for your welcome, General Eisenhower." He retrieved a single piece of paper from inside his uniform jacket. The King took a quick glance at the unfolded paper but did not read from it. "You are on the verge of embarkation for a glorious expedition to restore freedom to an entire continent and indeed the whole world. I wanted to convey my genuine admiration and respect. As we in the nautical services often say since the days of sail, Godspeed and following fair winds."

The generals applauded. The prime minister chose not to speak at the opening. Eisenhower returned to the podium.

"The weather is the last of our critical variables. I will defer the weather forecast to the end. First up will be General Strong, G-2." Eisenhower returned to his seat as the chief of intelligence took the podium.

"Your Majesty, Prime Minister. The enemy order of battle remains unchanged in the battlespace. We have detected no force movements into or out of Normandy. The enemy activities remain routine with low level training. The forces assigned to the 84th Corps also remain unchanged, with the headquarters located at Saint-Lô. The Normandy corps remains under the command of Army Group B, headquartered in Paris, which is Field Marshal Rommel. Most notably, the majority of the enemy's armored reserve is outside the operational control of Army Group B and under direct orders of the chancellor through Panzer Group West. FORTITUDE has not overplayed the enemy's preconception, and the status of the objectives is still positive. The precondition interdiction targets assigned to the combined air forces have been hit and broken. Two of those sites are under repair and will be hit again prior to D-Day. All plan prerequisites have been met, and we see no indications of enemy movement to alter those requirements. Any questions?"

None came. Strong nodded his head and sat down. Eisenhower returned to the podium.

"The other anomaly that cast a shadow over the plan was the Exercise TIGER disaster at Slapton Sands. I assigned General Bull, SHAEF G-3, to investigate the events, causal factors, and consequences relative to the OVERLORD plan. General Bull."

Bull replaced the supreme commander at the podium. He summarized the facts associated with the catastrophe. The number of missing had been reduced to a couple of dozen with virtually all of the missing being moved to the killed list. Some of the previous wounded also moved to the killed list with their passing under treatment. Bull also listed the lost or seriously damaged ships and other equipment. The exercise had proceeded as planned just after dawn and had concluded successfully despite the battle damage.

"The damaged ships, except for two L-S-Ts," Bull continued, "will be repaired in time to return to the active list for D-Day. The lost L-S-Ts will not be entirely compensated for, but we have adjusted the landing plan for D-Day to accommodate for the losses. As General Strong reported, we have not detected any evidence the enemy has understood or appreciated what they accomplished that night. More importantly, we have detected no reaction to the TIGER disaster. The enemy got lucky that night, and we suspect they saw Slapton Sands as just another training exercise of unspecified purpose. This leads us to the conclusion that OVERLORD has not been compromised. Any questions?"

Several questions came from the flag officers related to the security procedures in place that night. One particular question struck Bull, to which he responded.

"The E-boat base at Cherbourg has not been overlooked. The base has been on our pre-D-Day bombardment list. We have not hit the base until that time to avoid drawing too much enemy attention to Normandy. That evening, the ships operating south of Devon attracted sufficient attention to draw the E-boats out. In hindsight, we had insufficient radar-equipped vessels in the screening force. We will not have that problem before D-Day. One, the entire screening force from battleships to corvettes will have active radar. Two, the Cherbourg

E-boat base along with other E-boat bases from Cherbourg to Dieppe will be destroyed on D-2 by separated air raids, which is deemed sufficient to protect the invasion fleet without broadcasting the approach."

Bull's comment instigated a minor debate on those elements, but the plan remained unchanged at the end of the discussion. They dealt with a few administrative loose ends that were tied off.

Eisenhower announced, "This brings us to the weather. Group Captain Stagg, you have the floor."

Group Captain James Martin Stagg was a lifelong meteorologist assigned to the Royal Air Force Meteorology Office or Met Office. He chaired a joint, combined committee of meteorologists to produce the daily weather forecasts for the SHAEF staff.

"We have been watching the weather in North America and the North Atlantic for months now and using a variety of predictive tools to forecast the weather. We have reasonable success predicting the weather seven to ten days out. We are three weeks from the opening of the D-Day window on the 5th. We have assumed that the 5th is D-Day. We see a low-pressure system of interest moving across the Northeast United States. Based on similar systems and locations, that system may become problematic. With the assistance of the Commander Naval Forces, we have deployed an array of warships with a Met Office meteorologist aboard each warship to give us a stronger two-to-three-week predictive forecast. I can assure you," Stagg said, glancing at Eisenhower, "that we have gone to extraordinary lengths to give the supreme commander the most accurate weather forecast we can. As of this moment, we have insufficient information to suggest or recommend altering the current D-Day landing date. Any questions for the Met Office?"

None came. General Eisenhower stood at the podium again. "To summarize, in closing, we have a stable plan. We are ready to execute. The enemy has given us no hint or suggestion that conditions for execution are any different from our initial requirements. For the last three weeks, we will all be watching the weather."

General Eisenhower closed the meeting, and they disbanded. He thanked The King and the prime minister for attending. Wishes and blessings were exchanged among the three leaders.

———

Monday, 15.May.1944
OSS London Station
Nos. 70-72 Grosvenor Street
Mayfair, London, England
United Kingdom
18:25 hours

The day's mission had gone well. Mission accomplished. Brian felt good when he saw the message on the board from Colonel Bruce. Brian called and left a message that he would make the run into London once the squadron was released. Here he was.

Brian completed the security procedures without a hitch. *I wonder if they work around the clock?* Colonel Bruce had been notified of Brian's arrival and waited for him as the escort delivered him to the station chief's office.

"Thank you for making the journey into London, Brian. Our communications inadequacy is irritating and certainly cumbersome to you."

"No problem, Sir. It's usually easy for me to reach London as long as we don't get released too late in the day."

"One of these days, I'll get out to see your base at Debden. Did you fly today?"

"Yes Sir. Good mission. We got the job done, and everyone came home. A few holes in some planes but nothing serious."

"I received several HUNTER messages today. You can see them if you wish." Brian shook his head and waved his hand dismissively. "They confirm that Chip Warner carried your message to Mister Sales. Warner remained in Wichita for several days to assist your general manager in outlining the plan elements the O-S-S needs for future operations. Warner reported separately that he believes Sales has a firm grasp on the O-S-S requirements and the general size of the air service. They also indicated by several messages that B-A-S will have the necessary support to achieve the objective. General Donovan must present his transition plan to the president in the fall. He has requested a draft plan by the middle of July and a final one by September first."

"I assume Bobby accepted the timeline."

"Yes, he did. We'll have to establish some courier processes to ensure you have the products and time to adjust as you wish to meet the deadlines. By the way, Warner also issued a separate contract for the construction of an appropriately sized SCIF," pronounced 'skiff,' "or Sensitive Compartmented Information Facility, at the B-A-S location as a secure place where sensitive information can be created, handled and stored. The hiring of a few appropriately cleared people has been authorized to handle the associated paperwork."

"Thank you, Sir. So, the ball is rolling."

"That is my information. Although I'm not in the operational loop and just a communication conduit, and if you have no objection, I'd like to see the plan either during or after you've approved the plan."

"I see no problem."

Again, Colonel Bruce invited Major Drummond to share dinner with him. This time, Brian accepted. They went to the colonel's favorite restaurant and enjoyed purely social conversation. When they finished their meal, Bruce asked his driver to drop Brian off at Liverpool Street Station to at least cutout the Underground for his return to base.

———

Tuesday, 16.May.1944
Oxford Railway Station
Park End Street
Oxford, Oxfordshire, England
United Kingdom
11:30 hours

"**W**elcome to Oxford," Jonathan said as the two friends met and embraced on the platform.

"I've been here before," responded Brian.

Jonathan gestured toward the terminal, and they strolled side-by-side. "I didn't know that. Do tell, my brother."

"RAF Brize Norton is just to the west of the city. I had to go through primary flight training at Brize Norton before I met you at Hawarden and O-T-U-7."

"Well, how about that. Then, welcome back to Oxford."

When they made it outside the terminal, and before they hailed a cab, Brian turned to face Jonathan. "Why am I here? I came because you asked me to, but why am I here?"

"I'm sworn to silence on that query, I'm afraid. My sister asked me to ask you for this visit. I've done that. She asked me to escort you to University Hospital. I am about to do just that."

"You didn't answer the question."

"No, I didn't, because I can't. So, if you will, mate, let's get on with this. We can find a pub afterward to toss a couple of pints before we head back to the war."

Brian smiled and nodded his head. The two aviators went to the head of the taxi line. Jonathan gave the cabbie their destination.

———

Tuesday, 16.May.1944
Oxford University Hospital
Headley Way
Headington, Oxford, Oxfordshire, England
United Kingdom
11:55 hours

The receptionist in the main entrance lobby called Doctor Kensington. Squadron Leader Kensington and Major Drummond waited for Rosemary to appear, which came ten minutes later. Rosemary Kensington stepped smartly past her brother and embraced Brian, kissing him passionately.

Before Rosemary released him, Brian said, "Well, that was quite the welcome."

"Heartfelt, truly. Thank you for coming . . . both of you." Neither officer responded. "I'll treat you both to lunch. Follow me."

They did so. The walking conversation stuck to the common cordialities of family, health, and non-war-related activities, including Rosemary's experience as a full-fledged physician. Rosemary did not mention her meeting with Jonathan and Linda two weeks earlier, and Jonathan chose not to volunteer the information in the spirit of Rosemary's request.

The physician's dining room was only about half full. Rosemary led the two officers to a corner table with some separation. Their casual social conversation continued. Brian asked a direct question about the battle wounded she was treating, including the types of wounds. Rosemary handled the questions with ease, grace, and patience. The meal was decent, well-prepared, but not particularly noteworthy. All three of them finished.

Why the hell did she ask her brother, my best friend, to get me up here? Certainly not to buy us lunch and chit-chat. I can't stay here all afternoon. It'll take several hours to get back to Debden before the evening meal. "Thank you for lunch, Rose," Brian said, pushed back from the table, and started to stand.

"Wait," Rosemary protested. "I'm not done."

"Done with what?" asked Brian. He glanced at Jonathan, who only shook his head and shrugged his shoulders.

Rosemary smiled. "I asked my brother to ask you here as a favor to me. I thought you would be more likely to come if he asked you rather than me. I have a few things I want to say to you, and I have one request."

Brian nodded his head in agreement.

"I love my brother. He loves you . . . in a brotherly way. He has tried to protect me, and my heart has defied his advice. I felt something special when I first met you at home during Christmas of '39. I came to recognize that feeling as love, deep, genuine love. I have loved you ever since." Brian started to speak but stopped before a sound emerged when Rosemary held up her right hand palm out. "I'm not finished. Please let me finish." Brian nodded his head in consent. "It has taken me a long time to build up the courage to reach this point. Before you nearly interrupted me, I was at the point of saying that I know Charlotte loves you very much. I am certain you love her equally, if not more. I respect your marriage, and as much as I would love to have you as my husband, I know, recognize, and acknowledge that is impossible. You're in a very dangerous profession, and I could not forgive myself if I did not say the words and say them aloud with my beloved brother as a witness. I love you, Brian Drummond. I have loved you since I met you." Rosemary stared at Brian and held his eyes. "This is the point where you can speak."

Brian did not say a word for several seconds. "I have a million thoughts running through my brain. The one that seems the most relevant at this moment is I love you, Rosemary Kensington, in my own way, but your assessment of my relationship with Charlotte was spot-on accurate. I also say this in front of our witness." Brian smiled at Jonathan, who nodded his head in acknowledgment. "I am married to the woman who saved my life in more ways than one. She has borne our first child and first son. Charlotte is an important, if not vital, part of my life. I cannot and will not do anything to jeopardize my relationship with Charlotte."

"I am not and never will even suggest you do anything of the kind. I acknowledge reality, Brian. I can assure you. I just wanted you to know how I feel directly in my words and from my mouth. That said, I now come to my favor." Brian did not budge or blink. "I shall come directly to the point. I'm requesting your consent for me to ask Charlotte for you to do for me what you did for Mary Spencer."

"What might that be?" Brian asked with innocence and no expression or reaction.

"You gave the Spencers an enormous gift of two beautiful children—a son and a daughter."

Damn it all to hell! How the hell does she know that? Brian could not contain his reaction. Rosemary's statement shook him visibly. *What do I say?* Brian could only shake his head.

"I want a child. I want that child to be part of you that I can love with all my heart." Brian could still only shake his head, so Rosemary continued. "I will ask nothing whatsoever of either you or Charlotte. I have no interest in interfering with your lives, your marriage, your family, your relationship with Charlotte. I would like your consent to talk to Charlotte. With that, I will go to Standing Oak Farm and speak to her eye-to-eye. What say you?"

Brian opened his mouth, but no words came forth. He again could only shake his head. Brian looked to Jonathan and stared at his eyes as if the answers might be found there. "You want me to impregnate you?" he finally asked.

"Yes."

Again, Brian could only shake his head for several seconds. "How did I become a farmyard stud? I'm not some stud stallion."

"And I'm not some broodmare."

"I'm sorry. I didn't mean to suggest . . . ," Brian fumbled. He thought for a few more seconds. "I understand . . . no, no, I can't possibly understand how you feel. This is a free country. I've no right to decide whom you can or cannot talk to. If you want to talk to Charlotte about this, I won't stop you. But I really must warn her. She needs time to think about what you're asking of her . . . and of me."

"I'm not asking you to hide anything from her, but I am asking you to let me plead my case to her. I've told you how I feel. I intend to say the same thing to her. I don't want to lose either of you as friends. I'm only asking you both to give me a part of you that I can love . . . and love freely and openly."

"You're free to talk to Charlotte, Rosemary. I've no intention or desire to stand in the way of your freedom. I can't make any promises, Rose. In the light of your statement and request, I must ask, what are your constraints on what I can say to Charlotte?"

"In the spirit of your consent, I'll ask you only to allow me to present my request and reasoning directly to Charlotte. I'd prefer she not be hardened before I get a chance to speak."

"I think I can abide that request."

"I've spoken my feelings. I need to let you go, both of you. I know you have important jobs to do in our defense. God bless you both. Thank you for listening."

Rosemary walked with both officers to the main entrance. She hugged and kissed her brother and the person of her affection. With that, Jonathan hailed a cab, and both men departed.

Neither man spoke during the cab ride nor did they speak until they were 20 minutes into the train journey back to London. They remained together through the London Underground and finally split for separate trains back to their respective bases.

———

Wednesday, 17.May.1944
Standing Oak Farm
Winchester, Hampshire, England
United Kingdom
14:15 hours

Mabel had informed Charlotte and the crew at lunch that they had the largest greenhouse-grown produce delivery ready. Charlotte rode one of the horses to the Harris property for lunch with Mabel and her team. They walked through all five greenhouses that were in full production. The crew used any container they could gather up—crates, boxes, chests, even wooden deployment boxes provided by the American Army. They were ready. Charlotte marveled at the quantity and breadth of produce they were able to grow.

A small convoy of five Army, 2½-ton, 6x6, covered trucks arrived. A first lieutenant in green fatigues stepped down from the cab's passenger side of the lead truck.

"Good afternoon, ladies," the lieutenant greeted Charlotte and Mabel. "I'm Lieutenant Richmond with 9th Infantry logistics, and we are here to accept your vegetable deliveries."

Charlotte and Mabel introduced themselves. In an available moment, Mabel whispered to Charlotte that the Army had not sent the same man twice.

"How do you want to do this?" asked Richmond.

"The produce for delivery has been staged in the barn," Mabel answered. You can pull the trucks through one by one, and we'll load the containers, or you can back them up to the main door for loading."

"Either way works for us. I brought men to help with the loading. Let's go take a look at how you've got the boxes organized."

The ladies and the lieutenant walked to the barn. Ten women dressed in overalls stood by stacks of containers. Richmond inspected the various groupings.

"All this food sure looks good. On behalf of the U.S. Army, thank you so much for producing this for us. Given your organization, I'd say it's probably best to come through the barn. We can load one group on each truck and split the other two groups among the various trucks."

"Either way should work," Mabel responded.

Richmond went to the barn door at the back to inspect the access and then walked to the front door. He started barking orders for the drivers to drive around the back in line and enter the barn's interior for loading. At the same time, Mabel told the greenhouse crew how they would load the trucks.

Women and men worked together to load each truck as it came through. Richmond stood with Charlotte and Mabel to observe the loading process that took just twenty minutes. He tallied the count of each box and each content type.

"I counted exactly the number and types agreed." He reached into his uniform shirt pocket and handed a check to Mabel, who in turn passed it to Charlotte. The check was written for US$1,750, payable to Standing Oak Farm.

"As agreed, Lieutenant. Thank you for your business. We should have a partial delivery in three weeks with another full delivery in two months."

"I may not be here to accept delivery, but if we're not here, we shall pass the torch to our successors . . . probably our logistics depot in Basingstoke."

"With gratitude to the U.S. Army," Mabel said, "we're producing large amounts of produce. We're also working on preserving our excess produce."

"Do you have samples?" Richmond asked.

"Yes Sir."

Mabel found a cardboard box and placed a jar each of preserved tomatoes, new potatoes, carrots, and cucumbers, along with a sample of pickles and onions.

"Excellent. We'll evaluate these samples and perhaps place an order. It's a pleasure doing business with you, ladies. The troops will love fresh produce. Until the next delivery, good day, ladies." Richmond swung his right arm in a circle over his shoulder. The convoy headed back to their base.

"Gather up, ladies," Mabel commanded. The women formed a semi-circle around Mabel and Charlotte.

"We could not find sufficient champagne," Charlotte began, "so blueberry muffins will have to suffice for a celebration. We made our first major delivery. Well done to all of you. Keep up the great work."

Charlotte made a point of talking casually with each member of the greenhouse crew. They were all, to a woman, grateful for gainful employment and appreciated being busy. Charlotte remained for nearly an hour and then road her horse back to the main farmhouse.

Inside, at her desk, she looked at the check. *A handsome profit indeed.*

———

Friday, 19.May.1944
RAF Netheravon
Fittleton, Wiltshire, England
United Kingdom
14:40 hours

King George VI, Queen Elizabeth, and their oldest child, 18-year-old Princess Elizabeth had been invited to observe a major rehearsal exercise three weeks after the disaster at Slaptons Sands. The Royal family was doing their part for the preparations of British forces for the Normandy invasion planned for just two weeks' time. The King knew the plan was set, and success would soon rest in the hands of the paratroopers before them. The newly formed 6th Airborne Division was conducting a full division parachute drop and glider landing on the wide-open Salisbury Plain, six miles northwest of the famous pre-historic Stonehenge monument.

General Montgomery briefed the King and Queen as well as narrated the various phases of the exercise. They were conducting the rehearsal in the daylight on the virtually treeless grassland to avoid training injury, but their part of the OVERLORD Plan would be executed in the dark of night with a full moon in the hedgerow *boçage* terrain of Normandy and the additional physical countermeasures added by the Germans.

Brigadier Stanley James Ledger 'Speedy' Hill, DSO, MC, Commander of 3rd Parachute Brigade, 6th Airborne Division, stood with Princess Elizabeth. The next wave formation of 56 Dakota transport aircraft approached with a demonstrable drone of their engines. Men rapidly jumped from the airplanes on cue. The parachutes were extracted and streamed behind each of them man, and then it blossomed into a green hemisphere with the paratrooper suspended beneath.

"Oh my, I can't imagine," the Princess proclaimed.

"They are well trained, Ma'am," responded Hill.

"I don't think I could do it . . . jump out of an aeroplane into the air."

"Everyone feels that way at first, Ma'am, but good training helps us overcome that initial fear and trust the system. These troops," Hill said, pointing to the descending array of parachutes, "represent the fastest means we have to insert a major ground fighting force on the ground."

When the parachutists began landing, the Princess asked, "Doesn't it hurt when they hit the ground?"

"No, Ma'am. Landing safely is part of the training."

The Princess remained fascinated as she watched the paratroopers land. When she looks over to Brigadier Hill, he demonstrated the bent knee landing posture and gave a brief description of the paratrooper's landing technique. After listening to Hill's explanation, the Princess returned her gaze on the landing paratroopers. "They jump up right away, and they are running, so apparently it works."

"Yes, Ma'am."

The Royals watched the entire evolution with interest and concern. They talked with the officers and troops, and the King, his wife and daughter received loud cheers as they departed.

———

Monday, 29. May. 1944
Supreme Headquarters, Allied Expeditionary Force
Camp Griffiss
Warren Plantation and Sandy Lane
Bushy Park, Teddington, London, England
United Kingdom
07:05 hours

Beetle Smith joined the supreme commander in his office. "We just received confirmation from the last of SHAEF assigned units. The bases have been sealed. All leaves have been cancelled. Telephone communications except with the base commander offices have been preempted."

"We have lit the fuze," Ike mused. "We need to get this done. I shudder to think what might happen if we must unravel this monster."

"Quite so. Stagg is getting nervous, which is not a positive sign, but I remain optimistic. The leading elements have all been staged and reported ready for embarkation. Ships are filling every southern port. The Germans must know something is coming."

"Yes, they do, and they believe our landings will be at the Pas de Calais. The longer we can convince them to hold that notion, the better for OVERLORD."

"We also received confirmation from the chief of staff, the War Department, and even the president himself. We are a go for execution."

"Yea, verily! Now, we wait on the weather."

"Many of us are praying for acceptable weather so that we can get this show on the road. We have a long march to Berlin."

"That we do, and Churchill wants us to beat the Red Army to Berlin."

"I've heard the speech and the demand. The sooner we can get Georgie into the fight, the better."

"Agreed. Churchill made it very clear that he did not support any sanctions on Patton. He wants the 3rd Army under Patton in combat as soon as we can get him there."

"Georgie does have his advocates."

"And Winston is one of those," Ike commented. "OK, let's keep a close eye on any potential leaks. We need to keep a lid on this venture for another week."

"Everyone is prep'ed, Ike. We'll do it."

Smith departed, and they both returned to their paperwork.

———

Tuesday, 30.May.1944
Supreme Headquarters, Allied Expeditionary Force
Camp Griffiss
Warren Plantation and Sandy Lane
Bushy Park, Teddington, London, England
United Kingdom
15:25 hours

The request from Group Captain Stagg for an unscheduled meeting did not bode well for the day. With his consent to the request, Eisenhower asked for his chief of staff to join him.

Beetle entered Ike's office with a somewhat breathless Stagg. The RAF officer took several deep breaths to gain control of his breathing. "Thank you for seeing me, General," Stagg began. "We just completed our afternoon compilation of data from all available sources. I brought the general chart should you like to see the data," he said, holding up a large paper roll in his left hand. "The approaching low-pressure system we have been concerned about has been precisely located and measured. Our weather ships measured the surface pressure this morning at 9-9-5 millibars, which is stronger than we anticipated, and it's moving faster over open water causing high seas. The projected storm track is too close for my liking."

"Will it reach the Channel and Normandy?"

"Yes Sir."

"When?"

"Our best collective estimate is Saturday, the third, and may last 24 to 36 hours. It's fairly intense, not just a simple rain squall. As of this afternoon, this storm exceeds our tolerable landing constraints by several parameters that we cannot and do not control."

"Well, that is not good news, now, is it?"

"No Sir. I wish it were not so, but that is what the data tells us. We'll be more accurate as the system gets closer."

"I want a prompt briefing once you have your bi-daily forecast from now on until I tell you to stop. This is far too close for my liking," Eisenhower said in a commanding voice.

"We will make it so, henceforth."

The supreme commander lapsed into contemplation. Smith gestured for Stagg to depart, which he did. Beetle decided to remain just in case his boss might need something. A knock at the door brought them both back to an attentive state.

His secretary announced, "Sir, a special courier is here with proper identification and an urgent message."

"Send him in."

The man, dressed in a well-fitted business suit, entered Ike's office with a metallic case chained to his left wrist. "Good afternoon, Sir," the man said and noticed General Smith sitting to the side. He hesitated and gestured with his eyes that he did not recognize Beetle.

Ike asked, "Whom might you be?" The man shook his head and again gestured with his eyes.

Beetle volunteered, "Do you need me to step out, Sir?"

"No." Eisenhower looked at the man and proclaimed, "That is Lieutenant General Smith, my chief of staff. He is cleared for all T-S-S-C-I information I am. Now, one more time, who are you?"

"I'm Herbert Goodman, chief of the German desk at M-I-6. 'C' asked me to personally carry this message to you and answer whatever questions you might have."

Eisenhower gestured for the case as he retrieved the key chained to his belt from the inside of his trousers. He unlocked the case and removed a single sheet of paper with red-striped margins.

MOST SECRET - ULTRA

```
MOST SECRET ULTRA
SECRET
DATE 1539 10 MAY 1944
TO CG 91LID
FROM CIC AG B
BREAK
BY ORDER OF THE COMMANDER IN CHIEF 91LID SHALL
DEPLOY TO VICINITY OF PERIERS NORMANDY NO LATER
THAN 3 JUNE TO SERVE AS REACTION FORCE IF
NECESSARY UNDER DIRECT ORDERS OF CG 84 CORPS END
SECRET
DECYPHERED 0837 11 APR 1944
MOST SECRET ULTRA
```

MOST SECRET - ULTRA

Eisenhower held up the message for Beetle to read rising from the table. Ike waited until Smith looked up. "Get Ken Strong, Pink Bull, and their deputies now."

Beetle departed.

Brigadier General Thomas Jeffries 'Tom' Betts, USA, served as Strong's deputy G-2.

Major General John Francis Martin 'Jock' Whiteley, MC, served as Bull's deputy G-3.

Eisenhower looked at Goodman. "Both men are my intelligence chiefs, and both are ULTRA cleared." Goodman nodded his head. I assume this is from Army Group B."

"Yes Sir. Rommel himself."

"I don't recognize this 9-1-L-I-D."

"That's the 91st Air Landing Infantry Division, or in German, *91.Luftlande-Infanterie-Division*—an airmobile division, or as we call them, an airborne or parachute division."

"The commander?"

"*Generalleutnant* Wilhelm Falley. He was just promoted, and rightly so. He is an accomplished combat commander, and the 91st has near full strength, combat seasoned troops."

Smith, Strong, Betts, Bull, and Whiteley arrived. Introductions were made, although Strong and Goodman knew each other. Eisenhower shared the message with the generals.

"Periers is dreadfully close to the 82nd's drop zone," offered Strong. "Can you give us an hour to assess this development?" Eisenhower nodded his head. Strong handed the message back to Goodman, who secured the highly sensitive message.

"Do you need me for anything else?" Goodman asked of Eisenhower.

"If you have the time, I imagine you could be of assistance to the G-2 and G-3 for their quick assessment."

Goodman nodded and departed with the staff generals.

"Well, that throws a clot in the churn," Ike thought aloud. "Let's reconvene as soon as the staff has their preliminary assessment."

Smith nodded and departed.

———

Chapter 6

Our destiny exercises its influence over us
even when, as yet, we have not learned its nature:
it is our future that lays down the law of our today.
-- Friedrich Wilhelm Nietzsche

Friday, 2.June.1944
Forward HQ, SHAEF
Southwick House
Pinsley Drive
Portsmouth, Hampshire, England
United Kingdom
19:15 hours

The 19th-century manor house, five miles north of Portsmouth, had been chosen as the Allied Expeditionary Force forward headquarters for the invasion. Trees on the grounds obscured the view, but from the third-story, south-facing windows, they overlooked Portsmouth harbor. An observer had an impressive view of The Solent and the Isle of Wight when visibility was decent. Ships filled the available space on the water. After the heavy bombing of the Portsmouth dockyard during The Blitz, the Royal Navy moved its School of Navigation into the manor house. In 1943, with OVERLORD planning well underway, SHAEF assumed control of the building and prepared it to control the invasion. They called it SHARPENER.

"Well done, Beetle. Good choice."

"We can't see much from ground level other than trees, but when the visibility is good, we can see most of the estuary from the top floor. I need to show you the Map Room, the nerve center for the next few days and weeks."

Eisenhower gestured for his loyal chief of staff to lead on. They made their way to an interior large windowless room. A massive map of the entire Channel with the relevant coastal communities labeled on both coasts covered one entire wall, side to side, floor to ceiling. This was the main sea traffic control facility. The cleared lanes for the landing craft, and transports were displayed for each assault beach—Utah, Omaha, Gold, Juno, and Sword. The first two were American. Gold and Sword were British, and Juno was Canadian. The warships were each assigned positions around the traffic lanes with the destroyers closest to the beaches, then cruisers, and big-gun battleships on the outside. Each lane had channels for landing vessels going to and from each respective beach. Wooden chairs facing the map filled the room. This is where the generals would sit.

"Once you've made the decision to execute the plan," Smith said, "the room will be transformed into an array of working desks for each landing beach. The personnel on the desks will maintain the map with timely information on the progress of the landing force."

"When do the commanders arrive?" Ike asked.

"Ramsey is here already. He's upstairs at the moment. The others will all be here by twenty hundred."

"Once they are all here and settled, I want to gather up the command staff in here. I know they've all seen the map and the facilities, but I want to make sure I set the stage properly for the next few days."

"Do you want the general staff as well?"

"No. The command staff is sufficient for now."

"I'll go see to it," Smith responded and departed.

Eisenhower sat in a front-row chair and stared at the map. This map would rapidly fill with symbols and markers within the next few days. Up until this moment, the staff had conducted simulation rehearsals to validate procedures and means of communication. Nevertheless, they would all soon witness the largest amphibious assault in history. The gravity of this time in history was not lost on Dwight Eisenhower.

———

Saturday, 3.June.1944
Standing Oak Farm
Winchester, Hampshire, England
United Kingdom
14:05 hours

Charlotte looked up from her desk when she noticed movement outside the window. A taxicab descended the far side ridge. *That must be Mary.* Charlotte stood and went outside to welcome her guests.

Mary Spenser had both her children, Malcolm, aged three, and Charlotte, aged seven months, as well as their nanny Grace Perkins; Edith brought the boys, Todd and Ian. Todd was the oldest of the children. The older toddler children immediately fell into their own form of communication.

"Welcome back to Standing Oak Farm," Charlotte greeted her guests. The two embraced in the European custom. Next, she welcomed Grace and introduced her to Edith.

"Thank you, Charlotte. I need a good bolt of Scotch."

"Difficult journey?"

"Oh my, the worst. I had to pull rank several times, and the railway and roads are saturated with lorries moving all sorts of things south. The convoys took up both sides of the roadway in a few places. You are blessed to have this haven of peace and tranquility away from the maddening storm."

"Yes, I would agree. Let's get you a good tumbler of Scotch, and we can talk about your experience. At least, you and the children are safe."

"Is Brian still flying fighters out of Debden?"

"Yes, he is, so I get to see him from time to time." Charlotte paused as she poured a healthy glass of Scotch for her guest. She poured herself a smaller amount. Charlotte handed Mary her glass. They held up and clinked glasses. "To our husbands remaining safe," Charlotte offered a toast.

Mary gave her own toast. "May our lads end this bloody war soon."

"Hear, hear!" They sat in the comfortable chairs by the modest fire in the large stone fireplace. "I meant to ask earlier, where is Harriet? Surely you did not leave her at Harrow?"

"No, no. We closed up the house. Harriett decided she needed to visit her sister in the Midlands. It would've been nice to have her here. She is such a creative chef. We don't want to be a burden, and we should earn our keep."

"Nonsense, Mary. You're welcome anytime, all of the time, for as long as you wish. We've plenty of space, and this is a farm. We grow things to eat, and thanks to the American Army, we grow a lot more things to eat."

"Thank you, Charlotte. Doing some farm work will be good for my soul."

"We can give you as much of that as you want."

"May I ask, when was the last time you heard from Brian?"

"April, April 22nd to be precise. The telephone system has been rather chancy since the beginning of April."

"Hmmm."

"Why do you ask?"

"No reason." Mary paused for a moment. "Just curious. Hopefully, the telephones return to normal once our forces are established on the Continent."

"Hopefully. He tries to call me, to reassure me, when he's had a particularly difficult mission. He doesn't want me to hear about a bad mission in the newspapers. So it's nice to know that the potential to talk to him, even briefly, is possible."

Charlotte paused for a moment and then remembered the letter. She retrieved the note paper and handed it to Mary. "I received this in the post this morning." While Mary read Brian's letter, what there was of it, Charlotte swallowed another sip of her drink.

CENSOR PASSED
by authority of Supreme Commander
under 55 Stat. 840, Title III, §303

1st June 1944

Dearest Sweetheart,

    I miss you and Ian so much. So much is happening and   . We have been restricted   and our telephone connections have been   . We have also been informed that   are allowed. I think this may   we've been waiting for is coming soon, which is why we're restricted   . I have no idea when I will be able to see you or talk to you again, but I know this difficulty will end. It is just a matter of time.

    Please give Ian lots of hugs and kisses for me. I miss you both so much.

    With my great love for you,

                   Brian

Mary handed the letter back to Charlotte. "I've never seen anything like this. Has it happened before?"

"No. But, then again, Brian has never been much of a letter writer."

Mary giggled softly and then said, "John either." They both laughed together. Mary stared into the fire and finished her drink.

"I don't think you've seen our new greenhouses. Would you like to take a horseback ride to see our new additions, courtesy of the U.S. Army?"

"It's not exactly a grand spring day, and the clouds are thickening, but a good ride would be refreshing."

They saddled the horses. The clouds were indeed thickening and darkening, and the wind was picking up. Charlotte considered abandoning the ride, but she felt they could squeeze it in a ride if they made the tour a quick version. Then, the two ladies mounted and headed out at a trot rather than a saunter.

The expanse, quality of construction, and most importantly, the breadth of their utilization impressed Mary. She gushed about how much the farm had grown and what they were able to grow year-round. Charlotte explained the Army contract and their use of the excess. The greenhouses were producing quantities far beyond the farm's consumption. They talked about post-war business potential. Mary offered several great suggestions that Charlotte was most grateful for.

When they completed the quick tour of the greenhouses, they rode to the Harris property, where Charlotte shared her vision of advancing the productivity of the land. Mary conveyed her amazement at how entrepreneurial Charlotte had become.

In just the short time they had been out, the sky had darkened more, and wind velocity had increased. Eventually, they felt a few drops that stimulated Mary to heal her horse to a full gallop. Charlotte followed Mary's lead.

They made it back to the main house, took care of the horses, and entered the house before the rain started. Charlotte poured them both a glass of Scotch.

"The sky looks like we're in for some rough weather," observed Charlotte from the safety of the stone, main house.

"Indeed, and we made it just in time," Mary said and gestured to the window. The rain was clearly visible, and it was not vertical. "This is going to be a bit of a blow."

"Wrong time."

"Don't you always need rain on a farm?"

"In that sense, yes, of course, but the invasion is obviously close. Crossing the Channel in a storm will only help the Germans."

"I see your point." Mary thought for a moment. "I'm certain the generals are watching the weather as well."

"May God bless all those young men who are about to go in harm's way."

Charlotte stoked the fire just enough for a modest flame. She turned to ask Mary if she wanted a refresh, but Lionel and Horace entered before the words came out. Charlotte glanced at the clock. "Did you finish milking early?"

"No, Mum, we just returned from the morning delivery. It is absolutely crazy in Winchester, and this descending storm is simply making the situation worse—endless lines of lorries heading to the coast. The constables stopped us, I don't know how many times, and held us for hours. Craziest thing I've ever seen or experienced. Something big, very big, is happening."

"We are not supposed to know," Charlotte answered, "but I believe the long-awaited invasion of the Continent is upon us, and I also believe that qualifies as very big."

The family and crew of Standing Oak Farm were all safe and accounted for, including their student-worker Jacob Holden. They were late with the afternoon milking. Charlotte, Mary, and Edith jumped in to help with manual milking, while Grace tended all four children. They spent the next hour working to return to some semblance of a normal routine.

—

Saturday, 3.June.1944
Forward HQ, SHAEF
Southwick House
Pinsley Drive
Portsmouth, Hampshire, England
United Kingdom
20:55 hours

Only the command staff gathered in the Map Room in accordance with the OVERLORD Operations plan to make the launch decision.

"I think we're all aware of the weather situation," Eisenhower began, "so, let's have the latest forecast." The supreme commander nodded to Group Captain Stagg.

"I'm afraid, gentlemen," Stagg said, "I don't bear good news tonight. We're currently experiencing the leading edge of this low-pressure system. This afternoon, the surface pressure was measured at 978 millibars, which means the system has strengthened over open water. Most relevant to the launch decision, the Met committee arrived at a consensus on the approach and passage. Our best estimate is the worst of the storm will hit tomorrow evening in Normandy."

"The relevant question among so many is," Eisenhower interjected, "when will be conditions in the landing area diminish below our maximum threshold?"

"As of our last review," Stagg answered, "the best estimate we have is Monday afternoon. We'll have a better estimate tomorrow when we can see more of the storm."

"Let's table the weather for the moment. We'll come back to the weather. For this next discussion, let us assume the weather is not a factor. This would be for a 'go' decision for the 5th. I want your best, considered assessment. General Montgomery, what is the ground force recommendation?"

"We have a sound, workable plan. The ground forces are prepared, ready, and poised for this endeavor. I would say go."

"Thank you, Monty. Next up, the naval forces. Admiral Ramsey, what say you?"

"My position, and it is not the unanimous opinion of the naval forces, remains resolutely opposed. There are a million and one ways this affair can go off the rails. The timing and traffic control to transport so many troops and equipment to the beaches is so close scheduled for D-Day that any one of the moving parts could jam up the whole timetable."

"What would you have us do differently?" Eisenhower asked.

"Spread out the D-Day landing forces to two or three days . . . to buy us margin for failure. At present, it will take only one lucky coastal artillery round from the Germans to alter our very closely timed landing plan."

"That's not an option, Berty," protested Monty. "We can't achieve the force structure necessary to withstand the inevitable counterattacks within a day or two at the most."

"I understand the need, Monty. I truly do, but my job is to represent the position of the naval forces in this operation. That is my counsel."

"Very well," Eisenhower said to cut off the debate. "The air forces are next. Air Marshal Leigh-Mallory, your recommendation?'

"I think we need more time to prepare the periphery of the beachhead to buy the naval forces an extra day. I acknowledge that does incur some additional risk to the FORTITUDE deception, but a fortnight will not be costly to our plan. Therefore, I recommend we delay D-Day to the 19th, the opening of the next window."

Eisenhower looked at his deputy supreme commander, Air Chief Marshal Sir Arthur William Tedder, GCB. "We have pushed the planning and operational staffs to find the best balance between widely variant factors," Tedder began. "But, regardless of the work that has gone into the plan, I cannot see it as anything other than a very perilous affair. Berty's spot-on correct. Just one lucky shot by the enemy, and our best efforts could go sideways. So, my counsel, it's very chancy. I cannot tell what another fortnight will yield. Sir Trafford may be onto something by risking our FORTITUDE deception for an all-out concentration of the U.S. air forces and the R-A-F on isolating the beachhead." Tedder nodded back to Eisenhower.

"Brad?"

Lieutenant General Omar Nelson Bradley, USA [USMA 1915], currently held the position as commanding general, 1st U.S. Army, and would have the right flank of the invasion forces. "We have been over this plan scores of times. We've done our tabletop simulations dozens of times. Yes, this is risky. It's the most complex and largest amphibious operation in human history. It's a gamble, no two ways about it, but it's a good gamble. We're with Monty. I say we go."

"Last but not least, Beetle, your turn."

"I think we all know that it's time. If this weather can break to give us a low enough sea state in the Channel and acceptable surf on the beaches, then I say Brad's summary is it—a good gamble."

Eisenhower lowered his head and rubbed his temples. Smith recognized the signs and silently empathized with his commander. The supreme commander was suffering the pain of a pulsing migraine headache, undoubtedly brought on by the stress of the historic moment. Ike rose from the table, stared at the wall map with no vessels yet displayed en route, and paced through a few cycles. Finally, he moved behind his chair and placed both hands on the back. "I'm reminded of the phrase often attributed to the French philosopher Voltaire, 'Perfect is the enemy of good.' Far too many political and military objectives hang in the balance upon this decision. We'll never have a perfect ops plan, no matter how much we delay. We all have our doubts, our fears, but we must not be frozen into inaction by our worries. I truly appreciate your wise counsel. This brings us back to the weather. Group Captain Stagg, can we obtain measurements from ships and land stations that would give us a refined forecast on when conditions will drop below our maximum acceptable threshold?"

"Yes Sir. The ships and numerous land observation stations work around the clock. I will need to send a tasking order for them to take special measurements."

"Five o'clock tomorrow morning is the hard deadline for a launch decision to make the 5th for landing. You've got six hours. Send that tasking order to every relevant station."

"It will be done, Sir."

"Thank you. Now, it seems the likelihood of meeting our execution criteria is low. Use the ensuing hours to prepare your forces for at least a 24-hour delay."

"Just a reminder, General Eisenhower," Montgomery spoke up, "a 48-hour delay will force a fortnight delay to our next window for proper tides."

"Thank you, Monty. I'm keenly aware of that fact. We'll take this as long as possible. Unless anyone has more they wish to say, we're adjourned and will reconvene at zero four hundred tomorrow morning." Eisenhower remained seated, and Smith again recognized the sign. Once the room was cleared except for the two generals, Ike looked at Beetle and said, "I have a pounding headache. I'm going to lay down for a couple of hours to see if I can dampen this crusher."

"I'll keep an eye on things and hopefully give you some peace for a few hours. I hope you feel better."

"Thanks, Beetle."

Eisenhower went to his room. Smith went to the Operations Department office.

———

Sunday, 4.June.1944
Forward HQ, SHAEF
Southwick House
Pinsley Drive
Portsmouth, Hampshire, England
United Kingdom
04:15 hours

The command staff reconvened as directed. The weather was the sole topic. Group Captain Stagg stood with a long pointer stick with a red tip in front of the massive wall map. "As of two hours ago, the center of the low-pressure system was located over and transiting across Ireland. The track appears to be consistent with our prediction and should pass just north of us." Stagg used the pointer to show the predicted track. "Working against us is the inherent wind shift that accompanies a low-pressure system passage in the northern hemisphere, which will be from the south to north, making the surf conditions on the French coast more problematic." Stagg paused to allow for questions on his words so far. All eyes remained on the staff meteorologist, and no one spoke. "The Met Office expects to post gale warnings for the Channel later this morning. However, the question we are all most interested in, we are forecast to exceed the threshold of maximum winds, surf, tide, and cloud cover for the morning of the 5th."

"So, even if we postpone for 24 hours," Eisenhower interjected, "we will still face adverse weather conditions by decision time for a 6th D-Day."

"Yes Sir, that is the forecast. However, we will have another 24 hours of more precise measurements and thus a more refined forecast. From a meteorological perspective, we should know whether the storm passes swiftly enough by the next decision window tonight or early tomorrow morning. Conditions may be rough for the early transports, but they should be below our maximum landing requirements by the time they reach the beaches."

"High seas will be most uncomfortable," observed Bradley, "for the troops who must face the full force of the German coastal defenses. The reason we sought a sea state limit was to ensure soldiers were in fighting shape when they reached the beach rather than debilitated by seasickness."

"You are, of course, quite correct, Brad. Yet, we are faced with the risk of landing diminished troops in the initial waves, or a two-week delay and holding 160,000 men in marginal, cramped conditions. That said, we clearly do not have even marginal conditions for this instant decision moment. Therefore, unless there are any objections, we will delay 24 hours. Issue the appropriate orders immediately. We'll reconvene this evening for a decision on the 6th. Any questions or objections?"

"Given the terrible conditions just outside these walls," Monty added, "the postponement this morning is correct, and I support it."

"Hear, hear," contributed Leigh-Mallory.

"Very well. There is nothing more that we can do beyond waiting out this storm. Thank you, Group Captain Stagg. I know you and your colleagues will remain most attentive to the passing of this storm system."

"That I can assure you, General."

The command staff dissolved to tend to their respective responsibilities.

21:30 hours

Once again, the SHAEF command staff gathered in the Map Room.

"Only one thing left on the agenda. You have the floor, Group Captain Stagg," General Eisenhower said.

"The gale warning was posted for the Channel and both coasts at 11:00 this morning. We reached Beaufort 10, whole gale, with sustained winds of 58 miles per hour, at eighteen hundred this evening. Wind speeds are diminishing. Based on our measurements, we forecast conditions below the plan threshold values by tomorrow afternoon."

"It will be rough for the initial departures and the airborne troops who will land first," commented Bradley.

"Yes, it will," answered Eisenhower. "The wind velocity is going to scatter the paratroopers, but they've trained well for just that contingency, among many others, of course. So, they'll know what they're facing and can adjust accordingly. What about the surf at H-Hour?"

"The surf levels will be on the upper end of the acceptable scale but below the maximum heights at H-Hour and the initial beach landings. The surf and wind will improve steadily during the day. All of the weather criteria will be met before L-Hour for the first parachute landings and will be improving for the beach landings."

Eisenhower nodded his head and lapsed into contemplation. Certainly, all of the other flag officers of the command staff were undoubtedly silently considering their duties in the hours and days ahead. "We are about the send 5,400 assault craft and 156,000 precious soldiers into combat on the grand crusade to liberate Continental Europe from the Nazi tyranny. Once we pull the trigger on this behemoth, we are committed to winning the victory. One last time, does anyone have anything they wish to add for the decision process?"

"Nothing is ever going to be perfect, Ike," Monty said. "We all have our reservations, but now is the time. The plan constraints have been met or will soon be met. We're ready. The troops are poised and prepared."

"Anyone else?"

Ramsey shook his head in the negative. Apparently, he felt he had spoken his peace, and it was now time to act. The others remained silent.

Eisenhower was not going to take a vote. To him, silence means consent. It was decision time. He stood and went to the back of the room. The command staff sat at the table. The Channel map covered the entire far wall. Ike paced from one side to the other, alternating looking at the map and the floor. The president and the prime minister had chosen him for this moment, for this decision. The time had come.

22:45 hours

General Eisenhower returned to the table, placing his hands on the back of his chair once again. He looked each man in the eyes. "OK. We'll go."

With that simple statement, the largest amphibious landing in history had been set in motion. The command staff did not need to be dismissed. They knew all too well what had to be done now. The cascade of code word orders rapidly spread like a virus throughout the invasion force. The planning was done. As they had said many times, now, the fate of the operation had been placed in the hands of the boatswains, sergeants and soldiers. They would determine victory.

Ike turned to Beetle. "I'd like to visit the airborne troops before they load up."

"I'll see to it, Ike. How's your headache?"

"Surprisingly, diminishing."

"It's a helluva decision for any human being to have to make, but the deed is done. Now, we trust the troops. I'm glad you're feeling better. This may not be the correct time, but in the light of this momentous decision, I wanted to show you the final public notice to be released on Tuesday morning."

Eisenhower nodded his head and outstretched his left hand. Smith placed the sheet of paper in Ike's open hand. "This is the printed page complete with your signature."

SUPREME HEADQUARTERS
ALLIED EXPEDITIONARY FORCE

Soldiers, Sailors, and Airmen of the Allied Expeditionary Force!

You are about to embark upon the Great Crusade, toward which we have striven these many months. The eyes of the world are upon you. The hope and prayers of liberty-loving people everywhere march with you. In company with our brave Allies and brothers-in-arms on other Fronts, you will bring about the destruction of the German war machine, the elimination of Nazi tyranny over the oppressed peoples of Europe, and security for ourselves in a free world.

Your task will not be an easy one. Your enemy is well trained, well equipped and battle-hardened. He will fight savagely.

But this is the year 1944! Much has happened since the Nazi triumphs of 1940-41. The United Nations have inflicted upon the Germans great defeats, in open battle, man-to-man.

Our air offensive has seriously reduced their strength in the air and their capacity to wage war on the ground. Our Home Fronts have given us an overwhelming superiority in weapons and munitions of war, and placed at our disposal great reserves of trained fighting men. The tide has turned! The free men of the world are marching together to Victory!

I have full confidence in your courage, devotion to duty and skill in battle. We will accept nothing less than full Victory!

Good luck! And let us beseech the blessing of Almighty God upon this great and noble undertaking.

Dwight D. Eisenhower

"Well done, Beetle," Ike affirmed. "Thank you for the editing. You've made it far better, and my signature is essential." Eisenhower stared into Smith's eyes. "There is also the prospect this affair may go the other way. If it does, I consign this simple concession note to your care, just in case this endeavor meets failure."

Our landings in the Cherbourg-Havre area have failed to gain a satisfactory foothold and I have withdrawn the troops. My decision to attack at this time and place was based upon the best information available. The troops, the air and the Navy did all that Bravery and devotion to duty could do. If any blame or fault attaches to the attempt it is mine alone.

— July 5

"This will not be necessary, Ike. I have faith. I shall hold it devotedly. But, to be clear, if necessary, do you want it dated the 5th?"

"No. A couple of days ago, I jotted down these thoughts predicated upon the 5th as D-Day. If necessary, the concession must be dated by the order to evacuate the assault forces."

"I have confidence it shall not be required, Ike, but I shall loyally carry out your orders."

"Thank you, Beetle. Now, I need a couple of hours sleep before I meet the troops tomorrow . . . well, almost today."

Monday, 5.June.1944
USAAF Station F-356
Saffron Walden, Essex, England
United Kingdom
09:55 hours

"**W**e've been confined to base for a week. We haven't flown in days. The telephones haven't worked in weeks," grinched Second Lieutenant Lewis Adrian 'Antler' Henricks of Ithaca, New York, who was Sweet's wingman and the next to youngest squadron pilot by just five months over Boy Williams. Brian had been the youngest pilot in every squadron he had served until the 334FS replacements joined in September 1943.

No one took the bait. Brian remained in his chair, leaned back against the wall, and dozed as he often did to avoid silly conversations. Antler voiced the frustration of waiting for the next mission.

"Don't get your panties in a bunch, Antler," Dusty challenged. "I can't imagine any invasion going forward with the weather that just passed through. It would do us no good jumping into the air when we can't see the ground, no point if we can't see what we're supposed to be shooting at."

Spot on, Dusty, Brian thought with his eyes closed, not wanting to participate. *This waiting and restrictions are weighing on all of us. We all know the invasion is imminent. Let's get on with it. But there's no point complaining about things none of us control. The sooner we get on with whatever is going to happen, the better.*

The grumbling continued, and Brian tried his best to ignore the useless complaining. The grinding reached a level that exceeded Arnie's threshold of tolerance. "Looky here, gentlemen. We are restricted to base and cut off from the outside world because of operational security. The supreme commander wants no mistakes or foolish comments that might be useful to the enemy in anticipating the imminent invasion. Let it suffice to say, the long-awaited invasion of the Continent and the placing of sufficient combat forces on the ground in France for the march to Berlin will begin at any moment. Hell, for all we know, it may have begun already. Thus, my counsel is, put your frustrations aside. This will not last much longer. The invasion is very close. We are going to get very busy soon. Enjoy the peace while it lasts. Play checkers, chess, or read a book. For those who have been doing this for a while, the incessant complaining quickly becomes rather tiresome. Learn to live with it." Arnie did not wait for questions or comments. He went to his office and slammed the door, which knocked dust loose from the wall boards.

Brian saw several of the pilots look at each other with puzzled expressions. He closed his eyes. He heard several board games being set up. No one spoke. Brian was grateful for the respite.

"Hey guys, look at this," Salt Morton said at the doorway before he stepped outside.

Brian did not move or open his eyes. He heard muffled non-specific conversation away from the building. None of the words he could discern inspired him in his reserved state, that is, until he heard the term 'impressive.' Brian opened his eyes and lowered his chair. The ready room was empty except for Sergeant Ellison at his desk and Arnie Clark's closed door. Brian lowered the front feet of his chair to the floor.

"New paint job, Major," Ellison commented as Brian approached the door.

A quarter of their fighters had been returned to the flight line. Their tail designators and other markings remained the same except for stripes on the empennage and wings. Alternating white and black stripes, each 18 inches wide, wrapped around the tail and each wing without interfering with existing markings. The prop spinner and rudder remained the 334FS fire engine red. The other fighters continued to be towed from the maintenance hangars to the flight line.

"I guess they want us easily identified," pronounced Sweet.

"Yeah, which means we'll be heading to the beachhead soon," Dusty added.

"And, you rookies can stop whining," Salt said.

Brian watched the process. He eventually saw his QP-G Mustang being towed with Sergeant Tomlinson driving the small tug. Brian made his way to his assigned parking spot to await Tomlinson. He did not have to wait long. When Larson stopped, Brian grabbed a set of chocks and blocked the left main wheel. Larson disconnected the towbar and came over to Brian.

"I guess they want to spot you," Larson offered.

"So it would seem. They must have added the black stripes in between to make the white stripes stand out."

"Group ordered the stripes, but we were told the instructions came from the 8th Air Force. We programmed the radio for the anticipated operations, again, according to Group orders."

"Any other changes?" Brian asked.

"No Sir. She's the same old bird . . . just new stripes. If you'll excuse me, Major, I've got to get the tug back to the hangar."

"Sure, no problem. I'm just going to give her a good walk around. We're not scheduled or alerted to fly today. Is she loaded and fueled?"

"Yes Sir. Tiptop. Do you need me here?" asked Larson.

"No. Not necessary."

"They have us all helping with the stripes. We should have the whole group finished this afternoon."

"Hop to it, then, Larson. I have a feeling we're going to get very busy quite soon."

Tomlinson jumped on the tug and drove off, dragging the tow bar behind him.

Brian completed his walk around and climbed up on the left wing to scan the cockpit. All the switches were in the proper position for the aircraft's quiescent state.

Buddy Courtland appeared at the aft left wing root as Brian finished his cockpit inspection. Brian nodded to Buddy and closed the canopy. Then, he jumped off the wing.

"What's going to happen, Hunter?" asked Buddy.

"I don't know. This is my first invasion, just like you." They both laughed. "I suspect we'll be tasked to keep whatever enemy fighters and bombers are left in France away from the landing area, and then we will likely be given ground targets to hit to keep German reinforcements from reaching the beaches."

"A lot different from what you faced during the Battle of Britain."

"Yeah . . . that battle was a whole different kind of fight."

16:20 hours

"What are they holding us for?" Frog asked. "We've been sittin' here all day. The aircraft are painted, loaded, and ready. Yet, we've got no orders, and here we sit."

"It's wearing on all of us," Dusty responded. "This isn't going to last forever. The generals will pull the trigger soon, I suspect, if they haven't already."

One of the phones on Sergeant Ellison's desk rang. He lifted the handset to his left ear. "Three Thirty-fourth." Juli listened, not moving from the operations desk. "Yes Sir." Ellison left the handset off the cradle. He did not look at any of the pilots and went to the skipper's office door. In a soft but audible voice, Juli said, "Group on Blue." Ellison returned to his desk, checked to make sure Clark had picked up the phone, and then he returned the handset to the cradle.

After a minute of indiscernible conversation, Arnie hung up. He came out, walked to the door, and said as he passed, "No one leaves. I've been called to Group. We're not released. No one leaves," he repeated and then disappeared out the door.

18:05 hours

Clark's return brought all the pilots to silent focus by his entrance alone. He closed the main door and placed his hat on the corner of Ellison's desk. Arnie scanned the squadron pilots presumably to ensure every single one of his assigned pilots was present.

"Well, for you reprobates who have been grinding on about the restrictions, I can announce you'll be free of those constraints soon, but not tonight or for the next few days." Arnie paused but not a sound could be heard. "I am not authorized to say why, but rest assured, the reason for the restrictions will change soon. But this is not the purpose of holding you here. You are instructed to get a good night's sleep. The O'Club bar is closed tonight." That statement induced groans but no words. "The reason for all this is my general briefing tonight. We will reconvene tomorrow morning at zero three hundred for the initial mission briefing. This evening I will simply inform you all that we will be flying from before dawn to dusk. We will fly multiple sorties as fast as the ground crews can refuel and rearm our aircraft. The mission plan calls for the entire group to operate as a whole all day tomorrow and perhaps longer. The ground crews are being comparably prepared for what will most likely be an extraordinary day."

"Do you know where we are going?" Sweet asked.

"Yes, but I'm not authorized to disclose the mission details until our mission briefing tomorrow morning. I can assure you, we'll have no waiting tomorrow. We'll brief and go . . . and we'll fly multiple sorties."

"Can you at least tell us what type of mission?" Salt asked.

"No, I can't. Let it suffice to say these unusual procedures are consistent with the restrictions that have been in place in recent days. All the mystery will likely be removed tomorrow."

The invasion is finally here, Brian thought.

"Now, one last admonition, if anyone has booze in his room, leave the cork in the bottle. We need everyone tiptop and on point tomorrow. I do NOT," he said with emphasis, "want to deal with or even detect anyone in a compromised or diminished state. Tomorrow is too bloody important. No games, no equivocation, no excuses. Have I made myself crystal clear?"

"Yes Sir," came the collective reply in unison.

"Very well. The mess is holding evening meal. So let's get back to the mess, get a good meal and a good night's sleep. Breakfast tomorrow morning will be served an hour before our briefing time. Dismissed."

The pilots shuffled out of the operations building and climbed into the covered bed of a 6x6 truck. Sergeant Ellison switched off the lights and closed the door before they finished loading. Ellison was the last to board and the first to be dropped off.

They ate their meal of steak, baked potatoes with the fixin's, and fresh green beans with sauteed onions. Only water, milk, or iced tea were available to drink. The tinkle of utensils on plates remained the only audible sound. No one spoke.

With his hunger sated, Brian left the dining room. He looked at the six open, empty telephone booths and felt the urge to talk to Charlotte, but he knew that was impossible, at least for now. His book, still working on *A Tale of Two Cities*, would have to suffice until he was ready for sleep. The progress with the book was slow and haltingly steady.

———

Monday, 5.June.1944
USAAF Station T-486
Newbury, Berkshire, England
United Kingdom
18:25 hours

The airbase had been RAF Greenham Common until the fall of 1943, when the airfield was transferred to the USAAF and became the home of the 438th Troop Carrier Group's four squadrons of Douglas C-47 Skytrain twin-engine transport aircraft. The group was assigned to the direct transport support of the U.S. 101st Airborne Division that had its headquarters at the base and its regiments garrisoned in the proximate area. The group had been an integral part of the division training and preparation for the OVERLORD invasion.

Several hours earlier, General Eisenhower had visited the British 6th Airborne Division at RAF Tarrant Rushton in Dorset. He had talked with paratroopers with 'D' Company 2nd Oxfordshire and Buckinghamshire Light Infantry, who would serve as pathfinders for the remainder of the division. Eisenhower was not there for a command inspection. He offered words of encouragement, but what Ike really wanted was to listen to the troops. They extolled their mission and readiness for the night drop they had long trained for. They were eager for the night drop ahead. Morale was sky-high and rock-solid.

Eisenhower also saw the vast array of Airspeed AS.51 Horsa troop-carrying gliders with General Aircraft Hamilcar heavy equipment gliders interspersed; all of them staggered on the runway in the planned landing order. In addition, Handley Page Halifax bomber-tugs stood on both sides of the runway and the glider array. The division's 6th Airlanding Brigade troops were keen to show the supreme commander a Hamilcar glider with a Tetrarch Mk VII Light Tank snugly fit into the interior cargo space and chained to the floor. The glider troops with their tanks would land on and defend the east side of the Orne River and Caen Canal.

From RAF Tarrant Rushton, General Eisenhower arrived at the Greenham Common airfield. He made sure that the officers who stood to welcome him understood he was not here to see them, receive any briefings, or conduct any inspections. They saluted and left the supreme commander to his purpose.

The men of Company E, 502nd Parachute Infantry Regiment, 101st Airborne Division, were near their main and reserve parachutes and hefty equipment bags. They were approaching their rig-up time. Ike recognized that he had arrived just in time. Once they began to don their parachute harnesses, their minds needed to be on the task before them. He looked for the senior trooper.

"Excuse me, First Sergeant, I'd like to talk to your paratroopers."

"Yes Sir. Be my guest."

"How much time do I have?"

"As much time as you need, General."

"No. The mission you are about to embark upon is far more important than me. I'll not interfere with your timetable."

"Yes Sir," the first sergeant checked his watch. "Twenty minutes, General."

"That should be sufficient."

Eisenhower turned to the men who had gathered around the supreme commander. "How are you boys doin'?"

"Ready and raring ta go, General," a sergeant barked.

"Yeah!" shouted a bunch of the paratroopers.

"You're ready for the night drop?"

"You betcha, Sir. We've been trainin' for just this jump. We're just grateful to get to take the fight to the damn Nazis finally. We'll be runnin' to Berlin."

Eisenhower chuckled softly. "Don't run too fast, fellas. We've got to get the supply trucks ashore too. We've got to keep you guys in food, water, and ammunition."

"We trust you, General. Just keep the supplies comin'. We'll lead the run as fast as you can keep us in bullets. We're going ta smack those Nazi bastards up side the head."

Eisenhower smiled. "I must say, I came here to offer encouragement for all of you. Your jumping into Normandy tonight will open our first steps of a grand crusade to liberate Europe and end the tyranny of Nazi Germany. I visited your cousins of the 6th Airborne earlier this afternoon. I must tell you in all sincerity that you fellas have encouraged me. With such eager enthusiasm, we cannot fail."

"We'll get the job done, General," the first sergeant added.

Ike felt tears welling up. He quickly wiped both eyes. He had never jumped out of an airplane during the day, set aside at night. He could only imagine what the paratroopers would experience and face in less than six hours. Ike listened as the paratroopers cheered and pumped themselves up for what lay ahead.

"Thank you for allowing me to share these last few moments before you suit up and prepare for combat tonight. I shall leave you to your preparations."

"Three cheers for General Eisenhower," commanded the first sergeant. "Hip hip." "Hooray!" "Hip hip." "Hooray!" "Hip hip." "Hooray!"

Eisenhower snapped to a crisp position of attention and saluted the men of Company 'E.' He turned and marched off smartly to his limousine.

Kay Summersby held the passenger door open for the supreme commander. He stepped into the passenger compartment. Kay closed the door and drove away.

"To The Cottage, Ike?"

"No, Kay. I'd love to, but I must get back to Sharpener. Too much is beginning to happen, and I must be there. This is the night we have been planning for over a year. Tonight, it all begins."

"Sharpener it is."

Kay expertly transitioned through multiple checkpoints and traffic jams of the multitudinous convoys headed to the coast. The transformation of the still accumulating BOLERO forces into the OVERLORD assault force had been nearly completed, and within hours, the combat assault to free Europe and end the war would begin.

—

Monday, 5.June.1944
No.10 Annexe
New Public Offices
Whitehall, London, England
United Kingdom
21:10 hours

"The meal tonight was exquisite," observed Clementine, "even more so given our wartime rationing constraints. Mrs. Landemare outdid herself tonight."

"Uh-huh."

Clementine Ogilvy Spencer-Churchill, née Hozier, stared at her husband of 36 years, who was lost in thought. She knew the signs all too well. Something weighty occupied his consciousness. Only the two of them sat for dinner in the small Annexe dining room. The table had been cleared. His shoulders were slumped forward and his head down. He stared at the tablecloth.

"Are you well, Winnie?" Her husband did not respond. She touched his left forearm.

"Huh?" Winston looked up into his wife's concerned eyes.

"Is something wrong?"

"No. Why do you ask?"

"You've been somewhere else all evening."

"I'm sorry, Clemmie . . . too much going on."

Clementine smiled softly and held Winston's eyes. "Tonight is the night, isn't it?"

Winston initially shook his head, but then he changed to a nod. "You have known me for too many years."

"Never too many, Winnie, and I need many more."

"Thank you for that. Now, if you will excuse me, my dear, I must see what Pim has for me."

"I'll have your brandy waiting for you."

"Thank you, my darling."

The prime minister used the steel circular stairway to descend from the reinforced Annexe to the underground bunker known as the Cabinet War Rooms. Winston made his way through the maze of narrow corridors to the Map Room. A dozen Navy, Army, and Air Force personnel worked feverishly on statusing the large wall map of the Channel—a smaller version of Eisenhower's Sharpener wall map.

Captain Pim looked up from his clipboard, noticed Churchill, and walked directly to the prime minister. "The transit is well underway, Sir. Every element of the initial assault force has met their entry gates into the assigned lanes—so far, so good. All three airborne divisions have taken off and made for their routes."

"So, our long-awaited invasion is underway."

"Yes Sir."

"God's will be done."

"Yes Sir."

Churchill found an empty chair and sat down heavily without taking his eyes off the ever-changing ship and airplane markers being moved down the map toward the Normandy coast. The prime minister sat watching the map change with his forehead lowered as if he was about to charge the map. He ignored the frenetic activity in the room around him. The lead transports would not reach their planned off-loading positions for several more hours in the pre-dawn. As twilight broke on the eastern horizon, the vast armada would be within sight of the Normandy coast. He imagined what a German private, feeling safe in his bunker, might think when the sky lightened enough for him to see the bay that had been empty when the sun went down that is now filled to the horizons with thousands of ships.

When Prime Minister Churchill had seen the progress and the blooming of the invasion plan, he thanked the Map Room staff and Captain Pim for their devoted work and then departed before midnight. The singular thought kept returning to his thoughts as he walked. Three divisions of paratroopers would be jumping from their aircraft and releasing from their tow aircraft to begin the landing of 11 full-strength divisions, five brigades, and three specialized battalions on the coast of occupied France. Winston made his way back up the circular staircase to the Annexe.

Clementine waited patiently for her husband's return. She stood and handed Winston a generous snifter of his favorite Hine cognac.

Winston took a healthy swallow of the liquor. "Thank you, Clemmie. I needed that."

"How is it going?"

"So far, precisely to plan. The para lads will be jumping out of their aircraft within minutes. I must confess to my recurring thoughts of Gallipoli. We have much more immediate information today than we did twenty-nine years ago. That can be a blessing and a curse. The A-E-F staff is the best of both countries, and I believe in Eisenhower."

"You have done your part."

"Yes, we have. As Ike likes to say, it is up to the sergeants now. The months of planning and preparation have given the sergeants the best tools available in this world at this time."

Clementine stood with Winston as he finished his brandy. He briefly considered another dose but placed his glass on the table.

"Do you realize that by the time you wake up in the morning, twenty thousand men may have been killed?"

"Oh, Winnie! My God, I shall pray that does not happen, and you are wrong in this instance."

"I shall pray with you, my dear. Prayers are all we have to offer at this stage. There is nothing I can add now." Winston lapsed into thought for a few minutes. "I'm dreadfully tired. Let us go to bed. There is nothing more that can do done tonight."

They did not have far to go in the compact Annexe apartment designed and built to protect the prime minister during the horrific nightly bombing of The Blitz. Another day was done. Tomorrow morning would bring momentous events on the French coast of Normandy.

———

Chapter 7

Extinction is the rule;
survival is the exception.
-- Carl Edward Sagan

Tuesday, 6.June.1944
USAAF Station F-356
Saffron Walden, Essex, England
United Kingdom
03:20 hours

Arnie gave his pilots a thorough mission briefing for multiple sorties of essentially the same mission. The 4FG would work in concert with the 56FG to block the enemy road, rail, and river traffic through Rouen, Normandy, France, on the River Seine. The city was a critical transportation junction across the Seine between Le Havre and Paris. The two fighter groups would cycle through the blocking mission throughout the day. They would also provide air cover over the Rouen sector to prevent any German bombers or fighters from entering the OVERLORD beachhead area. The U.S. and British fighter groups were paired in a similar manner around the periphery of the beachhead area. Arnie confirmed for the pilots what he could not do last night—the invasion of occupied France had begun this morning. Their job was to keep enemy reinforcements from moving west.

The details of their mission were a bit unusual from what the 4FG pilots were used to doing. The 334FS would have the center section. The 335FS would have the northern sector, and the 336FS would have the southern sector. Horseback would supervise his three squadrons from a long racetrack three thousand feet above the high flights.

Each 334FS flight would cycle through the interdiction positions. Two flights would hold at Angels 15 to serve as air cover and observation. One flight would stage at Angels 5 to specifically observe traffic over the three roadway bridges across the Seine and the railway along the west bank of the Seine. The action flight would carry out strafing strikes on any and all military vehicles trying to move through their assigned area. The flights would cycle through the three altitude positions. Arnie cautioned them not to attack any target from the same direction twice. They were also all loaded with the mix of ball and armor-piercing-incendiary rounds to give each aircraft a broad spectrum of effects for the broadest array of potential targets.

Arnie made a specific point of discussing armor attacks. None of them had yet faced enemy main battle tanks and the heavy armor common to top tier tanks. The guidance provided by 8ᵗʰ Air Force Intelligence focused on diving attacks on the top armor. If vertical attacks are not possible or opportune, they should aim for the tracks—at least immobilize the tank.

Since the 4FG was the first fighter group into their assigned battlespace, their initial objectives were the known anti-aircraft batteries in and around Rouen. 'B' Division had two sites on the western portion of the city. Yellow Flight was assigned to an 88 mm *Flugabwehrkanone 36* at the northern tip of The Cross Island on the north side of the Corneille Bridge across the Seine. Brian's Red Flight would take on a quad 20 mm *Flakvierling 38* battery at the northeast corner of the Botanical Gardens on the western edge of the city. Once the anti-aircraft guns were neutralized, Red Flight would strafe each bridge to stop traffic across the bridges as they set up the blocking formation.

Horseback led the group into the air as twilight began to lighten the eastern horizon. The 334FS was the middle squadron for takeoff. Brian led his division in sequence for their section takeoffs. As Buddy rolled into position, Brian released his brakes and advanced his throttle for their takeoff. With his aircraft cleaned up and in the climb out, Brian switched to auxiliary fuel tanks. They would keep their main fuel tanks full as long as they could and keep their main fuel among the squadron aircraft as close to the same as possible. They wanted to jettison their drop tanks when they were empty, encountered fighters or anti-aircraft fire, or reached Rouen, whichever occurred first, but they would stay together. The group descended to a low level and crossed the coastline between Dieppe and Saint-Valery-en-Caux. The squadrons and flights split for their assigned targets.

Brian identified the Red Flight target well before it was in range. He could see the crew running to the gun mount, swinging the four cannons toward him, and loading the magazines. His gunsight reticle tracked nicely to the target that had not yet opened fire. Brian beat them to the trigger. The flashes danced all over the gun mount. Bodies of enemy soldiers exploded as the high-energy projectiles impacted them. Brian pulled up sharply and rolled into a steep left-climbing turn. He pushed on his throttle to ensure he was at full power at the emergency gate—the frangible wire that separated full from emergency power. Brian had eliminated the entire crew and irreparably damaged their quad-20. The other three pilots of Red Flight added more damage and followed their leader.

Brian scanned the sky around them. Every mission without German fighters seemed strange, almost suspicious. *Where were they? Why aren't they defending their territory? What am I missing?* Brian rolled over more to check on progress below them. When Blue Flight climbed out of the low position,

Brian descended Red Flight to the intermediate position, which gave him a better view of their assigned bridges and the rails along the river.

Even when Red Flight's turn arrived at the low action post, targets did not appear. Salt took some small arms fire from soldiers on the east bank and fired a burst, which easily dispersed the half dozen men and may have wounded several enemy soldiers.

The squadron cycled through two whole sequences. Red Flight had just completed their second low station stint and returned to the high station orbit when 56FG reported in. Horseback called bingo for the 4FG.

As the group joined up at Angels 15 for the return to base, they could easily see the columns of smoke rising from the coast to their west. *That must be the invasion landing area.*

After landing back at home plate, the aircraft were being refueled and reloaded. They carried out a quick collective debriefing. That was all they had time for. No tanks, armored cars, trucks, or even military motorcycles crossed their area. They asked about the invasion progress, but the Intelligence debriefers gave them nothing, either because they did not know or were not authorized to disclose what they knew even to American pilots.

The aircraft were all reported ready. Arnie cut the debriefing short. "Time to go. Let's mount up."

The 4th Fighter Group quickly set off on the second of their mission cycles for the day. The smoke over the western Normandy coast had increased. Billows of smoke from the naval gunfire from the array of warships partially hid the armada of transports disgorging divisions of combat troops onto the five OVERLORD beaches.

The 4th Fighter Group flew five sorties of their interdiction mission that day. Several convoys of trucks attempted to cross the Seine in the afternoon but were turned back with dozens of trucks destroyed. They had seen no tanks of any shape, size, or type. Likewise, they detected no enemy fighters or bombers in their sector that day. Yet, at the end of the day, as evening twilight descended into the darkness of night, it had been a costly day. The entire Blue Flight of 335FS had been lost, including their commander with two known killed in action, the other two missing. The 334FS lost the least but still lost.

Arnie's wingman in the first section of Blue Flight, Second Lieutenant Bradley Thomas 'Hick' Hickerson of Macon, Georgia, had been shot down during the fourth cycle and observed successfully bailing out of his mortally wounded Mustang. He was initially listed as missing in action and later confirmed as a prisoner of war confined to *Stalag Luft III.*

Tuesday, 6.June.1944
Forward HQ, SHAEF
Southwick House
Pinsley Drive
Portsmouth, Hampshire, England
United Kingdom
07:30 hours

General Eisenhower sat alone at the staff conference table that had been moved from the front to the back of the Sharpener Map Room. He remained fixated on the progressive status of units moving ashore on all five landing beaches. The huge wall map that had been empty 24 hours ago was now full of ship, aircraft, and ground combat unit symbols positioned appropriately. The map room was a beehive of activity as dozens of men and women received reports, moved symbols on the wall map, and placed new ones as their status changed. The hectic activity of the map room carried its own degree of fascination.

General Montgomery entered the map room and stood facing the map with his fists on his hips. Eisenhower glanced at his ground forces commander but returned his attention to the ever-changing map. Neither general disturbed the other. Monty eventually made his way to the conference table and sat next to and left of Ike.

"I must say, Ike, considering the enormity of this endeavor and yesterday's weather, I believe we are doing surprisingly well." Eisenhower chose only to nod his head. "We've had a few problems." Again, Eisenhower only nodded his head. "The winds and anti-aircraft fire on approach scattered all three airborne divisions. However, as we hoped and expected, they've dealt with the anomaly exceptionally well. They've control of each of their assigned crossroads, including the Caen Canal and Orne River bridges. The first waves have landed on all five beaches. I just received a report that the 2nd Rangers have scaled the cliff at Pointe du Hoc. They also reported the coastal guns had been removed since our last pass of our photo recce."

Neither general spoke for several minutes. Eisenhower was the first to break their private silence. "I worry too much."

Monty smiled and chuckled modestly. "We all do, Ike . . . a burden of generalship, I'm afraid. We've a long way to go for just today, and an arduous journey ahead . . . but to this early point, we are doing surprisingly well."

Eisenhower looked at Montgomery. "I trust your judgment, Monty, but we are a terribly long way from even calling this a foothold."

"True, but all beaches are doing well, actually ahead of plan, except for Omaha. The channelization of those ravines is proving to be more difficult than expected."

"There is nothing we can do. We don't even have enough room ashore to maneuver."

"True, but we are rapidly building to that point."

"None too fast for me. So much is riding upon what happens today."

Monty leaned toward Ike and whispered, "Did you see the Boniface about Rommel?"

"About his wife's birthday, which is today as I recall."

"More about him leaving his headquarters in Paris for their home in the small city of Herrlingen, a suburb of Ulm."

"Yes, I saw it."

"He left on the 4th, which tells me he did not suspect we were coming. He had to have indications but probably believed the storm on the 4th and 5th meant he could make it home for his wife's birthday before anything would happen. So, we have that jump. And, he wasn't due back until the 8th at his headquarters in Chateau de La Roche-Guyon, north of Paris, actually in the cave complex behind the mansion." Montgomery smiled broadly. "I suspect we caught him with his pants down. But, I also suspect he is, or soon will be, rushing back to his headquarters to resume command."

"A positive sign."

"You know, Ike, to me, I think it is the most positive sign we have yet detected. We achieved the surprise we needed. I hold no illusion that hard fighting is ahead, but Rommel's absence for a routine family event leaves me with a very encouraging feeling."

"Regardless, Monty, we must get sufficient combat forces ashore and establish a broad and deep enough beachhead to focus on the greater objectives. I doubt I'll be able to take a breath of relief and gratitude until we have expanded the beachhead beyond artillery range and can land troops and supplies at will."

"We'll get the job done, Ike. Now, if you'll excuse me, I'd like to go check on Brad. He's been intensely attentive on the evolving situation at Omaha Beach."

"By all means. I shall be here for a while."

Montgomery departed. Eisenhower returned his gaze to the wall map and his thoughts to the troops on the ground in France.

—

Tuesday, 6. June. 1944
West Wing
White House
Washington, District of Columbia
United States of America
19:55 hours

"**W**e're ready when you are, Mister President," the radio sound technician said.

Roosevelt quickly skimmed the typewritten message he was about to read. He liked the message. Franklin looked up and nodded to the technician.

"Soundcheck, please, Mister President."

"Testing, one, two, three."

"We're good. Standby." The technician waited at his sound control panel. A green light illuminated. "We are live in five, four, three, two." The man pointed at the president when the green light went out, and a red light illuminated.

"My fellow Americans: Last night, when I spoke with you about the fall of Rome, I knew at that moment that troops of the United States and our allies were crossing the Channel in another and greater operation. It has come to pass with success thus far.

"And so, in this poignant hour, I ask you to join with me in prayer:

"Almighty God: Our sons, pride of our Nation, this day have set upon a mighty endeavor, a struggle to preserve our Republic, our religion, and our civilization, and to set free a suffering humanity.

"Lead them straight and true; give strength to their arms, stoutness to their hearts, steadfastness in their faith.

"They will need Thy blessings. Their road will be long and hard. For the enemy is strong. He may hurl back our forces. Success may not come with rushing speed, but we shall return again and again; and we know that by Thy grace, and by the righteousness of our cause, our sons will triumph.

"They will be sorely tried, by night and by day, without rest until the victory is won. The darkness will be rent by noise and flame. Men's souls will be shaken with the violences of war.

"For these men are lately drawn from the ways of peace. They fight not for the lust of conquest. They fight to end conquest. They fight to liberate. They fight to let justice arise, and tolerance and goodwill among all Thy people. They yearn but for the end of battle, for their return to the haven of home.

"Some will never return. Embrace these, Father, and receive them, Thy heroic servants, into Thy kingdom.

"And for us at home -- fathers, mothers, children, wives, sisters, and brothers of brave men overseas -- whose thoughts and prayers are ever with them--help us, Almighty God, to rededicate ourselves in renewed faith in Thee in this hour of great sacrifice.

"Many people have urged that I call the Nation into a single day of special prayer. But because the road is long and the desire is great, I ask that our people devote themselves in a continuance of prayer. As we rise to each new day, and again when each day is spent, let words of prayer be on our lips, invoking Thy help to our efforts.

"Give us strength, too -- strength in our daily tasks, to redouble the contributions we make in the physical and the material support of our armed forces.

"And let our hearts be stout, to wait out the long travail, to bear sorrows that may come, to impart our courage unto our sons wheresoever they may be.

"And, O Lord, give us Faith. Give us Faith in Thee; Faith in our sons; Faith in each other; Faith in our united crusade. Let not the keenness of our spirit ever be dulled. Let not the impacts of temporary events, of temporal matters of but fleeting moment let not these deter us in our unconquerable purpose.

"With Thy blessing, we shall prevail over the unholy forces of our enemy. Help us to conquer the apostles of greed and racial arrogancies. Lead us to the saving of our country and with our sister Nations into a world unity that will spell a sure peace, a peace invulnerable to the schemings of unworthy men. And a peace that will let all of men live in freedom, reaping the just rewards of their honest toil.

"Thy will be done, Almighty God.

"Amen."

Roosevelt looked up. The technician held his left fist until the red light extinguished. "We are out," announced the sound technician.

"Thank you for your expert assistance," the president said.

"Thank you, Sir."

The president's longtime trusted confidant and friend Harry Lloyd Hopkins pushed Roosevelt's wheelchair from the study back toward the Oval Office. The president's military chief of staff, Admiral Leahy, walked beside them on the right. They did not return to the Oval Office, and the three men used the elevator to reach the residence. Dinner waited for them in the dining room. They talked while they ate, and each of them thought the broadcast had gone well—a tribute to The Longest Day.

———

Thursday, 8.June.1944
Standing Oak Farm
Winchester, Hampshire, England
18:10 hours

Charlotte's extended family sat at the now full dining room table for their evening meal. Mary, her nanny, and her children remained at the farm. Charlotte was progressively more impressed by how Mary and Grace fit into the farm's operations and their engagement with the farm's processes. Grace and Edith alternated with tending the children and assisting with the morning and afternoon milking. The half dozen new calves born in the spring were consuming some of their yield, but no one complained. The farm's milk herd continued to grow.

The children occupied the attention of the adults. The antics and interactions of the children kept them all entertained and enveloped in laughter. The children finished eating first before Edith and Grace finished, but they excused themselves, rose, cleared their plates, and then they took the children outside to play in the warmth and sunshine of the waning late spring daylight.

Horace, Lionel, and Jacob finished their meals and cleared their plates. They excused themselves to deliver the evening's products to town and drop Jacob off at his parents' home. Finally, they called it a night.

Charlotte refreshed a cup of tea for each of them. She cleared the remaining plates from the table but sat back down, sensing Mabel had more to talk about.

When Charlotte sat and took a sip of her tea, Mabel spoke, "I made a small delivery of vegetables to several restaurants in town. The American Army has disappeared as quickly as it appeared five months ago. Winchester is almost devoid of men in uniform, except an occasional military lorry driving south. They've gone somewhere.

"I also got a call from a man who introduced himself as Captain Henry Jordan; he prefers Hank. Anyway, Hank told me he had assumed supervision for our produce contract. He was based at some American supply depot in Basingstoke. Captain Jordan wanted us to deliver our products to their facility, but I told him we had no lorries and certainly not sufficient fuel. So, he agreed to come with a convoy of large lorries to pick up the next load in five weeks."

"Is that acceptable?"

"Yes, seamless from our perspective . . . as long as they do what they say. They still want everything we can produce. Captain Jordan asked to come down early next week to see the greenhouses and our program."

"Sounds reasonable."

"To me as well."

"Do you need me there?"

"I don't think so, but you're, of course, always welcome."

"Thank you, Mabel. I know you will handle things quite well. I will make time if I can help." Charlotte finished her tea. She gestured to Mabel if she wanted a refill. Mabel shook her head. "Are you happy here?"

Mabel laughed hard. "Oh my Good Lord, yes, Charlotte. You have been an angel, and this place is heaven for me . . . and for my son. Charlotte, Todd is thriving here—the peace, the life stimulation, the extra care. I could never afford to employ a nanny. Truth be told, I could barely afford to feed and shelter Todd and me. Charlotte, you saved me . . . and Todd . . . in more ways than I can count."

"Mabel, my dear, you saved me. There is no way I could have managed those greenhouses and the Army contract. Your skills have not only fulfilled today, but it has also opened a far wider tomorrow."

"So, we have a mutual admiration society."

"You two were made for each other," Mary interjected finally.

They all laughed. "There is that, and rightly so." Charlotte continued, "Changing the subject, I've not seen anything in the newspaper yet, or even on the radio, but something is happening now. The popular supposition seems to be that the invasion of the Continent has finally begun. Hopefully, this war will be over soon. The end will eventually come. The men will return home and want their jobs back. There will be changes for all of us."

Mabel looked intensely at Charlotte without speaking.

"I'm fairly certain John will choose to remain in the Air Force," Mary offered. "What do you think Brian will do?"

"I don't know. We've not talked about it. He loves flying, so I imagine he will want to find a flying job whether it is in the military . . . or perhaps our airline."

"At least you both have men to come home to you. But, your statement concerns me. What changes do you see for me?" asked Mabel, looking directly into Charlotte's eyes.

"Oh my, I'm so sorry to have concerned you, Mabel. Your job did not exist until you became the inaugural chief. The job is yours and will remain yours as long as you are happy and fulfilled. My statement was more directed at what can we do to ensure you remain fully engaged?"

"Are you asking for my opinions or suggestions?"

"Yes, absolutely. We are in this together, Mabel."

"And what about me?" Mary asked. They all laughed again.

"Sir John will return when this war is finally over," Charlotte responded, "but you are welcome to remain here as long as you wish. You both will always have a home here."

Edith and Grace brought the children inside as the shadows descended upon the exterior. Grace carried Baby Charlotte as each of the children hugged and kissed their mothers, and said goodnight to everyone. Grace shepherded the boys upstairs. Edith jumped into washing the dishes. Charlotte, Mary, and Mabel helped, and collectively, they made quick work of the evening's dishes and cooking utensils, pots, and pans.

When the kitchen was done, Edith went upstairs to help Grace finish putting the children to bed, and then both women came back down to join the other three women around the modest fire. They still pulled the blackout curtains even though none of them thought they were necessary anymore. They wanted to be good citizens until the precautions were no longer required.

———

Monday, 12.June.1944
HMS Kelvin
Offshore Sword Beach, Normandy, newly liberated France
11:40 hours

Prime Minister Churchill, Chief of the Imperial General Staff Field Marshal Sir Alan Brooke, and Winston's longtime friend and colleague Prime Minister of South Africa Field Marshal Jan Christian Smuts, OM, CH, PC, FRS, had visited and spent the night at Sharpener. They received an OVERLORD status briefing from General Eisenhower and the SHAEF command staff, and then they enjoyed an evening meal with the staff.

The three leaders boarded HMS *Kelvin* at Southampton earlier that morning. They sailed out of The Solent, to the east of the Isle of Wight and south-southeast directly to ship's shore bombardment station off Sword Beach.

The *Kelvin* was a K-class fleet destroyer that entered Royal Navy service in September 1939, when she joined the 5th Destroyer Flotilla of the Home Fleet. Lieutenant Commander Robert Meryon William MacFarlan, RN, served as *Kelvin*'s captain since February. The ship had six 4.7-inch naval rifles as twin mounts in three turrets—two forward, one aft—as the main armament. The warship was also armed with anti-aircraft guns, torpedo tubes, and depth charges for anti-submarine work.

Churchill, Smuts, and Brooke joined MacFarlan on the destroyer's bridge. Each of the members held a pair of binoculars. "We have been assigned a shore bombardment task. The main mounts will open up shortly."

"Thank you, Captain." Churchill had barely spoken his words when the warship's primary armament erupted.

The concussion of the 4.7-inch gun muzzle flashes startled all of the men on the bridge. They raised their binoculars.

"The initial target," the captain explained, "is the tree line on the far side of the bridge across the Orne River. Enemy ground units are counterattacking the airborne troops defending the bridge." They watched the shells explode on target. The dust had not yet settled when the destroyer unleashed another broadside salvo at the same target."

"Very impressive gunnery, I must say, Captain," Churchill offered.

"Our gunnery officer has worked hard to ensure our crews are up to the task."

"It shows," added Brooke.

"I do not know when the next call for fire . . ." Just then, a battleship several miles farther out into the Channel let loose a one turret, three-barrel, salvo that snapped the heads of all four men around to seaward. They could feel the concussion even at that distance. "Seems the big guns have a target. Nonetheless, I was going to say, I think the wardroom is holding lunch for you, prime minister."

"Shall we get on with it, gentlemen?" Churchill received confirmations from the others. "We've a full schedule today."

The three leaders followed MacFarlan down several ladderways and through a couple of passageways to a hatch that marked it as the entrance to a diminutive wardroom that served as the officer's mess facility.

"Attention on deck," commanded a Navy lieutenant still in full battledress.

"At ease, gentlemen," Churchill said.

With their three guests aboard their warship, they had a full table with just the department heads, the executive officer, and the captain. At Churchill's insistence due to the packed agenda for the day, they made the meal a working lunch, as the captain explained the ship's mission as the easternmost destroyer in the line. The primary mission was eastern flank security. They had a straight shot cleared lane to the east should any E-Boat or other threat to the invasion fleet present. Their weapons were manned 24 hours per day, including torpedo tubes and depth charges. Their secondary mission was naval gunfire shore bombardment to support the Army working ashore.

"Mindful of the time, Prime Minister, I do believe the admiral's barge is standing by to take you and your party ashore for your next event."

Churchill stood, followed by everyone else. "Thank you so much, Commander MacFarlan, for the transportation, the naval gunfire demonstration, and the excellent luncheon." Winston shook hands with each officer in the wardroom and thanked each one for his service to His Majesty.

Once again, MacFarlan led his guests through the innards of the ship, stepping out of a hatchway into what served as the quarterdeck at sea. Smuts and Brooke descended the short gangway to the waiting motor launch. Churchill saluted and requested permission to go ashore in the naval tradition. MacFarlan smiled, returned the prime minister's salute, and granted permission. As soon as Churchill was safely aboard the launch, the crew cast off and headed to the beach several miles away.

The distinct image of General Montgomery with his black beret and dual cap insignia standing boldly with his fists on his hips waited on the beach just beyond the surf line. Montgomery had worn the black beret since it had been given to him after Second El Alamein. He wore the beret with the original Royal Tank Regiment cap badge plus the British general's cap badge.

A small landing pier had been constructed for just such events. Monty saluted his three senior guests.

At Churchill's prior request, Monty conducted a short walking tour of the beach defenses not yet removed as well as a description of what the landing zone preparations had accomplished in the days and hours before the troops landed. Once the beach tour was complete, Monty led the three leaders to a command tent set up in a grassy flat spot beyond the sand.

After completing a general summary briefing, Montgomery provided his assessment of the trouble spots. "We did not get to Caen as quickly as we had hoped, and now we are faced with a bloody slugfest with the Germans in the town. We are now maneuvering to encircle Caen, but the enemy has effectively used his armor and infantry to thwart our attempts so far. Today is D+6. We landed two more armored divisions across Sword since D-Day, with the last elements of the 7th Armored Division landing across Juno this morning. I must say the Air Force and the Navy are doing a magnificent job at interdiction, holding the enemy's reinforcements away from the beachhead."

"They are not likely to hold them indefinitely," quipped Churchill.

"Yes, of course, which is precisely why we are working so hard on Caen. We'll take the city, but it has proven more problematic than anticipated.

"We are collectively experiencing more difficulty with these damnable hedgerows of the boçage country. We are making progress, but it is slower than expected. Nevertheless, the troops are finding rather inventive ways to overcome each obstacle.

"I must also say the high point so far, if there can be a high point in combat, is the 9th Infantry Division and the VII Corps have made excellent progress on Cherbourg. The enemy garrison knows they have no way out. We have seen evidence they are demolishing port facilities and fighting on tenaciously to buy time for more destruction in an attempt to deny the harbor to us."

"We need that port, General . . . however badly it is damaged."

"Everyone understands that requirement, Prime Minister. General Collins estimates they should take the city in a week, or two at the outside."

"The sooner, the better."

"Yes Sir."

Churchill displayed a demonstrable scowl. "The longer we are delayed here, the greater the risk of enemy reinforcement. The latest evidence we have is that Hitler remains convinced Normandy is a feint, and our primary invasion point is the Pas de Calais. His armored reserve remains in garrison with *Panzer*

Group West. Rommel has been incessant in his counsel that Normandy is the primary landing site. This charade cannot hold much longer. Rommel is convinced, although von Rundstedt is currently taking a more tepid but still supportive stance."

"Yes Sir. We land the 11th Armored and West Riding Infantry Divisions tomorrow."

"We're stacking them up on the beaches, General. We must move," Churchill said with considerable emphasis on the last word. "We cannot keep sending more divisions with no place for them to go."

"Yes Sir," responded Montgomery, wisely choosing not to debate the matter.

Churchill abruptly stood and stomped out of the tent. Smuts and Brooke nearly ran to catch up and only managed to reach the prime minister when he stepped onto the makeshift pier. They boarded the launch. Churchill sat heavily with his persistent scowl. Both Smuts and Brooke recognized the mood and did not intrude upon his contemplation. Both stood looking aft to take in the sights of Sword Beach and the remainder of the Normandy beaches that were now a beehive of activity—supplies being off-loaded and wounded being boarded.

Another destroyer took the party back to Portsmouth. Churchill had not said a word during the entire journey back to England.

———

Tuesday, 13.June.1944
No.10 Downing Street
Whitehall, London, England
United Kingdom
19:15 hours

The Churchill's guests for dinner included their youngest daughter Mary, Winston's longtime friend and currently Lord Privy Seal Lord Beaverbrook, William Maxwell 'Max' Aitken, 1st Baron Beaverbrook, and wartime colleague, friend, and currently Minister of Production Oliver Lyttelton, DSO, MC, PC, and Beaverbrook's successor.

The group was still enjoying cocktail hour when Captain Pim was announced. He went directly to the prime minister, leaned forward, and whispered. "We just received confirmation from the Home Office and Air Ministry that the first V1 flying bomb impacted and exploded at zero four twenty-five this morning. The bomb destroyed the Grove Road Bridge of the Great Eastern Railway. The loss of the bridge will affect rail traffic from Liverpool Street Station to Essex and East Anglia until the bridge can be repaired. The explosion collapsed numerous buildings near the bridge."

"Anyone injured?"

"Yes Sir. Fortunately, there was no rail or road traffic in the area at the time. Regrettably, the rescue services have recovered six dead so far. As of an hour ago, they are working on the rubble and are likely to discover more casualties. Several scores were injured, some seriously and may not survive. Hundreds are now homeless."

"Please inform the Home Office, I want their full report on my desk tomorrow morning."

"Yes Sir. My apologies for interrupting your dinner."

"Nonsense, Pim. I need information like this as soon as it is available. I must tend to my guests. I shall come to the Map Room after dinner. Perhaps the Air Ministry can backtrack to the launch site. I shall be down in an hour or two."

"Yes Sir. I'll see what they can do in that amount of time. For all we know, they already have the information."

"Excellent," Churchill added. "I'll see you then."

Pim nodded his head and departed.

Winston turned back to his dinner party, only to see Clementine's concerned expression. He smiled softly and shook his head.

"Is everything OK, Papa?" Mary asked. The Churchills' 30-year-old daughter currently served in the Auxiliary Territorial Service (ATS). In fact, all of their children served in the military.

All conversation stopped, and all eyes turned to Winston. "We have been watching and striking when evidence presents on a new German weapon they call the V1, or Vengeance One. The first impact on British soil occurred early this morning, six dead so far, but a railway bridge was destroyed and many homes."

"We've heard of these things," Mary said, "in my anti-aircraft gun unit. We've practiced drills against similar targets. They tell us these winged bombs fly until the guidance system cuts off petrol flow, and then they dive to the ground and explode."

"That is pretty much correct. We've not captured one yet to dissect it, but that is what we know."

"So, they don't care what they hit as long as it's London," Max interjected.

"Correct," Winston responded. "They use a fixed ramp to launch these diabolical devices, and so far, all of the ramps we've found are pointed directly at London Center. They have no guidance that we have yet discerned, but they do have a gyro-stabilization system that adjusts for air turbulence to maintain its prescribed course. Mary is correct, in that its terminal phase is determined by the fuel cutoff set before launch, which allows them to crudely compensate for the prevailing wind. But, to our knowledge, no adjustments can be made once it is launched."

"Countermeasures?" asked Lyttelton.

"Mary's anti-aircraft guns, for one. R-A-F fighters can shoot it down, but an exploding warhead would be dangerous to the pilot. The R-A-F thinks they might be able to tip it off course, wing to wing, since the fighters are faster than these flying bombs. The Research Office is working on other means, which is the most I can say at this juncture."

"Enough war talk," Clementine announced. "Dinner is ready."

Those who had drinks finished them or placed their glasses on the table. Then, they filed into the dining room and took their assigned seats. The dinner conversation proved much lighter and jovial, focused on family and the future.

———

Saturday, 17.June.1944
Cabinet War Rooms
New Public Offices
Whitehall, London, England
United Kingdom
11:15 hours

Winston was in a cantankerous mood when he entered the conference room with only the War Cabinet and Defense Committee—the ministers and their respective chiefs—in attendance. The prime minister did not wait for the regular meeting protocol. "Why must we listen to these wretched sirens all hours of the day and night?"

"We have treated the V1 like any other bomber approaching this country to allow our population to take cover," responded Home Secretary Herbert Stanley Morrison, PC, MP for Hackney South.

"The damnable Nawzees are launching these dreadful bombs around the clock. Our people can get no rest or accomplish any work. They are near constantly in air raid shelters."

"If we provide no warning, people might be caught exposed. These are no small bombs. They're nearly 2,000 pounders."

"I know the size and risk," the prime minister continued his protest. "What about warning of only those devices that make it through our defenses?"

"Not enough time," Morrison answered.

"We are trying to intercept earlier over the Channel," added Air Chief Sir Charles Portal. "But short of stationing a continuous airborne patrol, we are in a constant race against time. We have already placed fighter crews on alert duty, which removes them from availability for other missions like ground support in Normandy or daylight bomber escort for pointblank. We're in an incessant balancing act quite akin to what we faced during the great air battle—too many tasks, not enough resources."

"For all of us, do what you can to refine the interception percentage and reduce these nuisance sirens. Can I at least get relief for our people by not activating the sirens for single missiles?"

"There is substantial risk in that," objected Morrison.

"I understand that, but let us try it to see if we can find a better balance. We cannot allow the Nawzees to terrorize us into non-productive fear. Can we confine the warning sirens to areas of the city at risk . . . along the track? We know these buzz bombs fly in a straight line."

"That would take a significant refinement to our warning system," Morrison declared.

"At least evaluate the potential, Herbert."

"We will do so."

"I should add here on a positive note, Herbert, I read your extensive report on the Grove Road first attack on the 13th with keen interest. Well done. These despicable contrivances are coming at us too fast and too many to report on each one. Let it suffice to report on those that are substantively different from the Grove Road incident."

"Yes Sir. Thank you, Sir. We will make it so," Morrison replied.

"Thank you for indulging my annoyance. Now, shall we return to the established agenda for this meeting?" Winston paused but did not expect a reply to his rhetorical question. "Oliver, your report on war production status, if you please."

The War Cabinet meeting returned to the agenda and proceeded to the more routine elements of their wartime work. The gears of governance turned as their work was never done.

———

Monday, 19.June.1944
Circum 13° 20' North - 139° 51' East
Western Philippine Sea
Central Pacific Area

U.S. amphibious forces opened the Battle of the Marianas on the 15th with the landing of the V Amphibious Corps composed of the 2nd and 4th Marine Divisions and the 27th Infantry Division.

In response, the Japanese Imperial Navy sortied to oppose the landings on Saipan Island. The U.S. 5th Fleet maneuvered to engage the Japanese 1st Mobile Fleet. The Americans deployed seven fleet fast carriers, eight light carriers, and seven battleships to intercept and engage the Japanese force of three fleet carriers, six light carriers, and five battleships.

Naval aviation dominated the day. The aerial part of the battle became known as the Great Marianas Turkey Shoot due to the lopsided results. The Japanese lost roughly 600 aircraft versus 123 American losses, but they also lost two fleet carriers and one light carrier among other warships and support vessels.

Among the naval aviators who flew that day was Commander David McCampbell, USN [USNA 1933], who served as Commander, Carrier Air Group 15 deployed aboard the USS *Essex*. During his first sortie that day, McCampbell shot down five Japanese dive-bombers, and on the second sortie, he got two more Zero fighters over Guam Island.

Four months later, during the Battle of the Sibuyan Sea and part of the much larger Battle of Leyte Gulf, McCampbell would shoot down nine enemy aircraft in a single day. For both engagements, President Roosevelt would award McCampbell with the Medal of Honor in February 1945.

—

Monday, 19.June.1944
OSS London Station
Nos. 70-72 Grosvenor Street
Mayfair, London, England
United Kingdom
10:25 hours

The communications room supervisor personally brought up the latest classified message from the director. The captain handed the red-striped single page to the station chief.

TOP SECRET

```
OS
LONSTA OSS NR 512
TS 190907Z JUN 44 URGENT
FM 109
TO 105
T O P   S E C R E T
URGENT
BT
SINCE ENEMY USE OF EITHER ROBOT PLANES OR
ROCKETS APPEARS TO BE IRRECONCILABLE WITH GOOD
```

```
TIMING OR GOOD MILITARY JUDGMENT I AM LOOKING
FOR SOME RATIONALIZATION STOP DO THE GERMANS
BELIEVE THIS ATTACK OF SUFFICIENT VEHEMENCE TO
BE UNTENABLE TO BRITISH AMERICAN WAR EFFORT BY
THE MAINTENANCE OF SUSPENSE AND TERROR STOP
HAVE YOU LEARNED THAT ANY SPECIAL EXPLOSIVE
IS USED FOR THE FIRST TIME IN THESE WEAPONS
STOP IF NO ABNORMAL EXPLOSIVE IS INDICATED
WATCH KEENLY FOR EVIDENCE OF THE DISSEMINATION
OF ANY SORT OF CONTAGION NEAR TO PLACES HIT
STOP DOES WRECKAGE OF DEVICES INDICATE USE OF
GYRO STOP DO ROBOTS COME OVER AT DEFINITE TIME
INTERVALS AND HOW MANY IN 24 HOURS STOP ARE WE
USING RADAR DEFENSIVELY STOP GIVE APPRAISAL OF
AFFAIR STOP URGENT END
BT
NNNN
```

TOP SECRET

———————————

Chief London Station Bruce looked directly at the captain. "The requested reply will take a few days to compile. Acknowledge receipt. No response at this time. I'll retain and secure this copy."

"Thank you, Sir." The captain left and closed the door behind him.

Bruce read the message one more time, and then he pushed the INT button on his control panel. "I need the department heads now."

"Yes Sir," came his male secretary's reply.

While he waited, David re-read the message two more times and jotted down a few notes on a yellow-lined writing pad. Bruce was still working on his notes when the men assigned to each position arrived. Bruce pointed to the conference table. When all six men, the five department heads plus the station deputy, were seated, David grabbed the message and his pad, and joined them at the table.

"First, I just received this message from Director Donovan. Please read it carefully, and then we'll discuss the tasking." Bruce passed the message to his deputy on his right. He waited for each man to read it. When the message returned to him, he said, "We have a few days at most to prepare our response."

"We can answer most of these questions definitively now," answered his military department officer. "The mechanics of the V1 are well understood. However, there are a few details on the algorithms used in the autopilot that we can't know until we have a captured intact unit we can disassemble and thoroughly examine."

"Like what?"

"We have no evidence of special explosives. We cannot say either the British nor us have examined every V1 impact crater, but the Home Office report on the Grove Road impact, the first to hit England on the 13th, was spot-on correct and quite comprehensive. We confirmed the details ourselves. We detected no known chemical or biological agent, or any contaminant other than the explosive material itself. The warhead of the V1 is 850 kilograms of Amatol, a conventional explosive material that has been used in all forms of ordnance for decades."

"So, these things are just explosives, not carriers with spreaders of more dangerous substances?"

"Correct… none yet, and I think we can assure the director and Washington that we, and here I mean the British and American specialists are watching very carefully to see if Hitler's desperation resorts to more dangerous substances."

"OK," responded Bruce. "We're watching. Now, what of the other questions?"

"Within the purview of my department, yes, absolutely and confirmed by several independent means, the system uses a gyroscope, a rather sophisticated gyro. We've collected remnants from craters, but our primary source comes from photographs, sketches, and descriptions of reliable sources inside the special weapons facilities in Germany. Some of those sources are our direct agents. The guidance system is simple and yet impressive in its simplicity. The missiles are launched by catapult in a fixed general direction. A spinner on the nose enables a sequence of events with the guidance system based on gateway revolutions. The first gate enables the guidance system. Shortly after the PAC leaves the rail . . ."

"PAC?"

"Pilotless aircraft. Shortly after the PAC launches and the airflow has turned the spinner the prescribed number of revolutions, the PAC turns to a preset compass heading that it maintains until impact. No further guidance is possible, and the flight parameters cannot be changed in flight. The PAC flies to its preset altitude and heading, and its de facto speed is determined by the performance of the pulsejet on that particular PAC. The speed is fairly consistent but does vary. The second gate is roughly the Channel coast when again the spinner revolution count arms the warhead. The third and final gate is another preset spinner revolution count that cuts fuel flow, inducing a terminal dive to presumably impact and detonate in the designated target area.

Tables of settings for the field launch crews were developed at Peenemünde as the design solidified."

"Well," Bruce interjected, "that little treatise generated a whole bunch more questions, but that will suffice for the moment. What of the other questions?"

"The 'sufficient vehemence' query is a political question beyond my sphere. Regarding the time intervals, the Home Office created and maintains a file register of known data for each impact they receive a report. The local constabularies have been provided a checklist form to collect and report on impacts in their respective jurisdictions. One of my guys went through the file Saturday morning with the Home Office analyst assigned to study the file. We only have a week's worth of data, but so far, they come and can come at any hour of the day or night. There are no detectible trends or patterns. We are looking for those trends and patterns, but none yet. The last question regarding radar, yes, the PACs are detectable by radar. They're spotted when they climb into the line-of-sight dome of any particular radar unit. By the point of detection, the direction can be quickly determined since it is fixed. What we cannot determine is the range setting. I should add here that Prime Minister Churchill was apparently quite upset by the perceived incessant air raid warning sirens a couple of days ago and directed the Home Office to refine their warning criteria and look for ways to reduce the near-constant nuisance warnings. That is a whole other topic for discussion.

"Back to the salient question from Washington, yes, the British ground air defense system has demonstrated good results with S-C-R 584 radar directed Q-F 3.7 inch anti-aircraft guns. They refine their network, move gun batteries for better coverage, and use fighters to fill in the gaps. We should all recognize the extraordinary bravery and ingenuity of the R-A-F pilots. They lost one aircraft when the warhead exploded. The pilot was seriously wounded, bailed out, and was further injured when he landed hard due to shrapnel damage to his parachute. Another bold pilot used his wing under the PAC's wing to roll the device and upset the guidance. A little disturbance won't work since the PAC sees the bump, like turbulence, and easily recovers. However, if the pilot can significantly roll the PAC, it cannot recover and impacts prematurely—quite remarkable airmanship, I must say. The maneuver does damage the fighter's wing, but it is repairable, I'm told."

"OK," Bruce said. "We have a couple of days to prepare a response to the director's message. We do not have much time. We need a summary message and a more comprehensive report that provides all of the details we have collected. We should include the Home Office Grove Road report as an attachment and any other relevant reports in our submittal. We will send a special courier to ensure timely delivery. I will also add here that we do not," he said with emphasis on the last word, "enjoy indifference to the political questions. The director needs answers, and we will give him the best our judgment can produce. Further, we know the question of the V2 is not far behind. So, I would like to include at least a summary of our V2 appraisal in our response to the last question. Any questions?" He paused as if to allow for questions, and then he added, "I guess that was a silly question. We all have many more questions than answers." They all laughed at the chief's point. We've got work to do. I want the summary message and report by the end of the week. This is an ongoing attack, so we need to establish an 'as of' cutoff for the data we provide. We've got a lot to do. Let's hop to it. We're burnin' daylight."

———

Monday, 19.June.1944
Cabinet War Rooms
New Public Offices
Whitehall, London, England
United Kingdom
16:30 hours

In November 1939, just before a heavy snowstorm began, the British naval attaché to Norway discovered an envelope containing a seven-page report that soon became known as the 'Oslo Report." The officer forwarded the document to MI6. Most of the British intelligence community assessed the file as an elaborate hoax intended to mislead and distract British war preparations. However, one young scientist with the Research Office within the Air Ministry Intelligence Branch saw enough in the report to take it as a credible attempt to alert the British. The War Cabinet was not convinced. However, one man listened intently to Dr. Reginald Victor 'RV' Jones, PhD (physics), to support his work investigating the subjects illuminated. The man who felt more in RV's analysis was none other than Prime Minister Churchill.

Jones gradually obtained sufficient facts to validate the contents of the Oslo Report one by one. The key for one particular item described a rocket-propelled projectile came from a reconnaissance photograph taken over the German research center at Peenemünde in Northeast Germany. The shape the photo analyst saw was a shadow shaped like a bullet with fins. As they developed the data collection, they learned of the secret German development effort known as *Aggregat* (or Aggregate in English) missile program. One particular item of the initiative transitioned from an intended military weapon to a political weapon of terror. In that transition the fourth member of the rocket family—the A4—became *Vergeltungswaffe* 2, or Retaliation Weapon 2, V2 for short. The system used pressurized ethyl alcohol fuel and liquid oxygen oxidizer as the propellant. Guide vanes immersed in the engine exhaust adjusted the thrust vector for guidance while the engine was thrusting. When the motor was shut down, movable surfaces on each of the four fins controlled the missile's direction. A large, hardened gyroscope and analog computer provided guidance commands to the guide vanes. While the trajectory of the V2 was quite different from the V1, the flight guidance was similar—a pre-calculated azimuth from the launch site to the target and a fuel cutoff at a precise time to achieve the necessary range.

As the evidence accumulated in the spring of 1943, the War Cabinet established the CROSSBOW Committee chaired by Edwin Duncan 'Duncan' Sandys, financial secretary to the War Office, MP for Norwood, and the prime minister's son-in-law. Duncan married the Churchills' oldest child and daughter Diana in 1935. The CROSSBOW Committee led by Sandys included prominent scientists Edward Appleton, John Cockcroft, and Robert Watson-Watt.

The War Cabinet meeting was closed and compartment classified. The chairman of the committee would be the principal presenter. Also in attendance were the prime minister's scientific advisor Lord Cherwell, Dr. Frederick Alexander Lindemann, PhD (physics), PC, FRS, Baron Cherwell of Oxford, and Dr. Jones.

"The subject of this closed meeting is the German retaliation weapons," Churchill began. "As I believe everyone knows, the Nawzees began their bombardment of primarily London with their V1 pilotless flying bomb six days ago. We are still adapting to the challenges presented by these diabolical weapons. Duncan's CROSSBOW Committee has briefed us on the number two weapon in their arsenal. Let us start with a summary of what we know about the V2. Duncan, you have the floor."

"Thank you, Prime Minister," Sandys said as he stood in front of a blackboard opposite his father-in-law. "While the current storm outside does not help the combat operations, it has brought a respite in the V1 attacks. Moreover, the storm illuminates one of the vulnerabilities of the V1, namely it flies at comparatively low speed and altitude, and has turbulence limits. We are still evolving our defensive strategy against the V1, but we have marked successes despite the number of these devices coming at us."

"And failures," interjected Attlee, "like the Life Guards Chapel yesterday during Sunday services."

"With 60 plus killed," Morrison added.

"As of this morning, 700 flying bombs have been fired at Britain so far, with 200 shot down, 112 by anti-aircraft guns and 88 by fighters. Our success rate is improving by the day, but they still can get through--yesterday's tragedy being one of those exceptions."

"This meeting is about the V2," Churchill reminded everyone.

"The V2 and the V1 differences are substantial," Sandys resumed. "The V2 is propelled by a powerful rocket engine that burns ethyl alcohol and liquid oxygen. It has a 1,000-kilogram, high explosive warhead instead of an 850-kilogram warhead. The V2 flies at supersonic speeds on a predominately ballistic arc. The range is roughly 200 miles compared to the 150-mile range of the V1. The guidance principle used in the V2 is analogous to the V1—a preset heading based on the launch location and the intended target and a preset motor burn to achieve the ballistic arc desired. The other major difference is that the V2 flies above the weather because of the ballistic arc. Newer versions of the V2 are believed to employ radio transmission to provide more refined guidance and presumably achieve better accuracy. Later models will have an undoubtedly greater range—300 miles or more."

"OK, Duncan," Morrison interjected, "we understand the V2 is even worse than the V1. So, when can we anticipate these monsters coming our way?"

"Well, Minister, we do not have hard evidence of deployment. However, to answer your query, I should add at this stage that the American 9th Infantry Division is estimated to be within days of taking Cherbourg. In their advance on the French port, they have captured three V1 launch ramps and what appears to be a V2 launch site. They also captured both V1 and V2 devices intact. A joint M-I-6 and O-S-S London Station exploitation team is initially evaluating the devices before they are boxed up and moved to Farnborough for detailed examination. The CROSSBOW Committee will be directly involved in the deep evaluation."

"Countermeasures?" Attlee asked.

"Therein lies the rub, Sir. The short answer is none. The speeds the missile reaches, and the high ballistic flight profile make interception impossible."

"Impossible?" Churchill challenged.

"Yes Sir. The missile terminal velocity is supersonic—several times the speed of sound. Our evidence indicates the missile reaches an apogee of roughly 100 miles well into the thermosphere with terminal descent near vertical."

"How many of these V2s do they have?" asked Attlee.

"Our best estimate is roughly 2,000."

"Dear God above," gasped Morrison.

"Yes, our current assessment is rather stark."

"Indeed!" Attlee protested.

"We're searching the electromagnetic spectrum for the guidance frequency and transmissions. We're still looking for vulnerabilities, but the only potential is the radio guidance signal."

"What else do you need?' Churchill asked. "We cannot just sit here and take the pounding that the despicable corporal chooses to mete out to us. Not on my watch. Thus, back to my query. What else do you need to stop the scourge of these terror weapons?"

"Take the production, assembly, and launch sites as quickly as possible," muttered RV Jones.

"Easier said than done, Dr. Jones," Churchill replied in retort.

"My point, Prime Minister, is as Minister Sandys articulated, there are no known countermeasures that we have been able to ascertain or develop, at least not yet."

"We continue our urgent search," Sandys said.

"What say you, professor?" asked the prime minister.

Lindemann smiled. "I have nothing to add other than I can attest the committee is exploring every possibility up to an including wild ideas. Everyone working on this problem fully appreciates the importance. They know the implications of what they are trying to prevent. We have to hope we advance swiftly enough or find some weakness."

"I must say that is a rather bleak picture you have painted. Does anyone have anything else to add? Do any members of the War Cabinet have any further questions?" No one spoke for a score of seconds.

"I think we've heard more than enough, Winston," declared Attlee. "We realized the Miracle of Dunkirk. We turned back the enemy invasion we saw as inevitable. We survived The Blitz. We defeated the U-Boat menace. We'll beat this threat. I have faith. We must all have faith."

"Well said, Clement. Thank you. I do believe we are adjourned."

———

Wednesday, 21.June.1944
USAAF Station F-356
Saffron Walden, Essex, England
United Kingdom
05:45 hours

The special mission briefing was intriguing not so much for the content as the landing base. Operation FRANTIC served as a demonstration of Allied solidarity as well as Operation POINTBLANK target bombing, although Prime Minister Churchill believed the operation was little more than a stunt advocated for by President Roosevelt. The operation involved shuttle bombing missions carried out by the 8th Air Force in England, the 15th Air Force in Italy, and three airbases in Ukraine.

This day, the 4FG would escort B-17 heavy bombers of the 385th Bombardment Group on the 8th Air Force Mission 134 with an assigned target of a synthetic oil plant and storage depot at Ruhland, Brandenburg, Germany, north of Dresden. What made the mission unique was their planned landing site. The mission would conclude at bases behind the Eastern Front lines in Red Army occupied Ukraine. The bombers would land at Poltava while the fighters would land at Pyriatyn Airbase. They would remain a couple of weeks in a quasi-exchange mission with the Red Air Force. Another unique aspect of the day's mission included a small travel bag each pilot carried behind his cockpit seat.

"We hear y'all will take a little vacation with our Russian friends," Larson said as we walked around the QP-G Mustang fighter with Major Drummond.

Brian chuckled softly. "I wouldn't exactly say that, but we'll not be coming back to Debden for a few days." They finished the walkaround inspection in the dim light of morning obscured by low broken clouds. Tomlinson followed Brian onto the left wing root. Brian placed his small travel bag behind his seat and settled into his seat, strapping into his parachute and seat harness as Larson made radio and oxygen connections. "Thanks, Larson. I'll take good care of your girl. See you in a few days."

"We'll be here waitin' on ya, Major."

"Thanks, Larson." Brian quickly stepped through his pre-start actions while Sergeant Tomlinson jumped down off the wing and positioned the fire extinguisher for the start procedures. Again, the start was flawless without anomaly.

Arnie Clark led the group onto the runway, followed by 334FS and the other squadrons in order. The group takeoff progressed smoothly. They joined the bomber formation and took up their escort positions to protect the bombers. Brian kept up with the navigation on his map, although the lead bomber navigator held the responsibility for the entire combined formation. Their route avoided known anti-aircraft gun concentrations. The fighters watched and waited. The Germans had learned the procedural practices and how to shepherd the diminishing resources to the greatest effect. The German fighter pilots were imaginative and adaptive.

Occasional flak bursts hit the bomber formation without noticeable effect. It was not until they turned for their approach to the target that the enemy fighters appeared. The enemy usually went for the bombers, which gave the escort the advantage. This time, it was all fighters. *They're trying to strip our escort.* Flak shells burst among the bombers. The fighters remained too busy in their furballs to observe the bombing of the target, plus they were too high to see any detail. Then, clearly on signal, the Germans disengaged. Because of the nature of this particular mission, they did not pursue the retreating Germans.

By Brian's map, when they passed the Polish border, Horseback radioed, "Upper, Upper Six, looks like we have a shadow." A single Bf109 fighter stood off about two miles at their nine o'clock position, maintaining a parallel track. *He's reporting our position. They know we're doing something significantly different from our normal operations.* "Cobweb Red, take our tail."

"Wilco," Brian responded and then gave a head nod for his Red Section to roll left. He smoothly pushed his throttle to full power and spread the section for combat on a good intercept heading.

As they closed half the distance, the German dived for the cumulus clouds below them. They played hide and seek with the German for a quarter of an hour. The German was clearly not interested in a fight. He had a specific mission assignment he was not going to deviate from. After two cycles and the appearance of a He177A-7 reconnaissance aircraft flying substantially higher, the German fighter returned to base. Brian's Red Section made a couple of intercept attempts. Brian even tried a couple of very long-range shots without success like he had done with the high-altitude reconnaissance aircraft all those years ago. The German simply opened the distance as if trying to draw the fighter away for an ambush.

"Cobweb Red, Upper Six, enough. Return to your position."

"Wilco."

Their tail remained with them even as they descended for landing. The bombers headed for Poltava while the fighters would land at Pyriatyn. The Germans knew where they were. The landings were smooth and uneventful. The Soviets were waiting for them. They also saw American ground crewmen. They learned that Army Air Forces had established an Eastern Command to provide command and support for Operation FRANTIC.

Brian stretched and exercised his joints to vanquish the kinks induced by seven hours in the confines of the Mustang's cockpit. The wafts of burnt wood and cordite were unmistakable, even though the fighting on the Eastern Front was by now well to the west. They would be here for a few days, but they had no taskings at the moment. Their aircraft were refueled and rearmed.

———

Friday, 23.June.1944
No.10 Annexe
New Public Offices
Whitehall, London, England
United Kingdom
11:00 hours

So much had happened since their last meeting. Churchill was eager, perhaps even anxious, to gain General Eisenhower's perspective and plans. After the cordiality of friends, they sat for their private meeting.

"I have always admired the old adage never to ask a question I don't want to hear the answer to. So how bad was the damage?"

Eisenhower cleared his throat. "I'm going across tomorrow morning to meet with Montgomery and Bradley and see the damage for myself. According to the Met Office, the storm disrupted operations on the 18th as winds and sea state exceeded unloading criteria. By the 20th, the storm reached its peak and was wreaking havoc on the Mulberry harbors. The Met Office claimed it was the worst low-pressure system in the area in 50 years. The report I received this morning indicated Mulberry 'A' at Omaha Beach is completely destroyed. Mulberry 'B' at Sword Beach is seriously damaged. The engineers are still examining both structures. We will salvage what items we can from 'A' to repair 'B' as quickly as possible. Some units are down to three days of ammunition. We are preparing parachute drops and glider flights to resupply the most vulnerable units. The storm also slowed the capture of Cherbourg. Based on aerial photography, the engineers have laid out their plans to repair the port facilities as swiftly as possible. As of this moment, 'A' is gone, and 'B' may take a week or more to achieve even minimal operations."

"Well, Mother Nature was not on our side this week."

"No, she was not."

"With the street fighting in Caen and now this storm, we are much closer to a stalemate."

"The hedgerows are proving far more problematic than anticipated in the Normandy boçage country. The Germans are using the terrain and vegetation quite well."

"We've got to break out, Ike. We're dreadfully behind our plan, and every day we stay here, the more vulnerable to the mounting enemy counterattack we become. So, what are you going to do?"

"We are finalizing plans for Operation COBRA, which includes the deployment of Patton's 3rd Army to the right flank as quickly as possible and a massive aerial bombardment of key junctions and enemy concentrations."

"The sooner, the better, Ike. The longer it takes us to get out of the hedgerows, the closer we are to failure. We're already facing major German armored units, but Hitler still has not released the bulk of *Panzer* Group West. His restraint and paranoia won't last much longer. We've not yet seen or detected even a hint that the corporal's opinion is wavering."

"Agreed, Prime Minister. We all know we are racing against time. I can assure you, the ground commanders from General Montgomery on down are all keenly aware and sensitive to that race. I can also assure you that we are looking for every possible mechanism to break out of the beachhead into far more mobile warfare. We are close to securing the Cotentin Peninsula, which will enable us to redirect the combat forces to the breakout. Monty faces most of the German armor on the left flank, which is not good for the 2nd Army, but it opens the potential on the right flank. The ground commanders and I all agree; we'd rather break out of the beachhead without COBRA, but we're preparing for its execution."

"Thank you, Ike. I'm with you, but I'm getting nervous," Churchill said.

"We shall continue to strive to assuage your anxiety."

"Thank you."

The remainder of their meeting conversation turned to more personal family and social topics until they both had agenda items drawing them away. Finally, they parted with words of encouragement to each other.

———

Saturday, 24.June.1944
Pyriatyn Aeroport (designated USAAF Station 560)
Pyriatyn, Poltava Oblast, Ukraine
Soyuz Sovetskikh Sotsialisticheskikh Respublik (USSR)
10:15 hours

The 334FS remained at the field tent that served as their squadron operations center. For the third day, they had no taskings. Arnie had informed them yesterday that Eastern Command sought missions on the Eastern Front to assist the Red Army. According to Arnie, the initial declinations were cordial and polite, but recently, they had become more rigid and strident, as if, in Arnie's opinion, they were insulting the Soviet Air Force by even asking. But, the main topic among the American pilots this morning was a series of explosions last night that were closer than anyone felt comfortable with.

It was not until their assigned liaison officer appeared in the tent that they had a source for answers. Soviet Air Force Captain Sergei Petrovich Koronov had given them a thorough briefing and inspection of their Yak-9 fighters, which appeared similar to the P-51D Mustang. Koronov was rightly proud of their aircraft and their success against the *Luftwaffe*. He also spoke passable English, which made his liaison task easier.

"What were those explosions last night?" asked Salt.

"We thought we were well behind the front lines," Dusty commented.

Sergei answered, "Morning, gentlemans. So many questions. First, we are now more than 450 kilometers behind the current front lines, which is near the Polish border in our sector. Second, we do get visited from time to time. Third, I do believe your presence in Ukraine has attracted the enemy's attention. They tried to bomb us, bomb you, last night."

"They missed," Salt interjected, inducing laughter.

"Yes, they did with thanks to the Night Witches," Sergei explained.

"I've heard that term," Brian added. "What are the Night Witches?"

"In the case of last night's action, they are woman pilots of the 5-8-6 Air Regiment. They fly old Yakovlev number one fighters and specialize in night intercept missions."

"Female pilots in combat?" Sweet questioned.

"Yes, and they are very good at what they do . . . fearless, I think. They jumped the German bombers on their way here last night. The Germans dropped their bombs in fields and ran."

"How many squadrons in an air regiment?" Buddy asked.

"Four . . . with fifteen aircraft to each."

"Do they only fly at night?" Dusty asked.

"No, they fly in day as well, but they specialize in night attack."

"If you let women fly in combat, why won't you let us fly? We just want to help," pressed Dusty.

Koronov smiled and shifted his weight from foot to foot. He was clearly uncomfortable. "Not my choice. Way above me. I not speak to this matter."

"Can we fly your Yak Nine?"

Sergei shook his head. "I not know. I must ask my chief."

"We must ask our chiefs before any exchange," interjected Brian. "Nothing wrong with asking, but I must remind my mates that these are not our aircraft. They belong to the Air Force, and the Air Force has a direct, sole say in what is done with these machines."

Koronov laughed with a sense of relief. He was fascinated with the bombing raids on Berlin. Sergei asked incessant questions about the bombers, the escort procedures, and combat with the Germans over Berlin. He seemed genuinely disappointed that the fighter pilots did not find the occasion to observe the bombs exploding in the enemy capital.

The Americans were not allowed out of the small compound without their liaison escort. The frustration of their quasi-confinement made their visit to Ukraine less than they had hoped, but these were the times in which they lived.

———

Chapter 8

Great historical movements are never begun
for attainment of remote and imperfectly comprehended ends.
They demand something concrete to work for;
they need clearly defined, particular aims.

-- Auguste Marie Joseph Jean Léon Jaurès

Wednesday, 5.July.1944
USAAF Station F-356
Saffron Walden, Essex, England
United Kingdom
16:05 hours

The 4ᵗʰ Fighter Group had been in Ukraine for two weeks and had accomplished very little. The potential had been far greater than the realized achievement. They had done virtually nothing other than eat, sleep, and complain. Captain Koronov had proved to be a good and supportive friend who tried mightily to engage his American compatriots, but he had been removed from flight status to perform the liaison function with the 334FS. Koronov had felt the same frustration watching his comrades takeoff on several missions while the American pilots were present. The pilots shared many common views of the work they all did.

The 334FS had taken to the air this morning and had flown high over the Eastern Front unopposed, they had seen the dust and smoke in a broad line from the Baltic to the Carpathian Mountains. The sight illustrated the violence on the ground below them.

The dockyards at Kiel, Germany, had served as the return flight target for the bombers. The bombers encountered far less flak than they had at Ruhland on the outbound mission. The German fighters the 4FG had faced again focused on the fighter escort rather than trying to penetrate the escort cover to reach the bombers. As a result, neither the bombers nor the fighters suffered any losses of aircraft or personnel.

Brian had managed to catch a few glimpses of the bomb impacts that had appeared to be spot on the target. The smoke from the explosions and fires had soon obscured all of Kiel harbor and half of the city. Once they were clear of Germany and over the North Sea, Brian had jotted down on his thigh map, *'fighters, not bombers, something changed.'*

With the green of England in sight and still over the North Sea, the bombers had turned to the right, heading for their base. The fighter escort task was complete, and they had turned slightly left for Debden. Even with the broken cloud cover over the southeastern counties, England felt like home, and it felt great to see the sight of home. Horseback had called for the group's approach with all 49 4FG fighters landing by section in sequence.

"Welcome back, Major," Tomlinson said from the left wing root, as Brian shutdown the big Packard engine.

Brian raised his flight goggles and unfastened the left side of his oxygen mask. "Thanks, Larson. Great to be home and great to see you."

As Brian unstrapped and disconnected from his fighter, Tomlinson asked, "Did you have fun on your holiday?"

Brian laughed. "No holiday, and it was not what we expected."

"Now that it's all over, how far did you go?"

"We landed at a Soviet airbase at Pyriatyn, Ukraine, which is in Central Ukraine, on the east side of the Dnieper River."

"My God, that's a long way," Larson exclaimed.

"Yeah, seven hours worth each way."

"Better you than me, Major. I don't think I could do it."

As Brian stood to climb out of the cockpit, Larson jumped down off the wing. Buddy Courtland waited behind the wing.

"That was quite the adventure," Buddy announced.

"Yeah, it was. Great job, by the way, Buddy. I'm sure not how useful the shuttle missions are, given the Soviets' restrictions on us. But, it was a great idea. We did our best, but the Russians were reluctant partners, or at least the generals and commissars were."

The two pilots ambled toward the operations building. Blue Flight, 2ⁿᵈ Section Leader First Lieutenant James Edward 'Jimmy' Stonestreet, an Eagle Squadron alumnus, shouted to Hunter. "Red's up for debriefing."

"Thanks, Jimmy." Brian changed direction toward the intelligence building. He looked over his shoulder to see Salt and Horn following them.

Staff Sergeant Norman Bradford greeted Brian with a smile. "Welcome back, Major."

"Thank you, Sergeant Bradford. Great to see you again. You're still here."

"Yes Sir. Another few months at my request."

The two men stepped through the standard mission debriefing worksheet. Finally, they came to the last item on the checklist, the Additional Comments section.

"I have a few comments I'd like to add to my debriefing."

With his pencil poised over the open box on the form, Bradford said, "Shoot."

"First, from my perspective, I see very little if any benefit to these shuttle bombing missions. We spent two weeks at Pyriatyn Airbase, and all we did was sit on our hands. We were essentially confined to our camp. The Soviets would not allow us to fly, not even in combat support of their operations on the Eastern Front. I've no idea why, but it was an extraordinary waste of time and combat capacity.

"Second, our Russian liaison officer, Captain Koronov, deserves commendation for his exceptional work trying to keep us happy. He is a Yak-9 fighter pilot who spoke passable English and was just as frustrated as we were in not flying. Yet, he worked hard to paint a bright face to the situation.

"Third, on the night of the 23rd, the Germans attempted to bomb Pyriatyn. Although the bombs landed close enough to wake us all up, they failed. According to Koronov, units of the 586th Air Regiment intercepted them, causing the Germans to drop their payloads and run."

"The Night Witches."

"So, you know them."

"Yes, we've heard stories, an all-female fighter group, a heavy group. They have 60 aircraft for a full regiment compared to our 48 for a full group. According to our information, they have two other female regiments, a night bomber unit and a night dive bomber unit. The Germans coined the term, and the descriptor took root."

"Fourth and last comment, I wanted to note a difference in the German fighter tactics that seem to have changed. On both the outbound and inbound bombing runs, the German fighters engaged with us rather than trying to penetrate our cover to get among the bombers. Two missions in a row got my attention."

"I've noted each of your points. Anything else?'

"That should do it, Sergeant Bradford." Brian walked back to the operations building. The other Red Section pilots were already there. He did not have time to sit.

"Skipper wants to see you, Major," operations clerk Juli Ellison said as Brian passed his desk.

Brian pivoted and knocked on the commander's office door.

"Enter," commanded Clark. Brian stepped inside. Arnie gestured for him to close the door and then motioned toward one of the chairs across from his desk. He did not waste time with small talk. "As soon as Yellow is finished with their debriefing, I've got some announcements. First, I am tasked to inform you that your rotation waiver will be honored but will most likely affect your Army career. The War Office wants to minimize your continued exposure and capitalize on your substantial experience. You need to take some staff duty and probably some training assignment to pass on your knowledge. However, they acknowledge that the war is approaching its conclusion. With that, what say you?"

"Skipper, I left home in Kansas against my parents' wishes when I turned 18 in 1939 before the war started. I joined the R-A-F against the threat by the government of felony prosecution for my violation of the Neutrality Act. All I ever wanted to do was fly. I'm soldier enough to fly, but I'm not a soldier. I don't know what the end of the war will bring, but I will deal with what comes. If the Army does not want me, I will find another throttle and stick to wiggle somewhere else. I'm grateful for the War Office's respect for my waiver. If you're asking for my preference, I'll stay with my waiver."

"Against my better judgment, we'll accept your request. Sweet has also requested a waiver, and since he is an ex-patriot born and raised in London, his waiver has been granted as well. The other requests, and there are six others, have been denied. I'll recognize promotions that Group received while we were in Ukraine. More importantly, transfer orders for five of our pilots have arrived. We'll be losing many of our section leaders, which means we will need to quickly train replacements and reorganize."

"Who are we losing?"

"Jimmy, Dusty, Frog, Buddy, and Salt."

"Damn, that's a lot to absorb."

"Indeed, we're not going to be taken offline, but we'll have a period of light-duty, so to speak, while we make these changes and get the newbies spun up. It won't be the end of it either. The other Eagles remaining will be transferred in the next few weeks, but they will leave us at least by the end of the month."

"Lot's of change."

"An understatement. I'll make the announcements when we're done. You'll be given a three-day liberty pass tomorrow morning after muster. So go home, enjoy Charlotte and Ian, and come back refreshed. We're going to be busy."

"Yes Sir. Wilco."

Arnie stood and gestured for him to leave. Brian went to his empty chair in the back corner but did not lean back. "OK, gentlemen. I needed to hold everyone to make a few announcements."

First, Arnie promoted Jimmy, Frog, Salt, and Sweet to Captain, and Buddy and Rolo to First Lieutenant. Second, he announced the transfers of Jimmy, Dusty, Frog, Buddy, and Salt. It was going to be a big night of celebration and send-offs. Dusty, Frog, and Salt had been ordered back to the United States to training positions; they would be on their way before Brian returned from his three-day pass. Tonight would also be good-byes to his No.71 Squadron comrades, and Brian and Dusty went back to the great air battle. Arnie also outlined the transition training of the replacement pilots that would start arriving tomorrow. Surprisingly to Brian, there was minimal grumbling about the significant changes to the squadron. Arnie congratulated the promotees and the squadron for a job well done. He wished those leaving a safe journey and good fortune.

Before joining his mates in the O'Club bar, Brian tried the telephone again without success. At least he would soon see Charlotte, Ian, and Standing Oak Farm. Brian joined the squadron pilots and most group pilots in the bar for a beer before dinner in the mess. The other two group squadrons had similar changes. A raucous night of celebration began.

———

Thursday, 6. July. 1944
Standing Oak Farm
Winchester, Hampshire, England
United Kingdom
11:15 hours

Morty Jurdy drove Brian from the rail station and went through his passenger's unique routine. As Brian stepped out of Morty's cab, Brian watched Charlotte and Ian appear on the main house's front porch. Both of them waved. Brian waved back and truncated his usual admiration of the farm upon arrival. Morty deposited Brian in front of his wife and son.

Brian wrapped his arms around Ian, who wrapped his little arms around his father's neck. Mother joined husband and son.

"I've missed you so much, Major Brian Arthur Drummond," Charlotte whispered into her husband's ear.

"As I have missed you. So much has happened since I last saw you, talked to you, or even heard from you. It's so good to be home."

Brian kept kissing Ian's forehead as Charlotte held them both tightly. "I missed you so much," Charlotte repeated.

They eventually untangled and went inside. Brian was surprised to see Mary and learned that she had been at the farm for a month with her children, son Malcolm, and infant Charlotte.

After the evening milking and dinner, the crew drove the day's dairy products to the distributor in Winchester. Charlotte and Brian excused themselves. Mary understood the need for husband and wife to have a private discussion. They had so much to catch up on. As they went outside into the warm summer air before sunset, Mary returned to the book she was reading, Mary Wollstonecraft's *magnum opus, A Vindication of the Rights of Women*—the source of more than a few discussions among the farm's women.

Charlotte and Brian walked hand-in-hand to their bench under the massive oak tree. There was no need for a fire, and they even considered shucking their clothes for a refreshing dip in the pond. They laughed, and the thought passed.

"You start," Charlotte commanded.

"We just returned from Ukraine."

"Ukraine?" Charlotte said with incredulity.

Brian summarized the squadron's experience of the last two weeks. He then explained the changes the squadron faced in the next days and weeks. First, Brian confirmed that the OVERLORD invasion had begun in early June, and they had flown multiple missions in direct support of the ground forces in France.

Charlotte told Brian about the events on the farm and how proud she was of everyone's performance in making the farm's expansion possible. They both were pleased with the results and the prospects for the future, which brought Charlotte to the root of her purpose.

"A question we should have discussed years ago came up recently when Mabel and I discussed the future of greenhouse vegetable production." Charlotte paused. Brian looked at Charlotte and gestured with his eyes—and? "I assured her that we would find local markets for our produce and try to expand our operations. However, she needed assurance that she would have a job when the war was over. Mary thinks John will stay in the R-A-F, which brings me to my query. What do you want to do after the war?"

"First and foremost, I want to be with you . . . whatever that brings."

"Staying in the Army?"

"Arnie told me my waiver would be honored, so they're not going to ship me back to the States. He also told me it would likely limit my advancement. I confessed to him that I wasn't a soldier. I was a pilot."

"Does that mean you want to stay in the Army?"

"If they let me fly."

"But, the American Army Air Forces will not stay in England forever."

"No, probably not. You and the kids would have to transfer with me wherever the Air Force sends us."

"What about the farm?"

"From what you've told me, Mabel is doing a magnificent job with the greenhouse production. I suspect she would do a great job managing the whole farm. You've got an accountant to handle the financial side. It would be no different from Braddock and Atherton managing our Kansas properties."

"You can't fly forever, Brian."

"True. My mind knows that, but my heart wants to fly as long as I'm physically and mentally able."

"What if it's not the Army?"

"Well, to be honest, I've not thought that far. I suppose I could ask the R-A-F, and of course, we have our own airline."

"Where would we be based?"

"If it's up to the Army or the R-A-F, they will decide. My waiver is only for the mission limit rotation, which means it only lasts until the war's end. If it's our airline, I suppose we could be based anywhere. I've not had any conversation with Bobby beyond the potential O-S-S/S-O-E contract. By the way, have you heard anything back from Bobby on the air support proposal?"

"No. Should I send him a telegram?"

"Well," Brian paused to think, "no, he still has time. If we haven't seen a draft by the end of July, then we should ping him. We should get something soon. I don't know if Donovan or Selborne are expecting exclusive support or if a companion operation is possible. We have difficult decisions ahead."

"Do you still trust Bobby to make the correct decisions?"

"I have no reason not to. I'll do my best to support our combat operations, but we're in this together no matter what. So, if I'm not available for any reason, do the best you can. It will be correct for us."

"Really, Brian. I'm not a pilot. I'm a farmer."

"Business is business, my dear. Trust your gut. It will be correct. I have faith."

Charlotte shivered.

"Would you like a small fire?" asked Brian.

"Yes. It is cooling off. A little warmth would be nice. I've got one more topic to discuss before we go in to say goodnight to the children."

Brian had a nice modest fire going in a few minutes. Both of them enjoyed the soft aroma of an oak wood fire. He sat back down beside Charlotte and put his arm around her shoulders.

Charlotte turned partially to look directly into Brian's blue-grey eyes. "Rosemary came to visit as you told me she might last May." Brian's expression noticeably changed from attentive to concerned. "I guess you are becoming the farm stud quite in demand."

"And?"

"I understand why Rose wants what she wants. I talked to Mary about Rose's request. Obviously, she understands as well. How much farther is this . . . this . . . this service of yours going to go?"

"I've no idea, Charlotte. I never wanted it. Mary was very aggressive before I met you. I had no idea what her intent was at the time. After her purpose became known, I understood the second one. Rose is different. I'm far more concerned about you than any of this."

"I've no doubt, none, about your love for me, Ian, or our future children to come, just as I've no doubt about my love for you, Brian. Before I dragged your sorry arse out of the pond," Charlotte smiled and glanced at the pond in front of them, "I knew I would never love again. You changed my life, Brian.

Thus, there is no reason to be concerned about me. So, as to Rose's request, do you want to do it?"

"No, Charlotte, it is not up to me. I'm not going to decide this. It's entirely your decision to make. I appreciate Rosemary. She is a special woman and the sister of my best friend. I'll abide by your decision either way."

Charlotte changed her position, squaring out on the bench, and stared out across the water. Brian poked the fire to adjust the burning wood without adding more split logs. He did not want to interfere with Charlotte's contemplation. Several minutes passed before she turned back to face Brian. "I'm good with this, Brian. I believe Rose is sincere and earnest in her request. If we can help her, then I can accept it."

"Are you sure, sweetheart?"

"Yes. I'll only ask the same guidelines as we used in Mary's second session."

"Agreed, as you wish, my dear. Are you going to tell Rose?"

"Yes, I think it's only right."

"Are you going to say anything to Mary?"

"Yes. She has been most gracious in her counsel to me, as you should probably inform Jonathan, so he does not worry or speculate."

"Agreed.

They were well into twilight, and the temperature had cooled swiftly. Charlotte shook her head. "We really should get back inside. The children are close to bedtime."

Brian extinguished the fire. Wife and husband joined hands and strolled slowly back to the house. They were just in time to say goodnight to all the children. The adults, including Mabel, Grace, and Edith, joined Charlotte, Mary, and Brian in a semi-circle around the fireplace with a small fire more for aesthetics than warmth. They talked mainly of the children and their antics. Laughter was good for all of them.

Charlotte and Brian were the last to retire. Brian spread the fire's coals to extinguish the flame, while Charlotte switched off the few remaining lights and opened the blackout curtains for the morning sunlight to come. They made time to renew their intimacy before sleep claimed their consciousness. Brian enjoyed teasing her that they needed to stay in practice for the moment when she changed her mind about producing more children of their own.

———

Saturday, 8.July.1944
2238 Q Street NW
Washington, District of Columbia
United States of America
18:25 hours

His Secret Service driver stood outside the door while the other agent went to the front door of the Mercer residence. President Roosevelt watched the exterior events move slowly, too slowly for him. Lucy walked beside the taller, brawny agent with her flowing floral print dress fluttering in contrast to his stark dark gray suit. Her brilliant smile contrasted with his serious demeanor. Franklin was grateful for the diligence of his Secret Service detail, but he eagerly anticipated Lucy's company. The door opened. Lucy stepped in and sat beside Franklin. She leaned across and kissed him on the right cheek as the two Secret Service agents took their seats in the front of the Cadillac limousine.

"I can't tell you how great it is to see you again, Lucy."

"You didn't have to come pick me up. This is like a date, Franklin. It's been so long since we enjoyed a date. Yes, my dear Franklin, I am grateful beyond description that we have been able to reconnect."

"I wanted, no, I needed to pick you up."

The two talked of the first spring of their affair in 1914 before the Great War began. They remembered the fragrances of myriad blossoms, as the light breezes mixed those aromas.

Eleanor Roosevelt had been and remained at their Hyde Park, New York estate since the 23rd of June. She had a short trip planned to Dayton, Ohio, next week, and she would not rejoin with her husband until later in the month for his journey to a military conference in Hawaii.

The White House
18:47 hours

In a precisely choreographed routine, the duty head Secret Service agent pushed the president's wheelchair with Lucy walking beside them into the residence living room. Roosevelt went directly to mixing drinks for everyone, an activity he truly enjoyed with family and potentates. Lucy, of course, knew Anna, who introduced Lucy to her husband, Major Clarence John Boettiger, USA. John returned from Italy after the Tehran Conference. He now worked in the War Office, Department of Governmental Affairs. Also with them for the evening were Margaret Lynch 'Daisy' Suckley, a sixth cousin, intimate friend, often companion, and confidante of Franklin, and Laura Franklin 'Polly' Delano, another of Franklin's cousins and frequent traveling companions.

The small group enjoyed drinks, a good meal, and conversation mixed with laughter and joviality well into the evening hours. Not one word about the war or the elephant in the room was spoken or even hinted at by expression or gesture all night. It was a gathering of family and friends.

———

Monday, 10. July. 1944
E Street Complex
25th and E Streets, Northwest
Washington, District of Columbia
United States of America
07:05 hours

Reports, papers, requests, and the other incessant paperwork of a large organization, and especially an intelligence agency, occupied too much of Bill Donovan's waking hours. He started early and stopped late. Donovan strived to stay ahead of it, but it was an impossible objective. Ned did a magnificent job prioritizing the paper, but Bill's curiosity drove him to try to read and deal with as much more than he could.

The knock on his door preceded Buxton's entry. "We just received a VENGEANCE from Dulles in Bern. The V2s are coming."

Donovan extended his hand for the red candy-striped bordered message.

———

TOP SECRET - VENGEANCE

```
OS
BERNSTA OSS NR 127
TS 092152Z JUL 44 URGENT
FM 110
TO 109
CC 105
T O P   S E C R E T   V E N G E A N C E
URGENT
BT
MULTIPLE RELIABLE SOURCES HERE AND GERMANY
INDICATE HIGH COMMAND ORDERED EMERGENCY
DEPLOYMENT OF V2 STOP ONLY TARGET LONDON STOP
SOURCES ESTIMATE DEPLOYMENT WITHIN FOUR TO SIX
WEEKS MAX STOP URGENT END
```

BT

NNNN

TOP SECRET- VENGEANCE

"I'm tempted to question him on the details of Allen's sources and why this comes from Bern rather than London."

"You know he's got some unique sources inside the Swiss and German governments. We encouraged him to run with his sources."

"Indeed."

"This is saying London will start to get V2s in addition to the V1 onslaught they are currently dealing with. At least, the R-A-F appears to have eliminated the V3 site at Mimoyecques before it could be activated."

"Yeah, Number 6-1-7 Squadron, the Dambusters, dropped a set of Tallboy bombs on the 6th. Photo recon appears to confirm the site's destruction. An intriguing concept . . . a rail gun that accelerates the projectile. Unlike the V1 and V2, the V3 had a fixed direction. They could vary the range with the applied charge. The German special weapon developments are coming to operational deployment. In addition to the V-weapons, they are deploying rocket and jet-powered interceptors."

"Yeah, a whole list of them."

"Do we know if our friendly ace, young Brian, has encountered any? If so, does he have an opinion?" asked Donovan.

"They've encountered the Me262, the twin-jet fighter, in April. Limited encounters, although the frequency is increasing. They have not seen the Me163 rocket-powered fighter, yet. Do you want to send a message to Drummond?"

"No. Let's wait until we have more information. Anyway, let's get this to M-I-6 and scrub it for strategic distribution."

"We'll get it done. Anything for me, now, Bill?"

"Nope. Just wading through the paper for the time being."

"I'll leave you to it," Buxton responded and departed.

Friday, 14.July.1944
USAAF Station F-356
Saffron Walden, Essex, England
United Kingdom
11:45 hours

The 334FS was a different unit. All of the transferees had departed. Replacements had begun to arrive. Some of the newbies had never flown the P-51D and had little hands-on training for combat, and none of the replacements had combat experience. All of them had come from the Training Command. But, as with all things military, they all had to adapt to changing circumstances and conditions. The squadron picked up three replacements while Brian was on leave. First Lieutenant Erik Lars 'Swede' Vortiss, USAAF, of Mora, Minnesota, replaced Jimmy Stonestreet as Blue Flight's 2nd Section Leader. First Lieutenant Paul Lyle 'Pile' Logan, USAAF, of Eugene, Oregon, replaced Dusty Langford as Green Flight Leader. Second Lieutenant Jordan 'Jordy' Adler, USAAF, replaced Hick Hickerson as Arnie's wingman in Blue Flight. Other replacement pilots were reported to be en route. Today's mission would be flown with a short squadron. Brian's Red Flight was short two pilots. Horn Lee would fly as his wingman until a second section leader arrived. The new Green Flight Leader Pile Logan would fly with two wingmen until a new section leader joined the squadron.

The squadron had managed a trio of training flights to give the newbies time to learn their new airplanes, one flight of gunnery practice, and another flight as a squadron maneuvering in various formations.

The day's mission was expected to be a comparatively low-intensity escort task for a rather large unique mission known as Operation CADILLAC. The Germans had not mounted a major aerial threat in France in more than a year; the Intel guys did not expect that fact to change.

The 4FG would be one of ten fighter groups to escort nine B-17 and B-24 heavy bomber groups to seven designated sites across three areas in Central France—Vercors plateau, Limoges, and Chalon-sur-Saône. On this day and this mission, the bombers would not drop bombs and instead would deliver 3,791 containers with 417 tons of weapons, ammunition, and supplies to *Maquis* resistance fighters. It was a bit odd to be doing such drops during daylight, which suggested the areas for the two drops were considered comparatively safe. It was also the reason a squadron of fighters had been assigned to escort the bombers.

The 4FG would have one bomber group to the farthest of the seven sites—Vassieux en Vercors. The 334FS had been assigned the eastern flank of the bomber formation, going and coming. The 336FS would have the western flank, and the 335FS overhead. Brian's 'B' Division had the rear corner of the bombers, while Arnie's 'A' Division had the front corner. They joined up with the bombers before they crossed the Channel. As they approached the French coast between Dieppe and Boulogne to the west of the mouth of the Somme River, the formation descended to low altitude. The bombers followed a low-level zigzag route to the east of Paris to avoid all known anti-aircraft batteries and populated areas. No enemy fighters challenged them. Only occasional flak bursts dotted the sky above and behind the formation.

Half the bombers dropped their payload bundles by parachute in a large field northeast of Vassieux, and the remainder dropped their parachute containers southeast of the village. The Mustangs retained their drop tanks even after they were empty since they attained none of the jettison criteria other than empty. The bombers flew a different egress route in the same manner—a low-level zigzag.

The fighters had not fired a shot. None of the bombers or fighters suffered any damage or malfunction. The 4FG split with the bombers once they were back over England. They landed back at Debden. Mission accomplished without incident.

During June through September of 1944, the RAF and U.S. 8th Air Force flew a major supply drop each month for the *Maquis*. By the end of September, France would be liberated from Nazi occupation and the need for an active resistance had diminished substantially.

—

Friday, 21.July.1944
USS Baltimore
Broadway Pier
San Diego, San Diego County, California
United States of America
15:35 hours

President Roosevelt settled into the heavy cruiser's flag stateroom modified to accommodate his disability. He barely had time to survey his compartment for the journey when Admiral Leahy knocked and entered.

"The captain informed me that the ship is ready for departure tomorrow at dawn. The transit is planned for five days, but he indicated the weather and sea states are in our favor, which means we should do better than planned."

"Very good, Bill. Thanks."

"I just received confirmation from Chicago minutes ago that the convention has chosen Senator Truman as your vice-presidential nominee."

"Missouri?"

"Yes Sir."

"Henry Wallace was always a little too far left for the committee. Henry is a good man and does not deserve this snub, but he will take it like the professional he is."

"Truman won on the second ballot—1031 votes to 105. The committee gave you an opening, if you wish to contest the selection."

Roosevelt did not hesitate. "No. The party has spoken. We'll make do with the party's choice."

"Lastly, for now, I've been informed that Bill Donovan flew out here to speak with you before we sail tomorrow morning."

"Did he say what about?"

"No Sir, which probably means it's sensitive."

"Please show him in when he arrives."

"Yes Sir," Leahy replied and departed.

Roosevelt spun himself around a couple of times. Most notable from his survey was a lower set of portholes that allowed him to observe the exterior from his wheelchair. At the moment, his view was just of other warships at adjacent piers. Finally, when he had seen as much as he was going to see, Franklin moved to the special desk built to accommodate him and his wheelchair. He had just opened the case with his work papers for the coming conference. Leahy's knock stopped him.

"Excuse me, Mister President, Director Donovan is here."

Roosevelt nodded and gestured for the OSS director.

"Good afternoon, Mister President. Thank you for fitting me in," Donovan said as the stateroom hatch closed behind him. Donovan walked to face Roosevelt across the desk.

"This is quite unusual, Bill. Whatever is on your mind, let's have it."

"We, and here I mean M-I-6 and O-S-S, have confirmed from multiple sources that the R-A-F seriously wounded Field Marshal Rommel on the 17th. He was returning by automobile from a conference at the *1st S-S Panzer Corps* headquarters. The R-A-F reported that 6-0-2 Squadron had strafed a staff car near Sainte-Foy-de-Montgommery with positive effect. They killed the driver and bodyguard. Rommel was immediately evacuated to Germany."

"Good for the R-A-F. That will throw them a curveball."

"Yes Sir. I also received an ULTRA retransmission from London Station, which pertains directly to the assassination attempt on Chancellor Hitler last Thursday."

"What do we know?"

"From several of our direct agents in Berlin, the chancellor survived the attack. We have confirmation that it was a bomb in his Eastern Headquarters they call the Wolf's Lair. We are still trying to determine exactly what happened and why it failed. Another singular source reported that four officers were killed and 13 others were injured, some seriously."

"You said you had an ULTRA," Roosevelt commented.

"Yes Sir." Donovan opened his case, extracted the red striped border single-page message, and handed it to the president.

TOP SECRET - ULTRA

```
OS
LONSTA OSS NR 512
TS 210846Z JUL 44 URGENT
FM 105
TO 109
T O P   S E C R E T   U L T R A
URGENT
RETRAN ON PERMISSION UK FM AND DG SIS
BT
MOST SECRET ULTRA
SECRET
DATE 1621 20 JUL 1944
TO ALL RSHA
FROM RF RSHA
BREAK
BY DIRECTION OF THE LEADER USE ALL AVAILABLE
MEANS TO ROOT OUT CONSPIRATORS AT ALL LEVELS
BREAK NO ONE EXEMPT BREAK PRIORITY ONE ABOVE
ALL OTHERS BREAK LONG LIVE THE LEADER HAIL
VICTORY END
SECRET
DECYPHERED 0039 21 JUL 1944
MOST SECRET ULTRA
```

TOP SECRET - ULTRA

"I'm not sure I understand all that," Roosevelt said, holding up the highly classified message. "First, who sent the original message?"

"Himmler sent the message ostensibly by order of Hitler to the entire state security apparatus, all of which is under his direct control—the Gestapo, the S-D, the Security Police, the Criminal Police, and the Foreign Intelligence Service. Our analysis of this message suggests that Himmler has evidence that the conspirators and their supporters are far broader and more pervasive than just the attackers. We are trying to piece together what happened exactly, but we may not know until after the war. 'All available means' coming from Himmler and presumably Hitler, in our opinion, means the Gestapo is free to use any method, including warrantless search, torture, and even summary execution. We also suspect this message will make the ruthlessness of the Night of the Long Knives pale to insignificance. They will likely start with every single man at Rastenburg before, during, and after last Thursday's event. M-I-6 has field agent reports of gunfire in Berlin at the Bendlerblock, the headquarters of the Army High Command beginning Thursday night—most likely firing squad executions."

"How wide do you think this will go?"

"Our evidence so far suggests there will be few if any boundaries or limits to this . . . this . . . this vendetta. The endeavor will work its way outward from Berlin to all occupied territories and most likely around the world. If they can't reach someone, they may direct or encourage their foreign agents, supporters, friends, and sympathizers to take action."

'Here?"

"Yes Sir. They do not care about boundaries or laws."

"Please thoroughly brief the F-B-I."

"I will brief Director Hoover myself as soon as possible."

"Was the Thursday event related to what we discussed last January, the 15th, as I recall?"

"Yes Sir. We think it was precisely this attempt. They knew they had to move quickly. Decapitation would not be sufficient. Swift recognition by the British and us would add legitimacy to their *coup d'état*."

"Could we have helped?"

"I appreciate the question, Mister President, but I think your assessment and decision last January were correct given the circumstances. The conspirators came extraordinarily close, but not close enough for the Allies to take action. Now, the reprisals have begun. I had a SIGSALY conversation with Stewart Menzies yesterday afternoon. We considered extracting our in-country agents as the Gestapo's rabid zealousness might expose and compromise our personnel and informants in a kind of domino cascade."

"Were any of our folks involved?"

"No Sir . . . neither us nor the British. But, they might become collateral damage as the vindictiveness of the Nazis will offer virtually no restraints."

"Can we remove them?"

"Stewart and I both agree that extraction is not practical or even possible. We have advised our field agents to keep their heads down and take precautions."

"May God help and protect them."

"I'm afraid prayer is the best we can do until the storm blows over."

"We must finish this war swiftly to end the carnage."

"That would be a big step, but I suspect the level of malevolence will not diminish quickly."

"God help us all."

—

Saturday, 22. July. 1944
Omaha Beach
Vierville-sur-Mer, Normandie
Liberated France
07:30 hours

The day was D+46—a month and a half after the Longest Day. The 28th Infantry Division landed across Omaha Beach. The troops saw corners and pieces of the Mulberry 'A' artificial harbor's destroyed remains and the remainder of the German obstacle beach defenses not yet cleared by the engineers. The division served in reserve for their first week in France.

The 28ID would enter combat as part of the XIX Corps, 1st Army, during the Saint-Lô breakout. The author's paternal uncle, Staff Sergeant Herbert Davis Parlier, USA, served in the 110th Infantry Regiment, 28th Infantry Division, XIX Corps, 1st Army, 12th Army Group, through the breakout and the run across France. The division would soon transfer to Patton's 3rd Army through the remainder of the division's combat in France and into Germany.

———

Tuesday, 25. July. 1944
Norfolk House
No.31 St James's Square
St. James's, London, England
United Kingdom
18:35 hours

Lieutenant General Bradley arrived for an unplanned meeting with the supreme commander. He was still in his battle dress with his helmet under his left arm on his hip. His dour expression suggested an unpleasant conversation was coming.

"I didn't expect to see you here," Eisenhower said as Bradley entered after being announced. The door was closed. Bradley stood at attention and ignored Eisenhower's gesture to sit.

"I had to come myself and in person."

"OK. That sounds ominous."

"It is very serious, Ike. This morning, we executed the first phase of Operation COBRA as part of our breakout effort at Saint-Lô. I won't belabor this. More than 100 American soldiers were killed and nearly 500 wounded by our bombers. I am responsible, Ike. Therefore, I came to respectfully tender my resignation personally."

Eisenhower scanned Bradley's face and eyes. He was dead serious. This time, Ike more emphatically gestured for them to sit in the plush leather chairs facing each other.

"I know you don't joke around, Brad. I'm not accepting your resignation, but I am demanding an explanation. Give me what you know so far."

"First, Jimmy Doolittle knows the basics of what happened. He's already directed a full forensic investigation of the mission. We shall know more in a few days. Second, for what we believe are several operational reasons, the heavy bombers deviated from the plan.

"The first segment of aerial bombardment began at 09:38 when 600 British and American fighter-bombers attacked strong points and enemy artillery around Saint-Lô. In the next hour, 1,800 8th Air Force heavy bombers were supposed to carpet bomb an area along the Saint-Lô–Periers road, positions held by the *Panzer-Lehr-Division*. They were light on infantry, and that was the point we intended to punch through their line of resistance. The heavy bombers were supposed to drop parallel to the clearly visible straight road and on the south side. We do not yet know why they came in from the north and dropped perpendicular to the road. As soon as we saw what was about to happen, we tried to abort the heavy bombers, but we had no direct communications. The end of the carpet-bombing landed short on our troops on the north side of the road. The 1st and 30th I-Ds and the 3rd Armor Division, the vanguard of the VII Corps, were poised to launch their attack and took the friendly fire hits. To their credit, despite the terrible losses due to friendly fire, they launched their assault on time with good initial results."

"Such losses in combat are an unfortunate part of the process, Brad, and you know that."

"Yes, but apparently, the aviators tried to tell me about their difficulties with the plan, at least the heavy bomber portion, and I didn't understand. I made the decision to execute the plan. I'm responsible for the deaths of those soldiers. I am accountable. My resignation is the only option, Ike. I appreciate your understanding and perhaps even your tolerance, but my conscience is being crushed by what happened this morning, which is precisely why I'm here in person."

"Brad, the reason you make such a great general is your compassion for the troops you command. The pain of this tragedy will pass."

"I don't think so, Ike. One of those dead soldiers was Les McNair. I'm going to have to face Clare and tell her what happened to her husband of 39 years. They married the year after he graduated, for God's sakes."

Lieutenant General Leslie James 'Les' McNair, USA [USMA 1904] commanded the VII Corps. He had chosen to be with his men in a foxhole 30 yards from the Saint-Lô–Periers road. By war's end, he would be the most senior American general killed in Europe during the war, and he was killed by friendly fire.

Eisenhower stared intensely into Bradley's bespectacled eyes. "I'm going to ask you only once, Brad, are you capable of commanding troops in combat?"

"Yes."

"Then, I do not accept your resignation. Now, get back to your damn command. Let's get this breakout done and Georgie into open country, so he can do his thing. Is your headquarters still at Isigny-sur-Mer?"

"Are you sure, Ike?"

"Yes, I'm sure, Brad."

"We are still in Isigny, but we're about to move forward."

"Thank you for your proactive candor. I'll be activating the 12th Army Group in a few days, and you will command it. Court Hodges will take over 1st Army from you."

Lieutenant General Courtney Hicks 'Court' Hodges, USA, had served as Bradley's deputy in the 1st Army. He received an appointment to and attended West Point in the Class of 1909 but dropped out because of his inability to comprehend geometry. Hodges enlisted in the Army as a private in 1906 and was now in his 38th year of service.

"Court's a good man. He'll do well."

"I know . . . just as you have done and will continue to do, Brad. Now, it's too late for you to get back to your headquarters tonight. I'd like you to spend the night. Kay will drive us to The Cottage. We'll have a nice dinner and sit by the fire. Kay and I will take you back to Northolt first thing in the morning so that you can return to your command."

This time, Bradley stared at Eisenhower and scanned his commander's eyes and face, perhaps attempting to assess sincerity. "Thanks, Ike. I hope you're doing the right thing."

"I am, Brad. Trust me. We're both sorry for this tragedy, but it was not the first and certainly will not be the last. Remember Slapton Sands." Eisenhower stood and went to the hat rack beside his spacious desk. He grabbed his framed cover. "Now, I'll leave the office as is. Let's go get you fed and a good night's sleep."

———

Thursday, 27.July.1944
2709 Kalakua Avenue
Waikiki, Oahu, Hawaiian Islands
Territory of the United States of America
21:30 hours

President Roosevelt had decided to use the Waikiki beach estate of Christian Rasmus 'Chris' Holmes, II, who had committed suicide the previous February. The main building was a palatial three-story mansion complete with an exterior elevator that allowed the president to enjoy the full splendor of the palace and extraordinary view. When the war began, the estate had been made available to naval aviators for rest and relaxation when they were in Hawaii temporarily. The president commandeered the estate as his residence during his stay in Hawaii for the Pacific Strategy Conference. The principal reason for his presence was an intractable disagreement between the two senior commanders in the Pacific Theater of Operations (PTO).

On 30.March.1942, the newly created combined joint chiefs of staff agreed to divide command of Allied forces in the PTO. Commander-in-Chief Pacific (CINCPAC) Admiral Chester William 'Chet' Nimitz, USN [USNA 1905], had also been designated Commander-in-Chief Pacific Ocean Areas (CINCPOA), which included all the Pacific Ocean except a portion known as Southwest Pacific Area (SWPA). At the time, recently dislodged Commander U.S. Army Forces Far East (USAFFE) General Douglas 'Doug' MacArthur, USA [USMA 1903], was designated Commander-in-Chief Southwest Pacific Area (CINCSWPA). The SWPA included Australia, New Guinea, Borneo, Java, and the Philippines.

Nimitz favored and presented a direct island-hopping strategy through the Mariana Islands, Iwo Jima, and Okinawa in preparation for the assault on Mainland Japan. MacArthur wanted to return to the Philippines and then to Formosa (Taiwan) before the final assault on Japan. The B-29 Stratofortress heavy bomber had been declared operational the previous April. Tinian, the northernmost island of the Marianas, and Formosa were roughly equidistant from Tokyo (1,500 miles) and within the range of the B-29. The two commanders argued they could not do both, and their respective strategy was best. Reconciliation fell to President Roosevelt.

The president hosted the night's dinner for the principals—Admiral Nimitz, General MacArthur, Admiral Leahy, and Admiral William Frederick 'Bull' Halsey, Jr., USN [USNA 1904], the new Commander, 3rd Fleet. The vigorous debates of the last two days did not transfer to the cocktail hour or the dinner. While dominated by the Navy, MacArthur remained the *primo uomo* of the gathering. The meal proved to be far more exquisite than rationing would commonly allow. No one complained or objected. Instead, they enjoyed the meal together.

"Well, gentlemen," Roosevelt announced, "shall we retire to the library for a nice after-dinner brandy?"

Admiral Leahy pushed the president's wheelchair down the hallway to the wood-paneled room with full bookshelves from floor to ceiling with a rolling ladder on each wall. As was his practice, Roosevelt served up a brandy snifter for each man, including himself. They shared disassociated stories from their distant past for 30 minutes.

MacArthur leaned in and whispered, "May I have a private word, Mister President?"

"Certainly," Roosevelt responded, caught Leahy's eyes, and nodded toward the door.

Leahy put his unfinished drink on a nearby table and pushed the president's wheelchair into another room that was configured more like a conference room. Leahy positioned the president at the head of the table. Roosevelt gestured to MacArthur to sit to his left. Bill Leahy stepped toward the chair to the president's right.

"Private, if you please, Bill," MacArthur said in a commanding voice.

Leahy looked to the president, who nodded his consent. Leahy departed and closed the door behind him.

"Thank you for the courtesy, Mister President."

"Of course, General. What's on your mind."

"First, I would like to convey my sincerest gratitude for your efforts to resolve the disagreement between Admiral Nimitz and myself."

"It is unfortunate that the disagreement reached my level, but that reconciliation falls to me as commander-in-chief."

MacArthur did not continue for several seconds, perhaps to consider his words. "I must say Admiral Nimitz's strategy is laudable, but . . ." He stopped when Roosevelt held up his left-hand palm out.

"General, we are not going to discuss this strategic disagreement without Admiral Nimitz present. First, it is unethical, and second, I will not slight Admiral Nimitz, who has conducted himself properly and professionally throughout this conference."

"My apologies, Mister President. There were a couple of aspects of our respective presentations that were not discussed. I know you have a hectic schedule for your remaining few days on the islands, and I must return to my command tomorrow."

"Those are your choices, General. Shall I call for Admiral Nimitz so that we can continue this discussion?"

"That is your choice, Mister President, but I don't think it's necessary." MacArthur looked away from the president for several seconds and then back to Roosevelt's waiting stern gaze. "I am compelled to remind you, Mister President," MacArthur paused, as much to give the president an opening as to ensure he had the president's attention, "this is a reelection year, and your party has nominated you for an unprecedented fourth term."

"I'm keenly aware of that facts, General. Your point?"

"I dare say that abandoning 7,000 starving prisoners of war, survivors of the Bataan Death March, and 17 million Filipino Christians might well turn public opinion against you."

Roosevelt could barely contain his shock. He rolled his chair back as if he were going to leave and terminate the meeting. Franklin regained his composure, decided against fleeing from the fight, and moved his chair back into position. "No one has ever accused you of not being ambitious, General. I must say you are as arrogant as your detractors claim. For an active general to threaten the commander-in-chief may well be unprecedented in American history. No wonder you wanted a private audience, so you could maintain your plausible deniability of 'he-said-she-said.' Your presidential ambitions are scarcely disguised, General. Your Republican friends . . . ," Roosevelt paused and gestured for MacArthur to stop as the general leaned forward and started to respond. "I am still the commander-in-chief, and it is my turn to speak. Your Republican friends may well have coaxed you to run against me. If so, I will caution you to read the Constitution.

"Now, that said, we have a war to fight. I need you, and you need me. I'm not going to relieve you of command for conduct unbecoming and dismiss you from service, as is my inclination. If I detect even the slightest hint that you've engaged in politics at any level, I shall immediately order your relief of command and arrest. Despite your ego and sense of self-importance, you are just another general who serves at my pleasure directly."

Roosevelt did not wait for or expect a response. He continued, "As I stated this afternoon in closing our conference, I've heard both arguments. As commander-in-chief and president of these United States, I've many other factors beyond the military aspects to consider in deciding on our strategic approach. Once I have assessed the whole situation, orders will be issued by the War and Navy Departments. You will receive your orders shortly after my return to Washington.

"One last word, General, we will not talk of this conversation again. Do I make myself clear?"

"Yes Sir."

"Very well. Then, this regrettable discussion is concluded." Roosevelt rolled himself to the door. MacArthur stood but made no move to assist the president. Franklin opened the door himself. Leahy, who was waiting across the hall facing the door, jumped to help the president. "I'm done for the night, Bill."

The two leaders went directly to the elevator and the president's quarters. Leahy asked about the meeting, but Roosevelt refused to discuss what had just happened. The president left the closing of the dinner to his military chief of staff.

———

Friday, 28.July.1944
Cabinet War Rooms
New Public Offices
Whitehall, London, England
United Kingdom
14:30 hours

Secretary to the War Cabinet Sir Edward Ettingdene Bridges, KCB, MC, waited until the last second ticked over on the wall clock to signal the door guards to close the door and exclude any late arrivals. The full War Cabinet plus the Defense Committee—the defense ministers and joint chiefs—were the only attendees for this classified meeting.

"This meeting of the War Cabinet and Defense Committee will come to order," Sir Edward commanded. "On our only agenda item, Mister Morrison, your report if you please."

Home Secretary Morrison cleared his throat. "At 9:41 this morning, a V1 buzz bomb struck Lewisham High Street without warning. The explosion did considerable damage. The count as of an hour ago is 50 dead and 200 wounded, but the rescue service is still searching the rubble of several shops and flats. The number of casualties will most likely increase as the search effort continues."

Prime Minister Churchill sat at the head of the inverted 'U' table with his forehead down and a pronounced scowl expression. He was clearly not happy, but he chose to remain silent and listen intently as the conversation developed.

"How did this one get through?" asked Attlee.

"The radar data suggests they launched from a new site and found a gap in our radar-directed gun array," General Brooke responded.

"How many gaps do we have?" Attlee continued his questioning.

"We move batteries around and interlace them to cover potential approach lines from known sites," answered Brooke. "The Germans learned quickly that their fixed sites are extraordinarily vulnerable, especially with our predominant air superiority over occupied France. They started employing mobile launchers, or at least movable launchers. They move the launchers faster than we can get bombers to attack the sites. We can't be everywhere all of the time, and we don't have enough guns. It is also much easier for the enemy to change the guidance parameters of the buzz bomb than it is for us to move a Q-F 3.7 battery. We're also expanding our coupling of the Type 282 RADAR unit and the fire control unit to give the gunners better predictive aiming." Brooke looked at and nodded to Air Chief Marshal Portal.

"I can add that our fighter pilots have learned to fly just in front of the flying bombs. The aircraft's wingtip vortex is sufficiently strong to upset the missile guidance system. Unfortunately, when we so disturb the missile, we cannot predict where it will go."

"Better to explode in the countryside," interjected Morrison, "than in London center."

"True," Sir Charles responded. "The technique works and saves us wing damage and potential shrapnel damage from an exploding warhead. I only note that once the device is upset, we have noted very erratic, unpredictable behavior. The missile can go anywhere. I would also like to add that from the Air Force perspective, we have significantly improved the coordination between the ground and air defense units to keep our fighters out of the anti-aircraft fire zones. We are also evaluating fighter patrols over the Channel to pick up as many as possible over the water. There is still a risk to naval vessels moving back and forth in support of OVERLORD, but so far, that risk is lower than the countryside danger and substantially lower than the city peril."

"How about stationing destroyers on the likely flight paths?" asked Secretary of State for Foreign Affairs and Leader of Commons Robert Anthony Eden, MC, PC, and long-time MP for Warwick and Leamington.

"We, the Royal Navy," began First Sea Lord Admiral of the Fleet Sir Andrew Browne 'ABC' Cunningham, Bart, GCB, DSO with two bars, "are well beyond having insufficient destroyers for current taskings. If the War Cabinet wishes to alter our operating priorities, we can station destroyers in the Eastern Channel and Southern North Sea. Not all of our destroyers are equipped with radar-directed anti-aircraft guns, which means we would have to be very selective with respect to assignment."

More than a few attendees glanced at Churchill, anticipating the prime minister's contribution. Winston did not twitch or murmur.

Sir Edward took the initiative. "Does anyone have something else to add?"

"Yes," Home Secretary Morrison spoke up. "Lewisham was not the only misfortune we suffered this morning. Another V1 missile made it through our defenses and hit a Kensington High Street restaurant at lunchtime, killing 44 people and injuring several hundred. These terrible losses of innocent civilian lives are the direct consequence of our no warning order."

"Enough!" shouted Churchill as he slammed his open hand on the table. "I am as disturbed and troubled by these horrible events as anyone. The defense of the realm falls to me . . . and the War Cabinet. As we discussed at length, no warning has its consequences, just as incessant warning does. We simply cannot allow these damnable doodlebugs to paralyze the nation with fear. The chiefs have summarized our evolving countermeasures. I shall ask for the War Cabinet's concurrence for the First Lord and First Sea Lord to make a quick study of positioning an appropriate destroyer picket line in the Channel as perhaps our first line of defense. I would like to see our other areas of operations, and how we might backfill."

"We will see to it, Prime Minister," answered First Lord Albert Victor 'AV' Alexander, CH, PC, MP for Sheffield, Hillsborough Division.

"If my memory is correct," Churchill told the group, "we are stopping more than are getting through. We have not beaten this latest menace to the Home Islands, but defeat it we shall."

"We've all appreciated your optimism in the face of adversity, Winston," Morrison said, "but our people are dying under the onslaught of these killer machines."

"We overcame the enemy's superior numbers in The Blitz," Winston continued. "We shall overcome these devices as well. Does anyone have anything else to add?"

No one spoke. Churchill looked into the eyes of every man in the closed room.

General Brooke raised his left hand to shoulder height. "Before we adjourn, the War Cabinet might like to know that I received a message from General Montgomery just before this meeting. Despite the terrible tragedy of the 25th, the 12th Army Group's XIX Corps has taken Saint-Lô, and the combined XIX and VII Corps are prosecuting the breakout west of Saint-Lô. Generals Montgomery and Bradley are encouraged by the success of the combined armor-infantry forces. The Germans are being overrun before they can dig into the *boçage*. I must remind the War Cabinet the 12th Army Group has roughly 30 miles of boçage to fight through. However, if they can maintain the momentum, they should break out into open country within a week or two."

Various spontaneous exclamations temporarily filled the conference room.

"Godspeed and following winds to our forces on the Continent," the prime minister added.

"With that," Sir Edward announced, "we are adjourned."

—

Chapter 9

A love of liberty is planted by nature in the breasts of all men.
-- Dionysius of Halicarnassus

Tuesday, 1.August.1944
Headquarters, Special Operations Executive (SOE)
No.64 Baker Street
Marylebone, London, England
United Kingdom
07:15 hours

"If I am informed properly," Lord Selborne began, "you are headed off to France soon."

"Yes Sir," answered Trevor Anderson. "We jump in six days."

"You are a man of many talents, Trevor. You've joined the first of our new joint teams to deploy."

"Correct, again. It seems my language skills can be of some use. We will be jumping in with a large passel of the new incendiary devices."

"Ingenious little weapons and I dare say your usefulness goes far beyond your proficiency with multiple languages."

"Thank you for that, my Lord. I would like to think so."

"I wanted to catch you before you deployed to follow up on our conversations last May."

"Has there been any developments?"

"No, not in particular. I met with Mister Petrie yesterday morning on several other topics. He also updated me on the Philby matter." Cecil paused to allow for an opening if Trevor had anything to say or ask. "Petrie asked me to inform you, as the anonymous source, that M-I-5 has an open, low-grade investigation. Sir Stewart is aware of the open investigation, but he was asked to avoid any deviation from normal conduct and behavior. He said he could not predict the outcome, but he also asked me to convey his gratitude for your courage to raise the issue. The Security Service is watching."

"I truly hope my instincts are wrong."

"In this instance, the risk you are not wrong is far greater than the threat to your former Cambridge classmate."

"Thank you for that, Sir."

"One other question from M-I-5. Have you had any contact with Philby since your last encounter in May?"

"No sir . . . no contact of any kind."

"Just a reminder from Director-General Petrie, do not avoid contact with Philby and do not seek it either, unless under the direction and coverage of M-I-5. If you do make contact for any reason, no matter how slight, ensure you notify me immediately to protect your anonymity."

"For the next few weeks, I'll be out of the country and fairly well occupied. Nonetheless, you can count on my discretion, my Lord."

"Thank you, Trevor. Good luck with your mission. I eagerly await your return and debriefing."

"I'm just glad someone is watching. I hope to return in a week or two. Thank you very much for the update, Lord Selborne."

———

Monday, 7.August.1944
Vérignon, Provence-Alpes-Côte d'Azur
France Occupée
23:05 hours

Three hours in harness in the back of the modified Armstrong Whitworth Whitley Mark V induced an overwhelming urge to jump just to get out. It was not Trevor's first experience jumping from a Whitley at night, but three hours made this opportunity his longest mission. They did not call the Whitley the flying barn door for nothing.

The Project Jedburgh was a joint Allied program, with the OSS Special Operations (SO) branch, the British Special Operations Executive (SOE), and the French *Bureau Central de Renseignements et d'Action* (BCRA) involved. The name had been chosen at random by the Ministry of Economic Warfare, but many believed the program was named for the Scottish border village of Jedburgh. A typical Jedburgh team was comprised of a British SOE agent, an American OSS agent, and a French BCRA specialist. Trevor trained with Team JONAS for six weeks.

Trevor was the additional fourth for the three-man Jedburgh Team JONAS. The British member was First Lieutenant Jeremy 'Bolt' Thorne. The American was Second Lieutenant Tom 'Hammer' Kendall. The French member and the team's specialty radio operator was André *'Orage'* Beldroit. Their welcoming committee this night was expected to be the local *Maquis* unit.

The dim red 'prepare' light illuminated. The four men checked their harnesses and attachments, and then they checked the back of each other. Finally, they hooked their static line to the cable attached to the aircraft's interior. They would jump in reverse order, Trevor first, Thorne last, at 3,100 feet pressure altitude, 500 feet above the farm field elevation northeast of the village of Vérignon.

The interior red light blinked three times. Trevor opened the hatch and secured it. He instinctively tugged on his static line to ensure it was secure. The four jumpers shuffled into position. It was imperative that they left the aircraft as close together as possible to minimize their landing dispersion.

Three days after the full moon, the moonlight offered just enough light to see the hills, forest, and occasional clearings. Trevor could not see lights and did not expect to see any. Instead, the pilot would get a highly directional, narrow beam signal lamp, coded signal to indicate the correct location and safeness for the drop.

The green light illuminated. Trevor pushed out of the hatch, felt the drop, and then the welcome jolt of his parachute opening. He quickly did as he was trained and checked the parachute canopy—no missing or torn panels, all the risers and shroud lines were straight, not tangled—and then he checked his equipment and weapon's bags. Once he was satisfied, he was in good shape, Trevor looked around him. The other three were all in good shape as well. It appeared they were in the proper place, the correct field. He did not have much time and prepared for landing.

Trevor hit the ground and rolled. He jumped up, felt no pain, nothing broken or sprained, and collapsed the chute. He figure-eight'ed the parachute shrouds and canopy material, and then he placed the bundle in his parachute bag to make disposal easier. Next, Trevor attached his Thompson submachine gun to his cross-shoulder sling strap. He also felt to ensure the M1911 pistol was still in his shoulder holster under his jacket. The backpack remained intact and closed.

The small *Maquis* team joined them in the field.

"*Nous devons agir rapidement,*" one of the men said.

"*Oui,*" Trevor replied before the other team members joined them. Once all four team members were together with their *Maquis* escort, Trevor added, "*Ouvrir la voie.*"

The ten men jogged off toward the east tree line. A half dozen other well-armed *Maquis* fighters led the group to a small open trench they had pre-dug to bury the four parachute bags. Then, with the parachutes hidden, the group set out through the dimness of the forest with half the resistance fighters leading the way, and the other half bringing up the rear guard.

Their march in the forest darkness took 90 plus minutes to reach a small, poorly maintained forest hut with no discernible light. Most of the fighters deployed around the hut, disappearing into the shadows. The apparent *Maquis* leader gestured without words for them to enter the cabin. The interior darkness made the details difficult to see. A hidden floor door allowing just enough dim light to display a staircase showed the way. They descended the stairs, and the leader closed the door behind them all. The group waited in what appeared to be an anteroom with two tunnels. A single candle lit the room. They followed the leader down the right tunnel through several bends into a large room with tables, chairs, and signs of life.

The leader turned to face the Jedburgh team. "Welcome to Vérignon. I am Lion."

The light from the additional candles in the cave finally offered sufficient illumination for Trevor to recognize the man known as Lion. His name was Dr. René Beltron d'Avignon, MD, a prominent physician turned successful resistance fighter and the provincial *Maquis* commander.

André introduced the team. "I am Storm. This is Bolt," gesturing to Thorne, "Hammer," motioning to Kendall, "and Diamond." Trevor nodded his head.

Lion shook hands with each man. "In case we get stopped by *le Boche*, who speaks French?"

"We all do," responded Storm, "some better than others." They all laughed softly. "Diamond and I speak with native fluency. Diamond also speaks excellent High German and Polish."

"We are glad to have you with us. We understand you brought a special weapon?"

"Yes, we did," Bolt answered.

"Excellent. I know you have had a long day. We have prepared a dormitory so you can get some rest before we begin the training."

"Were you informed of our timing and purpose?" asked Bolt.

"Purpose, no. Timing, yes."

"Then, we have much to discuss and address in the next few days."

D-Day for Operation DRAGOON was planned for one week's time. Their immediate assignment was the isolation of the beachhead area—the Gulf of Saint Tropez. Three divisions of the 7th Army's VI Corps would land on the famous beaches and cut into the southern flank of German forces in the west.

They secured for the night. The guard watch would keep them all safe for the night. Storm sent their safe arrival message. They took a cot with a blanket for what remained of the night.

———

Tuesday, 8.August.1944
USAAF Station F-356
Saffron Walden, Essex, England
United Kingdom
08:10 hours

The 334FS finally returned to full strength last week. The last three replacements arrived in the previous two weeks. First Lieutenant Michael

Stephen 'Rocket' Springfield, USAAF, of Helena, Montana, became the Green Flight, 2nd Section Leader, with Stove flying his wing. First Lieutenant Gerald Adam 'Hole' Horten, USAAF, of Omaha, Nebraska, filled the position as Brian's 2nd Section Leader with Horn flying his wing. And last but not least, Second Lieutenant Karl Eugene 'Corn' Eiger, USAAF, of Hersey, Pennsylvannia, joined to be Brian's wingman. Corn was right out of the training command with barely a hundred flight hours. The two first lieutenants had served as plowback flight instructors. They had more flight time, more gunnery practice, but no combat experience. Like the other replacements, they would have to learn quickly in their trial by fire.

The 4th Fighter Group seemed to pick up more than their share of unusual missions, perhaps because of their experience, their combat accomplishments, or maybe simply the luck of the draw. Brian recounted for the replacements the frustration of the Eagle squadron pilots when the RAF held them back because of their unruly, rambunctiousness. For whatever reason, the day's mission was another one of those unusual missions.

Horseback would lead the entire group to escort one squadron of RAAF Beaufighters for a low-level attack on various known barracks and support facilities in and around Stavanger, Norway. Intelligence had given them good targets, and the joint command wanted a diversion for the Germans to think about, for assistance to the Normandy breakout and DRAGOON landings. The 4FG had been chosen because of their experience and their long-range P-51D fighters. The plan called for Horseback with two-thirds of his 4FG to trail the attack squadron by roughly five miles at an altitude of nominally 8,000 feet, or in sight. He would have 335FS and 336FS with him and manage the air cover to keep the German fighters at bay. They expected more fighters, perhaps not as thick as over the heart of Germany, but more than over France. The 334FS would stay low and flat with No.455 Squadron. 'A' Division would have the right flank, and 'B' Division would have the left. The primary objective was to protect the attack squadron. Their secondary mission, given no enemy fighters, would be to attack targets of opportunity. The high squadrons could join in once the Beaufighters were complete and out to sea on the way back to base.

No.455 Squadron was part of the ANZAC Strike Wing within the RAF. The squadron had Australian crews and flew the twin-engine Bristol Beaufighter Mark X manned by a pilot and navigator/radio operator and armed with 20mm cannons, and 0.303 machine guns, and on this day, configured to carry one Mark 13 torpedo or wing-mounted RP-3 3-inch rockets. On the day's mission, half the Beaufighters had torpedoes, and the other half had rockets.

On this launch, 334FS was the last squadron to take flight. They turned north-northwest along the English coast rather than south or east. Horseback chose a long chase join up to catch up to the squadron of Beaufighters at 8,000 feet altitude. They wanted to avoid the German radar units in Belgium and the Netherlands. The 334FS completed its join up and took their positions around the attack aircraft.

At the Edinburgh Estuary, the whole formation wheeled to the right and picked up a heading of 059º magnetic direct to Stavanger. Now, they only had to worry about a possible German radar picket ship in the form of a fishing trawler. They maintained their altitude to conserve fuel. The only vessels they had seen were along the British coast. Roughly halfway across the North Sea and 100 miles from the Norwegian coast, the Beaufighters descended to wavetop height. The 334FS stayed with the attack aircraft.

These guys like to fly low.

The Mustangs had plenty of power margin with the Beaufighters. The hazy conditions gave them five-mile visibility.

"Cobweb, Upper Six, trawler 10 o'clock, ten miles," Horseback radioed from his higher observation position.

"Upper, Cobweb Six, roger, break, Cobweb Red investigate."

"Cobweb Red, wilco." Brian nodded his head for the Red Flight to turn to the north. The four Mustangs spread out into a line abreast. The haze did not help. But, they did not have far to go at their speeds. The trawler appeared out of the haze directly in front of them. Brian adjusted his line-up slightly to the right, lined up on the vessel, placed the sight reticle short of the target, and broadcast, "Tally ho." By the time he finished, he saw the spinning radar antenna. "Bogey. Engaging." The trawler had a *Kriegsmarine* ensign and grew quickly in his sight. He squeezed and held his trigger down. All six wing-mounted, heavy machine guns erupted. Brian focused on the superstructure that held the radar antenna. Wood chips, flashes, splinters, and puffs of smoke marked the destruction of the superstructure. "Waterline," Brian broadcast for the rest of his flight as he banked hard right and pulled back firmly. Waterspouts and flashes on and around the trawler burst into his peripheral vision before turning away. He turned hard but remained mindful of the water just below him in the haze. Brian picked up Hole, completing his run and pulling off, and Horn made his approach to the target. He let up on his back stick pressure to avoid interfering with Horn's attack. By the time Brian regained a clear view of the vessel, the German radar picket ship was barely visible and was more like a boiling white spot in the North Sea. "Bogey eliminated," Brian broadcast. "No survivors."

"Well done, Cobweb Red. 0-7-4 at eight." Blakeslee provided just enough clues for their rejoining and did not add more information just in case anyone was listening.

Brian understood. He leveled his wings out on heading and reduced his throttle setting by five inches MAP. Corn was in position promptly. Hole and

Horn needed several more miles to catch up. The Beaufighters slowly appeared out of the haze ahead of them.

As soon as Sweet saw Hunter approaching, he moved his Yellow Flight wide, so Red Flight had a straight shot into the 'B' Division leader position. Brian slowly throttled back to match the speed of the Beaufighters and checked over his shoulders to check on the position of his 'B' Division.

"Bandits, two o'clock high. Becky engage," Horseback broadcast.

Brian did not have time to observe what was going on above and behind them. However, the chatter of aerial combat told them what they needed to know about the fighter situation. They had no enemy fighters, yet, at wave top height. Brian had confidence Horseback or Becky would tell them if the enemy fighters broke through or reacted to the low-level attackers. Several minutes later, as the furball fight boiled behind them, the coastline of Norway materialized out of the haze. It took the attack squadron leader a minute to determine their location and adjust their direction slightly to compensate.

The attack plan called for 'A' Division and the rocket attackers to cut across the peninsula to attack a variety of ground targets—fuel storage, anti-aircraft guns, barracks buildings, ammunition dumps, and enemy defense targets of opportunity. 'B' Division would stay with the torpedo attackers, who would round the peninsula in a reverse course for their torpedo runs down the channel. The torpedoes were intended for Axis transport and cargo ships as well as warships anchored in the harbor. Brian's fighters would engage any anti-aircraft guns that attempted to engage the torpedo Beaufighters. Red Flight had the east flank, and Yellow Flight took the west flank.

The four dock Beaufighters dropped torpedoes into the water. The stream of bubbles indicated the weapons were running straight and true toward the docks. Those aircraft turned hard right in sequence with 'A' Flight adjusting to their charges.

The other torpedo Beaufighters each took their assigned warships in the harbor—a cruiser, three destroyers, and two transport ships, both low on the waterline, which meant they were loaded with something. The three destroyers were trying to get underway to avoid the torpedoes running straight toward them. The warship Beaufighters banked hard left in sequence toward open water with 'B' Division laying down suppressive fire for their egress.

Several attack and fighter aircraft took hits and had damage, but they were all still flying. The two groups flew on parallel courses at low level until they were miles into the North Sea. After 20 minutes, in accordance with the plan, they began a cruise climb to reach better visibility and thinner air for better range. The higher altitude also offered a less turbulent ride. With better visibility, the three groups rejoined. The torpedo group was the last element to rejoin. Brian counted the attack and fighter aircraft with the entire formation stable at 8,000 feet and good cruise speed with sufficient fuel for the return. *All present and accounted for.*

On sight of the English coast, the Beaufighters broke off first since their base was closest. The 4FG Mustangs landed in the same order they had taken off. Once they completed all of their debriefings with the intelligence personnel, they were released for the remainder of the day.

The new guys chose to make a run into London despite the ongoing V1 blitz. Brian knew he did not have enough time to make it home to Charlotte and Standing Oak Farm, and he just did not feel up to a London adventure. They had reduced attendees for the evening meal, but it was a better-than-average meal. Brian figured a few beers with the remaining group pilots would prove to be a welcome relaxation.

"The phones are working, again," Sweet announced to the pilots remaining in the bar. A dozen pilots jumped to the bank of telephone booths.

I'll have to wait my turn.

Brian bought another beer. He checked on the telephone booths. At least one man waited outside each of the half dozen telephone booths. Brian returned to the gathering of 334FS pilots.

Brian casually kept track of the goings and comings. When the comings exceeded the goings, Brian drained his beer and excused himself. He would attempt a call to Charlotte, and then he was more interested in reading a little and going to bed early. He needed a good night's sleep. Only one other pilot waited. Brian let him take the next booth when it opened up. A few minutes later, another booth opened.

"Operator," the female voice said.

"Are the connections to the south coast working now?" asked Brian.

"Yes, they are. The coastal restricted zone orders were lifted on the 1st of the month."

"Finally. Were they implemented for the invasion?"

"We cannot discuss that, Sir. Did you want to place a call?"

"Yes. Winchester 4-3-7-9, please."

"One moment." The line turned silent a dozen seconds or so. "Go ahead."

"Standing Oak Farm," Mabel said.

"Mabel, this is Brian."

"It is great to hear you, again, Mister Drummond. Let me get Charlotte for you."

The clunk of the handset on the table told him she had left. Another clunk meant someone picked up the handset.

"Brian," came Charlotte's excited voice.

"I can't tell you how good it is to hear your voice over the phone after these months. I know I saw you a month ago, but we had a long mission today, and it's assuring to hear your voice."

"Is everything all right, Brian?"

"Yes. It was just a long day . . . successful . . . but long. I can't tell you over the phone where we were, but . . . someday."

"Everything is moving along swimmingly here. We made another large delivery of our greenhouse produce to the American Army earlier this week."

"You're doing so well, sweetheart. I'm so glad the restrictions have been removed."

"Me too. I could talk to you all night," Charlotte said, "but I'm sure you need a good night's sleep. So, I shall say I love you very much, and I miss you terribly. Now, I want you to hang up the telephone handset and head off to bed."

"I love you, Charlotte. Thank you for understanding. I am off to bed. Talk to you soon.

"Good night, my love."

"Good night, sweetheart."

———

Tuesday, 8.August.1944
No.10 Downing Street
Whitehall, London, England
United Kingdom
17:30 hours

Winston chose to walk back to No.10 after the meeting in the Cabinet War Rooms. The fine summer weather made the walk enjoyable and even refreshing. He felt the urge to find a bench, and just sit with no one interrupting the pleasure of the warm sunshine and light breeze bringing aromas other than cordite and burnt wood. But his thoughts about the pending meeting with the supreme commander kept him moving. There was only one subject for this meeting, although he wanted to get Eisenhower's latest assessment of the breakout at Saint-Lô.

Churchill barely made it back to his office when Duty private Secretary Colville announced General Eisenhower's arrival.

John Rupert 'Jock' Colville had been one of Churchill's private secretaries through the early war years. After two years on active duty, he returned to Churchill's secretariat staff last December.

Winston quickly found the message he needed for the meeting. "Let us not keep the supreme commander waiting. Please show the general in." Churchill stood and came around his desk to greet Eisenhower.

"Thank you for taking the time for me, Ike."

"I am at your service, Prime Minister."

The prime minister gestured to the low coffee table. The two leaders sat across from each other. "What is the latest from Normandy?"

"The 3rd Army broke out of *boçage* south of Avranches. They should be in Rennes tomorrow. They will seal off the Brittany peninsula in a few days, cutting all the German lines of communication to the western ports. The bulk of Patton's 3rd Army will soon turn and head east."

"What about the Brittany ports?"

"To be blunt, we will lay siege and starve them into surrender. All of their fuel, ammunition, and supplies of any kind will be cut off. They will be isolated islands until they surrender. While we know we must deal with those ports and their garrisons, our primary purpose is the advance to Germany."

"We look forward to great things from General Patton."

"We are putting him in his element with the forces he needs. We have high expectations as well. We shall soon see. George is eager to demonstrate what he has been training for all of his professional career. We shall soon see," Ike repeated.

"Excellent. The last two months have been excruciating. It is a relief to be out of those damnable hedgerows finally."

"We are agreed."

Churchill changed the subject and grabbed the single-page message. "As we discussed several weeks ago, the situation in Poland has become critical with the arrival of the Red Army." Eisenhower nodded his head in recognition. "Through the Polish government in exile, His Majesty's Government encouraged the Armia Krajowa, Polish nationalists, under the command of Polish General Count Tadeusz Bór-Komorowski, to take action against the German occupation forces. Komorowski sent this message. Churchill handed the paper to Eisenhower.

CONFIDENTIAL

```
DATE 04 AUG 44 1719 HOURS
FROM HOME ARMY POLAND
TO UK PM
BREAK
AS YOU ENCOURAGED POLISH HOME ARMY ROSE UP
AGAINST NAZI OCCUPATION FORCES BREAK RED ARMY
HALTED ADVANCE AT RIVER VISTULA AND REFUSES TO
ASSIST BREAK WHY THEY STOP BREAK NEED WEAPONS
```

AND AMMUNITION BREAK SITUATION DESPERATE SEND
HELP NOW END

CONFIDENTIAL

"We received that message this morning. I do not know why it took so long to reach my office, but it is clearly an appeal for military support. We know that two *Waffen-S-S* divisions as well as the notorious *S-S-Sturmbrigade Dirlewanger*—that gaggle of wild, bloodthirsty criminals—have been deployed to Warsaw to suppress the Uprising. So, as prime minister, I ask you directly, what can we do?"

Eisenhower nodded his head but did not respond immediately. Instead, he held the prime minister's gaze as he considered Churchill's query. "Prime Minister, with all due respect, my position as supreme commander has not changed. Warsaw and Poland are not in my theater of operations. I have no authority to exceed my command mandate."

"I give you that authority. We have to do something. The Russians are 20 kilometers away and holding back to let the S-S do their dirty work. The S-S animals are killing anyone and everyone regardless of age, gender, or any semblance of humanity to suppress the Uprising."

"Prime Minister, you are placing me in a very tenuous difficult position. However, if you and the president wish to amend my objectives, I stand and remain at your service."

"I have discussed this situation with the president, but we have not discussed amending your objectives."

"Then, that is the first step."

"Ike, we need a strong Polish presence to counter Stalin's apparent intentions to install a pro-Soviet puppet regime in Poland and probably the other Eastern European countries as well. They want the Germans to do their killing for them and eliminate any modicum of Polish nationalism."

"I think we all understand that, Prime Minister. I hold considerable sympathy for the initiative and courage of the Polish resistance. But, if I exceed my mandate, there are no boundaries to personal initiative. I will do my best to execute my orders, but I cannot exceed my orders."

"While I discuss amending your orders, I will ask General Alexander to attempt an aerial resupply to the Polish nationalists."

"Not my theater. Yet, as a military officer and a friend, I would not encourage that action. We have depleted the 15th Army Group for OVERLORD and DRAGOON. We have slowed their offensive operations. If we deplete their resources further, we may well force them into the defensive, unable to carry out offensive operations. My counsel, we must remain focused on defeating Germany as soon as possible."

Churchill shook his head in frustration. He stared and scowled at Eisenhower. "Very well, then. I am headed off tomorrow for talks with Generals Wilson and Alexander. I intend to watch the DRAGOON landings. Get General Patton into open country."

"Good luck, Prime Minister. The 3rd Army is on the verge of turning the corner on the Germans. We'll have him running soon."

Churchill nodded his head and returned to his desk, choosing not even to say goodbye. Eisenhower recognized the sign, stood, and departed.

———

Wednesday, 9.August.1944
Brignoles, Provence-Alpes-Côte d'Azur
France Occupée
09:50 hours

Jedburgh Team JONAS had brought two Firefly field tins each in their packs. Each tin was the size of a small coffee tin with a key attached at the bottom to open the container and held components for four devices—a charge cup, a detonator, and a trigger mechanism. Once assembled and the safety pin pulled, dropped into a fuel tank, the trigger dissolved in gasoline in roughly two hours. The fuse time varied with ambient temperature—hotter-shorter, cooler-longer. Firefly was not designed to explode like a bomb, although they occasionally did so. Instead, they were intended to blow an irreparable hole in the fuel tank and render the vehicle inoperable for at least several weeks, if not longer.

They spent two days training the *Maquis* fighters on assembly and function. They also rehearsed the extraction process to get the *Maquis* soldiers back to the forest and out of harm's way. Their targets were armored vehicles of a leading reconnaissance troop for the 11th *Panzer* Division. Lion had intelligence that the armor division would be deploying from Marseilles east toward the DRAGOON landing beaches. The objective was to cause the division to hesitate just long enough to investigate what happened and what to do about it. Lion did not know D-Day, but they certainly knew some major operation in their area was imminent.

Lion expected his *Maquis* troops to join other Résistance groups into more conventional formations as part of *Forces Françaises de l'Intérieur* (French Forces of the Interior; FFI). Part of the plan and the reason for Diamond's participation was the captured uniform he now wore. He was now in the persona of *SD Sturmbannführer* Hans Klein, complete with a functional *Parabellum-Pistole*

1908 (P08), more commonly known as a Luger for its designer Georg Luger. Diamond and Lion would play captor and arrestee if the situation warranted. For now, they observed the stretch of roadway where they calculated the Firefly devices would activate. They had no idea how many devices were actually inserted, but they hope to see the result soon.

"*Ils sont en retard,*" Lion muttered softly.

"*Oui. Patience. Ils ont peut-être commencé tard.*"

"*Non. Si les Boches sont quelque chose, ils sont pointilleux sur la ponctualité.*"

Lion's frustration with waiting for the as-yet unseen convoy had not bothered Diamond, but he did think, Perhaps the Fireflies activated early. Trevor only nodded his head in agreement. They lay on a thick bed of pine needles under a thicket of conifer trees. Their view was not unobstructed, but it covered several miles. The lead SdKfz 251 *Schützenpanzerwagen* half-track appeared heading east at a comparatively low speed, followed by another, and then the mass of a *Panzerkampfwagen VI* Tiger tank with its formidable 88mm main gun.

"*Ils sont là,*" Diamond whispered.

Another Tiger followed the first one. Their turrets were pointed 45° left and right in readiness. The tank commander sat up in their open hatches. They apparently did not feel an immediate threat. SdKfz 222 *Panzerspähwagen* wheeled armored cars alternated with Mercedes L4500A covered trucks loaded with soldiers. Two Tigers provided a formidable rearguard with their turrets pointed toward the rear left and right. The scouting unit was still moving with no apparent hindrance or particular caution.

Damn! Maybe the Fireflies didn't work.

They watched intently with their binoculars. The convoy moved at a steady but slow pace. They watched with frustrating impotence. Then, as the lead half-track partially disappeared behind the edge of a hill to the east, a waft of smoke rose from underneath the vehicle, but the vehicle kept moving. They watched with considerable interest. The second Tiger lurched to a jerky stop. The turret of the first tank swung around, searching for a target, anticipating an ambush. The turret spun several times but found nothing to engage. Black smoke began to rise behind the hill to the east. All the trucks stopped with large wet spots below them. The fuel on the ground found an ignition source. Fire enveloped the second truck. Soldiers bailed out as fire bloomed and ignited the uniforms of the last few soldiers to make it out. Soldiers in the other trucks and armored cars dismounted, spread out, and took up combat positions as if they were under attack, but no shots were fired. One other truck caught fire. The two functional tanks moved off the road and toward the middle of the column, with one on the north side and the other on the south side.

"*Mission accomplie. On devrait y aller, maintenant,*" Trevor whispered.

Lion nodded his agreement. They crawled backward slowly and as silently as they could manage. The Germans were going to be very angry. It would take some time for them to figure out what had happened to their armor-infantry column, but they would determine what caused the attack. The *Maquis* were confident there would be reprisals if the expected invasion did not divert the attention of the occupiers before they could figure things out and take action.

Their cover story was that Major Klein had noticed unusual behavior and was escorting his captive to Marseilles for questioning. They had a captured *Volkswagen Kübel* staff car stashed a mile away and guarded by a *Maquis* soldier dressed as an SS private.

They returned to the car. The guard and the car had not been disturbed. Lion and Diamond got in the back seat. The guard got behind the wheel and drove away. They needed to get beyond five miles from Brignoles to be outside the likely initial German dragnet to find the attackers of their convoy. Trevor kept the pistol in his lap just in case.

The trio made it back to the cave where the *Kübel* had been stored. Trevor changed out of his German uniform and back into his regular clothes. They had another long march of a couple of hours back to the mountain shack cave. The operators who executed the Firefly attack had made it back to their base ahead of Lion and Diamond.

Lion gathered up the entire group less the guards standing watch in the forest. He recounted what they witnessed at Brignoles. The soldiers cheered despite the risk of their discovery. The debriefing turned into more of a celebration of success than a stoic military debriefing. The agents who inserted the Firefly devices confirmed they had not been able to access two of the tanks. To Trevor's surprise, Lion managed to have a dozen bottles of champagne and ready for consumption. The gathering enjoyed a moment's celebration on a successful mission.

Diamond eventually found a private word with Bolt, as the commander of Jedburgh Team JONAS. "I presume you will have Storm send the mission accomplished confirmation tonight at our assigned window."

"Yes. Zero one fifteen Greenwich."

"Do you need my services further?" asked Trevor.

Thorne thought for a moment. "Fortunately, we didn't need your German language skills for today's mission, but it was encouraging to know you were here and prepared to assist. You've satisfied the task. I'll instruct Storm to add your extraction code."

"Thank you."

"I assume you will depart as soon as we receive confirmation of your extraction."

"That would be wise. It is a long journey to reach that point, and these times don't allow direct transportation."

"Thank you, Trevor. Now, it's probably wise to get some rest after a hectic day."

———

Saturday, 12.August.1944
Villa Rivalta
56 Via Posillipo
Posillipo, Napoli
Regno d'Italia
16:20 hours

Prime Minister Churchill opened the door to greet General Bill Donovan himself. "Welcome back to Italy and Rivalta, Bill."

"Thank you, Prime Minister."

Winston gestured to an open, airy, living room. They walked to a couple of rather pillowy chairs and sat across from each other. "Do I understand correctly that you are here for the same reason as I am?"

Donovan chuckled softly. "I would never be so bold to claim comparability, Prime Minister. I came to witness the DRAGOON landings."

"As am I."

"I'm also in theater to check on my field teams."

"You and Lord Selborne have done well, Bill. I received a rather sparse SOE message on the Jedburgh Team JONAS attack."

"We are still several days away from a proper detailed report. I can fill in perhaps a few more bits." Winston nodded his head. "The Firefly devices apparently worked as designed and intended. The team disabled an entire reconnaissance platoon, except two tanks. The entire action team made good their escape at least an hour ago. We did not receive confirmation until early this morning. The codes that were sent by the team indicate that the Firefly attack was very successful. We don't yet have an exact count, but the code the team sent meant 'very successful.' We'll find out exactly what that means in a few days."

"Well done, Bill."

"There are many other successes both in the north and especially the south. The resistance with Jedburgh assistance seems to be causing hesitancy or lashing out in directions away from the DRAGOON beaches. We should see the results in a few days."

"Excellent." They sat in rare silence for a dozen seconds. "Thank you for making time for me, Bill." Donovan nodded his head. "I understand you are meeting with Tito tomorrow."

"Correct."

Josip Broz was a long-term communist activist and leader of the Communist party in his native Croatia and Yugoslavia in general. He was commonly known as and preferred the moniker, Tito. Broz also led the most successful partisan network in the Balkans. MI6 fostered a relationship with Tito long before the war. The OSS was late to the party, but Donovan had met with Broz several times during his quasi-intelligence years before and during the early years of the war. When the Germans entered Yugoslavia, SOE assumed the lead for encouragement and supply of Yugoslav resistance, and Tito assumed the rank of marshal, having formed the Military Committee of the Communist party of Yugoslavia.

"I'm having him here for dinner tonight in a more social and lubricated environment."

"Your domain, Prime Minister."

"Yes, I suppose it is. Nonetheless, in the light of your meeting tomorrow, I wanted to discuss our approach." Donovan did not respond and only nodded his head in agreement. "We expect he will be accompanied by Brigadier Maclean, our lead SOE agent in Yugoslavia."

Brigadier Fitzroy Hew Royle Maclean, CBE, MP for Lancaster, was a Scottish soldier who had operated with the Special Air Service (SAS) in North Africa in true T.E. Lawrence fashion. His performance brought him to the attention of Lord Selborne and Prime Minister Churchill. Before the war, as a member of the Diplomatic Service, Maclean spent several years in Moscow and witnessed Stalin's purges up close. Churchill appointed Maclean to lead the SOE liaison mission to Yugoslavia.

"You are going to meet with Tito and Maclean at *Il Fortino*?" Churchill asked.

"Yes Sir . . . a nice peaceful secluded safe house."

"I really should visit your villa. What is your purpose?"

"Prime Minister, the United States has no intention of interfering with His Majesty's Government. On the contrary, we have been working with Fitzroy since we joined the fight."

"Sure, sure, I don't dispute our common purpose and intentions, but the president has asked you to assess Tito personally."

"Yes."

"His communist ties are troubling, especially given Stalin's undeclared intentions in Eastern Europe. Tito's partisans have been the most effective Balkan group against the Germans. If we use Tito against the Germans, he will gain strength in Yugoslavia. He wants to keep Yugoslavia united. My sense of the man is that Tito is quite independent-minded. He does not strike me as a Stalin minion, and as long as he maintains his independence and the independence of Yugoslavia, I think we can work with him. There is no doubt he will help us beat the Germans, but the question for us is what happens after the war is won?"

"We all have the same questions, Prime Minister."

"I should have thought of this earlier. Would you like to join us for dinner tonight?"

Donovan considered Churchill's invitation. "With respect, Prime Minister, I don't think that would be a good idea. Broz knows who I am and what I do. You represent the political leadership. He also knows I'm an intelligence officer. I appreciate the invitation and your confidence in me."

Churchill thought for a moment. "Perhaps, you are correct. We can make independent assessments and compare notes." Donovan nodded. "Given the timing with the pending invasion, we'll both be with the fleet. After the forces are ashore and hopefully stabilized, we can meet aboard *Kimberly*."

"We should be able to make that happen. Now, I should be leaving before your dinner guests arrive."

———

Sunday, 13.August.1944
Villa Il Fortino
Via Sopramonte
Isla di Capri, Campania
Regno d'Italia
09:30 hours

One of the OSS front guards entered the living room. "They're here." The man, carrying a Thompson submachine gun hanging on a shoulder strap, did not wait for an acknowledgment. He returned to his duty position. Amalfi Station had assigned an armed guard to remain out of sight on each of the four corners of the villa.

Bill Donovan heard the front door open. He stood to welcome his guests. Amalfi Station Chief Major Alfredo Stephano 'Al' Morelli entered first, followed by Marshal Tito and Brigadier Maclean. Tito was attired in a fresh, well-pressed, grey uniform with ornately embroidered flourishes. Morelli stepped aside. Bill extended his right hand to Tito. "Great to see you again, Marshal Tito."

Donovan had met Josip Broz Tito numerous times during various quasi-intelligence tours during the inter-war years. Bill knew Tito's politics and his ambitions. He also knew Tito's military record during the Great War. Tito was a natural leader, and he inspired loyalty in the men around him.

"You must be Brigadier Maclean," Donovan said to Fitzroy.

"I am indeed. Fitzroy Maclean, General Donovan. I have heard your name so many times. It's an honor to finally meet the man of legend."

"Legend, no, but please, Bill is sufficient."

Donovan nodded to Morelli, who excused himself and went back to the car to wait. The three men dispensed with their social amenities and sat on comfortable chairs and a couch.

"How was your dinner with Prime Minister Churchill?"

"We have growing number of your pilots and aircrew," Tito declared, ignoring Donovan's questions.

"We thank you for collecting, protecting, and caring for them."

"Honor." Tito looked at Fitzroy and spoke in Croat.

"Marshal Tito said they have 55, and they pick up more almost every day."

"What you want us to do with them?"

"We are arranging an extraction." Donovan looked at Maclean. "I understand you have two wounded SOE agents that need to be extracted as well."

"We've contacted Baker Street."

"Lord Selborne didn't mention it when I passed through London. Can they hold on for 10-15 days' time?"

"Yes. They will do what they must do."

"We will add them to the list and try to get to the extraction field sooner." Fitzroy nodded and explained Donovan's statement to Tito.

The marshal nodded his head and smiled. "Good. We ready."

"The aviators are looking at the moon, weather, enemy action and such. We will communicate the details as soon as they are settled."

Tito nodded his head. "Tell me, Bill, do you remember our last meeting in Zagreb?"

Donovan laughed. "Oh my goodness, how could I ever forget! You introduced me to Rakija."

Tito laughed heartily. "There are many factions in Yugoslavia, but Rakija unites us all. You did well with your first taste."

"Yes, I did. Very strong. It is not so easy to find outside of the Balkans."

"After war, I send a case or two."

"Thank you, Josip." Donovan paused for a moment. "Speaking of unity, I must say, President Roosevelt, Prime Minister Churchill, and even Premier Stalin are looking to the post-war years. We are nearing the end of this war. We shall all have to transition to peace, which brings me to my question. What is your vision or intentions for those approaching post-war years?"

Tito smiled. "My answer quite simple—freedom. Well, and unity."

"What does that mean to you?"

Tito smiled more broadly. "To borrow from your country, 'United we stand. Divided we fall.' You know my country rose from the pieces of the Great War. We see today the divisions in Yugoslavia. I want unity for our children, for the future."

"How does Premier Stalin fit into your vision for Yugoslavia?"

"He Georgian. He not even Lenin. He Soviet Union. He not Yugoslav or even Balkan."

"But, you share common beliefs," Donovan commented softly.

"No!" Tito exclaimed with force. "This not correct. We share nothing in common."

"Communism."

"No again. His communism is not my communism. We must be friends, or at least respect each other. I do not want Russians in Balkans any more than Germans."

Donovan paused to assess his position, decided he had enough, and chose to change the subject. "We will make the first deliveries on your list of requirements. The transport aircraft will carry those supplies when they fly in to extract our downed aircrews and evacuation personnel. You will need people and transport to unload the aircraft and move those supplies away from the landing field. The remainder of the supplies will be delivered in the following days to the coastal sites you have provided."

Tito shook his head and looked at Maclean. Fitzroy explained Donovan's statement in Croat. The marshal nodded his head and smiled. "We ready."

"We shall endeavor to meet your future requirements as well."

Maclean added, "Please excuse us, General Donovan. The marshal has a scheduled luncheon with Field Marshal Alexander in Naples, and we must be on our way."

As the three leaders said their goodbyes, Major Morelli reappeared. He would take the marshal and brigadier across the bay to Naples in one of the OSS high-speed motor launches.

———

Tuesday, 15.August.1944
HMS Kimberly
43° 18' North - 6° 41' East
Off Saint-Tropez, Provence-Alpes-Côte d'Azur
Golfe de Saint-Tropez, France Occupée
08:30 hours

The naval gunfire bombardment and initial waves of assault troops of the U.S. VI Corps had gone well. Operation DRAGOON had begun to land the lead elements of the 7th Army across French Riviera beaches from Cap Nègre to Pont des Trayas, just to the west of Cannes. Also part of the invasion force was the Free French 'B' Army. The DRAGOON objectives were the liberation of Southern France, driving north up the Rhone River valley, and joining the 12th Army Group. The supreme commander needed the port facilities of Marseilles to enhance the OVERLORD logistics capacity.

Prime Minister Churchill had been on the starboard bridge since dawn with binoculars, observing the landing of the 45th Infantry Division at Delta Beach. Lieutenant Commander James Wolferstan Rylands, RN, the captain of *Kimberley*, joined the prime minister and said, "Excuse me, Sir. General Donovan has arrived from *Tuscaloosa*."

"Thank you, Captain. Please show him to the bridge." Rylands turned to satisfy Churchill's request. "Wait. We may need to use your stateroom, if you've no objection."

"As you wish, Prime Minister." Churchill nodded, and Rylands departed.

Several minutes later, Bill Donovan appeared on the bridge wing. "Good morning, Prime Minister. So far, so good."

"It is indeed a good morning, Bill. These operations never cease to fascinate me, like watching a massive ballet play out before us." Both men stood at the railing, observing the myriad activities and movements toward the beaches while they talked.

"Quite so."

"Can we talk here, Bill?"

Donovan looked around, above and below the small bridge wing. "It appears safe enough."

"Excellent. What have you?"

"As we discussed in Naples, the Jedburgh teams in the area were quite successful. Some of the disabled or burned-out armored vehicles remain on the Brignoles Road west of town. The report I received last night indicated that the Firefly devices worked better than designed. The Germans tried to repair two half-track vehicles but abandoned the effort probably because they determined it was not worth the effort. Instead, they used a Tiger tank to push the hulks off the road and clear it."

"Well done, Bill."

"Thank you, Sir. I received a decrypt just before I departed for *Kimberley* this morning. O-B West informed Army Group 'G' that reinforcements would not be available since they were required for Normandy. He would have to make do with the forces he had."

Oberbefehlshaber im Westen (OB West), high commander in the West, commanded Army Groups B, D, G, H, and *Panzer* Group West. *Generalfeldmarschall* Gerd von Rundstedt had been OB West since 1942, but he was replaced by *Generalfeldmarschall* Günther von Kluge in July, when von Rundstedt failed to push back the Allied invasion exceeding Hitler's threshold of tolerance and advocated for surrender after the counter-offensive failed. *Generaloberst* Johannes Albrecht Blaskowitz served as the commander of Army Group 'G' in South France, and reported to von Kluge.

Churchill asked, "Have you detected any reinforcements heading toward France, north or south, or Italy?"

"Nothing out of the ordinary. In fact, there is less movement than usual, which probably indicates the Germans have curtailed normal rotations or leaves. The OB West message further suggests the Germans are stretched thin."

"I haven't been to the Map Room since yesterday. What is the latest on the counter-offensive they began on the 6th?"

"As of this morning, the Germans have 13 frontline armor and infantry divisions that are contained on three sides and in danger of being encircled between Falaise and Argentan. Some units have moved east, but the bulk of their force remains in frontal combat. We have no direct evidence as yet, but it appears they are going to fight to the end."

"That will do nicely."

"Quite so, and the 3rd Army continues to pour through the Avranches gap."

"Into open country."

"Yes. Patton's terrain."

"Closing the Falaise Gap on the German counter-offensive should help the 21st Army Group finally break out of the Caen containment."

"I would think so, and I do believe that it's General Eisenhower's view as well."

"Excellent. Field Marshal Wilson is expected back aboard *Kimberly* for lunch. Can you stay for lunch?"

Donovan glanced at his wristwatch. "I'm afraid not. In fact, the launch is waiting for me. A destroyer will take me about 20 miles out for a transfer to a Catalina. I'm headed to India, China and Australia."

"MacArthur."

"Yes. President Roosevelt approved his campaign to retake the Philippines, and we are trying to give him the intelligence to help the effort."

"I take it he is not receptive?"

"That is perhaps an understatement. He is very territorial, and he has never supported the O-S-S, but we keep trying to win him over."

"Are you taking the Catalina all of that distance?"

Donovan chuckled softly. "No Sir. That would take way too long. I've got a Constellation configured with a large auxiliary fuel tank—a very fast and comfortable aircraft. We'll stop in Samoa between Australia and Hawaii. I will meet with Admiral Nimitz before returning to Washington."

"Best be on your way, Bill. Thank you for the chat. It's always a pleasure."

Donovan saluted and departed. Churchill took a short break from his witnessing to watch Bill Donovan board the launch and head directly for an American destroyer.

———

Wednesday, 16.August.1944
Zeitz, Halle-Merseburg
Deutsches Reich
11:30 hours

The sole target below the 390th Bomb Group was a major synthetic oil plant operating in the outskirts of the city—Mission 175. The plant was owned and operated by *Braunkohle Benzin Aktiengesellschaft*, a consortium formed in 1933 with chemical company I.G. Farben to convert lignite coal into various synthetic oil products—high octane aviation fuel, diesel fuel, gasoline, lubricants, and paraffin wax. *Braunkohle Benzin AG* was often referred to by the acronym contraction of its name—*Brabag*.

One of the heavy bomber squadrons over Zeitz was the 569th Bomb Squadron, which was one of the 390th Bomb Group's four B-17 heavy bomber squadrons, all of which displayed a large Square J symbol on their vertical stabilizers. The 390th Bomb Group was part of the 13th Combat Bombardment Wing, 8th Bomber Command, 8th Air Force.

The 390th Bomb Group had taken off from Station B-153, the former RAF Framlingham located southeast of Framlingham, Suffolk, England, earlier in the morning. They generally had favorable weather and conducive thin clouds in the vicinity of the target. Their bombing run altitude was Angels 21—21,000 feet.

The Group's fighter escort kept the German fighters occupied and away from the bomber formation. Fortunately, they had not encountered any of the new German high-speed interceptors. Instead, the bomber formation had to deal with moderate-level flak bursts. The anti-aircraft fire damaged 88 of the bombers that day. One bomber, a Boeing B-17F Flying Fortress, serial number 42-29962 with the nose art name Dottie III, took a nasty hit that took out the Number 1 engine, causing a serious fire on the left wing. The crew could not maintain formation position, lost altitude, and flew erratically as they grappled with the damage and the threat. Finally, pilot First Lieutenant Robert M. 'Bob' Buckley ordered the crew to bail out.

From that moment, each member of the crew focused on their parachute and dropping out of their assigned egress hatches from the stricken aircraft.

Among the Dottie III crew that had to bail out on that Wednesday was Navigator First Lieutenant John W 'Jack' Stearns, USAAF, the maternal uncle of Dr. John W 'Jack' Rutherford, PhD (Aeronautical Engineering), an accomplished aeronautical engineer and colleague of the author at McDonnell Douglas Helicopter Company, now part of the Boeing Company. The Zeitz mission was Stearn's 26th combat mission, and he was wounded in the right hand by shrapnel from the flak shell burst. The crew made it out of the crippled aircraft except for Tail Gunner Staff Sergeant Herbert W. Harms, USAAF.

Angry armed farmers and soldiers waited for each crew member to land. The Americans were immediately captured, collected, and rendered to the POW camp *Stalag Luft III*, halfway between Berlin and Breslau, Poland, the same camp that was the site of the Great Escape on the night of 27/28. March.1944. As the Red Army advanced on the camp around Christmas, the Germans evacuated the prisoners and guards to *Stalag 7A*, an army POW camp at Moosburg, near München. Units of the U.S. 14th Armor Division finally freed the Dottie III aircrew along with 27,000 other Allied POWs at *Stalag 7A* on 29.April.1945. Jack Stearns arrived in New York City by ship and made his way home to San Diego, California.

Readers are encouraged to visit the 390th Memorial Museum located in Tucson, Arizona.

———

Thursday, 17.August.1944
Observation Post 417
Casali, Lazio
Regno d'Italia
10:50 hours

After returning to Naples from the DRAGOON landings, Prime Minister Churchill wanted to see the remains of the Monte Cassino Abbey. The advance of the 15th Army Group had been stalled since 2.December.1943 at the Gustav Line that was anchored by the German occupation of Monte Cassino. The Operation SHINGLE landings at Anzio in January failed to break the Gustav Line defenders. Allied commanders eventually approved the aerial bombardment of the Abbey. The initial air raid was carried out on the 15th of February and another bombardment a month later. The Gustav Line finally broke on the 18th of May, and the 15th Army Group advanced north, taking Rome on the 4th of June. Elements of the 5th Army took the historic city of Florence on the 11th of August, and the Allied Armies in Italy were preparing to assault the German Gothic Line south of Bologna.

Prime Minister Churchill and Field Marshal Alexander drove north from the Caserta headquarters in an American Jeep with two half-tracks armed with 50-caliber machine guns and a squad of troops each. The road and observation post at the hilltop south of the Liri Valley had not been used in months. Grass and other vegetation had grown, reclaiming the ground. At the disused post, the troops deployed to secure the site.

With the picturesque Liri Valley, even with the ravages of war before and below them, Churchill and Alexander raised their binoculars, looking across the valley to Monte Cassino.

"My God," Churchill exclaimed. "What a tragic scene! I visited the Abbey before the war. It was a magnificent building, glorious views, and a place of peace, tranquility, and contemplation. Now, it is nothing more than a pile of stone rubble."

"It is a horrible tragedy, but it had to be done."

"The necessity makes it no less tragic. I hope we can find the means to rebuild the Abbey back to its former glory. Can we go there?"

"No Sir. Since we took the Abbey, we have had a combined engineer company clearing the mines and unexploded ordnance to save the mountain. Unfortunately, they have yet to rebuild even a makeshift road to the summit."

"Well, then, perhaps we can ask the pilots to make a low pass or two over the mountain on the flight north to overfly Monte Cassino before turning west for his return to England."

"I think that can be arranged," Alexander responded.

Churchill returned his binoculars to his eyes and gazed at the demolished Abbey across the valley. Then, without taking his eyes off the Abbey, Winston said, "For six months, that perch held up two Allied armies." Alexander did not react. "In the three months since that mountain was finally cleared of Germans, the Allied Armies in Italy have marched north nearly to the Po River and liberated Rome and Florence."

"All true, Prime Minister."

"Humph," Winston grunted as he lowered his binoculars. The prime minister turned, stepped toward the Jeep, and said gruffly, "I've seen as much as I can from here. Let's get to the aircraft so I can get closer."

Churchill, Alexander, and their security entourage loaded up and headed down the hill. They drove south directly to Marcianise Airfield, built by the U.S. Army Corps of Engineers in 1943 to service Allied Forces Headquarters at Reggia di Caserta.

The Avro York C Mark I VIP transport aircraft known as Ascalon was ready, and the crew was standing by when the prime minister arrived. Churchill walked directly to the cockpit and informed the pilot of his requirements. Then, the crew began the process of bringing the large four-engine aircraft alive for flight.

———

Friday, 18.August.1944
USAAF Station F-356
Saffron Walden, Essex, England
United Kingdom
16:10 hours

The mission debriefing had taken much longer than normal, even for Brian. The 4FG had been one of four fighter groups escorting several bomber groups in a concentrated area bombing mission against a BMW aircraft engine plant at Berlin-Spandau, Germany. Nominally, the mission was similar to other missions in the vicinity of Berlin, but this one was quite different for the 4FG.

In the serious defense of Berlin, the mission bombers and fighters faced several squadrons of Me262 Swallow twin-jet engine fighters and a squadron of Me163 Comet rocket-propelled fighters. It was the first encounter for the 4FG, although reports of engagement by the revolutionary German aircraft had been accumulating since March with 8th Air Force G-2 Intelligence. Consequently, the debriefer asked a rather long list of relevant questions regarding the 4FG experience and insisted on extracting every detail he could from Brian.

When Brian returned to the 334FS Operations building, the main briefing room was a cacophony of noise, with roughly two-thirds of the squadron pilots present and embroiled in storytelling, discussions, and debate. Brian smiled and nodded to Sergeant Ellison. Then, he went to 'his' chair.

"What do you think, Major?" asked Corn.

"About what?"

"The only thing we're talking about since we got back . . . those new German fighters."

"They're very impressive," Hunter responded succinctly. He leaned his chair back against the wall.

"No, no!" exclaimed Stove. "Not this time, Major. Stay with us."

"Yeah, Hunter," added Second Lieutenant John Henry 'Jack' Jarvis of Austin, Texas. "You've got more combat experience than anyone else in the squadron, including the Skipper. None of us thinks any of us hit any one of those jets and rocketplanes, and they clearly got through our screen, dropping several of the bombers."

Brian grounded his chair. "Those new machines are very fast."

"Yeah, but what are we going to do about them?" Jack pressed.

"They are still aircraft flown by pilots. I didn't get the correct lead, but our bullets are faster than their aircraft. We'll learn how to fight them. The Comets get one pass, and they give us a clear flight path with that smoke trail from the rocket motor. We need to get some bullets in his face when he arcs over and begins his dive on the bombers. If we can disrupt his aim on his run at the bombers, then he's done. He doesn't get a second chance."

"How do we do that?" Corn asked.

"I didn't get an opportunity to try this, but if we can catch them as they are arcing over for their dive on the bombers, we can pull up and get off a few bursts before we run out of airspeed."

"That would leave us vulnerable," Pile commented.

"Yep . . . but not for long," Hunter added.

"Pretty risky," said Pile.

"Yep, again, but we've got to get guns on those bastards. We know where he's going. They seem to have a very predictable flight path, which means we can anticipate where they are going to be. It's all timing. I got a few shots," Brian continued, "but I was way behind him."

"What about the jets?" asked Rocket.

"I got off a few shots on those that passed through my area, but again, I was behind them," Brian answered. "We certainly can't chase them. Both are far faster than our Mustangs."

"How about catching them when they are landing?" Swede queried.

"Probably have regular fighters to protect the area when they have to slow for landing," responded Rocket.

"Hey, fellas, let's not forget our primary task on those missions is protecting the bombers. We cannot leave them until we know they are clear and safe."

"True," Swede added.

Arnie came out of his office. "Everyone done with their debriefing?"

"Yeah, Skipper," replied Rolo. "I'm the last."

"Very well, then. I'm sure this debate will go on for some time, so we're released. Let's go have a beer before supper."

Cheers and exclamations of approval added to the sounds of those pilots who had not doffed their flight gear. The squadron pilots and comrades from their sister squadrons filled the bar to standing room only. Hand gestures of recounted engagements and imagined future encounters kept the occupants in constant motion. There were nearly shouted verbal exchanges as the group of fighter pilots considered what had happened and how they might deal with future fights with these new German aircraft.

The energy of the excited pilots dampened somewhat during their evening meal but returned to full vigor as they returned to the bar after dinner. These were indeed challenging times.

The pilots learned that the restricted zone and telephone connections into or out of the restricted zone had been lifted and telephone service restored on the 31st of July. Brian wanted a shower and sleep, but it had been almost a month since he heard Charlotte's voice.

Brian took an open booth and gave the operator the number he knew by heart. Although their sortie rate remained higher than any semblance of normal, the telephonic services were returning to normal. The connection was made in short order.

"I love you," Brian said once he heard Charlotte answer the telephone.

Charlotte giggled. "You are so sweet."

"Not as sweet as you. It's been a very long, busy day, but I needed to hear your voice before I take a shower and get off to bed. I'm very tired."

"I'm all too willing to give you my voice, darling. It may have been a difficult day, of which you can't tell me over the telephone, but you are home safely, and that is what means to the most to me."

"Yes, I am. Anything new on the Home Front?"

"Everything is boringly normal. Nothing new from the States."

"Well, I guess that is good news."

"My sweet, you sound dreadfully tired. Thank you so much for your call. I am sated. Now, I want you to get off to bed."

"Yes, Ma'am. I love you. Have a good night."

They disconnected. Brian took a nice hot shower, took care of his nightly hygiene, and jumped into bed. He knew there was no hope of reading his book.

———

Tuesday, 29.August.1944
Avenue des Champs-Élysées
Paris, Île-de-France
Liberated France
13:30 hours

The 28th Infantry Division was chosen to march in the celebration parade. The entire 15,000-man 28th Infantry Division paraded down the length of the famous Parisian boulevard. Of course, General de Gaulle felt compelled to lead the procession—the victorious conqueror after all.

Among the 28ID soldiers that marched to celebrate the liberation of Paris was Staff Sergeant Herbert Davis Parlier, USA, the author's paternal uncle.

On the 1st of August, *General der Infanterie* Dietrich Hugo Hermann von Choltitz was promoted, and on the 7th, he was appointed as the military governor of Paris. He was often referred to as "The Crusher of Cities"—Rotterdam, Sevastopol, and now Paris. Events moved swiftly despite German resistance. The breakout of the Allied forces from the Normandy beachhead began on the 25th of July. The Falaise Pocket collapsed on the 21st of August. General Choltitz disobeyed Hitler's direct order and surrendered the Paris garrison on the 25th, despite the reprisals well underway in the wake of the July 20th assassination attempt on Hitler.

Operation OVERLORD was declared complete and closed on 30.August.1944. The Allies were firmly ashore. Nevertheless, the march to Germany and Berlin continued.

—

Wednesday, 30.August.1944
No.10 Annexe
New Public Offices
Whitehall, London, England
United Kingdom
19:30 hours

General Eisenhower was the prime minister's only guest for dinner this night. He was shown into the prime minister's small dining room.

"Pardon me for not standing," Churchill said and extended his right hand. The two men shook hands. Winston gestured to the seat beside him. "I took the liberty of pouring you a Johnny Walker Red."

"Thank you, Sir. How are you feeling, Prime Minister? I understand you've been ill."

"Yes, a touch of pneumonia, my nemesis, I'm afraid. Lord Moran has been a bit of a stickler, keeping me in bed all day, but I refused to be dissuaded from this discussion."

"I do bring good news. The 3rd Army continues to push hard east of Paris and the Seine. The 21st Army Group has crossed the Seine. Monty's and my forward headquarters remain in the vicinity of Caen, but we are preparing the move forward. This morning, with the ongoing logistics plan working well, although under considerable stress, I closed the OVERLORD plan. I must say General Patton's 3rd Army is challenging our logistics capacity. We need a substantial port much farther east than Mulberry 'B,' but Patton is doing what he does best—our *blitzkrieg* in German parlance. They've reached Verdun. They will make an attempt to take it quickly, but if not, they will bypass and isolate the German garrison."

"Good news, indeed. I've not been to the Map Room for several days now. I also must inform you, my dear Ike, that we will promote Monty to field marshal effective on the first. Others will follow shortly."

"And, I must inform you that I am taking command of the A-E-F ground forces also effective on the first so that Monty can focus on the 21st Army Group operations. Once the order is issued, Monty and Brad will report directly to me."

"Is that wise, Ike?"

"Yes Sir. It is essential. The 21st Army Group is falling behind the 12th Army Group. And, to be candid, I need to eliminate some friction that is counter-productive."

"As you wish, Ike. You are and shall remain the supreme commander."

"I can also report that General Patch and the 7th Army have captured Toulon, Marseilles and are advancing nicely to the north. We will transfer the 7th Army to SHAEF once the link-up has occurred or is imminent."

"You mentioned earlier that Patton has reached Verdun." Eisenhower nodded his head. "That puts them within striking distance of the German frontier."

The two leaders paused their conversation when dinner was served. They managed several bites of the fillet of sole, au gratin potatoes, and fresh asparagus. The stewards completed their service and departed, leaving the two war leaders alone again.

"The problem we face is the extraordinarily long lines of communications," Eisenhower continued. "Virtually all the combat supplies for the 12th Army Group are being off-loaded at Cherbourg. The 12th Army Group requirement is 14,000 tons per day of food, water, ammunition, and fuel. We're currently managing only 7,000 tons per day. We've moved every truck company we have to France to move these essential supplies forward. Now, we've added on 2,400 tons to feed Paris. As a result, we have been operating at dreadfully low levels of on-hand fuel and ammunition, and we may well have to pull Patton up rather than allow his tanks to run out of fuel."

"The professional German military officers know they are done," Churchill observed. "The evidence continues to mount. Some of them recognized that reality after Stalingrad in January of '43, but all of them saw the truth after the collapse of the Falaise Pocket. But that damn corporal will not let it end. I am certain you will solve the problem, Ike, which brings me to Germany. You've endured me saying it many times. We must meet the Soviets as far east as possible, and definitely, beat them to Berlin . . . not just to end the war in Europe but also to set the post-war peace. I fear Stalin will be just another conqueror rather than a liberator. If we are not aggressive and at the same time careful, we may well trade one war for another."

"We do not want that."

"No, we don't. We need to keep pushing."

"We will, Prime Minister, but we must never forget that a tank without fuel is just a big lump of steel that cannot do anything other than look menacing."

"True. We shan't allow that to happen," Winston proclaimed.

Eisenhower nodded his head. "The XXX Corps is across the Seine with the 11th Armor in the vanguard and Guards Armor, and they are advancing nicely. The Canadian I Corps is crossing the Seine near the river's mouth as we speak. We should have LeHavre soon, but their port facilities are limited, useful, yes, but limited, and won't be operational until we get the Germans pushed back beyond artillery range."

"That will help, but we really need Antwerp. Monty will get there. We'll take Antwerp one way or another.

"Resupply will be substantially better with Antwerp. Monty knows speed is of the essence to not give the Germans time to destroy any of the port facilities. Winter is coming. We will not reach Berlin before winter sets in, which means our troops will also have to fight the weather as well through to spring."

Churchill laid his utensils at the 4:30 position on his plate with the unfinished meal and pushed the plate away from him. Eisenhower did the same. "May I interest you in an after-dinner cognac?"

"Perhaps a short one."

"I must ask you to pour since Lord Moran has insisted on my immobility under his strenuous objection to my leaving the bed for this meal and conversation." Churchill frowned, shook his head, and pointed to the cabinet.

Two brandy snifters were on the cabinet. Eisenhower found the bottle of Hine Cognac he knew was Churchill's favorite. He poured three fingers for Churchill and barely one finger for himself.

Winston raised his glass. "To your continued success on the battlefield, Ike."

"Hear, hear, and to your health and swift recovery, Winston."

"Thank you, Ike. Lord Moran will get me back to peak health, of that I am certain."

The activities of their children in uniform and in service occupied their conversation through the general's brandy. They both enjoyed a little laughter recounting their antics in cajoling their children to produce grandchildren. Winston had a head start, but their shared experience of fatherhood was another common thread between the two leaders.

—

Chapter 10

The great tragedy of Science—
the slaying of a beautiful hypothesis by an ugly fact.
-- Thomas Henry Huxley

Wednesday, 6.September.1944
Standing Oak Farm
Winchester, Hampshire, England
United Kingdom
16:10 hours

Rosemary Kensington had arrived in the afternoon, spent the day with Charlotte, and would depart in the morning. She insisted upon bringing the news personally. Tomorrow, Rose would return to Carlingon Castle, Northumberland, to give the news to her parents personally as well.

"I am so happy for you, Rose. I know this is something you have wanted for quite a while now."

"I have you to thank, Charlotte. It would not have happened without your consent and support."

"I didn't do anything."

"Modesty and humility are attractive traits, but I meant what I said. None of this," Rose said, patting her lower abdomen, "would have occurred without your consent."

"Thank you for that. I'm just glad we could help. Now, it is that time of day and somewhat of a tradition. Since this is a farm, would you like to milk a cow? No requirement, just a friendly offer."

"That would be great."

"Ian and Todd are getting pretty good at squeezing a teat or two, but their attention span is fairly short."

"That would be fun just to watch."

"OK, then. I'd better call Brian and leave him a message. I've no idea when we might hear from him, but I'll feel better knowing that we tried."

"Sure."

Charlotte called the number she knew by heart. She left a short message with the mess corporal who answered the Officer's Mess telephone. She also made sure to ask the corporal to write on the note that everything was fine, and that she had good news from Rose.

Charlotte then called upstairs to let Edith know it was milking time. The boys recognized the term. Their screeches and heavy footsteps foretold their excitement. Todd was almost four, and Ian was passed his third birthday.

Edith joined them to shepherd the boys when they exceeded their capacity to focus. Both boys had been milking for six months. Neither one had yet made it through a full udder, but they still seemed to enjoy the process and participation.

Rosemary had more fun watching the boys but still managed to milk three cows before the crew had the remainder of the herd on the machines. Edith herded the boys back to the house to clean up for dinner. Rosemary and Charlotte returned to the house to clean up as well. Rosemary joined in the preparations of the evening meal. They were ahead of the crew.

"So, Mary and her children stayed with you?" Rosemary asked as they prepared the table for a country dinner.

"Yes, for two months. They returned home in early August. The craziness of the invasion preparations and the doodlebug attacks convinced her it was safer out here than in Harrow. It was a treasure to have them here. Malcolm and the boys became quite the knot."

"I'm so glad you could do that and enjoy that time together."

"It was a difficult time with all the invasion activity, but it was a delight to spend time with Mary and the children. We had no children here for so many years, but for those two months, we had a house full. I asked her to stay, but she insisted she had been away too long already."

"The buzz bomb attacks are still going on, are they not?"

"Yes, they are, but she was convinced she was safe enough in Harrow. I imagine she will be . . ."

The crew entered. Dinner was ready, and they had a team to feed. Horace reported that the afternoon's dairy products were loaded and ready for delivery this evening.

Laughter and joyousness filled the house. The boys provided the entertainment, as always. The meals at Standing Oak Farm felt very much like family affairs. Even Rosemary noted the mood. Horace, Lionel, and Jacob thanked everyone for the delicious meal, excused themselves, and headed into town for the evening delivery.

After the dishes, utensils, pots, and pans were cleaned up, dried, and put away, Charlotte considered escorting Rosemary to the bench under the big oak tree, but they were still waiting for Brian's call. It was unusually warm for being on the backside of summer in England, but it was still too warm for a fire. Charlotte asked just enough questions to keep Rosemary talking about her medical practice, which was dominated by treating battlefield wounds and injuries. They were interrupted only by goodnights and sweet dreams for Todd and Ian. Rosemary hugged and kissed the boys as well. Charlotte kept Rosemary talking until the telephone rang. Charlotte nodded to Rosemary, who smiled and shook her head. Charlotte stood and went to the telephone on the small table.

"Winchester 4-3-7-9." Charlotte waited for the go-ahead. "No, no problem. Everything is fine. Yes, good news." She listened. "Rose is here." "Spending the night." "Talking." Charlotte smiled. She turned to face Rosemary and held out the telephone handset. Rosemary shook her head. Charlotte smiled more broadly and shook the handset at Rosemary, who shook her head, huffed and puffed, and stood to take the handset from Charlotte.

"Hello," Rose said. "Yes, it's me." "I'm pregnant." "Yes, I'm sure, you twiddle. I received medical confirmation two days ago, and I just had to come to Charlotte." "I know. I am grateful beyond description to both you and Charlotte for your graciousness, generosity, and compassion. Thank you so very much, Brian." "No, I've not told anyone else. Charlotte was the first. You were second. I leave tomorrow morning for Carlingon to inform my parents." "No, not yet. I'll tell him when I see him." "Yes, you're welcome to tell him if you see him or Linda before I do." "Thank you again, Brian." Rosemary listened for a few seconds and then held the handset for Charlotte.

"Yes, my darling. Pretty good news, don't you think?" "Congratulations, my love." "How was your day?" Charlotte listened as Brian informed her of the squadron's long and costly day. "Get some sleep, my love. Please, please, be safe." "I will." "Good night. I love you," Charlotte said softly and placed the handset back in the cradle. She gestured for them to return to the chairs.

"I can't tell you enough how grateful I am, Charlotte."

The lady of the house smiled. "I understand that, Rose. I'm glad we could help. How do you think your parents are going to respond?"

"They will not be happy that I chose to bear a child out of wedlock, but at the end of the day, they will be overjoyed to have another grandchild."

"How will you manage your medical career?"

Rosemary smiled softly. "The same way you do."

"Yes, of course. So, you intend to continue your medical practice with the burdens of motherhood."

"Yes."

"Will you breastfeed your infant?"

"That's the plan . . . unless I can find a wet nurse I like. It's going to be tricky. I know that. And there are probably myriad elements of everyday life that I've not considered or resolved. But I've spent a lot of time thinking about this pregnancy. I'm sure I will have moments of doubt as to the wisdom of this decision, but I'm convinced it's right for me."

The women talked and shared into the wee hours of the morning in the nearly dark house. Charlotte offered to build a fire more for ambiance than heat, but neither wanted additional warmth. Instead, they laughed and enjoyed each other's company.

—

Friday, 8.September.1944
Cabinet War Rooms
New Public Offices
Whitehall, London, England
United Kingdom
21:30 hours

The War Cabinet and Defense Committee, plus Duncan Sandys as chairman of the CROSSBOW Committee, gathered in the closed door, classified conference room. The prime minister chose not to notify the support staff due to the late hour and the unscheduled meeting.

"Let us hop to it," Prime Minister Churchill declared and induced instant quiet. "Herbert, your report, if you please. What do we know?"

"Three hours ago, people in West London heard a sharp double boom. The evidence we have so far strongly suggests it was a V2 rocket. The missile impacted in Chiswick near the junction of Staveley Road and Burlington Lane, killing three people instantly, including a three-year-old girl." Churchill lowered his head, and a pronounced scowl creased his face. "Eleven houses were completely destroyed and another 15 seriously damaged. The missile left a deep crater 30 feet across."

"Both British and American radar picked up the launch," interjected Secretary of State for Air Sir Archibald Henry Macdonald 'Archie' Sinclair, Bart, Kt, CMG, PC, MP for Caithness and Sutherland, and 4th Baronet of Ulbster. Churchill gestured for the rest of the story. "The Air Intelligence Branch took the radar data and calculated the launch site was from near Wassenaar in Holland. The photo recce units will launch shortly after dawn tomorrow to survey the area. Bomber Command has been placed on alert for a short notice mission if we can locate the site."

"Excellent. Press the counter-battery fire to the fullest extent of our capability. Try not to involve innocent civilians."

"As you know, Prime Minister," added Field Marshal Brooke, "we have overrun and captured numerous launch sites and equipment from Cherbourg to Belgium. I should also report that Brussels and now Antwerp were liberated by the 11th Armored Division. The Germans abandoned both cities without a fight. They are putting up minimal resistance across the 21st Army Group area. We are seeing signs they are withdrawing behind the Siegfried Line in front of the 12th Army Group, where they may make their stand. Wassenaar is on the coast between Rotterdam and Amsterdam, and the vanguard of our ground forces is roughly 30 miles away. They shall not have that launch site much longer."

"All well and good, Brookie, but they can launch . . . ," Churchill looked at Sandys, "How fast can they launch these monsters?"

"Our current analysis indicates they have the potential to launch a V2 every 15 minutes from the same launcher if they have assembled rockets and sufficient fuel on hand. The rocket uses liquid oxygen as the oxidizer for the ethanol fuel. Liquid oxygen is very cold, requiring special handling equipment and procedures. They fuel the missile after it is erected on the launch stand. It is not a simple process. They cannot just stand the missile up and fire it. Practically speaking, we think one or two per day, firing from the same launcher, is more likely."

"Surely, they have more than one launcher," Attlee said.

"Yes, they most assuredly do. We've overrun dozens of sites so far, and the launcher that hit Chiswick is still ahead of us."

"They apparently overshot their target," commented Churchill.

"We do not know what their target was," Sandys replied.

"London."

"Yes Sir. I am only reflecting on the technical details. We have known for some time now that they intended to hit London. I am only stating that the scientists and engineers have not yet determined the accuracy of the guidance system. We assume they intended to hit London Center, but we do not know for certain."

"Understood," Churchill responded. "We must not allow the Germans to know where these one-ton bullets landed."

"Already done," Morrison immediately answered. "The Press has been informed that the explosion heard by many within five miles of the impact was a gas main explosion, which is not entirely wrong since the warhead ruptured a gas main."

"Fine. That story will work for a few of these things, but it will not work for all. The Home Office must devise other explanations for these explosions. There will be more."

"We are working on that aspect," Morrison responded. "The newspapers understand the importance of not confirming any impact for the Germans through our open Press. They understand. They are protecting the people and themselves."

"Please stay on top of it, Herbert. I would like your report on this strike as soon as it is available. Now, Brookie, you know the importance of Antwerp. When can we use the undamaged port facilities?"

"The Canadian 1st Army is on the left flank and clearing the coastal areas. They are working to clear the Beveland peninsula, and they must take Walcheren Island. In essence, we must secure both sides of the entire estuary before access to the Antwerp port facilities is safe for general operations."

"How long?" Churchill asked with irritation in his voice.

"I understand and appreciate your frustration, Prime Minister. This is difficult terrain, low-lying ground prone to flooding, marshy in places. Assault forces must cross multiple defended waterways. As of this morning, General Simonds's estimate is six weeks."

"Unacceptable. We need Antwerp today."

"We have Antwerp."

Churchill slammed his open palm on the table. "Damn it, Brookie. Antwerp does us no good if we do not have unfettered access to those port facilities. The supplies for the 12th and 21st Army Groups are stretched dreadfully thin. We're on the verge of halting offensive operations, especially for the 3rd Army without supplies. We barely manage half of the daily requirements, and all of those supplies must travel hundreds of miles to reach the combat units. We must clear the Scheldt sooner." The River Scheldt runs from France, through Belgium, and empties into the North Sea in the Netherlands. The key Belgian port city of Antwerp grew from Roman times at the head of the Scheldt Estuary, which controls access to the city. It was even more important in these troubled times.

"I will discuss the problem with Ike and Monty."

"As will I at my first opportunity. Is there anything else?" Churchill looked around the room. No one spoke. "We've had enough punishment for one evening. We are adjourned."

———

Monday, 11.September.1944
Headquarters, Special Operations Executive
No.64 Baker Street
Marylebone, London, England
United Kingdom
09:00 hours

Trevor sat alone patiently in the minister's conference room. He knew the meeting was with Lord Selborne because of the location, but he had not been informed of the subject or the attendees. They had already debriefed the JONAS mission, so Trevor was reasonably certain that was not the subject. perhaps they had a new task for him.

The first to join Trevor was Director of Operations and Training Major General Colin McVean Gubbins, CMG, DSO, MC. They exchanged pleasantries and nothing more. Lord Selborne entered less than a minute later, followed by Stanislaus 'Blocker' Pordonski.

Andersen had known and worked with the former colonel in the polish secret police until the Germans and Soviets overran and divvied up Poland.

Blocker had served with SOE since arriving in England. Diamond and Blocker had run several covert missions before the war. The most important was the capture of the current version of the German Enigma encryption device.

Trevor had not seen Stan since late 1940. They both had been very busy. Stan had successfully conducted several covert operations in his native Poland for the SOE.

"I recognize that you two glorious field agents haven't seen each other in several years," Selborne said, "but we really need to get this meeting started." Diamond and Blocker sat across the conference table from Selborne and Gubbins. "To ensure we're all on the same note, permit me to recount a few relevant facts. First, at the urging of the Polish government in exile, His Majesty's Government encouraged the Home Army . . ."

"*Armia Krajowa*," Pordonski interjected.

"Yes, the A-K led by General Count Tadeusz Bór-Komorowski."

"A good man, very capable," Stan added.

"I do not know the general, but I certainly trust your judgment. The A-K initiated numerous attacks on German forces in Warsaw on the 1st of August in anticipation of linking up with the Red Army, which had advanced to the Vistula south of the city. However, the Reds decided they needed to rest and resupply, so they pulled up and refused to assist the A-K."

"Fucking Communists," Pordonski muttered.

"You are not alone in that sentiment, Stanislaus. The government received the initial pleas for assistance from General Komorowski a month ago. There have been subsequent requests as well. General Eisenhower has not released the 8th or 9th Air Forces since Warsaw is outside his area of operations and beyond his charter. Prime Minister Churchill and President Roosevelt have repeatedly discussed the situation but cannot agree to retasking SHAEF. The prime minister has convinced Field Marshals Wilson and Alexander for the 15th Air Force to carry out some supply drops for the A-K, but they are not enough, and those missions are inherently perilous and costly. The Germans have moved two *Waffen-S-S* divisions, one infantry and one armored, to carry out the suppression of the A-K uprising. They have also deployed the *S-S-Sturmbrigade Dirlewanger* . . ."

"Those bloody fucking criminals," Pordonski nearly spit with disgust.

"Yes, they have quite the infamous reputation."

"Yes, they do. They have been more ruthless and inhumane than even the *Einsatzgruppen*. They kill, but the *Dirlewanger* kill with zeal."

"We have ample evidence to substantiate your assessment, Stanislaus. We are not here to commiserate about the mercilessness of the enemy fanatics. On the contrary, the prime minister has asked us to explore options and do what we can to assist the A-K while the Soviets watch."

"Do you have a few spare armies?"

"No."

"Yes, well . . . the *Dirlewanger* and the *Waffen-S-S* are ruthless, but they are also skillful fighters. We can only meet them with overwhelming force. Worse, as you indicated, there is no air support."

"We're thinking diversionary attacks," Gubbins said. "You know the country far better than we do. What about a high visibility, high impact, target or set of targets close enough that the Germans cannot ignore or discount. Something that gets their attention and draws off those forces in Warsaw that are trying to defeat the A-K."

"Hmmm." Blocker lapsed into thought. None of the others wanted to interrupt Stan's thinking. "I need some time to think. I know Poland, but I don't know the details of the German occupation. The security forces will be at their most alert and attentive state. We would need to find something we can get to quickly and is not heavily defended."

"I'm afraid we do not have much time," Lord Selborne said. "The situation in Warsaw is desperate."

Pordonski nodded his head in recognition and agreement. "Understood. Give us a day or two. I imagine this is quite sensitive, so probably not advisable to discuss with other knowledgeable ex-patriots."

"The risk is to you and Trevor. You two are probably best positioned to make that judgment."

"Then we best jump to it," Trevor responded.

"We will reconvene on Wednesday afternoon. So shall we say 16 hours?"

Trevor and Stan looked at each other and nodded their heads. The four men bid their adieu.

———

Monday, 11.September.1944
Gentigen, Moselland
Deutsches Reich

Elements of the 28th Infantry Division and the 5th Armor Division, part of the V Corps, U.S. 1st Army, reached the Our River near Gentigen—the border of Germany in their area of operations. They were the first Allied ground forces, east or west, to enter Germany. The vaunted German Siegfried Line of defensive fortifications loomed just a few miles to the east.

The immediate objective was to secure their footing on German soil. They expected to receive orders to probe the German defensive line. Corps G-2 Intelligence indicated determined resistance could and should be anticipated.

The troops talked about what they thought lay ahead. None of them were eager to find out, but they instinctively knew they would soon determine the actual deployment of enemy forces in front of them.

———

Monday, 11.September.1944
E Street Complex
25th and E Streets, Northwest
Washington, District of Columbia
United States of America
15:50 hours

Afternoon reports had been part of the OSS leadership routine since the inception of the intelligence / special operations organization. Ned Buxton had served as the deputy director from the outset and been a faithful assistant who maintained the office when Bill Donovan was on the road, as he often was. Wild Bill had just returned from an exploratory journey to South America.

"We received a congratulatory letter from General Arnold," Buxton announced.

General Henry Harley 'Hap' Arnold, USA [USMA 1907], had been the chief of the Army Air Corps since 1935. He led the air forces through the tumultuous years of very rapid expansion once the United States entered the war. Arnold had other notable firsts like the Women's Auxiliary Service Pilot (WASP) program, jet fighter development, and he was a staunch advocate for tactical and strategic airpower.

Buxton continued, "He conveyed his gratitude to the O-S-S for organizing the recovery of Air Force pilots from the Balkans."

"Have we received the final numbers?" Donovan asked.

"Yes . . . just this afternoon," he referred to a sheet of paper in his folder. "The 15th Air Force report indicates they pulled out 251 Americans, 6 British, 4 French, 9 Italians, 7 Yugoslavs, and 12 Russians from the Balkans, in total 289 Allied pilots, aircrew, and other personnel. The last aircraft took off just after twilight began yesterday morning."

"Five times the original estimate."

"Indeed!"

"The real credit must go to the pilots who flew those aircraft. I would bet good money each of those C-47s was overloaded, and it took exceptional skill and risk to get back in the air from unimproved fields."

"Tito did everything he said he would do."

"Yes, he did. Please prepare a letter of gratitude to Marshal Tito for his exceptional effort, not just collecting our downed aviators in their area, but also taking care of them until we could arrange the pick up."

"I'll take care of it right away."

"Did we receive any word on the supplies we sent for Tito's partisans?"

"Not directly. I'll ping the station chief to find out. I assume the delivery went as planned, or we would have heard complaints."

"True."

"How was South America?"

"Interesting and informative. Argentina is very unsettled. Germans seem to be popping up all over South America, especially in the Andes foothills of Western Argentina."

"Understandable. While you were gone, the German Desk notified us they were working on two relevant items, among many others. First, we have received indications of some secret society or organization to aid or facilitate the escape of S-S leaders. Their current working hypothesis is this new organization is arranging for the relocation of S-S officers to South America. You may have detected the backside or results."

"We must learn more about whatever that entity is. In fact, thinking about what I learned in South America, ask the German Desk to prepare a briefing for us as soon as possible on what they have so far and what their plans are to flesh out the picture. The image I have at the moment is that the rats sense the sinking ship, and they are getting ready to make a run for it. The S-S may well be preparing for the post-war years, whatever they will be for them.

"I managed to find a few private moments and conversations with a couple of S-I-E officers I've known since before the Great War, and I trust them."

The Argentine SIE was the *Servicio de Inteligencia del Ejército*, in English, the Army Intelligence Service, and dealt with both internal and external state security affairs. The SIE was the closest thing to an Argentine secret police organization as the country had at the time.

"According to these two fellows, independently, I might add, the Germans have been moving money, gold, silver, jewels, and other fungible assets to Brazil, Argentina, Chile, Ecuador, and even peru, which probably support the escape organization you mentioned earlier. The problem for us is J. Edgar Hoover. He believes to his bones that South America is his domain. He sees it as a criminal matter. While we cannot deny the criminal aspects, I see the intelligence facets as far greater. There is much to this story. I need to get caught up on what we know and what we don't know."

"I'll see to it pronto."

"You said there was a second matter."

"Yes. Again, the German Desk has fragments of information about troop and equipment trains moving west. Our field agents have not found out where those trains are going, but they think those trains are different. Something is brewing in West Germany."

"The U.S. 1st Army's V Corps entered Germany today. Montgomery is about to execute Operation MARKET GARDEN, landing an airborne corps across the Rhine at Arnhem in Eastern Holland."

"Yeah. But, they are slowing Patton because they can't get fuel or ammunition to his troops fast enough. So, they may stop him soon, until the supplies can catch up with the 3rd Army."

"So, what is the German Desk's best guess about the troop movements?"

"They are very careful with their speculation, but based on the information they have, their current hypothesis is a major counter-offensive."

"What do they hope to accomplish? They can't possibly win. They're flailing against the wind."

"Do you want me to pass the question to the German Desk?"

"No, not yet. We need to hear their unfettered view of the facts as they have them so far."

"Understood. They're going to fret about not having sufficient information or corroboration."

"I'm not interested in a finished report. I want to know what they know so far."

"Understood, Bill. I'll see to it. I'll get them to brief us in a day or two."

"That will do just fine."

———

Wednesday, 13.September.1944
Citadelle de Québec
Ville de Québec, Québec
Dominion of Canada
16:45 hours

Prime Minister Churchill and Science Advisor Lord Cherwell sat in two of the eight chairs in the secure, private conference room set aside for meetings such as this. Winston displayed more than a bit of irritation, which was not lost on Cherwell.

"Thank you for carving out a little time for me, Winston," Lord Cherwell said.

"I will always make time for you, professor. So, what is the urgency?"

"I recognize that you have a chockablock full schedule, and I confess to the overwhelming urge to take advantage of our friendship." Winston gestured for Cherwell to get on with it. "I also recognize this conference is about the post-war world. From the discussion this afternoon, I sensed that you are skeptical about Henry Morgenthau's proposal."

"He calls it the pasteurization of Germany. I have exactly the same impression as I did when the draft treaty of Versailles was presented, and we have now seen where that got us."

"I understand and appreciate your arguments, Winston, but I have a few other thoughts that I did not feel comfortable raising during this afternoon's plenary session, but I am compelled to offer to you for consideration." Again, Churchill gestured for the professor to say what he wanted to say. "The Morgenthau plan, as presented this afternoon, calls for the pre-war, pre-*Anschluss* borders to be restored, Germany to be divided into four smaller bits, and for Germany to be denuded of its industrial capacity."

"I know, Fred. I was there too," Churchill barked with mounting irritation.

"Sorry. I was simply stating the foundation. I see the Morgenthau plan in an entirely different light. As I see the plan, it would likely save Great Britain from bankruptcy by eliminating a dangerous competitor. With the elimination of the industrial capacity of Germany, Europe must turn to Britain. Somebody must suffer for the war, Winston, and it is surely right that Germany and not Britain should foot the bill."

"That is exactly the basis of the Versailles Treaty, and we bear witness to what that produced."

"Yes, we have. You know as well as anyone that Lend-Lease saved us from bankruptcy in '41. You also know that Lend-Lease will end at the war's end or shortly thereafter. We must do something to transition our wartime industry and economy to the reality of peacetime . . . and the new peacetime that we will soon live."

"In essence, you are suggesting we sacrifice Germany for our salvation."

"I do not see it that way. I see the post-war reality as just a transition of warfare. We will soon be fighting for our very survival on the economic battlefield . . . very much as we were during the summer of 1940. We are talking survival, Winston. We both have seen what German industry can do when turned by a despot for war-making purposes. You saw the train wreck coming years before it happened. Very few people listened to you before Hitler came to power and achieved his dictatorship with a wartime industry behind him. We also witnessed what German innovation has been able to accomplish. We see it virtually every day with those flying bombs and rockets from space."

"True enough, professor, and I do appreciate the recognition. You have given me more than a little to contemplate. Now, it appears the time has arrived for us to freshen up before cocktails and dinner. The president does enjoy being the bartender, and we must not disappoint."

Lord Cherwell smiled, nodded his head, and said, "Thank you very much for listening, Winston. I hope the conversation was useful."

"Most assuredly, professor."

The two men separated and returned to their quarters to prepare for dinner.

———

Friday, 15.September.1944
Citadelle de Québec
Ville de Québec, Québec
Dominion of Canada
17:35 hours

The fourth day of the OCTAGON Summit Conference had not been any easier than the previous sessions, but it was more conclusive. It was the conclusiveness that stimulated Secretary of State Cordell Hull to request a private meeting with his boss, President Roosevelt.

"What have I done wrong now, Cordell?" the president asked with a markedly sarcastic and irritated tone.

"I wanted to convey my disappointment in you and the prime minister for initialing the *aide-mémoire* endorsing the Morgenthau Plan for post-war Germany. I thought we had agreed that deeply punitive peace treaties do not ensure the peace."

"Who is president?"

"You are, Mister President. Of that, there is no dispute. To be blunt, Mister President, you have signed up the United States to the sterilization of Germany."

"I think that is the point, isn't it?"

"Mister President, please, I thought we had thoroughly discussed our post-war treatment of Germany . . . and Japan for that matter. I also thought we had agreed that the humiliation and subjugation of Germany after the war would quite likely lead to yet another war. The Morgenthau Plan may make sense from an emotional perspective, but it goes even farther in the negative direction than the Versailles Treaty."

"Cordell, I am not as foolish as you apparently think I am. The memo is a classified internal planning document. It is not for public release. The war is not yet won, Cordell, and far too much can happen in these last months of the war in Europe. Winston and I agree that the plan is the worst case. Neither of us expects the worst case, but at least we shall be prepared."

"If this plan leaks out, it will only ensure protracted fanaticism by the S-S, the Army, and even the populace. We need to win the war, not make the war more difficult to win."

"Point taken, Cordell. We still have a bumpy road ahead of us in both Europe and the pacific. We are not sharing this memo with Uncle Joe. This is not the policy of the United States or Great Britain. It is a planning document."

"I wish it had stated that. But, unfortunately, taken outside the context of this conference, which is entirely possible, the memo could easily be interpreted as Allied policy and intent."

"Have you discussed your view with Eden?"

"Yes, at the close of this afternoon's plenary session. He sees the memo exactly as I do. He indicated when we parted that he was going to have the same conversation with Prime Minister Churchill."

Roosevelt chuckled softly. "Well, then, Winston will have a fun moment to share."

"You can make light of a grave matter, Mister President, but we are discussing the future of the world."

"I appreciate the seriousness, Cordell. Thank you for sharing your perspective. Now, I need to change for dinner. With Winston present, it will be another long night ahead."

"Thank you for listening, Mister President. I'll see you at dinner."

"You betcha."

———

Monday, 18.September.1944
Hyde Park, Dutchess County, New York
United States of America
18:05 hours

The weather cooled off, but not yet sufficiently to initiate the glorious colors of autumn in New England. The two leaders transitioned from professional discussions to the more social conversations between two wartime world leaders who were truly friends. Franklin insisted, and Winston did not ask, but the host found a case of Pol Rogers champagne, not 1928 vintage but before the war. Winston always enjoyed chilled champagne before dinner. Franklin was all too willing to accommodate his guest.

"You've always been a most gracious host, Franklin."

"Thank you, Winston. I only try to reflect the generosity you have shown me over our years of friendship."

They held their glasses up in an unspoken toast to each other. "I must say, Franklin, OCTAGON was quite a successful conference, although our foreign ministers were none too happy with our initialing Henry Morgenthau's rather radical plan."

"Perhaps a serious understatement, Winston," Franklin responded with a mischievous chuckle. "Cordell had the audacity to lecture me on my responsibilities as president."

"Anthony was not quite that bad, but the meaning was just the same. As we have discussed, I am not an advocate of pasteurization of Germany, but there are some decent points in Henry's plan."

"On that, we are agreed. It was for that reason that I initialed the memorandum. As I told Cordell, I initialed it as a worst-case planning document."

"As we agreed."

"But, as Cordell informed me, that is not what the memo says. He's concerned about the document standing alone."

"That was not our intent."

"No, but that is how he sees the memo, and we have them as our counsel on foreign affairs. We must listen."

"Indeed. I think we do, but we do not have to agree. I believe we did the correct thing in setting the worst-case scenario for Germany."

"True enough."

"I'm always grateful for your indulging my complaints, Franklin, especially on the Tube Alloys problem."

"To be frank, Winston, I was surprised when you raised the issue. Until you made me aware, I, clearly and erroneously, assumed the Manhattan project was proceeding as we had agreed all those years ago."

"I repeatedly asked our participants to work it out with the project leadership. I do believe the team leaders have tried and received no consideration. Further, they perceive conditions are worsening. They feel excluded from decision-making. They tell me they are falling behind the development state. Lastly, I am not sure I know where we are with the Tube Alloy project."

"I am truly sorry, Winston. That has never been my instruction nor my intent." Roosevelt paused and looked at the house. Then, he signaled for someone to come.

Grace Tully came out to the patio table and handed a folder to the president. First, he initialed the memorandum, and then he passed the folder to Churchill. The prime minister read the document and initialed it before giving it back to the president, who read it one more time before closing the folder and handing it to Grace.

TOP SECRET - PARAMOUNT
MOST SECRET - TUBE ALLOYS

```
TUBE ALLOYS
AIDE-MÉMOIRE OF CONVERSATION BETWEEN THE
PRESIDENT AND THE PRIME MINISTER AT HYDE PARK,
SEPTEMBER 18, 1944
1. The suggestion that the world should be
informed regarding TUBE ALLOYS, with a view
to an international agreement regarding its
control and use, is not accepted. The matter
should continue to be regarded as of the utmost
secrecy; but when a "bomb" is finally available,
it might perhaps, after mature consideration,
be used against the Japanese, who should be
warned that this bombardment will be repeated
until they surrender.
2. Full collaboration between the United States
and the British Government in developing TUBE
ALLOYS for military and commercial purposes
should continue after the defeat of Japan
unless and until terminated by joint agreement.
3. Enquiries should be made regarding the
activities of Professor Bohr and steps taken to
ensure that he is responsible for no leakage of
information, particularly to the Russians.
```

FDR WSC

MOST SECRET - TUBE ALLOYS
TOP SECRET - PARAMOUNT

Once Tully was back in the house and the door closed, Roosevelt looked back at Churchill. "That is done. I think we agree that the memo accurately reflects our agreements."

"Yes, it does."

"I should say that Stimson and Groves briefed me before our Quebec conference. They told me the development team has determined that the design for the uranium device will not work for the plutonium weapon. They are confident the uranium bomb will work; however, they believe plutonium is a far more attractive material for full-scale production. Groves indicated the Site Y team has a series of tests coming up to evaluate a new technique to achieve critical mass, as they call it."

"Thank you for your update, Franklin. I eagerly await the results of their testing. I am fairly certain you are as anxious as I am to achieve a working weapon. We are closer to victory over Germany, so unlikely to be necessary. But the bomb may be useful against Japan."

Roosevelt noticed a signal from the house. "It appears dinner is ready for us."

Winston stood and pushed Roosevelt's wheelchair into the house.

—

Wednesday, 20.September.1944
USAAF Station F-356
Saffron Walden, Essex, England
United Kingdom
17:40 hours

The 4th Fighter Group flew two long ground support missions—RODEO 307 and 309—in direct support of Operation MARKET GARDEN. Each of the group's three squadrons had assigned target areas. Their mission instructions were simple—shoot anything German in their respective assigned areas. The 334FS had the terrain north of the Nederrijn River, the northern branch of the Rhine River, after the waterway split at the Dutch-German border. In addition, they covered Arnhem and Osterbeek, the operating area of the British 1st Airborne Division.

The daring and risky combined arms joint operation featured an armor-infantry thrust from Eindhoven through Nijmegan to Arnhem, and a bold airborne assault of the 1st Airborne Army. In addition, the operation intended to do an end-around the Siegfried Line, a reverse maneuver like the Germans carried out on the Maginot Line in the spring of 1940.

The squadron had been busy hitting tanks, artillery, trucks, and troops all morning. They returned to Debden just long enough to refuel, rearm, and get a bite to eat. The afternoon had been equally busy with more similar targets. They had only partially debriefed the morning sortie, which added length to the day's debriefing.

As Brian entered the ops shack, Sergeant Ellison looked him in the eyes and said, "Skipper wants to see you as soon as you completed your debriefing."

"Thanks, Juli." Brian did not stop to doff his flight gear. The door to Clark's office was closed. Brian knocked.

"Enter."

Inside, Brian saw Arnie Clark and Horseback Blakeslee standing in front of the desk with stern expressions. *What the hell have I done?* Brian quickly chewed on the day's events. *It's been a tough day, but there's nothing unusual.* "What's cookin'?"

"Have a seat, Hunter," Horseback commanded. Brian did as he was instructed. "There is no easy way to say this. The R-A-F intercepted a number of buzz bombs this afternoon. They deflected several bombs. One of the deflected V1s landed in Hampshire." *No, no, no, this can't be happening.* "Your wife and son have been taken to Hampshire Central Hospital."

"Are they alive?"

"We don't know, Brian. We only know what we told you. The fastest way to Winchester is in your Mustang. However, before I authorize your use of a government aircraft, I have to know you are safe to fly. This is a lot to take on, Brian. You've had a very long day already."

"I'm good, Colonel."

"Are you absolutely certain?"

"Yes Sir."

"Then you are authorized to use your fighter. We will alert Middle Wallop that you are coming, and I'll ask them to have a car and driver available to take you directly to the hospital. Do you need us to make any other arrangements?"

"Not that I can think of. I'll probably be at the hospital tonight. When do I need to be back?"

"None of us knows the condition of your family," Blakeslee answered. "Let's leave it like this. As soon as you can get a handle on the situation, let either of us know, and we'll go from there."

"What about MARKET GARDEN?"

"Don't worry about that. Sweet will handle your division. Now, get out of here while you've got daylight."

"Thank you, both. I'm gone." Brian ran out of the building and to his fighter. Tomlinson stood on the left wing root with the engine running smoothly at idle. Brian jumped up on the wing and into the cockpit. Larson made his connections while Brian strapped into his parachute and seat. After a quick check of his cockpit switches, he called for taxi and takeoff.

The controller cleared him at high speed, low level, across Northwest London to Middle Wallop. Brian kept the powerful packard at full power and radiators wide open. He touched down 25 minutes later, after sunset and into twilight.

The base commander was waiting along with a driver and a car standing at idle. "We don't know any more, Major," the wing commander said, acknowledging why the American major was at the RAF airbase.

"Thank you, Sir. Can your crews take care of my fighter?"

"Yes. We'll see to it. Our very best wishes are with you, Major. We stand ready to assist in any way possible. Now, you best be off."

"Thank you, Sir."

Brian got in the back seat. The driver moved swiftly to the main gate. Once they were outside the base, the driver picked up speed and switched on the car's siren and flashing blue lights.

———

Wednesday, 20.September.1944
Hampshire Central Hospital
Winchester, Hampshire, England
United Kingdom
20:15 hours

The hospital was all too familiar to Brian, having been here several times before, over the years, although on a couple of those occasions, he was unconscious upon arrival. He asked the receptionist about Charlotte and Ian. The only answer he got was that they were at the hospital and that he should go to the waiting room. He knew the way.

Brian was surprised to see Mabel. Even Horace, Lionel, and Jacob were present, having completed the evening product deliveries. Mabel was demonstrably distraught with reddened eyes, wet cheeks, and convulsive breathing.

"How are they?" Brian asked.

"We don't know, Mister Drummond," Mabel responded convulsively.

"What happened?"

"A bomb exploded east of the house. Charlotte and Edith had Ian and Todd out in the sunshine playing in the tall grass before the cows were turned out into that pasture. Ian was running ahead and was nearest the explosion. Charlotte must have seen the buzz bomb coming and jumped to protect Ian." Mabel started crying again. "Oh, Brian, it was so bad. All four of them are here."

"The hospital personnel have not given us any updates?"

"No."

"Before I jump into this, who is at the farm?"

"June."

"June?"

"Yes Sir. Mrs. June Sorvon Cranston, she is the farm's accountant."

"OK." Brian looked at the men. "I appreciate y'all looking after things, fellas, but morning milking will come soon regardless of what happens here. I suggest you go home and try to get as much sleep as you can. Please tend to the business of the farm. I'll try to get back to the farm as soon as I know something."

"Yes Sir," the three men responded in unison.

"May God bless and protect them," Lionel offered.

"Thank you." Brian waited for the three men to leave. Then, he turned to face Mabel. "I'm going to see what I can turn up for us." Mabel nodded. Brian headed for the double doors clearly marked MEDICAL PERSONNEL ONLY.

A nurse finally stopped him. "You're not allowed in this area."

"My wife and son were brought in this afternoon. I want to know their status along with our employee and resident—Edith Hanscom, and juvenile Todd Bloodworth."

"You will have to go back to the Waiting Room. I'll try to get one of the doctors attending them to give you information."

"Look, nurse. I appreciate your rules. I'm not budging until I know the condition of my family and residents."

"Sir, you are forcing me to call security."

"Then, call them! You need to give me something."

"Please go back to the Waiting Room. I'll come to you."

"No."

The nurse gyrated, started to turn away several times, and then she faced Brian. "You are a persistent sod, aren't you?" Brian only smiled. "Stand right here. Don't move. Give me a moment to see what I can find out."

Brian did as he was instructed. The nurse made several telephone calls, presumably to other departments within the hospital. She nodded and shook her head as she talked to whoever was on the other end. Finally, the woman in uniform stood and returned to Brian.

"I do not have a status on your wife or son, which could mean they are still in surgery or treatment. I've let the emergency department know that you are in the Waiting Room. Edith Hanscom is out of surgery safely. She is sedated and resting."

"Has her family been notified?"

"Yes, I believe so."

"And Todd Bloodworth?"

"He has been treated. He is safe. He is also sedated and resting. Mrs. Bloodworth can see him. A nurse will come to the Waiting Room to escort her to his bed."

"Thank you. I appreciate your patience. Please let me know as soon as my wife and son finish treatment."

"I know the emergency staff will do so. They know you are here."

Brian nodded and returned to Mabel. He recounted the information the nurse had given him. Mabel collapsed into a chair. Brian put his left arm around her shoulders as she cried softly with relief.

A different nurse entered the room, saw Mabel, the only woman in the room, and said, "Mrs. Bloodworth?"

Mabel jumped up. "Yes."

"Your son is stable. He is sedated and resting for his body to relax and begin healing. If you want to see him, I will take you back."

Mabel looked at Brian as if to ask, do you want to come?

Brian said, "Go ahead. I really should stay here just in case the medical folks come with news on Charlotte or Ian." Mabel nodded once and left with the nurse. Brian sat down, took off his uniform tunic, and loosened his necktie. *This is a major area hospital. Why am I the only one waiting? Maybe I can quickly visit Mabel and Todd . . . and maybe Edith. Naw! I can't. They might come with news at any minute.* Brian stood and began nervously pacing like a caged lion. Millions of thought fragments surged through his consciousness.

The clock on the wall displayed quarter past ten when a middle-aged man in a white lab coat entered the Waiting Room and stepped directly toward Brian. "You must be Major Drummond," he said.

"Yes. I am," Brian answered as he stood.

"I must ask you to sit down," the doctor instructed.

"I'm OK. Give it to me straight."

"Very well. I'm Doctor Nolan. I treated your wife."

"And?" Brian said impatiently.

"She is in serious condition, Major. She has several broken ribs, a rather nasty compound fracture of her left arm, and multiple shrapnel wounds. But, beyond the pronounced risk of infection with her injuries, the most significant issue is her brain. She has a serious concussion and remains in a coma."

"Is her brain OK?"

"As far as we can tell, yes. There appears to be no lasting damage, but we will not know until she comes out of the coma, and we can evaluate her properly."

"Is there anything I can do?"

"Pray and wait."

"Can I see her?"

"Yes, but there is not much to see. She is fairly well bandaged from her injuries. They were far too close to that explosion."

"I was told it was a deflected V1, which carries a nearly one-ton warhead. Yes, that is a helluvan explosion. What of our son?"

"He passed away. He . . ."

Brian collapsed to his knees, and his forehead hit the floor hard. He heard nothing else. Brian felt only blackness. The darkness held him crumpled up on the floor for an indeterminate amount of time. Brian eventually felt the doctor shaking his right shoulder. After several minutes, Brian heard what he thought was 'do you need assistance'? He raised his head and torso but remained on his knees. Wiping away the wetness on his cheeks, Brian turned his head slightly to see the concerned expression of Doctor Nolan looking down at him.

"Are you all right?" the doctor asked.

"No. I'm not all right. Our son is dead, and my wife is in a coma . . . and the world is in a bloody fucking war that has taken both of them from me. So, no, I'm definitely not all right."

"Do you need a sedative?"

Brian shook his head and stood. He was a good head taller than the doctor. "No, thank you. I need my family."

Nolan nodded his head. "Unfortunately, I cannot alter reality. I must return to my duties. Would you like to see your wife?"

Brian only nodded. Doctor Nolan escorted the Army aviator to the critical care ward and a bed with sheet curtains pulled out on both sides. *My God, he's right. She isn't recognizable under all those bandages and bedding.* Brian leaned forward to where he thought her left ear was under the bandages and whispered, "I'm here, sweetheart. You're safe. I love you very much." When he stood and turned back to find Doctor Nolan, he was gone, and two nurses stood dutifully at the foot of the bed. *One of those nurses looks familiar.*

"We will take good care of her, Major Drummond," the familiar nurse said. "I would like to say it is good to see you, again, but I know this is a grievous time for you. We are so deeply sorry for the loss of your son. We'll do our best to ensure you do not lose your wife." Brian felt tears well up in his eyes as he nodded his head and turned away. "It's quite all right."

"My apologies," he said, looking at the recognizable nurse. "You seem familiar, but I don't remember your name."

The woman giggled softly. "I don't recall ever giving you my name, but I was one of the nurses that treated you at the end of July and again in September. My name is Lester, Nona Lester." Brian shook her hand, and then he looked to the other nurse and extended his hand.

"I'm Mercy Smith. Nice to meet you, Major Drummond."

"An honor to meet you both."

"Respectfully, Major," Lester began, "there is nothing you can do. As such, I would encourage you to go home and get some sleep. If she regains consciousness, we will telephone you promptly."

"Anytime—day or night." Brian turned back to Charlotte. *Damn, I can't touch any spot of her. I've no idea what is underneath the bandages.* He leaned to her left ear. "I love you, my lovely. Rest and heal quickly." Brian gave her an audible air kiss. "I love you, Charlotte Drummond." *All I can smell is antiseptic. I never knew how much I miss her scent.*

Brian straightened up, took a deep cleansing breath, and turned. Mabel was standing with Nona and Mercy. "How is Todd?"

"Compared to the others, he is stable, and his wounds are fairly minor. He was extraordinarily lucky. How is Charlotte?"

Nona volunteered, "She's in a coma with a serious concussion, along with multiple wounds, broken bones, and burns." Brian nodded his concurrence. Lester looked across her shoulder at Mabel. "He needs to go home and get some sleep, and he probably needs something to eat."

The two visitors left their contact information with the nurses and said goodnight. Mabel used the old Hillman car. *She knows the streets and route.* Brian asked her to drive, which she was willing to do. During the drive, Mabel recounted what she learned from Edith, which was not much more than they already knew. Edith was watching Todd, who was behind them, when she heard Charlotte scream before the explosion knocked her off her feet. Mabel was grateful Todd was the least injured but felt profound guilt that she was relieved while Ian was dead and Charlotte was in a coma. Brian listened, but he was too tired to talk.

———

Friday, 22.September.1944
Project Y, Los Alamos National Laboratory
Post Office Box 1663
Los Alamos, Los Alamos County, New Mexico
United States of America
10:20 hours

The 7,300-foot elevation and pine-scented mountain air were always welcome features of the project Y site . . . well, except in the dead of winter, but it was late summer and still warm.

Commanding Officer of the Manhattan Engineering District Major General Leslie Richard 'Dick' Groves, Jr., USA CEC [USMA 1918] had just arrived with the foreknowledge of the important test scheduled for this morning. He made his way directly to the office of the director. Dr. Julius Robert Oppenheimer, PhD (Physics), had been director of the laboratory and the Site Y work since the outset of the project in 1942, just a few weeks less than Groves.

In July, the technical team had abandoned the gun method for the plutonium weapon. The technique was theoretically acceptable for the uranium device, but plutonium proved more problematic, and yet it was a more attractive material for their purposes—nuclear fission. This morning's test was known as the RaLa experiment, which referred to the use of radioactive lanthanum (RaLa, ^{140}La) to validate the implosion technique scientifically.

"Welcome back to Los Alamos, General," Oppenheimer said as Groves entered his modest office and he stood.

"Thanks, Oppie. I've been on pins and needles all week."

Oppenheimer smiled and bowed his head slightly. "I suppose I could have some fun with that . . . but I won't. The test went off as planned this morning. We have several days of analysis to be precise with the results. The preliminary assessment by the test team offers good and not-so-good news."

"Well, then, give me the bad news first," Groves insisted.

"The test did not achieve the results we hoped."

"I'll need a little more detail than that."

"The initial assessment is encouraging. We recorded a gamma-ray burst, which indicates we achieved compression. However, the timing on the explosive lenses was off. As a result, we did not achieve symmetric compression."

Groves thought for a moment. "We've discussed the lensing technique. What did you use as a detonator?"

"We used a multipoint Primacord system. The target was compressed but distorted, so not acceptable for our purposes. They are making some adjustments and preparing for another test in a couple of weeks. I think it is safe to say we saw enough in this morning's test to get us far closer than we were yesterday."

"That seems like a positive step."

"It was, General. It was. We built Technical Area 10 (TA-10) in Bayo Canyon for just these tests after Serber convinced me it might work last fall. When we finally realized the gun technique would not work with plutonium, we shifted all of our efforts to RaLa. For the process to work, each explosive lens must detonate within microseconds of each other to compress the plutonium core to critical mass density."

"Is that the last critical milestone?" Groves asked.

"No, but it is a 'Do not pass GO. Do not collect $200' gate. I've asked the electronics team to investigate the potential of an electrical trigger to solve the timing issue. We must conduct several more tests of the current system to determine consistency, and we will explore what we can do to make the Primacord detonate more predictably."

"If I understood your earlier statement, the RaLa technique looks like it might work."

"Correct."

"Then, what's next?"

"Once we achieve the proper timing on the explosive lenses, we need to achieve the proper neutron flux as part of the implosion process. Too much or too little . . . neither is acceptable. The science tells us we should be able to use a seed construction embedded at the center of the plutonium core, but that part doesn't matter if we can't achieve the precise symmetric compression of the core to critical mass."

"Do you need anything, Oppie? Is there anything I can do to help?"

"No. Not yet. We do not have a workable solution just yet, but this morning's test suggests the necessary precision may be within reach. I'm more confident this afternoon that we will solve the timing problem."

Groves nodded his head as he considered the information. "Very well, then. That's the way I'll report it. Please keep me informed, as you have done."

"I will certainly do that, General."

"I will add here that both Oak Ridge and Hanford are moving along nicely to supply the required quantity and purity of both uranium and plutonium for full-scale devices, assuming you can solve the implosion design problem."

"I feel much better today than I did yesterday that we might actually find the solution. We are quite mindful of Voltaire's succinct observation that "*Le mieux est le mortel ennemi du bien.*"

"Perfect is the enemy of good."

"Exactly."

———

Sunday, 24.September.1944
Hampshire Central Hospital
Winchester, Hampshire, England
United Kingdom
15:25 hours

Brian had been at Charlotte's bedside since early this morning, as he had been every day since he arrived on Wednesday. He continued to whisper into her bandages where her left ear was. He had found a few patches of undamaged and unbandaged skin on her right forearm. Brian gently stroked those patches of skin and kissed them repeatedly in his efforts to connect with her unconscious soul as he had done since the incident.

Unrealized time passed with his hand on Charlotte's right forearm and his head on the bed beside her when he eventually felt a hand gently shaking his right shoulder. Brian raised head, blinked several times to focus his mind. Looking to his right, he saw Edith standing next to him. He smiled softly.

"My apologizes, Mister Drummond." Brian shook his head not wanting to speak. "Colonel Clark called the farm. He said it was urgent that he talk to you, so I drove here straight away."

"Thank you, Edith. Can you stay here with Charlotte while I find a telephone?"

"Yes Sir."

Brian patted Charlotte's forearm and went to her left ear to tell her that Edith was here with her. He had to call the squadron. He got no reaction, and he did not expect any response. He just wanted her unconscious mind to know. Brian looked across Charlotte's immobile body to Edith. "I'll be back as soon as I can."

"Take whatever time you need, Major. I'll stay here with Mrs. Charlotte."

"Thank you," Brian answered.

The ward nurses had 101 reasons he could not use the ward telephone. For his efforts, the nurses eventually took Brian to an unoccupied doctor's office that had an outside functional telephone. She closed the door behind her, leaving Brian alone for his telephone call. The operators took not quite a minute to make the connections.

"Three three four," Sergeant Ellison answered.

"Juli, this is Major Drummond. I received a message to call Colonel Clark."

"Yes Sir. He's waiting for your call. Stand by . . ."

Presumably Juli Ellison went to Clark's office to tell him that Brian was waiting on black phone.

"Clark," came the Skipper's voice.

"Hunter."

"First, how's Charlotte?" Arnie asked.

"Still in a coma I'm afraid. I'm at the hospital for the fourth day since the impact. The doctors remain optimistic, but she's still in a coma, and there's almost nothing of her not bandaged and braced."

"I'm sorry all this has happened, but I need you back. Horseback has been supportive, but we've gone as far as we can go."

"I understand, Skipper. It's too late to get back tonight."

"Tomorrow will do but I need you back."

"No problem, Skipper. I'll take the first train out in the morning, which should get me back to base by noon."

"That will work. We'll probably be in the air, so tomorrow afternoon will be sufficient. I'm sorry we can't give you longer, Brian. My very best wishes for Charlotte's speedy and full recovery."

"Thank you, Sir. See tomorrow."

Brian hung up the handset, sat for a few moments to consider the remainder of the day and tomorrow, and then he returned to Charlotte and Edith.

"Anything change?" Brian asked Edith.

"No Sir."

"I'll have to leave tomorrow morning to catch the first train to London. I must return to my squadron and the war."

"I'm sorry you must go, Major," Edith added. "If I may ask, how much longer is this dreadful affair going to persist?"

"I wish I knew." Brian whispered his love to Charlotte, went around the bed, and repeated his routine with Charlotte. He pulled up a wooden chair, sat next with Edith, and placed his left hand on Charlotte's right forearm. "We are a lot closer to being done with this war . . . at least in Europe. The Allied Expeditionary Force is tapping on Germany's door and approaching the Rhine. I'm no general, but we've gone a long way east since June."

"That sounds good."

They sat together in silence as Brian softly stroked Charlotte's arm. Brian repeated his verbal and touch assurance to Charlotte several times in between visits by one of the ward nurses to check Charlotte's vital signs.

After what had to be an hour based on the nurse checks, Brian looked across his left shoulder at Edith. "I'd better get you back for supper."

They said goodnight to Charlotte. Brian told her that he had to go back to work, and others would look after her. They checked out the nurses. Brian informed the nurses of what was happening, and to keep the farm and him informed.

On the drive back to the farm, Brian asked Edith to stand in for him with Charlotte. He wanted to know the moment Charlotte regained consciousness. Edith agreed to be his eyes and ears.

They made it back to the farm in time for dinner. Brian informed the crew of Charlotte's status, his return to the squadron, Edith's assignment to stand in his stead-at the hospital, and his gratitude for their extra work during this very trying time. Brian considered going back to the hospital after the crew disband but decided he should get a good night's sleep.

———

Friday, 29.September.1944
SHAEF Forward
Trianon Palace Hotel
1 Boulevard de la Reine
Versailles, Île-de-France
France libérée
13:15 hours

"**P**ink is getting the latest from the lines. He'll be up here shortly," offered Beetle Smith.

"That's fine, Beetle. It gives us a few extra minutes to enjoy this rather opulent headquarters."

"No point living in tents when we can commandeer hotels like this," Smith said, swinging his left arm around the expansive penthouse suite.

"True. I'm not complaining, but I suspect General Marshal will counsel me about having a bigger, more elegant office than the chief of staff or even the secretary."

Smith chuckled softly. "A necessary risk, Ike. You are the supreme commander of the greatest land army in history. By the way, Monty is in Brussels. Brad is at Verdun. And Jake is at Dijon and closing nicely."

Forward elements of the 6th Army Group (6AG) had pushed north from the DRAGOON landings in Southern France and linked up with the right flank of George Patton's 3rd Army on the 11th of September. By prior coordination and agreement, the operational control of the 6AG was transferred from AFHQ to SHAEF on the 14th. The 6AG was under the command of Lieutenant General Jacob Loucks 'Jake' Devers, USA [USMA 1909], a classmate of George Patton.

"Pink should be here by now. Let me go check on where he is."

"Sure. You've given me plenty of paper to go through."

Smith left for several minutes. Ike was still in the middle of a supply status report from the staff G-4 when Beetle returned with the SHAEF G-3 Major General Pink Bull. Eisenhower rose from his desk and went to the conference table in front of the large wall map of Western Europe. Eisenhower and Smith sat across the table from the map. Bull stood to the map.

"My apologies, General. The temptation of ever-changing field status kept me collecting more information." Eisenhower chose to simply nod his head. "Starting in the north, The 21st Army Group salient, the troops call Hell's Highway from Eindhoven through Nijmegan to link up with the airborne forces on the far side of the Nederjin, has attracted considerable enemy attention. Field Marshal Montgomery is driving to solidify the link-up. The bridges over the Nederjin and Waal, the lower Rhine in the Netherlands, are still standing.

So far so good. The Germans have made several attempts to destroy the bridges and collapse the salient without success. The enemy has substantial forces in the area, and there will be heavy fighting ahead, unfortunately.

"The Canadian 1ˢᵗ Army is working on opening the Scheldt," Bull said pointing with a wooden, red-tipped pointer to the islands at the mouth of the Antwerp estuary. "They are preparing for amphibious assaults on Walcheren and Beveland Islands next week. The pocket from Zeebrugge to Temeuzen on the south side of the Scheldt is still holding out, but they have no means of resupply, reinforcement, or relief. It is only a matter of time."

"And blood," Eisenhower grumbled.

"Yes Sir, regrettably." Bull paused to allow for comment. None came. "The 12ᵗʰ Army Group is up against the Siegfried Line across virtually their entire front. Of particular note, the 1ˢᵗ Army has just three divisions—the V Corps – the 4ᵗʰ and 28ᵗʰ Infantry, and the 5ᵗʰ Armor—defending 70 miles of that frontage. They are very thin." Eisenhower did not react and only nodded his head and grunted. "The 3ʳᵈ Army has met significant resistance at Metz. The Germans have reinforced Fort Driant—a hilltop redoubt—that they apparently intend to defend. It has a commanding view of the surrounding terrain and presents a problematic situation for the XX Corps. The 90ᵗʰ Infantry Division crossed the Moselle north of Metz and ran into the *17ᵗʰ S-S Panzergrenadier Division*, which is fully manned and amply supplied. Their first attempt to encircle and cutoff Metz failed. I might add here that General Patton is not happy with being drawn up by the lack of supplies that have been diverted for MARKET GARDEN. The 3ʳᵈ Army is short on fuel, artillery ammunition, and clean water." Again, Eisenhower did not respond and only stared at the map.

"Where is General Patton?" Beetle asked.

"He's at his headquarters at Etain, about 15 miles forward of General Bradley's headquarters at Verdun."

Eisenhower finally spoke. "I'd better go visit Georgie. MARKET GARDEN is our best shot for swiftly getting across the Rhine and cutting off the Ruhr Valley industrial area. We need to weaken the massed German forces behind the Siegfried Line to avoid a bloody slugfest. I know Patton is frustrated. Pulling him up short has a negative side in that it allows the Germans to move reinforcements into the area. Once the 21ˢᵗ Army Group is firmly across the Rhine with substantial forces . . . well, we will re-align. We need those port facilities at Antwerp."

Every general in the European Theater understood the importance and necessity of the Antwerp port facilities. General Bull keenly understood that reality. Neither Pink nor Beetle could add anything.

"What about the 6th Army Group?" Eisenhower asked.

"They are advancing nicely and filling in between the 3rd Army and the Swiss border. Intelligence says the Germans have reinforced Colmar, south-southeast of Strasbourg. The 6th-A-G supply line is Marseilles, not quite Cherbourg, but still stretched. General Devers indicated they're ready for full combat. Colmar may be that test."

"OK," Eisenhower responded. "I've got what I need. Thanks, Pink." Ike looked at Beetle. "Let's set up Brad for the morning, and then I would like him to accompany me for the talk with Georgie. We've got to stay focused on the realities of what we face. I know George is chomping at the bit, but he's part of a much larger team. I'll lay it out plainly for him. We'll try to make it a day trip."

"I'll see to the arrangements post haste. I'll confirm the details this afternoon."

"Thank you, gentlemen." Eisenhower stood and went to his desk. Smith and Bull departed.

—

Chapter 11

It is the disease of not listening,
the malady of not marking,
that I am troubled withal.
-- William Shakespeare
(2 Henry IV, Act 1, Scene 2)

Monday, 2. October. 1944
Cabinet War Rooms
New Public Offices
Whitehall, London, England
United Kingdom
16:05 hours

Prime Minister Churchill pushed the button on his desk panel for his duty private secretary.

"Yes Sir," Jock Colville answered.

"Didn't I have a scheduled four o'clock appointment?"

"Yes Sir . . . the Minister of Economic Warfare requested the appointment this morning."

"Thank you, Jock. We'll give him another ten minutes, and then we need to move on."

"Very well, Sir. I'll call his office to see if there is a problem."

"Fine. Thank you, Jock."

Churchill returned to the last SHAEF field report, which always captured his interest. The latest progress in the Netherlands, Luxembourg, and now Western Germany was vastly more encouraging reading than those bad days during the worst of the Battle of the Atlantic. Montgomery continued his effort to make the most of MARKET GARDEN's less than ideal result. The stagnation of George Patton's 3rd Army after his brilliant dash across France was heartbreaking, but Winston agreed with Eisenhower's decision to divert thinly stretched resources to MARKET GARDEN.

The sound of the buzzer broke his concentration. "Yes, Jock."

"I called the ministry. His office indicated he left half an hour ago."

"Has he been in an accident?"

"I also checked with Scotland Yard, and they have no reports of traffic accidents in the area. Oh wait . . . Lord Selborne just arrived in fine form. Shall I send him in?"

"Yes, please. No need to keep the Earl waiting."

A few seconds later, a double knock preceded Jock's entrance. "Lord Selborne is here, Prime Minister."

"Please show the minister in."

"My apologies, Prime Minister . . . traffic and security was a little more suspicious with you down here."

"You are here, now, safely. You have news?"

"Yes. This afternoon, we received independent confirmation that General Komorowski surrendered the polish Home Army yesterday."

"That is most unfortunate but not unexpected given the Red Army's total indifference. What of the team you sent in to help?"

"They are still in the country. Two of our best men."

"Who are they?"

"Blocker and Diamond."

"Diamond, you say. I've met him several times before the war."

"He has exceptional skills that have proven to be quite effective."

"Are you going to leave them in Poland?"

"I'd prefer not. The Germans are retreating, and they are under considerable pressure, or will be when the Red Army picks up the offensive again."

"I suspect that it will be their last push when they resume the offensive. We must get to Berlin first." Churchill stared at Selborne.

"I am unclear here what you are implying, Prime Minister. Are you suggesting we endeavor to slow down the Red Army . . . to work against their advance on Germany?"

"Interesting thought . . . but, no. I'm not suggesting that we take action against the advance of the Red Army. I was simply offering an observation. What is your recommendation with regard to your in-country agents in Poland?"

"They could not help the Polish Home Army. M-I-6 has intelligence assets in Poland. I would like to withdraw our agents as soon as we can transmit the extraction code and recover them."

"With the loss of the Home Army, conditions in Poland are going to get even more hectic, chaotic, and uncertain. We don't need those good men mixed up in the turmoil of the German fighting retreat. I approve your recommendation. The usefulness of your field operatives in Poland is much less today."

"Very well. Thank you for your time, Prime Minister, and I offer my apologies for my tardiness."

"Life happens to all of us, Lord Selborne. Thank you for the briefing."

Selborne nodded his head and departed.

———

Tuesday, 3.October.1944
Office of the Director, Office of Strategic Services
National Institutes of Health Building
2430 E Street Northwest
Washington, District of Columbia
United States of America
08:15 hours

"Cecil confirmed the surrender of Komorowski and his Home Army in Warsaw," Ned Buxton observed.

"A somber and tragic affair," added Donovan.

"The Red Army could have saved them."

"Yes, they could have, but I think the Soviets decided it was best to let German bullets kill Polish nationalist forces rather than Soviet bullets."

"Damn Russians are a ruthless bunch, aren't they?"

"An understatement, I'm afraid, Ned. What is the latest on the German troop movements west?"

"The German Desk indicates the evidence continues to mount. However, they still do not clearly understand the purpose."

"What do the British think?" Bill asked.

"They see similar evidence. So, M-I-6 has issued a warning to the War Ministry and SHAEF that the movements suggest a major counter-offensive. The obvious focus would be Arnhem, but our guys indicate those units have not shown up in Dortmund or Münster, which might suggest they are not destined for Arnhem."

"There are too many of these reports to be ignored. We must find out where they are going. Have we advised the War Department or SHAEF?"

"No. The analysts are still uncertain. They want to find the destination."

"Understandable. Aerial photography has not helped?"

"The Germans have apparently been very clever with their camouflage. The Desk has asked the field agents to get a few photographs of the trains to gain some clues on the camouflage techniques to help the photo interpreters, but nothing yet."

"Troops and tanks must be going somewhere. They can't just disappear," Donovan mused.

"Indeed!"

"Such troop movements west do not make sense when the Germans are on the run in the east."

"Perhaps they are reserve units Hitler has held in abeyance."

"Perhaps," Donovan lapsed into contemplation. "Maybe they are new units . . . Hitler Youth or that new People's Storm we've been hearing about."

"Could be. One thing is for certain. Something is up. They are building forces somewhere in the west for an unidentified action. That is our challenge."

"With evidence mounting, we must prioritize this issue, Ned."

"I'll see to it. By the way, I received a private from London Station that Selborne met with Churchill and discussed the situation in Poland. Selborne wanted to withdraw his agents deployed to help Komorowski and apparently thought Churchill was hinting at using those agents to slow the Red Army."

"My, my, my . . . I'll have to talk to Cecil about that the next time I'm in London. Churchill has been obsessed with the Russians squatting on Eastern Europe. He's convinced Stalin has no intentions of restoring sovereignty in the countries they occupy, which is precisely why he pushes Eisenhower to meet the Red Army as far east as possible."

"I suspect he's not far from what we may well face in the post-war world."

"Agreed. It won't be a pretty world."

"No, it won't, and we must be prepared for both, which is exactly what I'm emphasizing in the transition plan."

"What's your read of the president? Will he buy it?" asked Ned.

"The plan will emphasize his thoughts from our first discussion in late '39. He'll tweak it, as he always does, but yes, I think it will be exactly what he wants."

"What did you think of the air plan that Chip submitted?"

OSS-BAS Project Officer Major Chester Hugh 'Chip' Warner, USAR, OSS code 743, had been the primary liaison and contract officer with Bainbridge Air Services from the inception of their operating relationship.

"As our British friends like to say, spot on! Chip did a magnificent job with Mister Sales. Has our hero reviewed the plan?"

"No, not yet, that I know of."

"Let's get his endorsement. It is his company, after all."

"Do you want me to handle that aspect?"

"No need, Ned. Warner or Sales can handle that task. I'd just like to have his consent before submitting the overall plan to the president next month."

"We'll get it done this month."

The two leaders turned their discussion attention to the war in Asia and the pacific. The Battle of Peleliu, codenamed Operation STALEMATE II, had begun on the 15th of September, and it was not going well. The cave-by-cave, crevice-by-crevice, bloody fight was giving the Army and Marine Corps a bitter foretaste of what lay ahead at Iwo Jima and Okinawa. Bill Donovan had made little progress with General MacArthur, but he had taken the initiative to insert agents on Mindanao, Luzon, and Formosa. The OSS was providing valuable intelligence, but MacArthur remained reticent to acknowledge the service's contribution. Such was the nature of the intelligence business.

———

Thursday, 5. October. 1944
Combined Services Detailed Interrogation Centre
Trent Park
Cockfosters Road
Enfield, London, England
United Kingdom
14:30 hours

The intelligence chiefs gathered at Cockfosters Cage at the request of Colonel Kendrick—Lord Selborne for SOE, General Sir Stewart Menzies for MI6, Director-General David Petrie for MI5, and Colonel David Bruce representing OSS. Bruce was the newest member of the group, but he was well known to the group. The social amenities were quickly dispensed with.

Colonel Thomas Joseph 'Tom' Kendrick was a career intelligence officer within MI6 and founder of MI19, the POW interrogation service. Cockfosters Cage, as the estate was known, specialized in an innovative form of interrogation. The entire estate—rooms, benches, walking paths, trees, bushes, virtually everything they could devise for installing and wiring of surreptitious microphones—so analysts could listen and record casual conservations between German, flag rank, prisoners of war. Kendrick devised, developed, ran, and now commanded Cockfosters Cage.

"Thank you for coming on such short notice, gentlemen," Kendrick said. "I must remind us all that this meeting, words, and products are classified most secret and compartmented as ANGEL.

"We recorded a conversation last Saturday, and we just completed our transcription and analysis."

"These things happen when they happen, Tom," Sir Stewart responded. "Let us have it."

"The conversation occurred between five generals, including our newest guest General Wahle, the commander of the 47th Infantry Division captured at Mons. The group gathered at the far end of the garden in a secluded spot. The center of the conversation was General von Choltitz, who has been here for a little over a month and raises an important question for the government."

"What do they call him?" Selborne asked.

"The Crusher of Cities," responded Menzies. "His reputation in Rotterdam and Sevastopol supports the moniker."

"In this recorded conversation with his brethren, he explains his conduct and gives us a view of his actions in Paris.

"Here is our current listing of focus guests," Kendrick added. He passed a clearly marked paper to each leader to be collected up and destroyed after the meeting.

MOST SECRET - ANGEL

```
     Current focus list; 5th October 1944; 08:00
BAS -- Generalmajor Gerhard Bassenge - Luftwaffe
          (9 May 1943)
BRO -- Generalmajor Friedrich Freiherr von
          Broich - Heer (12 May 1943)
CHO -- General der Infanterie Dietrich Hugo
          Hermann von Choltitz - Heer (25 August
          1944)
CRA -- General der Panzertruppe Hans Cramer -
          Heer (12 May 1943) transferred USA
CRU -- General der Panzertruppe Ludwig Cruwell -
          Heer (29 May 1942)
LIE -- Generalmajor Kurt Freiherr von Liebenstein
          - Heer (13 May 1943)
NEU -- Generalleutnant Georg Neuffer - Luftwaffe
          (9 May 1943)
SPO -- Generalmajor Hans Graf von Sponeck - Heer
          (12 May 1943) transferred USA
THO -- General der Panzertruppe Wilhelm Josef
          Ritter von Thoma - Heer (4 November 1942)
WAH -- Generalmajor Carl Richard Heinrich Wahle
          - Heer (4 September 1944)
```

MOST SECRET - ANGEL

"Just a question at this juncture," Petrie asked, "what determines the transfer of a detainee? And where do they go?"

Kendrick answered, "Simply put, usefulness. Some are not talkative. Some are disruptive to the productive conversations we seek. For example, on this version of the list, Cramer was a staunch Nazi and repeatedly tried to intimidate the anti-Nazis. He provided no information, and he directly stymied the others.

"In contrast, Crüwell is also a dedicated Nazi, but he argues with the anti-Nazis, which often pulls valuable information out for our microphones. Crüwell was not in the subject conversation, which was probably by the participants' design and intent. We do make efforts to subtly stimulate conversations by planting reading material in German and English. To answer the where, once we release them, they are transported to the United States and Canada. Most go to Camp Clinton, near Clinton, Mississippi."

"Pardon my novice-ness here," said Bruce, "what other techniques were used to get the Germans to talk without making them suspicious?"

"Quite all right," Menzies interjected, "we are colleagues here. Go ahead," he said, looking directly at Kendrick.

"Our most effective tool is Lord Aberfeldy."

"Aberfeldy?"

"Yes, actually, Major Ian Moore, an M-I-19 officer, in the form of a nobleman and distant cousin of King George VI, assigned as a welfare officer charged to look after the health and well-being of the German general 'guests' as we call them at Cockfosters. Aberfeldy is quite skilled, well-rehearsed, and very effective at stimulating conversations. He has convinced many of the generals that he is sympathetic to the Germans and their plight."

"Thank you," Bruce acknowledged.

Kendrick nodded. He passed a packet of several stapled pages, all marked the same. "Here is the translation transcript of the original German conversation at issue."

MOST SECRET - ANGEL

```
    Excerpt of conversation: BAS, BRO, CHO, THO,
& WAH; 30th September 1944; 14:37
BAS What is your story?
WAH I was captured near Mons a month ago.
BRO Belgium?
WAH Yes. The Mons pocket. We could not retreat
        fast enough. Paris fell faster than we
        expected, and we were overrun.
THO Well, you are with the rest of us now.
WAH The corporal made another speech before I
        was captured.
THO We heard it . . . heard on the radio.
BAS Really? I didn't listen to it.
```

WAH Neither did I. The blithering idiot! If
    only the German people as a whole would
    suddenly rise up and refuse to carry on!
    But they are all scared stiff now, of
    course. They're all afraid of that bloody-
    minded, blood-thirsty hyena.

CHO In those last days before our surrender of
    Paris, the Leader sent me a direct message.
    It said, 'Paris must not fall into enemy
    hands except as a field of ruins.' Can you
    imagine? Such a historic and beautiful
    city, and he wanted me to destroy it for
    spite. We planted the explosive. We were
    ready, but I refused to issue the order.

BAS What about your family?

CHO I fear for them, but I had to do the
    correct thing. Nordling assured me he
    would save my wife and children.

THO You are not alone.

BRO Have you heard of your family since you
    surrendered?"

CHO Not yet, but I remain hopeful.

BRO You saved Paris but what about Sevastopol?

CHO The worst job I ever carried out —
    which, however, I carried out with great
    consistency — was the liquidation of the
    Jews. I carried out this order down to the
    very last detail.

BAS Quite the contrast. You carry that burden.

CHO We all share the guilt. We went along with
    everything, and we half-took the Nazis
    seriously, instead of saying to Hell with
    you and your stupid nonsense. I misled my
    soldiers into believing this rubbish. I
    feel utterly ashamed of myself. Perhaps we
    bear even more guilt than these uneducated
    animals.

BRO Maybe the Leader did not know what was
    going on.

```
THO Of course, he knows all about it. Secretly,
    he's delighted. Of course, people can't
    make a row - they would simply be arrested
    and beaten if they did.
WAH After the assassination failure, Freisler
    and the SS have gone crazy. Worse,
    Reinecke has joined them in that damnable
    kangaroo court.
THO He is a disgrace to the uniform.
CHO Reinecke is such a common commercial
    traveller, such a vulgar horrible fellow!
End of relevant conversation.
```

MOST SECRET - ANGEL

"That was quite the little clutch, wasn't it," Petrie mused aloud. "Who is Reinecke?"

"General of Infantry Hermann Reinecke," answered Menzies. "He was assigned to the so-called People's Court. General Wahle is spot-on correct. The Nazis have gone over the top in the aftermath of the assassination attempt on the 20th of July. This is like an extended Night of the Long Knives. They've gone after anyone and everyone who might have even heard a rumor. They've included others they were just unhappy about. They've executed people who have been in concentration camps for years. It is crazy. Further, this conversation validates that the professional military was involved and culpable. So, we've cautioned our assets in the country to keep their heads down and don't take unnecessary chances."

"As have we," Selborne added.

"Likewise," contributed Bruce.

"The question before the government, before both governments, is the disclosure of this material in the inevitable war crimes investigations and trials. The evidence is overwhelming, disgusting, and repulsive."

"What do you suggest?"

"The techniques and equipment are too bloody important. We can certainly devise means to make the prosecutors aware of what we've learned in the 'M' Rooms," the label the professionals gave to the microphone rooms where they listened to the German conversations. "These transcripts must be used in court where they will be subject to cross-examination."

"That is a very tall order, Tom," Menzies said. "Choltitz confessed to war crimes and crimes against humanity. Are we to ignore what we have learned here?"

"No, Sir Stewart. These transcripts might help guide the investigations, but these means and methods are vital and must be protected. We may need this capability after the war."

"That is an ugly thought," Selborne said.

"But it's accurate and appropriate," added Bruce. "The concerns for Stalin's intentions after the war are mounting daily."

Menzies looked at each of the other men. "Are we in agreement? Are we unanimous?" Each of them provided their affirmation. "Very well, then. I'll raise the issue with the prime minister. I suspect he will not be pleased. He has had his mind set upon prosecuting these barbarians to the fullest extent of the law, our knowledge, evidence, and outrage. But I will convince him."

"With your permission, I will brief General Donovan and leave the convincing of President Roosevelt to him."

Sir Stewart chuckled more visibly than audibly. "That should do quite nicely. Does this satisfy your concern?" he asked Kendrick.

"Yes Sir."

"Do you have anything else for us to discuss?"

"No Sir. There is so much actionable intelligence, insight, and clues in these transcripts just since our last meeting, but those elements are being processed by the normal intelligence processes."

"Very well, then, we are adjourned."

———

Saturday, 14.October.1944
96-311 Park Lane
Mayfair, London, England
United Kingdom
18:45 hours

Sarah Churchill had decided to take the weekend for decompression and a little alone time. She had a rare two-day leave from her photo interpretation unit at RAF Medmenham. The booms and tremors of V1 doodlebug flying bombs and V2 rockets still occurred, but blessedly, they were becoming less frequent. Her lover of many years now, U.S. Ambassador Gil Winant, felt compelled to be with her father at Chequers. Sarah missed Gil, but her need for solitude exceeded her hunger for companionship, intimacy, or pleasure. That would come, but the weekend was for recharging.

After a hot bath and short nap, Sarah stood in her small kitchen debating with herself what she was going to prepare for her dinner. In the end, she decided simpler was better. Sarah had half a jar left of a magnificent country blackberry jam, and she still had a little butter. The chief cook at the Medmenham mess hall had set aside a small loaf of fresh-baked bread that she brought with her. Sarah carefully sliced off three half-inch pieces from the loaf, toasted them, and spread them with scarce butter and blackberry jam. She savored the flavors and acknowledged the goodness with aural affirmation. Sarah had just finished the second piece when the telephone rang.

"Mayfair 5-7-1-3," she answered.

"Sarah, it's me," came the voice of her sister-in-law Pamela Beryl Churchill, née Digby, who was still married to but essentially estranged from her older brother Major Randolph Frederick Edward Spencer-Churchill. Randolph was working for Brigadier Maclean with Tito's partisans in the Balkans. "I really need to talk to you."

"Sure."

"No, I can't talk about this on the phone. I need to come over for a chat eye-to-eye."

"Something serious?"

"No . . . just thoughts overwhelming me."

Sarah loved Pamela as a sister, but she also felt a twinge of irritation that her quiet time was being intruded upon. At the bottom line, she could not resist Pamela. "I don't have much to eat."

"I've already eaten."

"Very well. Come on over." Pamela had her own apartment that was still paid for by her long-time lover W. Averell Harriman.

Sarah finished her third piece of toast and another cup of tea. She cleaned up the kitchen, opened a nice bottle of cabernet sauvignon with two glasses, and then decided to freshen up for her own sense of well-being. The distance between their apartments would take 15-20 minutes to walk and 5-10 minutes, depending on how easily it was to hail a cab.

Re-reading Emily Brontë's 1847 novel, *Wuthering Heights*, had occupied Sarah's limited available reading time, but she loved the story and the writing. This reading was her third pass through the classic novel. Nevertheless, she managed seven pages before the brass knocker at the front door announced Pamela's arrival.

The two women hugged and kissed cheeks as the true friends they were. Sarah poured the wine for both of them. They toasted each other and the coming peace. The couch worked for both of them as they faced each other sideways from the ends. Sarah gestured for Pamela to speak.

"I miss him so much, Mule," Pamela began, using Sarah's childhood familial nickname reflective of her stubborn streak. "It will be a year next week. I had so hoped Ave would take me with him, but he chose Kathy instead."

"She is his daughter, Pam."

President Roosevelt had appointed William Averell 'Ave' Harriman to be U.S. Ambassador to the Soviet Union, and the Senate confirmed the appointment. Harriman took up his new position on 23.October.1943. He was reportedly the fourth richest man in the world. Harriman had chosen his younger daughter Kathleen Lanier 'Kathy' Harriman to be his principal assistant and hostess for social events for his duty as ambassador.

"Of course, she is, but I sleep with him, and he is such a damn good lover."

"So you have told me more than once, Pam." They both laughed hard.

"Where is Gil, by the way?" Pamela asked.

"He's with Poppa at Chequers."

"Why aren't you there?"

"Several reasons, I suppose. First, they are discussing something serious. We've been giving them too many reasons to ask questions. Gil's still married, after all."

"As are you, Mule." They laughed again.

"And you, Pam. I also needed a quiet weekend to relax."

"And I'm imposing on your quiet time."

"Not to worry. So you just wanted to tell me you miss Ave?"

"That was the opener, Sarah."

"Well then, what is the rest of the story?" Sarah jumped in.

"To be blunt, I think I'm a genuine courtesan. I truly love sex. I thrive on it; even bad sex is good sex. The worst of it is I've tried to fill the void of Ave's absence with lovers. I think I'm getting a reputation."

Sarah laughed and fidgeted. "I think you crossed that threshold some time back." Again, both women laughed. "Now, on this quiet Saturday evening with a nice wine, my prurient curiosity has been stimulated."

"Who?"

"Yes."

Pamela giggled demurely and took another sip of her wine. "I've told you about Jock Whitney." Sarah nodded. "He is quite the fun fellow, skillful in bed, but he's not Ave. I enjoy pleasure with Jock, but afterward, it makes me miss Ave more. After we became intimate, I learned that he supplanted Ave as London's wealthiest American, and to my surprise, he's married to Betsey Cushing, ex-wife of James Roosevelt, President Roosevelt's oldest son."

"Small world."

"Indeed. I don't think I've told you, but I've had an on-again-off-again affair with Ed Murrow, the broadcaster, and now Ed's boss's boss Bill Paley, the founder and chairman of C-B-S. They are interesting characters. Bill is not over here that often, but when he does come, he calls me. And, of course, I must do my part for military morale. I've seen American General Fred Anderson, an

Air Force leader, and the most surprising is Peter Portal, Chief of the Air Staff. I think he's genuinely infatuated with me."

"Your cup runneth over."

"I guess so, huh. My sexual appetite is largely satisfied, but I still miss Ave even more. I want to go to Moscow, but he has not invited me. I would be lost in Moscow without him."

"Pamela, you have so much here. I know you love Ave, but would you really go to Moscow?"

"If I could, I would."

"You were sure happy while he was in London."

"Yes, I was, as you are with Gil."

"Quite so, and listening to you and your exploits has certainly aroused my yearning.

"I'm sorry to have disturbed your weekend, but I just needed to ask you that question."

"I've not heard a question."

"What do you think of my desire to go to Moscow to be with Ave?"

"Pam, have you written to him?"

"Yes, of course, and he has replied."

"But, he's not invited you to join him?"

"No, not yet, but I've not asked him either."

"So, you want my opinion?"

"Yes. That's why I'm here. You're my best friend. I trust your opinion and judgment."

"Thank you for that, Pam, as you are mine." Sarah paused in contemplation. Pamela watched but did not break her best friend's thinking. Finally, Sarah turned and looked directly into Pamela's eyes. "You must decide for yourself, Pam. You asked for my opinion, and I shall offer it for your use in the decision-making process."

"OK, Mule. I appreciate your reticence, but I came to your flat to talk, for you to hear my views, and to hear your view. So, please, let me have it."

Sarah smiled and nodded her head. "If it was me, I could not go without an invitation I tested. Sometimes men say things in the heat of the moment that they do not mean. But, even if he did invite you, I would still recommend you test it. You don't know anyone in Moscow other than Ave and Kathy. You would be alone more than not, Pam."

"OK, OK, you've talked me off the ledge."

"The other element in all that is you'd have to find a military transport and a sponsor."

"Wouldn't Poppa do that for me?" asked Pamela.

"I'd be afraid to ask him. You are still married to his only son and my only brother."

"Good points." Pamela thought for a few moments. "Thanks for listening, Sarah. You are a true sister and best friend." She finished her wine and stood. The two women hugged and kissed cheeks. Pamela left to return to her apartment. Sarah sat back down, finished her wine, smiled, and then she picked up her book to read about a bygone era.

—

Monday, 16.October.1944
Standing Oak Farm
Winchester, Hampshire, England
United Kingdom
11:15 hours

Charlotte saw the main farm for the first time since the tragedy three weeks ago. This morning, Mabel had picked her up when she was released from the hospital. Charlotte had awakened from her coma four days ago and remained in the hospital to evaluate her for any residual brain injury. She still had bound ribs and an over-the-elbow cast on her left arm. The stitches closing a dozen shrapnel wounds had been removed last week, and her injuries were still healing and sore. Blessedly, they had avoided any signs of serious infection. The women had talked in general terms about the weather, cooking, and work clothing. They avoided the war, the farm, and the tragedy.

Over the last rise, Charlotte saw the main house, barn, outbuildings, and corral fencing. "Where is everyone?"

"They are about, I am certain. After all, this is a working farm," Mabel observed, inducing laughter, which caused Charlotte to wince in pain. "I'm so sorry, Charlotte," Mabel added.

Charlotte held up her right hand, gesturing to stop, as she clutched her lower chest with her right arm. "This is life, Mabel. No pain, no gain."

Mabel stopped the car at the front door. She anticipated Charlotte's query. "I'll move the Hillman to the vehicle shed once I get you inside and sitting by the fire." Charlotte nodded her head in agreement. Mabel jumped around the car to assist Charlotte in standing and cradled her right arm in case she wobbled. They moved slowly to the front door. Mabel opened the door, stepped inside, and held the door open for Charlotte, who entered first. People filled the living room, dining area, and kitchen.

To Charlotte's surprise, Countess Selborne, Grace Palmer, stood in front of the crowd. "Welcome home, Charlotte. We gathered to embrace you with love."

Tears swiftly welled up in Charlotte's eyes and descended her cheeks. So many of her friends: Mary Spencer and her children, Linda Kensington, and now a noticeably pregnant Rosemary Kensington. The dairy and greenhouse crews were all present and cheering. They surrounded Charlotte, hugged, and kissed her, bringing more tears. Most of the crew were also among the well-wishers, including most of the greenhouse personnel. Then, Charlotte saw Edith holding Todd's right hand. Edith smiled and released Todd. The nearly four-year-old ran toward Charlotte, who slowly knelt and extended her arms to embrace the charging boy who almost knocked her over.

"Love you, 'Sharley,'" Todd said.

"I love you, Todd."

Todd pulled back just a little to stare at her arm cast. "Does it hurt?"

Charlotte giggled softly, giving her a few bolts of pain in her ribs. "No, Todd, it doesn't hurt. That is why they put this cast on me, so my arm can heal properly."

"Where is Ian?" Todd asked innocently. "I miss him."

Charlotte collapsed into a heap on the floor and began wailing loudly, almost screaming. Her breathing became convulsive. She felt hands touching her, but it did not soothe her or dampen the excruciating void Charlotte felt that was draining the life out of her. Worse, Brian was not here to soften her grief. The hands stroked and patted Charlotte's back, and none of them even attempted to divert her from her grief. Ever so slowly, Charlotte's cries subsided. When she finally lifted her head and wiped her cheeks with her right sleeve, Todd stood in front of her with a very worried expression.

"Are you all right, Sharley?"

"Yes, Todd, I miss Ian too. We love you, and we are grateful you are all right."

"What do you say?" Charlotte heard Mabel command behind her.

"Thank you, Sharley."

"You are most welcome, Todd." Charlotte felt firm hands lifting her to her feet. She turned to face a sea of worried faces. "My apologies. I miss him so much." Charlotte sucked in several convulsive breaths. All the voices spoke words of sympathy, condolence, and support. "I am not much of a hostess."

"Nonsense," Mary objected.

"Does Brian know?" asked Rosemary.

Charlotte looked at Edith who stepped forward. "Yes ma'am. I called Major Drummond immediately once Mrs. Drummond had awakened and she had been initially evaluated by the doctors four days ago."

"I got to talk to him yesterday evening," Charlotte added, "with Edith's vital assistance."

"Why isn't he here?" Rosemary aggressively barked.

"He has a war to finish," interjected Grace with solemnity on behalf of the unspoken husbands, brothers, fathers, and uncles still engaged in the fight.

"They are not here, but they are not forgotten. John has always said no news is good news," Mary offered. "He is probably swamped, Charlotte."

"This damnable bloody war has cost us all far too much already," Charlotte mumbled.

Lady Grace Selborne stepped toward Charlotte and wrapped her left arm around her shoulders. "We are all here to support you, Charlotte. We feel your loss. These are tragic times with tragic consequences. Fate brought you to this moment. Please do not forget that we are all here for you and your family."

"I know, and I thank you, Lady Selborne. Thank you all for your support." Charlotte felt the bone-numbing darkness of the profound fatigue of her continuing physical recovery and burgeoning depression rapidly descending upon her. "Now, I truly appreciate your generous display of affection and caring, but I'm terribly exhausted. I need to lay down."

The chorus of voices encouraged Charlotte to tend to her health and well-being. Charlotte nodded her head, waved to everyone, and went to her bedroom. She did not have the strength to remove her clothes and collapsed onto the bed. She pulled a blanket over her and fell into a deep sleep.

—

Friday, 20.October.1944
Leyte Island, Philippines
Occupied Territory of the United States of America
10:00 hours

The 96th Infantry Division had sailed aboard USS *General John Pope* and four other transport ships on 27.July.1944 from San Francisco for Honolulu, Hawaii. The division was billeted in tent camps at Schofield Barracks for six weeks of jungle and operational training. They had additional stops at Eniwetok and Manus Island, where they transferred to an array of Landing Ship Tank (LST) amphibious assault ships for the final approach to Leyte Island.

This was J-Hour of A-Day of Operation KING TWO—the invasion of Leyte Island and the return of U.S. forces to the Philippines, and the fulfillment of General MacArthur's vow in 1942—"I shall return." The 96th Infantry Division, known as the Deadeyes, had landed the 382nd and 383rd Infantry Regiments at J-Hour across Orange and Blue Beaches between Dulag and San Jose.

MacArthur debarked from USS *Nashville* and waded ashore at Red Beach, Palo, Leyte, fulfilling his promise to the Philippine people. At 13:30, accompanied by Philippine President Osmeña and some of his immediate staff,

Commander-in-Chief Southwest Pacific Area General Douglas MacArthur waded ashore in thigh-deep water. He had returned with the U.S. 6th Army to liberate the Philippine Islands. That afternoon, MacArthur broadcast, "People of the Philippines, I have returned! By the grace of Almighty God, our forces stand again on Philippine soil."

The author's father, Sergeant Charles Fredrick Parlier, served as a squad leader in 'A' Company, 1st Battalion, 381st Regiment, 96th Infantry Division, XXIV Corps, 6th Army.

—

Friday, 20.October.1944
USAAF Station F-356
Saffron Walden, Essex, England
United Kingdom
17:15 hours

Brian thanked Tomlinson for taking such great care of his Mustang and apologized for the holes in the aircraft. It had been a very long, intense day. He ambled toward the intelligence debriefing building with the recognition that the 'A' Division was ahead of his 'B' Division, and they would have to wait their turn with the debriefers. Other members of his division quickly caught up with him.

"That was a helluva day," Corn stated.

"Yeah, it was," added Sweet.

Brian would only nod his head in agreement.

The guys seemed more tired than talkative, which was perfectly fine with Brian. He preferred other members of his division go ahead of him, which they did. Hunter was the last of the 334FS pilots, and to his surprise, his debriefer was none other than Staff Sergeant Norman Bradford, the 8th Air Force intelligence analyst.

"I'd like to say it's great to see you again, Sergeant Bradford, but I'd prefer to get something to eat and go to bed."

Bradford smiled. "Understandable, given what I've learned from your comrades already," he said, gesturing to an open booth they used for these mission debriefings. Once inside, Bradford closed the door. They sat opposite each other across a small table. Brian recounted his takeoff configuration—half ball and half armor-piercing machine gun ammunition, and two, three-tube rocket launchers under each wing. Each tube held a 4.5-inch M8 rocket carrying a 4.3-pound, high explosive warhead.

Brian began to recount his observations from the mission. "We hit the known anti-aircraft sites near simultaneously as a squadron with what appeared to be success. 'A' Division found two new sites, previously unknown; we found one. Once we took out those sites, 'B' Division climbed to our perch altitude of Angels Five to provide air cover while 'A' Division went to work on our primary target, Fort Driant at Metz.

"We saw a squadron of 1-oh-9s and prepared to engage, but they were headed somewhere else. We kept an eye on them to see if they might double-back, but they never did. Other than that sighting, we encountered no air opposition.

"When 'A' Division expended their rockets, we traded places. We descended on Fort Driant and set up a clover-leaf attack pattern over the target. 'A' Division had done a pretty good job. It took us longer to find new or still functional targets in and around the fort. I shifted our targets to doors, hatches, and openings, in principle to skip shrapnel into the interior. I've no idea whether the shift was successful.

"Jack Jarvis took a hit in his engine, giving him a rough runner. He diverted to A-96 and landed safely."

Advanced Landing Ground designated A-96 opened for Allied aircraft on the 29th of August. The airfield was locally known as Toul/Ochey Airfield and was operated and staffed by the 9th Air Force, located 13 miles southwest of Nancy near the village of Thuilley-aux-Groseilles and had a history going back to the Great War.

"I will comment here that the M8 rockets we used had minimal effect on the stone and concrete of the fort's construction. We needed much more powerful weapons. Also, the M8 rocket is not a particularly precise weapon. It seems to wiggle in flight, making it difficult to achieve precision. Nonetheless, numerous fires were burning by the time we finished, and nothing moved. It looked to me like we accomplished what we were assigned to do.

"The Skipper changed our mission to use more of our machine gun ammo. We sought targets to the east of the fort and Metz--tanks, trucks, a few howitzers, and some troop concentrations. We shot those up pretty well. When the Skipper called bingo, we headed home initially at a low level looking for more targets. We found none . . . just Allied forces. I guess our passing was kind of an airshow. We saw troops waving and cheering as we passed.

"Once we were well clear of the front lines, the Skipper climbed us up to Angels Eight for better fuel consumption, although we still had plenty, and to cool the engines. Landing back at base was uneventful."

Bradford finished jotting down his notes. "Very thorough, Major," he announced. "Anything else?" Brian shook his head. "Thank you very much. Have a good night."

When Brian left the debriefing room, the other rooms were all open. Some intelligence analysts were sitting at a common conference table, working on their processing of the debriefing worksheets.

Brian was somewhat surprised that the squadron operations building was still open and the lights were on. As he entered, he was genuinely surprised to see all of the squadron pilots sitting and Arnie sitting in a chair facing the group. As Brian hung up his flight gear, Arnie stood and said, "Hunter, front and center." Hunter's puzzled expression invoked laughter and ribbing from some of the other pilots. "Attention to orders." The pilots stood and came to a position of attention. "The Secretary of War takes great pleasure in awarding Major Brian A. Drummond his senior pilot wings in recognition of the collective five years of service in the U.S. Army Air Forces and the Royal Air Force as an American volunteer, and the accumulation of 3,117 flight hours, including 277 combat missions with 23 credited aerial victories, and he's not done, yet. Congratulations, Hunter." Clark removed Brian's pilot wings and replaced them with his new senior pilot wings. The gathering applauded and cheered.

Sweet shouted, "Drinks on Hunter." Brian shook his head. "Nope, no excuses, Hunter. You know the drill."

The pilots congratulated Brian. They closed up the ops building and went directly to the Officer's Mess since they were approaching the end of the evening meal. Brian wanted to fall into bed, but he stuck it out and had a couple of beers with the squadron and some other group pilots.

When he was able to break from the celebration, Brian stopped at the bank of telephone booths. Several were empty. He chose one, closed the bifold door, and asked the operator to connect him to the farm.

"Standing Oak Farm," came Edith's distinct soft voice.

"Evening, Edith. How is Charlotte?"

"Not good, I'm afraid, Major."

"What's wrong?"

"Mrs. Drummond is very depressed. She has withdrawn. We can't get her out of bed. She won't eat. We are all very worried. Mrs. Kensington is here now. Would you like to talk to her?"

"I'd like to talk to Charlotte. Please tell my wife I'm on the telephone, and I need to talk to her."

"Very well."

Brian heard the handset being placed on the table, and then he heard Edith talking with Linda about Brian's request. They presumably went to the master bedroom together. Brian listened hard but could not hear anything other than the crackling of the fire.

The handset rumbled off the table. "Brian, it's Linda. She says she can't talk."

"We've got to get her out of bed, and she must eat."

"We all know that, Brian."

"Has she eaten anything since she has been home?" a worry husband asked. "Has she eaten anything?"

"Yes, spotty. Charlotte has had toast and scones with honey, some soup here and there, and some tea."

"Are the doctors any help?"

"No."

What the hell am I going to do? What can I do? She is dying slowly. I can't talk to Arnie tonight. I can't talk to him tomorrow morning because we're flying first thing. I'll talk to him after we're done. He'll probably not be happy to hear my request, but I've got to do something.

"Are you still there, Brian?" asked Linda.

"Yes, yes, sorry, I was just thinking what I can do." *I can't tell her we're flying tomorrow.* "Please keep trying to get her out of bed and moving, and she must eat proper food. She loves Shepherd's Pie."

"We've tried that several times."

"Please keep trying. Tell her how worried we are. I'll try to get home as soon as they'll let me go." Linda did not respond. "We've got to break her out of this depression. Churchill calls depression the Black Dog, and the Black Dog is smothering her."

"We'll keep trying, Brian. We all acknowledge how serious this is. Now, you'd better get to bed. You must tend to yourself."

"Thank you, Linda. Please thank Edith and everyone for their efforts to help Charlotte. Good night." Brian hung up the telephone handset and sat in the booth, lost in his thoughts. He felt a dark, heavy blanket descending upon him. *I've got to shake this off before I fly.* Brian eventually made it to his room and collapsed into bed.

———

Wednesday, 25.October.1944
Leyte Island, Philippines
Occupied Territory of the United States of America
03:55 hours

As the 381st Infantry waited to land later in the day, the troops were brought up to the main deck by the sweltering tropical heat even at night, and more significantly, by what sounded like thunder. The troops watched what they thought was lightning. The flashes beyond the horizon to the southeast preceded the rumbling thunder roughly 20 seconds later.

What the Army soldiers did not learn until later, they witnessed naval history in those early morning hours—the Battle of Surigao Strait. Six American battleships crossed the 'T' in a classic maneuver bringing the maximum firepower onto the minimum enemy answering fire. The Americans opened fire beyond the maximum range of the Japanese. It would be the last battleship-on-battleship naval engagement in history. It was also the first time since the Battle of the Saintes in 1782 that a 'crossing of the T' had been successfully used by ships of the line. Of particular note on the night's engagement, five of the six American battleships involved had survived the damage inflicted at Pearl Harbor—*Pennsylvania, California, Tennessee, Maryland,* and *West Virginia.* The USS *Mississippi,* with her 14-inch main battery guns, rounded out the battle line. As fate would have it, the most effective of the six American battleships that night were the most seriously damaged warships at Pearl Harbor. They had been repaired, retrofitted, upgraded, and modified to include the most advanced fire control radar of the era. In 18 minutes, the American battleships fired three hundred 2,700-pound 16-inch and 1,500-pound 14-inch rounds that devastated the Japanese task force. The cruiser line had fired four thousand 8-inch and 6-inch shells.

After observing the 'lightning and thunder' of this historic naval engagement, the 381st Infantry Regiment was released as the 6th Army reserve, went ashore later that day, and joined the combat operations on Leyte.

The previous day, during the Battle of the Sibuyan Sea, Commander Air Group 15 was embarked aboard *USS Essex.* Commander David McCampbell, USN [USNA 1933], flying an F6F-5 Hellcat, shot down nine enemy aircraft during a frenetic aerial battle. His wingman shot down six other aircraft that day. McCampbell had to land on the USS *Langley* with the *Essex* deck unable to recover him. His engine quit from fuel starvation before he could disengage from the arrestor cable, and his starboard outboard gun only had six rounds remaining.

Added to his accomplishments during the Marianas Turkey Shoot, McCampbell was awarded the Medal of Honor for both events by President Roosevelt in February 1945. He was the only pilot to achieve ace-in-a-day status twice. McCampbell finished the war with 34 confirmed aerial victories. He was also awarded the Navy Cross for gallantry in combat the following day—the 25th of October 1944.

His son, David Perry McCampbell, is a United States Naval Academy classmate of the author in the Class of 1970.

—

Thursday, 26. October. 1944
Standing Oak Farm
Winchester, Hampshire, England
United Kingdom
12:05 hours

The journey home had been more anxious and apprehensive than any previous trips to the farm. Brian had called twice when his mission day was complete, and both times, Charlotte was sleeping. He had thought it was best she sleep, if they could not get her out of bed. Mabel and Edith, at separate times, had voiced their concerns for Charlotte's emotional and mental health. They said she was physically healing nicely, but they were concerned about her full recovery. Mabel had told him about their friends who had set up a schedule so that at least one of them was present at the farm to care for Charlotte and nothing else.

Once again, Morty Jurdy met Brian at Winchester Station and transported him to the farm as he had done many times. Morty stopped at the crest as he had always done, but this time, Brian waved him on to the house. His principal concern was his wife's well-being. Morty stopped at the front door. No one came outside to meet him. Brian paid the fare plus a handsome gratuity.

Brian entered the quiet house. Hearing the door, Linda Kensington looked over her shoulder as she stood at the kitchen counter making cookies, or biscuits as the British called the edibles. Brian walked to her. They kissed cheeks in the European style, although she kept her dough covered hands away from Brian's uniform.

"Welcome home," Linda said.

"Thank you." Brian unbuttoned his overcoat, gestured with his head toward the coat rack by the front door. Brian removed his overcoat and uniform tunic and hung them up, the overcoat on an open peg and his tunic with an available wooden hanger. He returned to stand at arm's length beside Linda as she worked.

"Thank you for taking the time to care for Charlotte."

"My pleasure, Brian. She is a jewel, and each of us has felt honored to help her."

"Is she sleeping?"

Linda smiled and shook her head. "She has been very depressed. It has been a concern for all of us. Based on what the others have said, she has rarely gotten out of bed. A few times to take a bath, but she has missed many more meals than she has made."

"That's not good."

"As with all of us, Charlotte must process her grief in the best manner for her, but we are all worried, Brian."

Many thoughts swiftly ran through his mind. "Who has been managing the business?"

"June, pretty much oversees things, but Mabel has been handling the greenhouses, and Horace keeps the dairy running smoothly. June had to go into town this morning, the bank I think."

"OK. I'm here now, for the next two days. I'm going to try and get her moving, again."

"Just be careful, Brian. Don't push too hard. She is hurting terribly."

"I'm hurting, too, Linda. Ian was my son as well. Death is part of my job, unfortunately, and there is a war to fight and win. Jonathan is as much a part of that process as I am. Nonetheless, thank you for your candor. Now, let me see what I can do to help Charlotte."

"Good luck, Brian."

Again, he just nodded his head. Brian took off his necktie, hung it up with his uniform tunic, and opened his collar. He walked to the closed bedroom door and stared at the lever handle. Brian took a deep breath, bracing himself for what he might see, and knocked softly twice before he opened the door. The room was dark and smelled antiseptic, like a hospital. Brian closed the door quietly after him and stood for a few seconds to allow his eyes to adjust to the darkness. The shape on her side of the bed did not move. He waited a little longer to ensure he could see anything that might be on the floor before he slowly and quietly stepped toward her side of the bed. Brian knelt beside Charlotte. Only her face was visible between the sheets and under the covers. Her eyes remained closed and did not twitch. Her breathing was regular, shallow, and slow. She seemed peaceful.

Brian did not move or speak, and purposely kept his breathing as inaudible as he could. He had no idea how long he was in that position. His knees began to hurt, but he refused to budge.

Eventually, Charlotte blinked her eyes open, smiled meekly, and extended her right arm from under the covers. She placed her hand behind Brian's neck and pulled his face toward her, so she could kiss him.

"I love you," whispered Brian.

"I have missed you so much." Tears quickly welled up and descended across her face to the pillow below.

"I have missed you, but I'm here now."

"Are you all right?" Charlotte asked.

"Yes. But more importantly, how are you?"

Charlotte closed her eyes and sobbed visibly but not audibly. Tears streamed across her face to the pillow. "I'm dead, Brian. I'm simply dead," she answered without opening her eyes.

Brian chose not to react to her words of depression, misery, and sorrow. He felt her pain, but he could not say it to Charlotte. "Let's get you back to living."

"No. I can't."

Brian kissed Charlotte's forehead, swiped away her tears, and then he kissed her on the lips. "It's a gorgeous day outside . . . a little on the chilly side, but still a beautiful day. I want you to put your feet on the floor. I'm going to open the curtains."

"Brian, I feel so hollow. I feel dead."

Gently stroking her forehead, Brian leaned forward to kiss Charlotte several more times. "You are not. You can feel my touch. You know I love you, Charlotte Grace Tamerlin." She smiled several times briefly and opened her eyes.

"I'm such a muddle."

"Nonsense. We signed up for the long haul . . . for better or worse. We will get through this together. Now, let's get you moving." Brian did not wait for a response. He reached under the covers, grasped her legs, and slowly pulled her legs out. Charlotte sat up on the edge of the bed. Brian was shocked how much weight she had lost. Brian stood and slowly opened the curtains. The brightness hurt his eyes, and Charlotte placed both her fists in front of her eyes.

"It hurts, Brian."

"I know . . . because you are alive." Brian embraced Charlotte under her arms and lifted her to a wobbly standing position. *My God, she's so thin. I can't imagine how long it has been since she has moved or even eaten. First things first. I've got to get her moving and feeling again.* Charlotte stood still as he removed her nightgown. He found a light soft shirt and added a heavy flannel shirt before supporting Charlotte as she haltingly stepped into her overalls. He helped her sit on the edge of the bed. It took him a few minutes to find nice wool socks and a pair of boots for her feet. Brian brushed her hair as best he could, and then he found a tie to pull her hair back into a short ponytail.

Satisfied he had dressed her for the chill of the autumn air in Hampshire, Brian wrapped his arms around her frail torso as he supported her right arm with his right hand. They shuffled to the front door.

"Well done, Brian," Linda said, as she intercepted the Drummonds at the front door. "I assume you two are headed to the oak tree bench. I made you a couple pieces of toast with butter and boysenberry jam. I'll escort you to deliver your toast."

"Thank you, Linda," whispered Charlotte. "You are such a big help. Everyone is so supportive."

The gravel walk to the massive oak tree proved to be more challenging for the weakness of Charlotte's deteriorated state. Once they reached the bench, Brian lowered Charlotte to the bench, and then he turned to making a modest fire. Linda sat with Charlotte and held the plate, as Charlotte slowly and gratefully consumed the toast.

Once he had a nice comfortable fire going, Brian sat down on Charlotte's left side.

Charlotte looked to her left at Brian. "Do you want some?"

"Sweetheart, you're the one who needs to eat."

Charlotte smiled and returned to her toast. Another two bites, and she finished. "Thank you so much, Linda. You are such a dear."

"Thank you, Charlotte. Would you like anything else?"

"No, thanks."

"Then, I will leave you to get reacquainted." Linda stood.

"Thank you so much, Linda," Brian added.

Brian put his arm around Charlotte's shoulders. "Are you warm enough?"

"Yes, dear . . . quite comfortable. You did an excellent job with the fire." She looked into her husband's eyes. "What did you want to talk about?"

"I'm here for you, Mrs. Drummond. I have no topic. We can talk about whatever you want to talk about. My objective was to get you out of bed, into the fresh air, and let you feel life, again. Smell the earth and the smoke from the fire. Feel the breeze. Hear the birds chirping and singing their songs. I'm your husband, Sharley." They both laughed at Todd's moniker for Charlotte. "I'm here to listen to you, to whatever will help you feel better. We have a long and fruitful life ahead of us . . . together."

"I hear you, Brian. And, I know you are correct." Charlotte stared straight ahead.

I know better than to intrude upon her thoughts, She'll speak when she's ready to speak. Brian sat quietly and kept his gaze straight ahead across the lake to the green, grassy hills beyond. *I love this place. I love this woman.* Uncounted minutes passed as Brian sat patiently. He stood a couple of times to tend the fire, returned to the bench, and tried to ignore the shiny reflective streams on Charlotte's cheeks. Brian could not hear her cry, but he knew she was weeping in silence.

"It was all my fault," Charlotte finally muttered.

"No!" Brian protested sharply but stopped when she held up her right hand.

"I killed our son, our precious little boy. If I hadn't allowed them outside, he would still be alive and thriving."

Brian jumped to his feet and spun to face Charlotte. "Stop, sweetheart. It was good for the boys to play in the tall grass. You could not, no one could predict an errant, deflected, buzz bomb would land on the farm. Fate happens to all of us. I live with that reality every day. There is nothing you could have done."

Charlotte only shook her head slowly. Brian stepped to Charlotte, knelt in front of her, grasped her wet cheeks, and looked deeply and affectionately into her bloodshot eyes. "You caused none of this. I know you are grieving and must process your sorrow in a manner best for you." Brian kissed Charlotte several times and wiped her cheeks, but the tears still descended her cheeks. "I wish I had some magical touch to remove all the pain consuming you, Charlotte. All I have to offer is my love for you. You may not feel it or even sense it, but 'This too shall pass.' I can only love you, and convey my love for you, and hope my love brings you out of the very dark place you are in right now."

Charlotte could only nod her head slightly. "I appreciate your sincerity. I don't know how you can love me, but I'm grateful for your love. Now, I'm exhausted. I need to lay down."

"We've been in the fresh air for . . . ," he glanced at his wristwatch, "20 minutes. It's a good start to get you back on your feet. Just one more question before I help you inside." Charlotte nodded her head in consent. "Who has been managing things here and with the States?"

"June, mostly, but Mabel and Horace, also"

"I have yet to meet June, but I really must do so."

"Yes, you should. If you don't catch her this afternoon, she should be back tomorrow morning. I need to introduce you."

"Not necessary. Your health is far more important. I'll find her and introduce myself. Now, let's get you back to bed."

Brian assisted Charlotte in standing. He would return to quench the fire, but it was OK for now. Supporting her, Brian walked back inside with her. She did not want to remove her clothes and just asked for a blanket so she could rest comfortably. Brian felt that decision alone was a positive sign.

With Charlotte peaceful and settled, Brian made sure the fire was completely extinguished and then returned to the kitchen. He briefed Linda on what he felt about his chat with Charlotte. Grace Palmer was scheduled to assume the duty tomorrow morning. Linda informed Brian that June had left for the day, so tomorrow would be the day for his introduction.

Brian needed to get a reply to Bobby Sales regarding the OSS-BAS air plan that he had reviewed this week. The correct way would be to have June reply to Bobby by telegram, but he did not want to wait another day. Brian went to the telephone and asked for a connection to London Station. Fortunately, Colonel Bruce was available. Brian briefly conveyed the essence of the Drummond family situation and specifically his successful review of the air plan. Bruce accepted the task to inform Sales and the E Street Complex of Brian's approval of the OSS-BAS air plan. Brian returned his attention to Charlotte.

———

Friday, 27.October.1944
Camp Elsenborn
Bütgenbach, Belgium
20:00 hours

Before the arrival of the American Army, the camp had been known as *Truppenübungsplatz* Elsenborn or Elsenborn military training area in English. The Belgian Army, and even the French Army, on invitation, used the facilities before the war. It was used by the German Army after the invasion of the Low Countries and France in 1940. Camp Elsenborn was two miles north of the village of Bütgenbach, three miles southwest of the German border, and just a few more miles to the Siegfried Line inside Germany that was the current front line of combat.

The stage had been hastily constructed using the terrain to form a rather nice pseudo-amphitheater. The United Service Organizations Inc. (USO), an American nonprofit-charitable corporation, was founded in February 1941, to entertain members of the United States Armed Forces and their families.

The evening's USO show at Camp Elsenborn featured Marlene Dietrich, a very popular actress and entertainer. She sang, danced, and performed comedy routines. Marlene was a German-born immigrant and naturalized American citizen who was a fervent anti-Nazi. She had and continued to work with the OSS to counter German propaganda and reduce German morale. Marlene had been advised numerous times not to go so close to the front-line combat operations, but she felt a duty to take the risks. When asked why she took such risks to entertain the troops, Marlene repeatedly answered, *"aus Anstand*—out of decency."

Among the audience for this particular USO show were members of the 28th 'Bloody Bucket' Infantry Division on a brief respite from combat.

Five days later, the 28ID returned to the front to join the beginning of the Battle of Hürtgen Forest, a brutal, bloody, tree-by-tree fight with desperate German forces. The battle had a profound impact on Staff Sergeant Herbert Davis Parlier, the author's paternal uncle and the younger brother of the author's father. What we know today as Post Traumatic Stress Disorder (PTSD) would eventually claim Herb Parlier's life three decades later, when the untreated turmoil became too much.

Unbeknownst to the American Army, the conifer tree canopy of *Hürtgenwald* was the staging area for the massing of German forces that American and British Intelligence agencies suspected were moving west, but they could not locate. The German units disappeared into the forest. The battle would last until it was subsumed by the looming and much larger winter battle. The Germans initially called the counter-offensive *Unternehmen Wacht am Rhein* (Operation WATCH ON THE RHINE) to suggest a defensive affair based on the Rhine River. The actual plan was *Unternehmen Herbstnebel* (Operation AUTUMN MIST). The Allies would soon call the winter struggle the Battle of the Bulge.

Chapter 12

No man can be ignorant that he must die,
nor be sure that he may not this very day.

-- Cicero

Wednesday, 1.November.1944
Office of the Director, Office of Strategic Services
National Institutes of Health Building
2430 E Street Northwest
Washington, District of Columbia
United States of America
07:05 hours

The reports were mounting more swiftly that something big was looming somewhere on the Western Front. Bill Donovan did not like the impressions the reports were leaving in his thoughts. He felt a threat agonizingly close that none of them could see, touch, or hear, but they knew it had to be out there and close. The Service had pulled out every available tool and still could not clarify what was happening beyond their biological senses. His intuition was screaming at him, but they had to have facts for the field commanders to believe the intelligence.

The Soviets were making progress in the Balkans, which Tito found useful to his aims of liberating and unifying the Balkan regions. The advance of the Soviets forced the Germans to withdraw from Athens and Greece, offering more combat units for whatever was building in the West. The Red Army remained less aggressive on the Eastern Front, apparently content to allow Hitler to thin his forces in Poland for movement to the west. Donovan pressed the buzzer button for his trusty deputy.

"Yes, Chief," came Buxton's voice over the speaker.

"Do you have a few minutes for me, Ned?"

"Sure, Boss. I was just coming to see you. Be right there."

A few minutes later, the knock on his office door announced the arrival of Ned Buxton. Closing the door behind him, Ned took the cushioned chair next to Donovan's modest desk.

"You had something," Bill said as Ned sat.

"A message from Bruce last night confirmed Major Drummond has reviewed and concurred with the air plan."

"Excellent. Good to go."

"That was the last piece."

"I'll finish it up."

"Bruce's message also informed us that Brian's son was killed by a deflected V1 flying bomb, and his wife was seriously wounded and is struggling with recovery. One other child and the nanny were also wounded but not seriously."

"I'll send a personal of condolence and speedy recovery to Brian and Charlotte."

"Do you want me to prepare a draft for you?"

"No, thanks, Ned. I'll do a note in my hand. Anything else . . . before we jump to my topic?"

"Nope."

"I've been reading the latest reports on the situation in Western Germany. Neither the British nor we have pinned down the German forces being moved west that we've seen for several months now. Reading last night and this morning, I passed my patience threshold with uncertainty. Something is going to happen soon. Would you please contact B-A-S and get me a Connie ASAP for London? I want to take Magruder and Köhler with me."

Brigadier General John Logan Magruder, USA [VMI 1909], had served as Deputy Director of Intelligence since the formation of the OSS. Helmut Karl Köhler had been the chief of the German Desk within the Secret Intelligence Branch since Magruder convinced Bill Donovan he was the best man for the job. Despite his name, Köhler was a native-born American and career intelligence analyst. The German Desk had 23 analysts to cover the torrent of intelligence coming from the field.

"Are you sure you want to do that, Bill, to clear out the Intelligence Branch?"

Donovan laughed modestly. "Hardly, but it is a nice sentiment . . . and I'll return them in a few days."

"Is this really that serious?" asked Ned.

Donovan leaned back in his chair and smiled briefly. "The succinct answer is yes. The slightly more elaborate answer is that I have exactly the same feeling I had in November of '41. My gut is telling me something big is afoot. Our collective intelligence community must take a position based on the data we have. SHAEF, oh hell, the War Department, the chief of staff, even the damn Army G-2 are convinced the Germans are done, that the troop movements could be for a host of reasons. Hell, one colonel in the G-2, I've no idea who he is, had the audacity, or perhaps outright ignorance, to suggest the Germans might be moving west to surrender to the Western Allies. The Germans are in trouble. They know the war is lost. The ANGEL information reinforces that notion. And yet, my experience tells me never to underestimate the will of the Germans to fight. These troop movements are not for surrender. They are moving for a fight, a counter-offensive. I can feel it."

"That seems pretty bold based on the data we have."

"Perhaps, but nobody said the intelligence business was easy."

"When do you want to leave?"

"This afternoon or evening, if B-A-S can swing it. Also, I'd like to depart from Anacostia . . . fewer eyes to notice."

"I'll see what they can do and let you know ASAP. I'll also alert Magruder and Köhler."

"Make sure they, specifically Karl, are prepared to present our data and their best guess of what it means. I intend to discuss this matter with them during our transit. Next, I'll take care of notifying Stewart and Cecil. Finally, I'm going to ask that we include Jumper Pike. We need his insight."

"There's a lot that needs to happen in short order. So I'd better hop to it."

Donovan only nodded and returned to his reading.

———

Wednesday, 1.November.1944
Bainbridge Air Services, Inc.
Wichita Municipal Airport
Wichita, Sedgwick County, Kansas
United States of America
10:15 hours

Bobby Joe Sales had just returned from an early morning personal flight in one of his surplussed Grumman FF-1 airplanes and was at his desk for 20 minutes when his secretary Helen Burbidge, a 28-year-old Municipal University of Wichita graduate and English major, stood at his open door and said, "Mister Sales, Colonel Buxton on line two."

"Thank you, Helen. Please close the door." Bobby waited for the door latch to click before pushing button two and lifting the handset to his left ear. "Sales," he said.

"Mister Sales, Colonel Buxton, I have a very short fuse request for special transport."

"How can we help?"

"We need a Constellation, the V-I-P version, if available, to transport three individuals and their baggage from Bolling Field at Anacostia to R-A-F Northolt in London."

"When?"

"This afternoon or evening."

"Whoa, that is short fuse. Hang on a moment, let me check my board and crew." Bobby examined the status board on the wall across from his desk. One of the BAS Lockheed Constellations had been configured with custom executive seating with plush reclining seats facing each other across a retractable

table; they called it their Very Important Person (VIP) bird. The designated aircraft was serviced and available. Next, he checked the four aircrew boards. Only two stewardesses were needed for such a small passenger list, and he had two experienced women, so that was good. The only Constellation-rated pilot available was one of the female pilots and a female flight engineer, but he had no copilots for an afternoon departure. Plus, they needed to depart from Wichita within the next three hours to make Anacostia in the afternoon. "OK, Ned, are you still there?"

"Yes."

"The V-I-P aircraft is available. I can put together a minimal crew, but I will have to fly copilot for this mission."

"Can you handle that?"

"Yes. How long will we be gone?"

"There are still some arrangements to close, so my answer will be a bit soft. If everything can be put in place, it should be only a day or two in London and then return to Washington."

"That should work. I'll need about an hour to confirm the crew. I'll put the aircraft on alert right now. Unless you hear back from me, we'll assume everything is a go. Could you have someone obtain clearance for us to land and takeoff from Bolling?"

"I'll have one of my folks get on it right now. Thanks, Bobby. One last stipulation . . . this is a secret mission, so appropriate controls are required."

"Understood . . . and no problem."

"We'd better talk again before you take off from Wichita to tie off the details . . . too many loose ends."

"Agreed, and wilco, as we say in the flying biz."

"Thank you for your quick response, Bobby."

"No problem, Ned. That's what we're here for."

They hung up. Bobby punched the button for Operations and informed the duty desk that serial number 2066 needed to be prepared for a one o'clock departure for an extended special mission. He asked Helen to check on the chosen aircrew and have them prepared for early afternoon departure, and then he asked her to find Francis June 'Franny' Billings, who had been promoted to aircraft commander five months ago and to ask her to come to his office pronto. The copilot usually did the flight planning, but Bobby had too many other tasks to complete. Franny was onsite and happy to do the planning. They had a lot to do to perform this flash mission.

———

The day's mission was CIRCUS 213, another bomber escort assignment for the 334th Fighter Squadron. Their target was the massive I.G. Farben Leuna Works at Merseburg, Saxony-Anhalt, Germany, 15 miles west of Leipzig. While the Leuna Works produced many chemical products and had been extensively bombed by both the 8th Air Force and RAF Bomber Command, they would focus on the synthetic oil production facility within the massive plant. The Leuna Works were heavily defended, and they were likely to face the full scope and force of the German air defense system.

There was no pretense of misdirection on this mission. The bombers and fighter escort formed up over the North Sea, took a slight dog leg to avoid the defenses of the Ruhr Valley, and then went directly into the heart of Germany and the Leuna Works. Belgium and the Netherlands had been cleared. Allied ground forces had penetrated the German frontier in multiple places, enabling the squadron's P-51 Mustang fighters to hold their external jettisonable fuel tanks until they were empty into Germany, giving them full internal fuel tanks for the fight ahead. The 334th had the front left corner of the massive bomber formation. The weather was perfect all the way to Leipzig. The bombers were stacked from Angels 22 to Angels 25. The fighters were spread out 2,000 feet above the top of the bomber formation.

A few flak bursts kept the bomber guys alert but caused no apparent damage or deviation by the bombers. The right-side escort reported a squadron of Fw190s below and south of the formation headed in the opposite direction. Brian never saw them, and they were no factor in their mission.

"Bandits, ten o'clock climbing. Looks like two Comets so far."

Brian saw the exhaust trails climbing straight up. Then, as the smoke trail began to arc over above them, the smoke stopped, and the diminutive interceptors disappeared.

"Cobweb, Upper Six, you've got 'em."

"Roger, Upper Six. Break, Cobweb Red, you've got position."

"Roger, Cobweb. Break, Red Two, let's go," Hunter pushed his throttle through the emergency gate and up against the hard stop, and then Brian pulled back smoothly, raising the nose to where he expected the *Komet* to dive on the bombers. Canopy glint briefly marked the German's flight path. Brian adjusted his flight path slightly. *I can't hold this attitude forever*. The tiny speck began to grow. *He's growing faster than my airspeed is decaying*. Hunter moved his sight pipper where he wanted it and squeezed the trigger. All six guns erupted and shook the slowing fighter. He let up, moved his pipper down, and depressed the trigger again. The *Komet* grew faster, and then the flashes spotted the interceptor just before it exploded into myriad fiery fragments.

Brian rolled right and pulled back until he felt the shudder of stall as the underside of his fighter was peppered by shrapnel. His aircraft fluttered and stalled. Brian neutralized his controls and pulled his throttle back to idle. Tracers flashed upward. The second *Komet* dove past him and through the bomber formation. Getting his fighter flying again took his full attention. The nose finally dropped. Airspeed increased quickly. Brian simultaneously pushed his throttle forward to full power and pulled back on his stick. Brian looked over both shoulders. *No chasers. Corn is in perfect combat position.* Brian quickly scanned the sky around him. They were behind the bomber formation. No sooner had he returned his nose to the horizon with the machine accelerating nicely a squadron of *Schwalbe* fighters approached the bombers from the left rear and apparently unaware of Hunter and Corn.

"Bandits, eight o'clock high," Brian radioed. "A squadron of Swallows."

The world's first operational turbine engine fighter, the German's named *Schwalbe*, the German word for Swallow. The moniker was hardly appropriate for a bird with enormous teeth—four 30mm cannons in the nose. The twin-engine fast fighter was sometimes referred to as *Sturmvogel*, German for Storm Bird. The Germans had their eyes on the bombers and their escort and had not seen the two Mustangs trailing the large formation.

"Tally ho!" responded Upper Six.

Hunter hand-signaled Corn to move to the left side and take the rear of the Germans. He was going to take the lead enemy fighter. The Germans would be crossing in front of them but well beyond the maximum effective range of the Mustang's guns. *It's the best shot we're going to get, and we can't pass this up. We'll only get one shot.*

Brian mentally calculated the German's fast crossing rate and the range for his aim point and lead. *This is going to be a very long-range shot.* The lead computing sight had no value for this situation. Hunter moved his aim point a little higher and right. He squeezed the trigger. The guns all fired. The tracers arced up and began to fall before the element burned out. Hunter quickly adjusted right and a little higher and fired one last burst. Corn's tracers arced out as well. The ballistics and engagement trigonometry were well beyond any of their experience due to the high speed of the *Komet* and *Schwalbe* aircraft. To his surprise, Brian saw two flashes on the leader's wingman. Fire erupted on the right wing, then the engine exploded. Several seconds later, the right wing broke, flying up and over the jet, and then the fighter instantly entered a high-rate spiral dive.

"Got 'em," Corn broadcast.

The 334FS pilots maneuvered to engage the descending German fighters. *It's too dangerous to chase the Germans—potential friendly fire.* Brian rolled to keep his section above the fight just in case one or more Germans chose to pull up into a high perch for reengagement. Hunter continuously scanned the sky, expecting the Germans to send more fighters. Then, flak bursts began blooming ahead of and among the bomber formation. They're close to their target. The *Schwalbe* aircraft hit a half dozen bombers, two of which could not maintain position. The Germans used their speed differential to disengage and dive away. The bombers pressed on through the flak as they always did. Several more bombers were hit and damaged by the flak bursts.

Brian's head remained on a swivel in constant motion. The entire bomber formation wheeled right after they had dropped their bomb loads on the chemical plant and synthetic oil refinery. Then, when he could catch a glance at the ground, he witnessed the strings of explosions, the dust, dirt, and debris of major bombing, and the black boiling smoke of petroleum burning. *Looks like they're spot on the money with hundreds of 500-pound high explosive and incendiary bombs.*

Headed back to England, the bombers stabilized their formation positions. The bombers that could not maintain position were left to hobble back as best they could. The fighter escort was doing the same. Hunter and Corn descended and rejoined in position. They expected the German fighters to renew their interception operations.

On the return leg, the 4FG had the southside, and the 56FG had the northside of the bomber formation. They were headed to a pivot point 30 miles south of the Ruhr industrial complex. The Germans returned. The 56FG engaged with success. The 4FG shifted to cover the bombers while their brethren achieved some victories and needed little assistance from the 4th.

As they passed over the Rhine and the Siegfried Line, they could see smoke and dust of combat below them, but they were too high to see any details. Upper Six released the 56FG to descend for targets of opportunity in support of the ground forces. The 4FG remained with the bombers for the return to England. Brian continued to check his gauges to ensure he could take appropriate action should he have a slow leak of lubricant, coolant, or hydraulic fluid. The powerful Packard engine continued to hum along nicely. It had been a good day, but Tomlinson and the group maintenance folks probably had a lot of repair work to perform tonight.

After the debriefings, securing, and eating a simple but edible evening meal. Brian headed directly to the telephones as he had done almost every night since the explosion.

"Standing Oak Farm," Charlotte announced.

"It is so great to hear your voice, my darling. Are you feeling better?"

"I still have my moments, but your insistent love helped my climb out of the hole I was in."

"I'm so glad and relieved that you're moving and presumably eating."

"Yes, I am. I had dinner with the crew tonight. Mary has the duty, and she brought Harriett, who made a sinfully delicious cake to celebrate my return to living."

"Excellent. I wish I could have a piece."

"I know it's a silly question, but when do I get to see you again."

"You know the answer. We're still very busy. I can't talk about what we are doing, but it is good."

"As much as I would enjoy talking to you all night, you need to get to bed to stay sharp. I'm feeling much better. I'm up and dressed. I'm eating good food expertly prepared. I'm surrounded by friends who love me. And, I have a husband who has saved me and loves me bunches."

"Bunches is a serious understatement." They both laughed. *It's better than the best symphony to hear Charlotte laugh, again.*

"Now, I'm mindful of my responsibility to protect you, my lovely. Get yourself off to bed and a good night's sleep. I want you fresh and ready for tomorrow's work."

"Yes, ma'am. It's so great to have you back. Good night, sweetheart."

———

Friday, 3.November.1944
Headquarters, Secret Intelligence Service
No.54 Broadway
Westminster, London, England
United Kingdom
09:15 hours

The gathering of senior intelligence professionals had been delayed a day to allow the SHAEF G-2 Major General Sir Kenneth Strong to fly in from their headquarters at Paris-Versailles. Major General Sir Stewart Menzies hosted the meeting in his secure conference room. OSS Director Major General Bill Donovan had requested the urgent meeting. With Donovan was Chief London Station Colonel David Bruce. Also in attendance were Minister of Economic Warfare and Chief of SOE Lord Selborne, and the Director Naval Intelligence Vice Admiral Sir Geoffrey 'Jumper' Pike, who had been asked to attend by Bill Donovan. Magruder and Köhler were with their MI6 counterparts.

"We are getting a late start. Bill, you requested this special meeting. You have the floor."

"Thank you, Sir Stewart. We have all been watching the Germans move substantial forces to the west. To my knowledge, none of us have localized where these units are and what their mission or intentions are. To be frank and candid, I am disturbed that we are not taking this developing situation more seriously."

"Bill," interjected Menzies, "I must interrupt." Donovan nodded. "I think we all feel the seriousness. I think we are agreed that the German armor, personnel, and supply movements to the west are troubling. M-I-6 just received this ULTRA decrypt early this morning. Thus, I doubt it has made it through the normal distribution." Sir Stewart passed the single page, red-striped paper to Donovan.

MOST SECRET - ULTRA

```
MOST SECRET ULTRA
DATE 2232 2 NOV 1944
TO PM UK FM FO
FROM STATION X
SUBJECT MOST URGENT ULTRA
SECRET
DATE 1751 1 NOV 1944
TO ALL UNITS AUTUMN MIST
FROM ARMED FORCES HIGH COMMAND
BREAK
EFFECTIVE IMMEDIATELY STRICT RADIO SILENCE
WILL BE MAINTAINED BREAK NO EXCEPTIONS BREAK
NECESSARY COMMUNICATIONS BY COURIER ONLY BREAK
HAIL VICTORY HAIL HITLER END
SECRET
DECYPHERED 1921 2 NOV 1944
MOST SECRET ULTRA
```

MOST SECRET - ULTRA

Donovan remained quiet and contemplative as the ULTRA message was passed to each person at the table. Finally, when the message made it back to Menzies, Donovan spoke. "Has anyone established what AUTUMN MIST is exactly?"

"We have only seen references," Selborne contributed.

"Just that message alone suggests it is an offensive operations plan."

"Winter is near," Strong said. "There is snow on the ground in parts of the front lines."

"Are you suggesting there will be no German offensive despite the intelligence of major armor and infantry units moving west?'" Donovan asked.

"Our opinion is," answered Strong, "the additional German forces are reinforcements for the defense of the Siegfried Line. Therefore, our assessment is the enemy is unlikely to attempt a winter offensive."

Donovan leaned forward on the table with both his hands initially balled into fists, but then flattened out his hands on the table before he spoke. "As I recall, the prevailing professional wisdom in the spring of 1940 was an attack through the Maginot Line or the Ardennes Forest was impossible, and we know how that worked out."

"I will add here," Pike offered, "underestimating the Germans is a grave mistake. This is not my area of responsibility or expertise; however, I do believe General Donovan's instincts regarding the ambiguities of the German movements are well-founded in their operational history."

"Has General Eisenhower accepted the G-2 analysis?" asked Donovan.

"It is not my place to speak for the supreme commander. However, I will note here that we have insufficient forces to defend the entire front."

"Translated into practical terms, that means the area you least expect a strike may well be the point of attack. Our forces are deployed for offensive operations. The German forces are likely deployed for their offensive operations that will probably be focused on where we are weakest. We can only give the operational commanders the best intelligence we can collect. I wish we had clear-cut evidence that needed no analysis or interpretation, but such conclusive intelligence is rare. I asked for this meeting because my sixth sense is rumbling like it was in the fall of 1941. I failed to convince the powers that be then, and I have no intention of making the same mistake again."

"What do you propose, Bill?" Sir Stewart asked.

"First, is there anything any of us can try that we have not tried already?"

"I've lost two valuable field agents already," Selborne answered, "trying to traverse the region south of the Ruhr, west of Koblenz, and north of Saarbrücken. The loss of those agents is additional evidence in my mind. So, I tend to agree with Bill."

"Sending more agents into the area will not serve our purpose and only get more good men killed or captured," added Menzies. "We have tasked photo-reconnaissance, including several dangerous low-level missions, to crisscross that region. We found nothing. We keep looking, but we have found nothing."

Donovan continued, "The Germans are going to attack during the dead of winter in the most difficult terrain they can find. To me, that is the Ardennes region."

"That's a guess," responded Strong. "You have no intelligence to substantiate that hypothesis."

"Agreed," Donovan answered. "It is only a hunch and a hunch at the very best. I think we are doing everything within the constraints of our tools and capacity. My objective for this meeting was to find consensus, hopefully, unanimous agreement."

"I agree," said Lord Selborne. "Bill's hypothesis makes the most sense of our facts."

"And I agree with Lord Selborne," Jumper Pike offered.

"While I certainly appreciate Bill's initiative and his hunch, as he calls it, I urge caution. With such a weak factual basis, we stand the risk of biasing the combat commanders to a condition we do not know will happen. We suspect the Germans are massing forces in the Ardennes area, but we do not know why they are doing so nor what their purpose is. I believe we should advise the leadership of our facts and allow them to draw the conclusions they see. We have kept the SHAEF informed of the facts we have. They know what we know. According to General Strong, the supreme commander does not agree with the measure of seriousness endemic with Bill's hypothesis. The best I can say is, I am neutral. With that," Menzies looked at Donovan, "have you conveyed your position to President Roosevelt?"

"Yes."

"And yet, apparently the president has chosen not to intervene."

"Correct."

"Have you discussed this matter with the prime minister?"

"No."

"Humph." Menzies stared at Donovan for several seconds and then looked at Sir Kenneth. "General Strong, your position?" asked Sir Stewart.

"I hold the same caution of which you speak. I can assure you all that I will convey the contents of this meeting to the supreme commander. Nonetheless, out of profound respect for the O-S-S director, I would encourage General Donovan to go to Versailles and discuss this issue with General Eisenhower directly."

"I agree with that as well," Menzies said.

Donovan nodded his head. "Agreed. I'll leave for Paris this afternoon. To summarize, we are not in agreement on the meaning of the intelligence we have. If I may state it, our official collective position is that we have concerning facts, but we have insufficient information to establish enemy intentions."

"That is an accurate summary." Heads nodded in agreement.

"Very well. That is how I will present it to General Eisenhower. Thank you for your time and contributions. I'll fly to paris this afternoon. Would you like to hitch a ride, Ken?"

"Yes, I would, Bill. Thank you very much. I am certain your carriage is demonstrably better than the shuttle."

———

Friday, 3.November.1944
Standing Oak Farm
Winchester, Hampshire, England
United Kingdom
11:10 hours

Her appointment with the doctor had gone well but was disappointing. He wanted her cast to remain on for another two weeks. Charlotte's other wounds had healed nicely. He was quite happy with her physical progress. Charlotte also shared her emotional struggle. Brian had gone a long way to pulling her out of the deep hole she was in, and the ladies had helped immeasurably. Mary and the children were coming down to spend the weekend. Further, each time Rosemary had the duty, she provided additional perspective as a practicing physician.

Charlotte was feeling better and doing better in great measure due to the love of her husband and their friends. She had tried to do some milking with one hand. Unfortunately, the effort proved to be too much too soon.

The taxi approaching over the far ridgeline crest caused Charlotte to stand, but the cab did not stop at the crest, so it was not likely Brian. She went to the front door and stepped out on the stone porch as the taxi came to a stop on the gravel.

Bobby Sales stepped out, closed the door, and the cab drove off. "Surprise!" he exclaimed.

"Welcome back to Standing Oak Farm. To what do we owe the pleasure?"

"We had an urgent, special mission . . . very short fuse . . . but I'm here in England, now, so I thought I would drop in to say hello. I am so sorry for your loss. I hope you are feeling better."

"Thank you for your kindness, Bobby. I have my ups and downs, but I am much better, well, or at least more functional than I was a few weeks ago. The crew will be having lunch soon. Please join us."

"Thank you, Charlotte."

"Can you stay here for a day or two, until you have to go back. We are a bit discombobulated due to my . . . my . . . my state, but as with me, we are functional."

"If it's no trouble, I would love to. It would give us a chance to talk, if you're up for it. A lot is happening at B-A-S."

Charlotte took Bobby inside and introduced him to Edith and five-months pregnant Rosemary, who were busy preparing lunch for the crew. Mabel had taken Todd with her for the day. The friends had collectively agreed that Charlotte's progress with recovery had not reached the threshold of self-reliance, although Charlotte had no intention of discussing her depression and their friends' response with Bobby.

Mabel did not return to the main house for lunch, choosing instead to have lunch with her greenhouse crew. Jacob was in his last year of school and would reach conscription age in less than two years. Bobby proved to be quite the jokester for the lunchtime entertainment at the table.

When the meal was done, and the dishes cleared, cleaned, and put away, Charlotte, Bobby, and Rosemary sat around the modest fire in the large, brick fireplace. Edith went outside to help Horace and Lionel with cheese production. She had agreed with Charlotte's insistence that she remain with the family despite Ian's passing. Charlotte knew they would have more children eventually.

Rosemary had not finished her explanation of the connection with the Drummond family and her presence at Standing Oak Farm when the telephone rang. She stood to answer. "Winchester 4-3-7-9, Standing Oak Farm." "Yes." Rosemary looked at Bobby. "The call is for you."

"Sales." "Yes." "Wow, that's quick." "Sure." "On my way." Bobby looked at Charlotte. "My apologies. I've been recalled. My principal wants to take off this afternoon for an unplanned leg."

"It's quite all right, Bobby. I understand. Where are you going?"

"I can't say, I'm afraid. What is the quickest way back to Northolt?"

Charlotte thought for a moment. "The train to London leaves in 45 minutes."

"I can drive you," Rosemary offered. "No, better yet . . . Grace will be here in a few hours. Charlotte, you should be fine for a few hours. Then, perhaps, Edith can drive Bobby and I to the rail station, so I can get back to Oxford early."

"You've been most helpful, Rose. That should work just fine. If you would be so kind to retrieve Edith from the barn, we can get you and Bobby on your way." Rosemary nodded and departed. Charlotte looked at Bobby. "I'm sorry we did not have more time, but business is business, is it not?"

"Yes, I'm afraid it is. I don't know if we will come back through London, but thank you for lunch, Charlotte. Please pass my respects to your husband." Sales stood.

"I will be sure to do that the next time I see him." Charlotte stood and gestured to the front door. ". . . whenever that might be." They both chuckled as they walked outside.

Edith and Rosemary stopped the dark green 1936 Hillman Minx Magnificent Saloon automobile in front of the house. Rosemary got out, ran into the house, and grabbed her bag. She came back out, dropped her bag, grasped both of Charlotte's cheeks, and kissed her on the lips. "Thank you, my dearest Charlotte. Continue your magnificent recovery. See you next time."

"Thank you, Rose." Then, as Bobby got in the back seat, Charlotte added, "Fly safe, Bobby. Good luck."

"Thanks, Charlotte." Bobby waved, got in the car, and closed the door.

Charlotte remained outside, and watched the car climb the hill until it disappeared over the crest. "Well, that was quick," she said aloud to no one. Satisfied they were gone, Charlotte went back inside, made herself a cup of tea, freshened the fire a little, and sat back down with her book. When Brian told her he was reading Dickens' *A Tale of Two Cities*, Charlotte decided to re-read the classic novel as well.

15:20 hours

The unique crunch of a car's wheels on gravel caught Charlotte's attention. After setting her bookmark, Charlotte closed her book and went outside to see who had arrived.

A nice maroon 1939 Rover 20 Sports Saloon automobile came to stop off to the side of the gravel forecourt opposite from the barn complex. The sun reflection of the windows prevented Charlotte from recognizing the driver. Grace Palmer, Lady Selborne, emerged and waved. Charlotte returned the gesture. The vehicle was new to Charlotte.

"It is getting a smidge chilly for horseback," Grace announced.

"I have not seen you driving, and I had not seen your automobile before. Very nice, I must say."

"Simple but functional," Grace added.

Charlotte suggested they go inside and where she informed Grace that Todd was with Mabel at the Brownfield greenhouses. She also told Grace that she needed to check on Edith.

Charlotte checked the vehicle shed. Both the Hillman and the Bedford flatbed were parked in their spots. Charlotte was somewhat surprised she had not heard Edith's return. Next, she poked her head inside the clean room. Horace, Lionel, Edith, and now Jacob were finishing up the day's cheese production. Satisfied everything was as it should be, except for her obliviousness to the return of either vehicle, Charlotte returned to the house and joined Grace in front of the fireplace. She sat after freshening the fire.

Charlotte explained Rosemary's early departure with Bobby Sales and his short visit.

"I trust you were not left unsupported," Grace responded.

Charlotte smiled. "I enjoyed reading for a couple of hours in front of the fire. I truly and deeply appreciate the loving support of everyone. I was in a very dark place a week ago, but I think I have been improving since Brian dragged me out of the house. Of course, I still have my bad moments, but I think I'm improving. This war cannot end soon enough for me."

"Several senior officers we know said they think the war will be over, at least in Europe, in a month or two at the outside. None too soon for me, and I'm sure . . ." Grace was interrupted by the sound of another automobile on the gravel outside.

"Seems to be a hectic day for visitors." They both laughed. Charlotte stood, followed by Grace. They walked outside just in time to see Marlene Dietrich exit Morty Jurdy's cab. "Marlene, what a delightful surprise."

"Oh my!" exclaimed Grace from behind Charlotte.

"Good afternoon, darling," Marlene in her distinctive German-accented sultry voice. She embraced Charlotte and kissed both cheeks. Marlene then extended her right hand to Grace. "Hello. I'm Marlene."

"Of course, you are," Grace responded meekly.

"And you are?"

"Oh, sorry, Grace Palmer, Countess Selborne." The two women shook hands.

Marlene turned to face Charlotte. "Please forgive me, Charlotte. I don't usually drop in unannounced, but I just had to flee London."

"Is something wrong?"

"Yes, dreadfully. I am besieged by reporters asking incessant questions, most of which are foolish or ridiculous fluff. I have been a prisoner in my hotel room. The hotel manager was most gracious in helping me escape and board the train. I just had to get out of London, and you were my first thought. I hope you don't mind, Charlotte."

"Of course not."

"I am so sorry to intrude when you have company."

"Oh, I'm not company, Miss Dietrich." All three women laughed. "I'm here for our friend," Grace said, nodding to Charlotte.

"Please, Grace, I prefer Marlene." She looked at Charlotte. "What is this?" Marlene asked, tapping lightly on Charlotte's arm cast.

Charlotte nodded. "Shall we go inside out of the fall chill? We can talk inside. Would you like something to eat?" Charlotte asked Marlene.

"A biscuit and a cup of tea would be delightful."

The ladies went inside. Grace offered to make a good pot of tea. Charlotte gestured to the plush chairs by the fireplace. Grace placed a plate of fresh cookies on the table, a cup and saucer for each woman, and poured the tea for each of them. Charlotte started to tell Marlene what had happened on the 20th of September but choked up several times. Grace picked up the telling, knowing the story well.

"Dear God above!" Marlene nearly cried. "I had no idea. I am so terribly sorry, Charlotte. In my ignorance and selfishness, I have dredged up and re-inflicted your grievous wounds."

Charlotte shook her head and waved her right hand. "No, no, Marlene. You had no way to know, and I'm in the process of facing our loss. It is part of my healing." Charlotte wiped away her tears, cleared her throat, and said, "What has brought you back to England?"

"I just completed another U-S-O tour, entertaining the troops. My last performance was in Eastern Belgium, only a few miles from the German border and the frontlines. It was very exciting, and the troops were most appreciative. I thought I might see Brian."

"He's been very busy, flying quite a bit. He was here for a couple of days last week and pulled me out of a terrible depression. Grace's husband the Earl Selborne is Minister of Economic Warfare. Their estate borders ours. We're neighbors." All three ladies giggled softly.

"We all have our duty to the war effort," Marlene said.

"Yours is far more dangerous than ours," Grace said to Marlene, who shook her head. "Neither of us have been anywhere, even remote from the frontlines."

"I don't have a husband," Marlene confessed softly, "especially a husband in uniform. Both of you are married to fighting men. I am in awe of what you do for our freedom."

"We don't fight," protested Charlotte.

"No. True. But, your part is far more difficult. You wait and support. I admire you both."

"Thank you for the recognition, Marlene, but you are world-famous. Everybody knows you and your support of the troops."

"Which is why I am here." All three of the women laughed hard and fed the laughter of the others.

"You are welcome to stay with us as long as you wish."

"Thank you, Charlotte. I would like to at least spend the night in this peace and tranquility."

Tears welled up in Charlotte's eyes. She tried hard to mask the effects of the bolt of lightning that struck her. *It wasn't so peaceful or tranquil six weeks ago.* "As long as you wish," Charlotte muttered.

"May I use your telephone? I should let my assistant know where I am."

"And dinner time is approaching. I should put together a meal for the crew and us," Grace said as she stood. She showed Marlene the telephone, told her how to get a line in rural England, and then she set to the task of meal preparation.

Charlotte remained in her chair, although the fire needed some attention. She lowered her head and swiped away the tears descending her cheeks. *Why God? Why did you take an innocent little boy? He didn't do anything wrong or sinful. He was just beginning to live life.*

———

Monday, 6.November.1944
Room 5E766
Pentagon Building
Arlington, Arlington County, Virginia
United States of America
08:05 hours

"Thank you for giving me a few minutes," the chief of staff said as he entered the secretary's office.

Stimson gestured to the plush leather chairs around a small round coffee table.

"As you know, Jack Dill passed on Saturday," General Marshall began.

Field Marshal Sir John Greer 'Jack' Dill, GCB, CMG, DSO, had been in the United States since December 1941 as Head of the British Staff Mission to the United States. Dill had been Chief of the Imperial General Staff, Marshall's counterpart, from May 1940 until he departed for the United States. George Marshall saw him as a friend and kindred spirit, who proved to be a vital contributor to the war effort and kept the British and American actions coherent. Sir John had been diagnosed with aplastic anemia, a serious blood disorder, in 1943. As his health declined, George Marshall arranged for Sir John and Lady Dill to spend the summer at The Greenbrier resort in White Sulphur Springs, West Virginia.

"Yes. Very sad. He was a good man," Stimson offered.

"Yes, he was, and I will add from my perspective, he was vital to our collective war effort. A keen mind. A true friend. I could babble on singing his praises, but I'm mindful of the time. I had personal and private discussions with both Lady Dill and Ambassador Lord Halifax about a memorial service at the National Cathedral and Sir John's interment here at Arlington."

"Only the president can authorize that," Stimson said.

"Exactly why I'm here."

Stimson nodded his head. "Quite appropriate, George. Would you like me to gain the president's consent?"

"Yes Sir. I'll gladly discuss the matter with the president, but only with your approval."

"I'll take care of that part with the president. This afternoon, I've got a scheduled meeting with the president to discuss the Manhattan Project. I'll raise this matter first, so I don't forget."

"Thank you, Sir. One more item, if you don't mind." The secretary nodded his head to go ahead. "I'd like to work with our friends in Congress for sanction to install a statue at his gravesite. He loved horses, one of many likes we shared. Nancy was stunned and eagerly agreed."

Nancy Isabelle Cecil Furlong, née Charrington, lost her first husband in 1940, the same year Jack Dill's first wife passed. Brigadier Dennis Walter Furlong had been killed while inspecting a British minefield on a Yorkshire beach during the dark days of the invasion threat. Nancy married Jack on 8.October.1941, and she left England for the United States, three months after their marriage. Sir John and Lady Dill were both very popular in wartime Washington.

"There is only one other mounted equestrian statue in Arlington National Cemetery—Major General Philip Kearny, the Union general killed at the Battle of Chantilly, right after Second Bull Run."

"Do you think you can swing it?"

"I've talked to some friends. I think we can gather the necessary funding from private donors, so we don't need public funding, only authorization. Nancy and Jack were very well-liked professionally and socially."

Stimson thought for a moment. "Congress is always tricky, George. You know that. I've no problem with you working on an authorizing resolution. My only caution is don't compromise or overcommit the department or yourself."

"You have my word, Mister Secretary," Marshall said. "Thank you for your time and support."

President Roosevelt gave his permission for Sir John Dill to be buried in Arlington National Cemetery—his burial plot is Site S-29 in Section 32. Congress passed Joint Resolution Recognizing the outstanding service rendered to the United Nations by Field Marshal Sir John Dill [PL 78-516; 58 Stat. 835], and President Roosevelt signed the joint resolution into law on 20.December.1944.

On 1.November.1950, President Truman unveiled and dedicated the statue of Field Marshal Sir John Dill mounted on a horse by renown American equestrian sculptor Herbert Chevalier Haseltine.

———

Tuesday, 7.November.1944
Residence
The White House
Washington, District of Columbia
United States of America
23:55 hours

Gathered in the residence around the radio were Eleanor, Anna and Franklin Roosevelt as they listened to the progressing election results. Also listening to the radio with the family were Admiral Leahy, Harry Hopkins, and 'Pa' Watson. As the broadcaster reported the incoming results, Hopkins kept a tally sheet.

Harry was the first to speak in over an hour. "Well, Mister President, by my count, you just passed 266 electoral votes."

Anna Roosevelt initiated applause, cheers, and congratulations.

Franklin raised both hands. "All of you are veterans of these elections. You know quite well that it is not over until the last vote is counted and more importantly, the joint session of Congress officially counts the Electoral College votes from the states. I am encouraged by the early results, but we must cross all the 't's and dot all the 'i's."

"Just enjoy it, Franklin," Eleanor scolded her husband. "You've won by a good margin. You can finish what was thrust upon you."

Franklin nodded his head in agreement. Applause erupted again. He enjoyed the praise and prospects of another four years in office. Franklin agreed with his wife. He needed to finish his charge to defend the nation. Eventually, the president raised his left hand. "I truly appreciate the enthusiasm, but I am tired and must retire for the night. Please feel free to remain as long as you wish. You will not bother me. We'll pick this up in the morning."

Eleanor and Anna kissed Franklin on the cheek before he turned his chair and wheeled himself to his bedroom.

President Roosevelt extended his historically unprecedented administration with a fourth electoral win. When all the votes were counted and the constitutional process was fulfilled, the Roosevelt-Truman ticket had won 53.4% of the popular vote and, more importantly, collected 432 electoral votes to Thomas Dewey's 99 electoral votes. He carried 36 of 48 states and benefited from a 64-30 majority in the Senate, and a 254-165 majority in the House of Representatives. It was the lowest but still substantial legislative margin Roosevelt had achieved since he became president.

—

Monday, 11.November.1944
No.10 Annexe
New Public Offices
Whitehall, London, England
United Kingdom
08:15 hours

The day's schedule for the prime minister was a planned day trip to Paris to join General de Gaulle in France's first Armistice Day celebration since 1939.

There was much to rejoice in with nearly all pre-war French territory liberated. More importantly to the Allies, the Scheldt Estuary had finally been cleared of Germans and declared secure three days earlier. The first supply ships had tied up at the Antwerp docks and were being unloaded 24 hours a day, seven days a week until the logistics corps caught up with the supply deficits for the frontline units. The 12th and 21st Army Groups were into Germany and through the Siegfried Line in several places. Yes, there was much to celebrate.

The day's duty private secretary John Peck met Prime Minister Churchill as soon as he emerged from his small bedroom. "Slight change of plans, I'm afraid, Prime Minister."

Churchill looked at Peck but did not speak. He raised his eyebrows as if to gesture 'and.'

"I was just informed that Paralos, the newly modified C-54B Skymaster for your transport, is not quite ready for service. So I called the squadron transportation office to inquire about Ascalon or any other executive transport aircraft."

"Are you trying to tell me, John, the trip is canceled?" Churchill said with demonstrable irritation.

"No Sir, not entirely. I was informed that a C-47 Dakota is available and ready, but it is configured with troop seating."

"Is this some backhanded way of telling me that I'm losing favor with the Air Force?"

"No Sir. Definitely not. I'm convinced this is just the fate of the moment. The other V-I-P transport aircraft are either undergoing required maintenance or are away on other missions."

"Well, I suppose, if it's enough for our parachute troops to go to combat, then it's good enough for me."

"The aircraft and crew are standing by at Northolt, so we should be on our way."

"Then, we'd better hop to it."

Prime Minister Winston Churchill arrived safely in Paris later that morning. He participated in numerous Armistice Day celebrations enhanced by the liberation of France. Churchill managed to have several chats with General de Gaulle, the self-anointed leader of Free France. They discussed a wide variety of topics, including current combat prospects on the western frontier, post-war reconstruction, post-war governance, and even Stalin's intentions in Eastern Europe. France was still under Allied military governance, but they both knew elections were coming.

———

Saturday, 18.November.1944
Oval Office
The White House
Washington, District of Columbia
United States of America
14:30 hours

"Good afternoon, Mister President," Bill Donovan said.

"Great to see you, Bill. So, today is the day."

"Yes Sir, Mister President. I hand-delivered the proposal, which is rather lengthy and detailed, along with my cover memorandum to Miss Tully for processing."

"Fine. I look forward to reading your proposal. Can you give me the gist in a few sentences?" asked Roosevelt.

"Of course, Sir," Donovan took a moment to frame his response. "As we have discussed more than a few times, I am proposing a central intelligence authority reporting directly to the president to filter, coalesce, analyze, and present essential strategic intelligence to the president and the government."

Roosevelt nodded his head as he thought for a moment. "Yes, we have discussed a centralized intelligence organization many times over the years. So, what is different now?"

"In short, the war will be over soon. But, with unfolding events in Eastern Europe and China, the president will need a broad, high-level view of events and the people behind those events. My criticism of the pre-war intelligence apparatus has not improved, and if anything, the factionalism has been more calcified and entrenched. The predominant motive seems to be protecting their turf, their domain, rather than fulfilling essential elements of information."

"Bill, I am not ignorant of the problem. I will also say here between us, as I will eventually say in public, you've done a yeoman's job at pulling together the strategic level intelligence I so desperately needed. I am enormously grateful for your selfless service since our very first chat on the topic all those years ago. You have suffered the burden of that factionalism you illuminate. I also acknowledge that it's an unnecessary burden. Yet, the president cannot be the arbiter of that factionalism."

"I am proposing that the director of the new post-war agency serve as that arbiter. You will note that I am not proposing that we consolidate or subsume any of the various intelligence organizations. I agreed with your decision that the O-S-S should report to J-C-S. The intelligence O-S-S dealt with was largely military affairs; it made sense. The post-war years will not be military in nature. In the peace, necessary intelligence will be mostly political and international."

"Agreed, Bill. I think you've captured the essence of my concerns. I will not be president forever, and I'm determined to pass along an appropriate national intelligence organization that buffers, filters, and coalesces, as you say, the strategic level intelligence that future presidents will need. So let me ask you, where do you think we will feel the most resistance to such a centralized national intelligence organization?"

"That's a far sportier question. Based on my experience over the last five years, I would say the G-2 and N-2. However, I'm compelled to note that J. Edgar Hoover will likely make his resistance personal."

"What about State?"

"I think they will see such an organization as a positive change to level things with the Army and Navy."

Roosevelt nodded his head in contemplation. "I need to study your proposal. We must face the resistance and deal with it. Please allow me some time to review your proposal. I'll certainly call you if I need more information or an explanation. In this instance, I think this office should handle the solicitation of comments from the affected government agencies. Please keep this between us until we have some meat to chew on. I do not want premature debate until we are ready."

"Mum's the word, Mister President."

"Who knows about this proposal?"

"Only Ned Buxton and myself, although cognizant individuals within O-S-S are aware of the details in their areas of expertise."

"Fine. Let's keep it that way for now. Silence. No leaks."

"We will do our part."

"Thank you for your exceptional work, Bill, all the way around. Now, let me change the subject before our time is up. What is going on along the Western Front?"

"I am convinced the Germans are preparing for a major counteroffensive, most likely in the area of the Ardennes Forest."

"Like 1940."

"Yes, except it's the dead of winter now with deep snow on the ground, and they're striking out from the defensive."

"And you think they will risk such an offensive given the pressure being applied by the Red Army in the East?"

"We don't have clear, unequivocal intelligence, Mister President. Allied forces are thinnest in that area. The Germans are quite familiar with the region. The terrain and our deployment favor their limited offensive forces and reduce our air superiority. We have flown numerous photo reconnaissance missions over the area, trying to locate those forces without success. Our collective air forces have no identifiable targets. The British have taken a more cautious interpretation of the available facts. I met with British intelligence chiefs two weeks ago, and then with their consent, I met with General Eisenhower the next day. He is not convinced our assessment is correct. The Allied Expeditionary Force is focused on resupplying the frontline forces and preparing them for the final spring offensive. The supreme commander is concerned about the intelligence but not sufficiently for redeployment of his forces."

"Are you going to ask me to intervene?"

"No Sir. Definitely not. I hold General Eisenhower in the highest regard, and I have insufficient evidence beyond my gut feeling to warrant intervention. If the Germans do attack, the A-E-F will deal with it."

"What would be their objective for such a counteroffensive?"

"We do not know. They've been very disciplined with their communications ...couriers only. ULTRA has given us nothing. If I were the German commander, I would strike as fast and as hard as possible to Antwerp to close the port and split the 12th and 21st Army Groups. I would try to compel an evacuation of the 21st Army Group like the B-E-F at Dunkirk."

"That's pretty bold."

"Yes Sir. No one has ever accused the Germans of not being bold."

"Oh so true, Bill. Now, I'm afraid our time is up. Thank you so much for everything you have done, not least of which is persisting against the factionalism you mentioned. I will study your proposal with keen interest. I intend to discuss distribution for comment with you before this proposal moves beyond you, Buxton, and me."

"As you wish, Sir. You can count on us."

"I know I can, Bill. Good day to you."

Donovan left the Oval Office. Treasury Secretary Morgenthau was waiting for his appointment with the president. Donovan waited. Once the next meeting was underway, Grace returned to her desk. "Is everything OK with my memo and proposal?"

"Yes Sir. I've registered the SECRET document, and it will be in the president's evening reading box."

"Thank you, Grace. The president is expecting it. Good day to you."

Donovan departed the White House and returned to his office in the E Street Complex.

———

Sunday, 19.November.1944
Cabinet War Rooms
New Public Offices
Whitehall, London, England
United Kingdom
16:10 hours

"Excuse me, Prime Minister, a courier has just arrived with a most urgent."

"Let's have it, Jock."

A younger man Winston did not recognize entered his small underground office. The manacled case he was carrying in his left hand was all too familiar. The prime minister retrieved his personal key.

Before opening the classified case, Winston faced the man, who appeared to be in his late 30s or early 40s, and looked sternly into his eyes. "I do not recognize you, young man. But, before I can take the next step, I must know who you are and why you are here?"

"Yes Sir. My name is Brewster, Henry Brewster. I am the language specialist assigned to the German Desk. 'C' asked me to bring this message to you. We believe understanding one keyword may require my language skills."

"So, if I call 'C,' he will verify your identity?"

"Yes Sir, he most assuredly will."

Churchill thought for a moment and then nodded his head. He gestured for the case to be placed on the desk. Winston opened the case and extracted a single red-striped border message.

MOST SECRET - ULTRA

```
MOST SECRET ULTRA
DATE 1323 19 NOV 1944
TO PM UK FM FO
FROM STATION X
SUBJECT MOST URGENT ULTRA
SENSITIVE
DATE 1007 19 NOV 1944
TO ALL ARMED FORCES
FROM ARMED FORCES HIGH COMMAND
COPY RSHA
BREAK
ALL OFFICERS AND SOLDIERS MUST BE REMINDED OF
THEIR DUTY TO THE FATHERLAND BREAK FURTHER ALL
PERSONNEL MUST BE REMINDED OF THE TRADITIONAL
GERMAN PRINCIPLE OF FAMILY CLAN LIABILITY FOR
THE FAILURE OF ANY SOLDIER TO PERFORM HIS DUTY
TO THE FATHERLAND BREAK HAIL VICTORY HAIL
HITLER END
SENSITIVE
DECYPHERED 0951 19 NOV 1944
MOST SECRET ULTRA
```

MOST SECRET - ULTRA

Churchill gestured to the leather chairs around the coffee table. "Before we get to the meat and potatoes, this message was deciphered before it was sent."

"No Sir. The Germans use Berlin time as their time standard, while we use Greenwich Mean Time, rather than Double Summer Time."

"Ah, very well. For all such messages I have read over the years, I never noticed the difference. We're deciphering in near real-time."

"Yes Sir . . . thanks to Colossus and the Hut 8 analyses."

"Turing."

"Yes Sir," Brewster answered with a hint of surprise that the prime minister would even be aware of Alan Turing, "and Joan Clarke, Gordon Welchman, and others."

"Our golden goose continues to lay golden eggs. We must jealously protect our goose. You mentioned a word."

"The German word used in the original message was *Sippenhaftung*. The strict translation is clan liability. In essence, the family or clan will suffer the consequences, if a soldier fails to do his duty—cowardice, desertion, whatever the S-S doesn't like. They are telling the lot of them, regardless of rank, that they will bring the hammer down on families and even friends. Our analysis in this context is far more serious. We believe Rommel's death on the 14th of October was not a battlefield wound, but rather an induced suicide."

"Induced?"

"Our guess is, the S-D likely assessed he had foreknowledge of the 20th of July plot and did nothing. Because of his status as a national hero, Rommel was probably visited by at least two generals, possibly one of them in the S-S, and gave him a choice of suicide or having his family face *Sippenhaftung*. We will not likely know until a post-war investigation can determine what happened. No one in S-I-S or O-S-S believes he died of war wounds, and yet they gave him a state funeral. The point is, given the ruthlessness of Himmler's R-S-H-A, the state security apparatus is probably stepping up their retribution against anyone even remotely involved or aware of the assassination attempt, or even dissidents who have existed at the fringe. The fact that Keitel would send out a message like this when they are so close to defeat is probably a measure of their vengeance and desperation, and we suspect it is a warning shot to their forces in the East, South, and West."

"AUTUMN MIST?"

"Yes Sir . . . probably most specifically those forces in the West. Germans are highly unlikely to surrender in the East. We have already seen German forces just giving up to the Western Allies to abandon the war and avoid the Eastern Front and the Red Army."

"That is an interesting assessment, Mister Brewster. Thank you very much. If you would be so kind, please convey to 'C' my genuine appreciation for sending you along as the courier for this one." Churchill handed the message back to Brewster, who put it back in the case and locked it. The prime minister thanked Brewster again. The courier departed. "Well, well, well," Winston said aloud to himself.

———

Wednesday, 29.November.1944
Leyte Island, Philippines
Liberated Territory of the United States of America

The 96th Infantry Division, XXIV Corps, 6th Army had been fighting in the central highland mountains for more than a month against a determined enemy. Rugged terrain, the density of the jungle, and heavy rains made the fight even more intense.

As twilight led into darkness, the troops heard the enemy vocalizations that often preceded mass charges by the Japanese. Sergeant Parlier was desperate to find cover for his men to defend themselves if the *banzai* charge materialized. Enemy foxholes were scattered across the mountain clearing, but they sometimes boobytrapped the fighting holes. Needing to move quickly before darkness fell, Sergeant Parlier ran from hole to hole, firing his rifle into the bottom of each hole. Unfortunately, one of the former enemy foxholes indeed had a mine in the bottom. The explosion nearly killed him and irreparably damaged his left eye, shattered his tibia shaft in multiple places, and sprayed his body with shrapnel. Sergeant Parlier was rapidly evacuated to a field hospital for stabilization of his numerous wounds.

On 31.December.1944, General MacArthur publicly declared that enemy organized resistance had ceased on Leyte Island. Pockets and stragglers fought until mop-up operations were concluded on 8.May.1945. The Philippine Islands were not liberated until the end of the war when the Japanese Imperial Forces surrendered on 15.August.1945. Individual soldiers held out in the jungles and mountains of various islands into the 1970s, when the Emperor and Japanese government joined the campaign to repatriate the holdouts.

As Sergeant Parlier's medical evacuation progressed, he eventually ended up at the Veterans Administration Medical Center in Topeka, Kansas, where he endured multiple additional surgeries, protracted recovery, and rehabilitation. His body was no longer the same and left him permanently disabled but functional. The author became all too aware of his father's sacrifice that sparked his curiosity about the war.

In hindsight, General MacArthur's gambit at redemption failed. Yes, he did return to the Philippine Islands as he promised. Arguably, the Philippine campaign attracted the attention of the Japanese to a sufficient extent to justify the commitment of diminishing naval assets to the naval battles of Leyte Gulf, which essentially ended major naval operations by the Imperial Japanese Navy. However, the expenditure of valuable ground resources did not contribute directly to the defeat of Japan.

———

Chapter 13

The mass of men lead lives of quiet desperation.
What is called resignation is confirmed desperation.
-- Henry David Thoreau

Thursday, 7.December.1944
Office of the Director, Office of Strategic Services
National Institutes of Health Building
2430 E Street Northwest
Washington, District of Columbia
United States of America
14:10 hours

The field reports from Western Germany slowed to an intermittent trickle. Most folks would react to the paucity of additional information or detectable activity as a crisis passed. Bill Donovan was not most people. He felt the comparative quiet in more ominous terms. The frustration of not having conclusive intelligence made Donovan's irritation all the more difficult to bear. He knew in his gut that something was about to happen. The director had tried to convince the powers that be of this instinctive hunch. The generals listened. They asked cogent questions and offered appropriate curiosity, but in the end, they were not convinced to redeploy based on such skimpy, disconnected information. Now, time would have to tell the tale.

Donovan read the latest reports coming from his OSS agents in South America, especially the southern continental countries. Germans were appearing in greater numbers. So far, several dozen had been clearly identified as SS men, although virtually all of them were not in uniform. The uniformed SS men were associated with diplomatic or embassy functions. Beyond their sheer numbers, the tacit support or blind eye by area governments made identifying and keeping track of the Germans problematic. The Germanophiles in South American governments outnumbered those who objected to the migration. His agents saw the results but pinning down the exodus to the mysterious ODESSA remained elusive.

The SS-led Alpine Redoubt seemed a little closer to tangible reality. Both MI6 and OSS field agents in München reported more SS men of all sorts moving through the city. OSS Bern Station reported non-diplomatic overtures by known SS senior officers to sympathetic Swiss governmental officials. Hard work by members of Bern Station over the last few months transformed the misty overtures into valuable intelligence information. The impression offered by Bern Station was that the Germans wanted to reassure their Swiss neighbors that their pending moves were no threat to Swiss neutrality. The German government, in other words the Nazi party, intended to move from Berlin to Berchtesgaden, Bavaria, Germany, with that corporal's mountain chalet, the Berghof, as the new capitol. The Obersalzberg region and surrounding mountains were foreboding enough to garner attention, since the National Socialist German Workers Party began and grew from the beer halls of Münich and Bavaria.

The intelligence told General Donovan and his colleagues something was afoot. Somehow, the potential of an SS-led mountain redoubt attracted more interest and attention than the potential of un-located enemy armor and infantry forces. Donovan knew and agreed that neither MI6 nor the OSS possessed conclusive, unequivocal intelligence that ODESSA or the Nazi Alpine Redoubt existed or even might exist, but information from a wide range of independent sources and collection agencies was sufficient to say that both SS activities were likely valid, accurate and active.

Donovan looked up to take a break from the report he had been reading when he saw Ned Buxton standing silently in the open doorway. "How long have you been there?"

"A few minutes. You were pretty intense on that report. I didn't want to interrupt your reading and thinking."

Donovan lifted the voluminous report. "The latest analysis from the German Desk on the Nazi Alpine Redoubt. What brings you to my doorway?"

"Well, I bring notification and confirmation that you have been promoted to the rank of major general."

"Wait a minute. I thought I was a two-star for over a month."

"You deserve more than two stars, Bill."

"Ned!" Donovan protested.

"That's my fault, I must confess. I overplayed the process. Once the Armed Services Committee approved the list, I knew it was a done deal."

"Ned, my God, it's not done until Congress approves the list and the president signs the bill. I appreciate your enthusiasm, loyalty, and energy, but the law is the law."

"My apologies, Bill, but it's official now. Congratulations."

Donovan nodded and looked back at the report on his desk.

"One more thing," Ned said. Bill nodded his head with demonstrable irritation. "Dulles just confirmed that Heisenberg will be in Zürich for a scientific conference on the 18th."

Werner Karl Heisenberg was a German theoretical physicist and one of the key pioneers of quantum mechanics. He was also the 1932 Nobel Laureate in Physics 'for the creation of quantum mechanics, the application of which has, *inter alia*, led to the discovery of the allotropic forms of hydrogen.' But, more important to the Allies, Heisenberg was considered the scientific leader of the German atomic weapon development program. He had been a target of MI6, SOE, and the OSS since the Allied joint nuclear weapons development program known as the Manhattan Project began.

"Signal Moe, the mission is a go," Donovan commanded more tersely than he intended.

"We will make it so," Buxton responded. "Door open or closed?"

"Open is fine, Ned." Bill looked up from the report and connected with Buxton's eyes. "My apologies for being so sharp. These damnable reports from Western Germany trouble me greatly."

"Understandable. They trouble us all. They'll resolve themselves eventually."

"Yeah, I just hope not adversely. We are not done with this fight just yet."

"Agreed. Call me if you need me. I'll continue to keep an eye on the day-to-day operations."

"As I know you will. Thanks, Ned."

Buxton nodded and disappeared. Donovan returned to his reading.

———

Wednesday, 13.December.1944
Headquarters, 3rd Army
No.4 Rue d'Auxonne
Nancy, Meurthe-et-Moselle, Grand Est
Liberated France
09:30 hours

General Patton met the supreme commander at the front entrance to the commandeered residence that served as the 3rd Army headquarters. "Welcome back to Nancy, General."

"Thanks, George."

"Not quite Versailles, but this mansion serves our purposes. Most of the staff are next door."

"Better than a tent, especially in this winter cold."

"Most assuredly."

"Something's brewing out there. Let's jump right on the beast."

Patton led Eisenhower to his Conference/Map Room. A large map covered one wall. The 3rd Army corps and division deployments were marked on the acetate overlay—3rd Army in blue grease pencil, 1st Army flanking units in green, and 7th Army flanking units in brown. The known German deployments were shown in red.

Patton began. "We finally pushed the Germans out of Metz. They withdrew across the border and behind the Siegfried Line defenses. We chose not to pursue them with winter weather gripping the region and my tanks short on fuel and ammunition."

"The intelligence boys continue to voice concerns about German redeployments. The O-S-S believes the signs point to a German winter counteroffensive into the 1ˢᵗ Army sector."

"What does Hodges think?" asked Patton.

"He accepts the potential but doesn't see the probes he would expect for a major offensive, plus there is nearly a foot of snow on the ground in his sector. So, we've thinned him out as far as I dare. How is your resupply going?"

"From my perspective, much better than it was a month ago. We're still not up to snuff yet, and we estimate it will take another month to flesh us out supply-wise for the spring offensive. However, opening Antwerp has helped enormously."

"Which brings me to the object of my visit. What is your plan for crossing the Rhine?"

"We've completed our reconnaissance of the approaches and suitable crossing sites. As long as we get fleshed out with our offensive supply stocks, we'll be ready to go by late winter, or early spring. I think the best crossing point is south of Mainz and Frankfurt at Oppenheim. That site gives us the best approach and east bank terrain for rapid exploitation."

"The Germans have substantial forces in Wiesbaden, Darmstadt, and Frankfurt. Aren't you concerned about a counterattack while you've got minimal forces on the east bank?"

"By spring, we'll be pressing them at multiple sites along the Rhine. They won't know where it's coming from. We'll use our artillery and air superiority to isolate the beachhead until we can get proper forces ashore on the far bank."

"It's risky, George."

"War is nothing but risk. Monty's thrust at Arnhem may not have been the success we all anticipated, but it fits the German mindset. Monty is across the Rhine, and he'll exploit the crossing."

"He's planning another major combined airborne and amphibious crossing in the spring to break the stalemate they're in at the moment."

"We'll get across the river sure enough, but the real question is where do we go after Frankfurt?"

"Both the O-S-S and M-I-6 are reporting increasing references that the S-S is thinking about tomorrow. The evidence is certainly not conclusive or irrefutable, but the information is troubling. They call the organization ODESSA. It's apparently some kind of escape, relocation, and re-identification organization for S-S men, especially the officers and hierarchy. But, it is the rumors of an S-S redoubt in the German and Austrian Alps that is the most worrisome to me. In those mountains, they could extend the war for years. We must end this war. Anything that might extend the war is simply not acceptable."

"You're going to turn the 12ᵗʰ Army Group southeast," Patton stated, more than asked.

"Yes. We can't take the risk that the intelligence is correct. I would rather head off such an initiative before it becomes reality than risk the potential of having a protracted fight in those mountains."

"Churchill will not be happy."

Eisenhower smiled. "That may be the understatement of the century, George. My orders are to win the war as soon as possible. The prime minister is obsessed with post-war Europe. For the record, I believe Prime Minister Churchill is precisely correct regarding Stalin's intentions in Eastern Europe, and between you and me, I think the president is too soft on Stalin and the Soviets. Regardless, our job is to win the war as quickly as possible. The politicians handle the politics. Whether the intelligence is correct or not, we cannot allow the Germans and especially the S-S to have that redoubt for continued resistance. The reality is the division of post-war Germany will likely thrust the Alpine Redoubt on us alone—not acceptable."

"Makes sense, Ike, but I think I can strike out to Berlin. Once we are through the Siegfried Line and across the Rhine, the Krauts will be on the run. We can beat Monty and especially the Russkies to checkmate, Ike, and if we get there quick enough, we might even capture that bastard corporal before he can off himself."

Eisenhower smiled and held Patton's eyes. "I'll keep that in mind, George, but let's focus on getting your Army across the Rhine."

"You've got it, Ike. We'll be ready to go in six weeks. We'll get this done in fine fashion."

"Of that I am confident, George. Now, I need to get along to Court and close out with Brad later this afternoon."

Patton walked the supreme commander to the door. A ¾-ton command car waited to take Eisenhower back to the airfield.

—

Saturday, 16.December.1944
Clervaux, Clervaux
Liberated Luxembourg
08:29 hours

A massive German artillery barrage began in the winter, near early morning darkness at 05:30 and lasted until 07:00. The 5ᵗʰ and 6ᵗʰ Armor Armies launched their attack out of the forest cover into the freezing mist and deep snow. Operation AUTUMN MIST began. The German counteroffensive soon involved nearly the full breadth of the 1st Army sector. The weight and fury of the initial German attack forced the thinly deployed scattered American units to carry out hasty fighting withdrawals. Numerous attempts to establish new defensive positions also swiftly failed under the onslaught.

Unbeknownst to the Americans in the days after the attack began, the German *150.Panzer Brigade* deployed as part of the initial assault force. *Waffen-SS Obersturmbannführer* Otto Johann Anton Skorzeny commanded the special German unit, the same man who commanded the Mussolini rescue mission the previous year, among other special missions. The unit had 20 captured Sherman tanks and 500 collected English-speaking Germans dressed in captured American uniforms and equipment. The mission of the 150th was to roam behind U.S. lines, spread confusion, and take the Meuse River bridges for the run to Antwerp. Skorzeny's actions were directed by the plan for *Unternehmen Greif* (Operation GRIEF).

The Germans intended to hit hard and move fast to break the Allied front lines and split the British and American army groups. The German *6. Panzerarmee* under the command of *SS-Oberstgruppenführer und Generaloberst der Waffen-SS* Josef 'Sepp' Dietrich hit hard and met stronger than expected resistance from the thin U.S. 1st Army units. Prisoners of war were considered an unnecessary distraction from their vital mission.

One of the 6th Armor Army's assault units was *Kampfgruppe Peiper*, led by *Waffen-SS-Obersturmbannführer* Joachim Peiper, who was responsible for many atrocities throughout the war, including what became known as the Malmédy Incident and the Wereth Eleven Massacre. The following day after the initial assault began, his troops killed hundreds of unarmed American prisoners of war rather than deal with guarding and caring for the captives—the Americans were summarily executed and left in the snow.

Peiper would stand trial with others at the Dachau military tribunal for the Malmédy Massacre. He was sentenced to death but avoided the hangman's noose when the U.S. military governor of the American Sector of Occupied Germany commuted his sentence. Peiper was eventually released from prison in December 1956 and was assassinated by a French anti-Nazi group on Bastille Day, 14.July.1976, at his home in Traves, France.

Saturday, 16.December.1944
Supreme Headquarters, Allied Expeditionary Force
Trianon Palace Hôtel
1 Boulevard de la Reine
Versailles, Yvelines, Île-de-France
Liberated France
10:45 hours

"Excuse me, General," said his *aide-de-camp*, Major Julius 'Juli' Calhoun, USA, from Macon, Georgia, who had been promoted in November last year. Eisenhower looked up from his reading. "General Bradley has arrived."

"Thanks, Juli. Please show him in as soon as he makes his way up here."

"Yes Sir."

Eisenhower finished reading the logistics report, made notes, and placed the document in his outbox. He closed the message folder and put things in their proper place before he stood. As he moved around the desk, Bradley entered.

"Good morning, Brad. Welcome to Versailles."

"Thanks, and good morning to you, Ike." He went directly to the large window overlooking the Versailles palace grounds. "Oh my, such opulence . . . and to think, some folks thought they were entitled to live like that," Brad said, as he swept his hand across the scene beyond the window.

"It is impressive, isn't it? We could probably spend weeks in that palace just to see the artwork in there. But, you didn't come all this way for the royal sights."

"No, I didn't."

Eisenhower gestured to the comfortable chairs arranged in a circle. They sat opposite each other.

"I'm dangerously short of infantrymen, all ranks up to first sergeant. We really must do something about replacement troops. Hodges's 1ˢᵗ Army is spread dreadfully thin. Spring will be here before we know it, and we need those replacements for the offensive."

"I sent an urgent to the chief and the War Department. They know our situation. I also asked the E-T-O staff to scrub the staging divisions of their replacement troops and send them forward as soon as possible."

"We need 'em quickly, Ike. By our count this morning before I departed, my Group alone is down twenty-three thousand plus. We will be hard-pressed for the spring offensive. Georgie is in the best shape of my three armies, but even he is short."

"I understand, Brad . . . truly. Unfortunately, the War Department has begun to close the tap on all specialties."

"Too soon, Ike, too soon. We have not won this thing yet. That intelligence about unaccounted-for German divisions is more than a little concerning."

"You are not alone, Brad. As always, we'll do the best we can with the resources we are given."

"Just very frustrating. We must . . ." Bradley stopped with a knock at the door.

A lieutenant colonel Eisenhower remembered was assigned to the SHAEF G-3 Operations Department, but he could not remember his name, opened the door, and partially stepped into the opening. "Excuse me, General, I was sent by General Bull." Bradley stared at the colonel, and Eisenhower nodded his head. "We're receiving reports from the 5th and 8th Corps of the 1st Army of major armor-infantry attacks. The best we know at the moment is the two penetrations are in each of their zones. Both Corps have reported what they believe to be fresh Tiger and Panther tanks."

"Fresh?" Eisenhower asked. "What do you mean by fresh?"

"They appear to be brand new tanks. They all have *Waffen-S-S* markings. The G-2 is trying to identify the units involved, but the unverified indications are the lead elements are from the *1st S-S Panzer Division* in the south and the *2nd S-S Panzer Division* in the northern salient."

"Is this the counteroffensive the intelligence fellas suggested was in the wind?" Eisenhower mused in almost a mutter.

"Depends on the magnitude," commented Bradley. "This could be just a strong probe."

"Seems odd . . . if the information proves correct, to use top-tier armor units for a probe."

"Agreed." Bradley looked at the colonel. "What is behind the lead elements?"

"We asked, but it's too early to tell, but the answer we did get was quote, Tigers and Panthers are coming out of the trees, unquote. The 90-minute artillery barrage before dawn suggests it's far more than a probe."

"Thank you, Colonel. Anything else?"

"No Sir. By your leave, Sir." Eisenhower nodded his head. The colonel closed the door. Ike stood, went to his desk, and pushed a specific button.

"Yes Sir," came Beetle's voice over the communications box.

"Beetle, Brad is here. Would you mind joining us, when you are able?"

"I'll be right there."

Less than a minute later, Beetle knocked and entered. "Mornin', Brad."

"Good morning to you, Beetle."

Eisenhower gestured for Smith to sit on one of the chairs between them. "Pink is developing reports of German armor-infantry attacks in the 1st Army's zone, 5th and 8th Corps sectors. They're not yet sure how big the two thrusts are."

"The German counteroffensive the O-S-S was predicting?"

"Could be, but based on what we know so far, it could be just a strong probe at this stage."

"What do you need me to do?"

"Stay on top of the G-3, make sure the G-2 is plugged in tight, and get the O-S-S and M-I-6 liaisons engaged quickly. If this is the attack the O-S-S has predicted, we'll need to seriously redeploy our forces. Alert Monty and Jake. We may need to shift forces to reinforce Hodges. Keep me posted as best you can."

"I'm on it." Smith left.

"I've got to get on the secure phone to Washington and London," Eisenhower stated.

"And, I'd better get back to my command pronto," added Bradley.

"Thanks, Brad. I'll keep the pressure up for your replacement troops. I suspect you're going to need more. Good luck, Brad. Give me your best assessment as soon as you get back to Verdun."

"You know I will. Thanks, Ike. We'll handle whatever started this morning."

"Go get 'em, Brad." Bradley and Eisenhower stood, shook hands, and then Bradley departed. Eisenhower went to his desk and sat. He took a deep breath and exhaled audibly. He lifted the secure telephone handset and told the duty Signal Corps sergeant his first of a half dozen secure telephone calls—General Marshall.

—

Monday, 18.December.1944
Eidgenössische Technische Hochschule (ETH) *Zürich*
No.71 Rämistraße
Zürich, Kanton Zürich
Schweizerische Eidgenossenschaft [Swiss Confederation]
17:35 hours

Swiss graduate physics student Otto Berman sat quietly in the back of the modest seminar room, listening intently to the day's various lectures. The Federal Institute of Technology of Zürich and the Department of Physics sponsored the one-day atomic physics conference. Head of the ETH physics Department Professor Paul Hermann Scherrer hosted the colloquium. Very much offended by German National Socialism, Scherrer had been the source of Allied intelligence through his relationship with OSS Bern Station Chief Allen Dulles. The professor knew there would be at least one OSS agent in the audience as well as German SD bodyguards for the conference's featured speaker.

Among the attendees and lecturers for the academic conference was none other than *Doktor* Werner Karl Heisenberg, PhD (Theoretical Physics). The

Allies believed Heisenberg was the chief scientist, comparable to Oppenheimer for the Manhattan Project, for the German nuclear fission development program. Beyond the half dozen SD 'bodyguard' minders with Heisenberg for the conference, he had one of his disciples and former students with him. *Doktor* Carl Friedrich *Freiherr* von Weizsäcker, PhD (Physics), would add his work on solar fusion processes to the forum.

What the professor did not know was Student Berman was actually OSS special agent Morris 'Moe' Berg. When Berg was recruited for the OSS after Pearl Harbor, he was playing for the Boston Red Sox as one of their catchers. Berg was conversant in ten languages, including German, Italian, and French. As a consequence of his language skills and keen intellect, the OSS trained him to have a working knowledge of atomic physics, including the essential critical factors of nuclear fission. With his expertise and training, Berg had been imbedded with various Alsos teams as they investigated Italian, German, and French nuclear research centers in liberated lands. Alsos was the codeword provided by General Groves for the collection, analyses, and exploitation of European nuclear research that might even remotely contribute to any German atomic weapons development. Alsos meant grove in Greek. Under Berg's suit jacket, he wore a shoulder holster that held a Walther PPK semi-automatic pistol with a threaded silencer attached. He also had a small case sown into the lining of his suit jacket that contained a capsule of potassium cyanide to prevent his interrogation by the Germans if he was captured.

He had nearly finished his work at the University of Pisa when the coded message from E Street eight days ago directed him to Zürich. The station chief confirmed the latest information and his mission.

Berg listened intently to the lectures all day in German. He took copious notes as much to help him document the conference as well as help coalesce the critical question of his mission. Was Germany close to an atomic explosive device?

Heisenberg's lecture at the end of the day dealt with S-Matrix Theory—an alternative to local quantum field theory as the basic principle of elementary particle physics. The lecture had absolutely nothing to do with fission. Yet, since it addressed elements of atomic-level physics, Berg could not relax. He knew enough to recognize they were tiptoeing at the edge of fission physics, and just a few words might shift the lecture into the area of immediate concern. Heisenberg kept his lecture at the elemental level with no detectable, even distant, hint at the necessary research to achieve a fissionable device.

The conference concluded. Professor Scherrer invited the attendees to his residence for a casual dinner party that night. Berg feigned attention to his notes so that he could watch the departure of the two German physicists. Nothing untoward or even sensitive appeared. The six minders followed their charges quietly.

Monday, 18.December.1944
No.84 Gloriastraße
Zürich, Kanton Zürich
Schweizerische Eidgenossenschaft [Swiss Confederation]
21:30 hours

Moe Berg tried his best to play the part of the meek, shy, introspective graduate student, Otto Berman, as much to protect his limited knowledge as to allow him to listen. Professor Scherrer hosted a modest but elegant dinner party for the conference attendees at his residence.

Berg moved around the room as a curious graduate student among practicing physicists like Scherrer, Heisenberg, and von Weizsäcker. To his amazement, Berg noted that none of the SD minders at the lecture were in attendance. Other ETH physics professors and graduate students were also present. The social conversation remained focused primarily on relationships, families, friends, and colleagues. He passed on the cocktails, wine, or any form of alcohol, knowing the critical decision was still ahead of him. Berg listened intently to the words exchanged among those present.

The dinner was an elegant and delightful meal unburdened by wartime rationing of common foodstuffs. Berg sat across from and two chairs down from Heisenberg, close enough to hear the German physicist's words clearly. Dinner table conversations remained light and airy—not one word of fission, atomic weapons, or even the war.

After dinner, professor Scherrer announced, "Shall we take our cognac in the library?"

Berg pushed back from the table and stood slowly. He smiled and nodded his head. He tried not to look directly at Heisenberg, who went to Scherrer. Moe saw them talking with his peripheral vision but could not hear a word. It appeared the German was excusing himself. Berg made his way to the coatroom. "Leaving Doctor Heisenberg?" Moe asked in his best High German.

"Yes. It's been a long day for me."

"I need to leave as well. Would you mind if I walk with you?"

"Of course not. It would be nice to have some company."

Both men donned their overcoats and hats. Heisenberg added a neck scarf and gloves. Berg had gloves but chose not to wear them just in case he needed a precise touch. He also left the top two buttons on his overcoat unfastened for easy access to his shoulder holster. Finally, they said their goodnights and departed. Berg let the German lead. They walked a dozen yards before Berg was the first to speak.

"I enjoyed your lecture, Doctor."

"It is a favorite topic of mine."

"But, you won the Nobel physics prize more than a decade ago for quantum mechanics, and scattering matrix theory seems to detract from quantum mechanics."

"Oh no, not in the slightest. You are a graduate student, as I recall. Correct?" Berg nodded his head. "You have much more to learn. For example, the matrix is simply a mathematical expression to predict elemental behavior." Heisenberg paused and then changed the subject. "What is your area of interest?"

Berg did not hesitate. "I am intrigued with Otto Hahn's fission experiments six years ago."

"In what way?" Heisenberg asked as they walked.

"The potential energy source is enormous. Such research might lead to virtually unbounded energy supply."

"In theory. The question of control becomes paramount. The potential is certainly present. Spontaneous, uncontrolled release of that energy potential is extraordinary. But we . . . ," Heisenberg stopped and turned to see why his walking companion was no longer beside him.

Berg had stopped, had swiftly and smoothly drawn his pistol, and aimed the weapon at Heisenberg's chest. His right thumb pressed lightly on the pistol's safety, but Berg had not yet disengaged the safety.

Heisenberg froze and did not take his gaze off the pistol aimed at his chest. Berg did not move either. The pistol's safety remained engaged. Heisenberg's focus shifted from the pistol to Berg's eyes rapidly several times. "You are not a graduate student, are you?"

"No, I'm not," Berg answered in his native English.

"American?"

"Irrelevant!"

"You are here to kill me?" Heisenberg asked in his native German.

"No, not precisely," answered Berg, shifting back to German. "My charge is to assess German atomic weapons development. You are the chief scientist and head of that development effort. I am authorized to terminate you, if I believe you and your colleagues are advancing atomic weapons development."

"And do you believe we are close to achieving a workable device?"

"If I did, you would already be dead, and most likely, I would be dead too."

"Yes, I understand. *Reichsführer* Himmler sent along watchers with me to ensure I did not threaten the state's position. I will confide in you that we were pursuing nuclear power and weapons development. I will also emphatically state that neither me nor even one of my scientific colleagues supported the development of a nuclear explosive. Most of us abhor National Socialism and what that ideology has done to our great country, but we are Germans. We love our country. For us to stop development by any means would have been a death sentence for each of us." Berg did not budge or twitch. His stern, focused expression did not change. "The attack on Norsk Hydro in 1943 and especially the destruction of the heavy water supply in February of this year ended our development effort. We have done virtually nothing since. The government has lost interest and is currently distracted by other programs."

"How far did you get?" Berg asked in German.

"We certainly validated the Hahn reaction finding, but we never achieved a sustained reaction. We were and still are a long way from a nuclear explosive. We know such power is theoretically possible, but none of us is convinced such devices are practically achievable."

Berg stared at Heisenberg but did not alter the aim point of his pistol. His thoughts churned away on the facts he had and considered the veracity of Heisenberg's words. The intelligence he had been presented during his training had not identified any requisite industrial concentration to produce a fission device. Heisenberg's words complemented the information he was aware of. The exigent decision was his and his alone. The fact that the German physicist acknowledged the early development and indirectly indicated that Heisenberg's statement was likely correct.

Berg returned his pistol to his shoulder holster. His stern expression did not change as he said, "Go in peace, Doctor." He started to turn and stopped when Heisenberg spoke.

"Wait! Please, who are you, and whom do you work for?"

Berg did not hesitate and reverted to English. "You have more than I should have disclosed. Unfortunately, I cannot answer your questions. Good night, Doctor." Berg turned and walked away confidently. They both would live to see another day.

———

Tuesday, 19.December.1944
Headquarters, 12th Army Group
Verdun, Meuse, Grand Est
Liberated France
08:20 hours

The nondescript, gloomy, school building, not far from the Meuse River, housed the main headquarters of General Omar Bradley's Twelfth Army Group. The thick, low, solid overcast near foggy conditions amplified the chill of the winter scene. This particular morning, a converted classroom with an array of small-scale maps that together covered the entire western front from Switzerland to the North Sea covered the walls. The latest Allied deployments and the known enemy unit locations were annotated on the acetate overlays on the maps.

Two days prior to the Winter Solstice, the dawn meeting brought two of Bradley's three army commanders to meet with the supreme commander. With the blackout curtains installed and still closed, and minimal interior lighting, reading the wall maps remained difficult. Generals Bradley, Patton, and Lieutenant General Jacob Loucks 'Jake' Devers, USA [USMA 1909], Commanding General, 6th Army Group, holding Bradley's right flank. Eisenhower was the last to enter, followed by Deputy Supreme Commander Air Chief Marshal Sir Arthur Tedder. General Hodges, Commanding General of the 1st Army, would normally attend such a meeting, but Eisenhower wanted him focused on the defense against the German advance.

Eisenhower began, "The present situation is to be regarded as one of opportunity for us and not of disaster. There will be only cheerful faces at this conference table."

"Hell," interjected Patton, "let's have the guts to let the pieces of shit go all the way to Paris. Then we'll really cut 'em off and chew 'em up."

Eisenhower scowled at Patton but chose not to react. He looked at the SHAEF G-2. "General Strong, the current intelligence situation report."

General Sir Kenneth Strong described the ground situation as of the prior midnight. Two main prongs of the German attack had penetrated the 1st Army lines by 20 miles so far. The German 6th Panzer Army was the northernmost in the V Corps sector, while the German 5th Panzer Army was on the outskirts of Bastogne in the VIII Corps sector. The 101st Airborne defended Bastogne with elements of the 9th Armor and 28th Infantry, while the 82nd Airborne fought against the northern salient near Spa.

"Thank you, General Strong. We're here to consider our counterattack and relief of the 101st. Tony McAuliffe knows the importance of the road junction at Bastogne. If he can hold it, the obstacle will slow the German advance substantially. Unfortunately, we have insufficient forces in the area to prevent the 101st from being surrounded."

"That bastard," snarled Patton in reference to the German commander, "has put his cock in a meat grinder, and I've got ahold of the handle!"

Everyone chuckled, including Eisenhower.

"OK, Georgie, I'll bite," Ike responded. "What can you do?"

"I can attack with three divisions in two days."

Muttered expressions of incredulity filled the room.

"Your confidence is noted, George," Bradley reacted. "This is a serious issue."

"I am serious, deadly serious. The 4th Armor has been resting and refitting. They are fully stocked and ready. The 26th I-D is in Metz, rested and ready. I'll pull the 80th I-D since they are the least engaged. We'll attack north from Metz—hard, fast, north through Arlon."

Eisenhower looked at Devers. "Can you shift two or three divisions north to back up the 3rd Army?"

"Not necessary," Patton jumped in and volunteered.

Eisenhower looked at and nodded to Patton, and then he looked back at Devers.

"We're dealing with the Colmar Pocket."

"At present, Colmar is not as important as Bastogne," Ike replied.

"Do you want us to withdraw?"

"No, Jake . . . just hold what you've got. Seal off Colmar. We need to deal with this German counterattack, and at present, Bastogne is the key."

"Lay siege?"

Eisenhower smiled. "For lack of a better term, yes."

"Very well. We'll find the divisions and move them north to cover the 3rd Army."

"OK, George, get your boys on the road as soon as possible. Brad, please inform McAuliffe that the cavalry is on the way. Don't fail us, George. This is too damn important."

"By your leave, Ike, I need to get back to Nancy and get this show on the road."

"Good luck, George," Ike said. "Bring home the bacon."

"We will."

Patton returned to his headquarters directly and immediately set in motion the charge, assembling the chosen combat divisions under Major General John Millikin, USA [USMA 1910], Commanding General III Corps, to relieve the garrison at Bastogne.

General George Patton stayed true to his word and estimate. At 16:50 on 26.December.1944, the lead elements of III Corps—Company D, 37th Tank Battalion, 4th Armored Division—fought through German defenses and reached Bastogne, ending the German siege. The link up with the 101st Airborne Division in Bastogne took place one week to the day after the commanding general of the 3rd Army made the commitment to the supreme commander and their colleagues.

On a personal note, the author's paternal uncle, a member of the 28th "Bloody Bucket" Infantry Division, remained engaged in combat on the shoulder of the southern salient throughout the Battle of the Bulge.

The German winter counteroffensive failed and was spent when Hitler authorized a fighting withdrawal on 7.January.1945. The frontlines before the attack had been restored by 25.January.1945. Hitler never again launched an offensive in the west on the scale of AUTUMN MIST. Prime Minister Churchill publicly stated, "This is undoubtedly the greatest American battle of the war and will, I believe, be regarded as an ever-famous American victory."

———

Thursday, 21.December.1944
Bainbridge Air Service, Inc.
Wichita Municipal Airport
Wichita, Sedgwick County, Kansas
United States of America
09:15 hours

"**M**ister Sales," Helen Burbidge said, interrupting Bobby's reading of the latest service report, "Mrs. Bainbridge is here to see you."

"Yes, by all means." Sales marked his place, stood, and walked around his desk just as Gertrude Bainbridge entered. "Good morning, Gerty. To what do I owe the pleasure."

"I received a telegram for you from Charlotte late yesterday afternoon."

"That's odd. Why didn't she just send it to me directly as she has done so many previous times?"

"She did not say. If I was to guess, I suspect she and Brian wanted me to be aware of the contents as a board member."

"Sounds serious."

"Depends upon your perspective, Bobby. Here, read for yourself." Gerty handed the yellow envelope to Sales.

Bobby gestured to the comfortable chairs. They both sat across from each other. He extracted the message and read it.

———

Western Union

Telegraph Company

TELEGRAM

DECEMBER 19 1944

```
TO BOBBY JOE SALES
CO GERTRUDE BAINBRIDGE
   BAINBRIDGE RANCH
   RURAL ROUTE 14
   WICHITA KANSAS USA
IT IS THE INTENTION AND EXPECTATION OF THE
OWNERS TO OPERATE BAS AS A COMMERCIAL AIRLINE
WITH OR WITHOUT PENDING CONTRACT NEGOTIATIONS
STOP PREPARE FOR TRANSITION TO PEACETIME
```

```
OPERATIONS STOP PUBLIC INFORMATION INDICATES US
WASP PILOTS AND AIRCREW MAY BE AVAILABLE STOP
PLEASE INVESTIGATE TO ENSURE ADEQUATE FLIGHT
AND MAINTENANCE PERSONNEL FOR FUTURE OPERATIONS
END
                    CHARLOTTE DRUMMOND
```

"You read it?"

"Yes."

"That's quite a statement," Bobby declared, holding up the telegram. "We've received no feedback from Major Warner or anyone else in the government."

"How do you view the contents of the telegram?" asked Gerty.

"Well, it's a fairly bold statement. We're a long way from the size of United, American, T-W-A, and the like."

"Is it not apparent they intend to transition B-A-S?"

"Yes, that is explicit. We've got a lot of work to do to make that transition. We've talked to a number of WASPs. I think we've got a good start on that element. I'll also say we've got a good operating model that should be scalable. Part of our task will be finding aircraft for the fleet. At the bottom line, it's reassuring to know Brian and Charlotte intend to operate an airline regardless of any O-S-S contract. I must also say, as I will to Brian and Charlotte, that if we receive a contract from the O-S-S, I suspect they may expect, if not demand, exclusive operations."

"Is that a problem?"

"No, absolutely not. I just want to manage expectations."

"One of us needs to acknowledge receipt," said Gerty.

"I'll take care of that. I'll give them a short summary of our status on each point and a sketch of my plan."

"We need to reassure our employees as well."

"Indeed. I'll see to that also. It's encouraging that they are thinking of the post-war future for B-A-S." Bobby paused for Gerty to see if she had anything else to say. "It's a bit early, but since you're in town, can I take you to lunch?"

"I've got some errands to run before heading back to the ranch, but lunch would be nice. What about noon at Gordon's Café downtown?"

"Good choice. I'll see you at Gordon's at noon."

Bobby escorted Gerty back to her automobile and saw her on her way. He returned to the office and dictated to Helen a reply to Charlotte's telegram. She would take care of sending it. Once satisfied with his response, Bobby returned to his service report until it was time to leave to meet Gerty as agreed.

Sunday, 31.December.1944
USAAF Station F-356
Saffron Walden, Essex, England
United Kingdom
07:15 hours

The 334FS had been forewarned and briefed for the day's mission in the early morning darkness. The weather guessers had forecast that the fog and low clouds that blanketed the entire Ardennes region for the last week would finally break into scattered clouds. Today would be the first day since the raging battle in the Ardennes began—the first day the aviators could join the fight.

The 334FS pilots knew what was happening in the Ardennes Forest region of the Belgium-German border and North Luxembourg. Today would be an all-out air offensive, striking heavily at everything associated with the extraordinary winter counteroffensive.

The mission plan called for the 334FS to escort a squadron of B-24 Liberator heavy bombers to the carpet bombing of a railroad junction near Jünkerath that the 8th Air Force G-2 indicated was also the likely headquarters of the I *SS Panzer* Corps. The target sat behind the Siegfried Line inside Germany, 22 miles east of the critical road and rail junctions of St. Vith, Belgium. They would keep their external fuel drop tanks on until they were empty or enemy fighters closed to engage. The potential for enemy fighters existed, but it was expected to be low since the *Luftwaffe* had contracted in an attempt to protect vital industrial and governmental sites. Once the bombers were safely on their way home, the 334FS would revert to a ground attack mission against advanced German armor forces just five miles from the Meuse River Bridge at Dinant, Belgium. They expected to have sufficient fuel for the day's operation. The central question was whether they would have enough ammunition.

The Eastern horizon began to appear as morning twilight lightened the sky when Brian nodded his head to Corn for throttle and take off. The section takeoffs progressed smoothly. The squadron formed up in a box of finger four flights. They climbed into the dawn and bright sun ahead of them. The rendezvous with the 785th Bombardment Squadron proved easy enough despite the morning sun in front of them. The mission plan called for the bombers to use a comparatively low altitude for better accuracy since anti-aircraft fire was expected to be light to non-existent in the highly mobile situation.

The squadron took their escort position—'A' Division in the forward corners; 'B' Division at the aft corners. The whole formation turned southeast over Antwerp, which would line up the bombers on the long axis of the rail yards at Jünkerath. The flight remained at Angels 15 for the long run to the target.

Damn, look at all these aircraft. Brian had not seen so many aircraft at different altitudes and on various routes all over the region of Southeast Belgium. Brian, like his brethren, continuously scanned the sky. None of them detected any German fighters, and no flak bursts interfered with the bombers. The bomb bay doors opened in unison, as if on command, and the sticks of bombs dropped near simultaneously. Brian scanned the sky around him a couple of more times as the bombs fell. Finally, the bombers began their right turn to the heading for home. The fighters adjusted to maintain their position around the bombers. For the first time since he had been flying bomber escort missions, Brian watched the string of explosions and shockwaves radiating out from each bomb explosion. Dust and black oil smoke soon billowed up, obscuring the subsequent bomb hits, but the shockwaves disturbing the smoke and dust marked each detonation. Toward the end of the strike, a bomb apparently impacted a railcar carrying ammunition. The massive domed shockwave flashed outward, dwarfing the specks of the 500-pound bombs. *Man oh man, that is impressive, and that was only one squadron. Looks like they were spot on the target.* They stayed with the bombers until they were past Brussels on the return leg. Other bomber squadrons were heading back to England on the left and right, above and below, while other bomber formations were headed into the target area. Brian saw Arnie's wings wobble like a wave to the lead bomber.

"Cobweb, we're complete. Secondary mission," Arnie broadcast and peeled off to the left and began to descend.

The squadron rejoined and reformed as briefed into a box formation of flights with each flight in a finger four. Brian's 'B' Division was abreast of and half mile to the right of Arnie's 'A' Division. They began to jettison their external fuel tanks. Brian switched his fuel selector to the main tank and jettisoned his tanks. They split the distance between Charleroi and Namur. They leveled off at 5,000 feet and shifted to a flights-in-trail formation. Arnie led them into a wide orbit around their assigned target area. Smoke and dust roughly delineated the front lines. The Dinant Bridge remained intact, but five miles was very close. They could not see signs, but they had been briefed that the British 6th Airborne Division was deployed on the west bank of the Meuse River. Brian only saw a couple of M4 Sherman tanks of the U.S. 2nd Armor Division and assumed the bulk of the division's tanks were hidden or camouflaged. The 9th Armor Division with the 28th 'Bloody Bucket' Infantry Division were working the south shoulder of the salient roughly 10 miles away. They could easily identify the line of German Tiger tanks on the road heading to Dinant. *They have to know we're here. No signs of anti-aircraft fire. Why aren't we talking to those guys on the ground?*

"Cobweb, enemy tanks on the road. Here we go." Arnie rolled his flight from the east with the sun to his back. The fighters fired at the rear of the heavy tanks. Impacts dotted a half dozen of the lead tanks. Some of the German tanks left the road, trying to find cover. *No detectable effect.* A handful of the lead German tanks pressed on. Green Flight followed with similar results.

"Cobweb. Cobweb Red, we're going to extend. We're going for the tracks of the lead tanks."

"Cobweb Red, go for it."

Brian continued on the orbit to the north and the broadside of the Tigers. The muzzle flashes indicated the Germans were firing their 88mm main battery guns. "I'll take the lead tank. Pick your targets. Go for the tracks," Brian radioed to his 'B' Division. Corn followed his leader into a dive. The other 'B' Division sections followed in sequence.

Trees and bushes intermittently blocked sight of the distinctively shaped tank but not enough to disrupt Brian's aim point. *I can't see the tracks, but I know where they are.* Brian squeezed the trigger. All six heavy machine guns erupted. The tracers chewed up the vegetation adjacent to the right side of the lead tank, and bright flashes were clearly seen on the tank's lower hull. The Tiger veered toward him into vegetation and stopped. Brian fired another burst at the turret before he climbed and rolled to the right to rejoin the orbit.

"Great shot, Hunter. Disabled the bastard. His right track is behind him on the road. Cobweb, let's go for the tracks."

Tracers scattered behind Brian as he climbed away. Corn was closing on his position. Brian returned to his position in the orbit and throttled back to help the join-up with his division. Brian hand signaled Corn and Hole to take up singles in trail to spread his eight aircraft. *According to the intel blokes, we can't penetrate the Tiger's hull or turret armor, but we can sure chew up the interlaced roadwheels and tracks. An immobilized Tiger is a better target than a maneuvering Tiger.* Brian scanned the skies as he waited his turn at the tanks. Several tanks appeared to be disabled. Crews had dismounted to assess the damage and begin repairs as best they could. Those exposed enemy soldiers were now targets. They also tried to hit tanks that had chosen to hide among the trees. The vegetation diminished the effectiveness of their ammunition. *But, even if we can't penetrate the hull armor, our 50-caliber impacts will definitely rattle their cage.*

Arnie shifted their attack heading several times as they went after the troops they could see. On several pullouts, Brian could see American soldiers on the ground, on trucks, and on tanks cheering and waving their hands. On the last climb away from his attack, when he saw the cheers, Brian felt compelled to add a victory roll as he climbed away from the attack ground.

Brian leveled off in the orbit and throttled back slightly to hold his position. He scanned the sky, looking for bad guys. None.

"Jordy Winchester," Adler called his out of ammunition state.

"Swede Winchester."

"Cobweb, we're bingo." Clark rolled out of their orbit, set course for home, and climbed away from the battleground.

Brian rolled across the orbit with an intercept heading and pushed his throttle forward, not quite to full power. He looked over his shoulder. The rest of the division followed his lead. Arnie leveled out at cruise power and Angels 15 for the transit home. Other squadrons of bombers and fighters of all types, both American and British, were easily seen en route, presumably to the Ardennes region. The 335FS was preparing to takeoff as the 334FS landed. The 336FS was already in the air.

Tomlinson was standing next to Brian on the left wing root before he moved the mixture lever to cut-off. He opened the canopy and unfastened the left side of his oxygen mask. "No holes. Just fuel and ammo. We need a quick turn. We're probably going back out as soon as the birds are ready."

"You got it, Major."

Arnie was sitting on the edge of the table in the bullpen. He looked at Hunter as he stepped into the operations building. "We're going back up as soon as the birds are turned."

"That's what I told Tomlinson."

"Great move on those Tigers, going for the tracks."

"Thanks. At least those beasts are immobile for a while, but we've got to get through that armor to take them out. We need the rockets."

"Can't do that today, but you've got a point. We've at least slowed them down and kept them away from the Dinant Bridge. The cannon cockers might be able to finish them off. Group is workin' with 8th Air Force on whether or where we go next."

"There has to be a way for us to get through the damn armor on that beast. How thick is the top armor?"

"Our intel guys should know. I don't."

"We might be able to get through with a more vertical attack."

"Worth a try."

"Not much of a lead required with tanks. No air cover and no anti-aircraft fire to contend with them makes them easier targets, even if we can't kill them with the ammo types we have."

One of the colored telephones on Sergeant Ellison's desk rang. He lifted the red handset. "Three-thirty-fourth." "Yes Sir." Juli held the handset out toward Arnie. "Group C-O, Sir." Arnie gestured to his office. Ellison listened and then returned the handset to the cradle once he heard the skipper answer. The green phone rang. "Ops," said Ellison. "Yeah, thanks." He hung up the handset. "Maintenance reports all of the aircraft are ready," Juli said softly to Brian.

Hunter nodded his head and then walked to the intelligence shack. He did not recognize several of the current debriefers, but Staff Sergeant Bradford appeared to be finishing up with Stove. Brian waited for Bradford to finish his notes. Finally, the sergeant stood and came to Brian. "Your turn, Major?"

"I can do it, but I have a question first."

"Shoot."

"What is the armor thickness on a Tiger tank?" Brian asked.

"The hull is just under four inches. The top and bottom are an inch thick."

"So, we're not likely to get through with our 50-cal ball ammo."

"No, not likely. Plus, you must deal with the obliquity angle, which makes any armor plate thicker because you are trying to penetrate at an angle." Brian nodded his head as he considered the information. "Let's get your debriefing done."

"The skipper's probably getting another mission briefing, so I don't know how much time we've got."

"We'll get as much as we can," Bradford said and returned to his debriefing room. Brian sat across the small desk.

Brian recounted the details of his participation in the morning mission. He got through the initial bombing escort mission and into the ground attack portion when Sweet knocked and opened the door.

"Skipper's got another mission for us."

Brian nodded in acknowledgment, and then he nodded to Bradford, who gave him a shoo gesture. Brian and Sweet were the last two to join the rest of the squadron.

"We're going back up as soon as I can give you the intel and objective," Arnie Clark began. "We're going directly to Bastogne."

"Yeah!" came several spontaneous exclamations.

"I understand and appreciate the sentiment, gentlemen," Arnie continued, "but we need to get back in the air, so please hold your enthusiasms for the Germans. Intel from the front reports placed the *1st Waffen-S-S Panzer Division* northeast of the Bastogne town center. This unit has history, but that is for another time. The division is giving the 101st a helluva time. Our mission is to stop them."

"With bullets?" protested Sweet, the only remaining RAF No.71 Squadron pilot.

"It's what we've got. No rockets this afternoon."

"Intel says the hull armor of a Tiger is four inches thick," Hunter interjected. "The top and bottom armor are only one inch."

"We can't get through an inch of steel plate armor with ball ammo," Sweet objected.

"Enough guys," Arnie commanded. "We have what we have. You did a pretty good job on the tracks. Let's immobilize the bastards. Then, the cannon-cockers and bazookas can finish 'em off. Hunter is going to try a top shot. We can all look for an open hatch. Some high-energy 50-cal rounds bouncing around the interior might well set off some ordnance. So, if you see any German tanks with open hatches, aim true, and douse the suckers. If they're buttoned up, go for the tracks like we did this morning." Arnie finished the administrative elements of the briefing, including communications, external fuel tanks, and control measures. "Let's mount up."

The 334FS took to the air in the early afternoon. Even with best of mission plans, they would be returning to base well after twilight. They stayed comparatively low at Angels Five. They would head straight for Bastogne and hold their external fuel tanks until they descended for their attack.

The smoke of fires rising from villages, roads, and forest trees marked the frontlines. "Cobweb, artillery has their turn first. We'll hold south at this altitude. Throttle back to max endurance."

"Wilco, Cobweb," Hunter broadcast. They entered a long racetrack holding pattern and throttled back to 22 inches MAP for maximum endurance or loitering time. Corn swung back and forth from side to side in a perfect combat spread position as they made their turns. With the squadron stable in holding in trail by sections, Brian kept his head and eyes moving continuously. *I don't want to be the first to face German fighters in this state.* Brian stole glances at their target area and marveled at the effects of medium and heavy artillery. The artillery guys scored at least two direct hits as secondary explosions undoubtedly marked the elimination of another couple of German tanks.

"Cobweb, our turn. We're cleared hot." Arnie and Jordy rolled out of the holding pattern and began their attack dive to their assigned target area.

"Wilco," radioed Hunter for his division.

Swede led his section and the line of sections out of the holding pattern and into a wide orbit around their target area. When they saw Arnie and Jordy pull off and climb into their position in the evolving orbit. Swede and his wingman, Second Lieutenant Gregory Bradford 'Jerk' Harrison, USAAF, from Butte, Montana, made their attack runs. As Hunter waited for his turn, he spent more time trying to locate the tank he planned to attack. Tracers rose from the ground, indicating an effort by the German armor force to defend themselves from their tormentors. Brian mixed his air scans for enemy fighters with the ground scans for a worthy target as he kept track of the sections ahead of him. *I think I've got one . . . a Tiger in hull defilade with tree branches for camouflage.* When Rocket and Stove made their runs, Hunter signaled Corn for their attack. He set up for a medium-angle diving attack. *He's buttoned up.* Hunter fired a good burst and pulled off. As he rolled left and pulled up into a climbing turn, he witnessed the multiple impact flashes on the hull and turret. *No secondary effects.* Hunter used his intermittent ground scans to search for his next target.

The forest below them made observation of targets and the bullet impacts of his brethren far more difficult, if not impossible, with one exception. It looked like Sweet's bullets managed to get inside a Panther tank that had erupted in a spectacular blooming explosion of white, orange, red, black, and grey billowing plumes. *I look forward to hearing the story of that one.* Brian scanned the sky. *No fighters . . . yet.*

Brian periodically checked on Corn. *Perfect.* As he approached his next rotated perch position, he could not find much. *I wonder what the others were shooting at. The burning hulk is obvious, but no target. The tank I hit hasn't moved. I guess I'll have another go at that Tiger again.* Movement caught his attention just as he began his roll into his attack dive. A Tiger lurched out of the trees onto the road. The tank's commander was sitting high in the open hatch. Hunter rolled hard back to the right, nearly inverted into a far steeper dive, and retarded his throttle to near idle. As he settled his gunsight pipper on his new target, he thought, *Damn, he doesn't see, hear, or sense I'm coming.* Hunter stabilized his pipper on the man in the open turret hatch and squeezed the trigger for a longer than usual burst. Brian pulled back on his stick as hard as he dared, straining against the g-force on his body. When the nose rose above the horizon, he pushed the throttle forward through the emergency gate wire to demand war emergency power. His aircraft was dangerously close to the trees, but his Vertical Speed Indicator needle went positive. Brian felt the shockwave concussion shake his fighter and heard the sharp ringing of fragments against the underside of his aircraft.

What Hunter could not see as he fought to recover from his steep dive was his converging bullet streams shredded the man in the hatch to a red vapor. Sufficient rounds ricocheted through the interior metal walls and equipment. Several 50-caliber rounds penetrated the stored 88mm rounds staged for rapid loading. The resulting explosion killed the remainder of the tank's crew instantly and blew the entire turret off the hull.

Once back in their orbit, Brian quickly looked for Corn. He signaled for a belly check. Corn disappeared underneath Brian's fighter. When he returned to his wing position, Corn signaled. *Hydraulic leak. Slight coolant leak. No oil leakage. I need to bingo. I'll have no landing gear or flaps.* "Cobweb, Cobweb Red, bingo, hydraulic leak, may have more."

"Roger, Cobweb Red. Good luck. Nice shooting."

"Sweet, you've got Baker. Corn, we're bingo."

"Roger," Sweet replied.

Brian set a course northwest on a direct heading back to Debden. He also climbed to Angels Ten to give himself a little more room if he needed to jump. Corn remained off his left wing to keep the setting sun behind him and a little lower than usual to keep an eye on the underside of Hunter's wounded fighter. Transiting over friendly territory made the return to base easier. Brian kept a close watch on the aircraft's fluid pressures and temperatures. Hydraulic pressure dropped to zero over the Belgian coast, but the oil and coolant temperatures and pressures remained normal. Brian signaled to Corn to switch to Button Able—their inter-aircraft frequency. "How's it look?"

"Don't see any more red fluid."

"'Cuz I'm out. Pressure's zero, no bounce. I'm going to have to do an emergency extension, and I'll need you to confirm I'm down 'n locked."

"No problem, Hunter. Don't see any oil or coolant."

"Thank goodness for small favors. My temps and pressures remain steady and normal. OK. Stay with me to the flair but go around to land singly. Switch Button Charlie, so we can get this show started."

Brian heard "Two," which was Corn checking in on frequency. "Garter, Cobweb Baker, at 25 miles at Angels Ten, flight of two, squawking Two."

"Cobweb Baker, Garter, we have you. Cleared to enter and descend."

"Roger, Garter. I've lost hydraulics. Requesting straight into Carmen."

With clearance, Hunter began a gradual descent and reached pattern altitude for Debden before they made the coast. He signaled Corn that he was slowing below the landing gear airspeed limit of 170 MPH. Throttling back below 17 inches MAP, the landing gear unsafe horn sounded. He advanced the throttle to hold his altitude and 150 MPH. He lowered the landing gear handle. *Nothing.* Brian retarded his throttle to confirm the warning horn and then returned the throttle to power for level flight. He pulled the Landing Gear Fairing Door Emergency Release Handle just above the Hydraulic Pressure Gauge. The Gear Unsafe red light illuminated with the audible clunk of the uplocks releasing. Brian pushed the rudder pedal to the right, yawing the aircraft. That might have one gear locked. He pushed the left pedal, heard another clunk, and illuminated the green Gear Safe light. Brian depressed both brake pedals. *Feels like normal pressure, so I should have brakes.* The wheel brakes were separate independent systems.

"Garter, Cobweb Baker, going off frequency for a moment."

"Cleared."

Brian held a single finger for Corn to switch to Button Able. "Check my gear."

A few seconds later, Corn came back. "They look down and locked, Hunter."

"Thanks. I've got a Safe light. Let's switch back to Charlie."

"Two."

"Garter, Cobweb Baker, looks like I've got my gear down and locked."

"Roger, Baker, switch to Carmen."

"Thanks, Garter, switching."

"Carmen, Cobweb Baker, with two at one point five, five miles out for straight into Two-Eight. Runway in sight with lights. I've got no hydraulics. Gear appears to be down and locked, green light, but I'd like the crash trucks just in case."

"Roger, Baker, rolling the crash trucks. Wind is two-two-zero at five. You're cleared straight into Runway Two-Eight."

"Baker cleared to land."

With no flaps, Brian would be landing faster than normal. He slowed early, opened the canopy just in case, and checked on Corn. His wingman was in a tight position, off his right wing with his gear and flaps down. He began his flare early to touch down on the approach numbers. Out of his peripheral vision, Brian saw Corn pass him swiftly at full power, and his gear and flaps coming up. Hunter touched down softly, smoothly, without a bounce, just past the approach numbers. He gently applied brake pressure slowing his fighter. With the aircraft at taxi speed well before the turnoff, Brian raised his right hand with his thumb up to signal that everything was good. The crash trucks stayed with him to the squadron parking area. Brian stopped in his parking spot and set the parking brake.

Larson was on the wing as Brian shutdown. "What happened?" Tomlinson asked.

"Took some shrapnel. Lost hydraulics. Everything else seemed to be OK." With the aircraft secured, Brian got out of the cockpit and remained on the wing to watch Corn land normally in the diminishing light. *The squadron's going to land in the dark.*

Tomlinson used a flashlight for both of them to inspect the damage. The stain of the lost hydraulic fluid was quite apparent. The aircraft had more damage than he expected.

Damn, I'm lucky one of those holes didn't puncture a wing tank. Better lucky than good.

"We'll give her a thorough look-see this evening," Larson announced. "Can't make any promises until we open her up."

Brian nodded and went to the other side of his aircraft as Corn taxied into his spot, shutdown, and joined Hunter behind his left wing.

"Everything OK," Karl Eiger asked.

"Yeah, landing normal . . . just being safe."

"Good. Any word on the squadron?"

"Nope, not yet."

"They're going to be landing in the dark."

"Yep, but at least we are safe enough to turn the runway lights on."

The two pilots went inside to warm up by the coal stove heater. Ellison informed them the squadron had not reported in yet. When Hunter and Corn took the edge of their chill, they went to the Intel Shack, completed their mission debriefings, and returned to the Ops Building.

Brian recounted what had happened during his last attack. Karl embellished the story with a dramatic description of the Tiger tank exploding. As they stood by the stove, Eiger asked Brian about the long days during the great air battle. The Spitfire flew more often but on shorter missions than the Mustang had done today, but the fatigue was just as numbing.

It was 70 minutes after evening twilight when one of Ellison's desk phones rang. Juli lifted the blue handset. "Three Thirty-fourth." "Yes Sir. Thank you, Sir." Juli hung up. "Squadron's inbound," Ellison announced.

Brian went outside into the cold air to watch the squadron land. He could hear the Packard engines humming at low power. Karl joined him. The runway lights were switched on to full intensity. The first landing light shone brightly in the darkness on short final. The sequence repeated itself 14 times without a single hiccup. No losses.

As Arnie approached the building, he said, "Glad you made it back. How bad was it?"

"Tomlinson thinks they might be able to repair the bird tonight. Shrapnel pocked the underside and took out my hydraulics. Everything else was good."

"That was a helluva shot, Hunter. Well done! Just too close."

Arnie immediately jumped on the telephone to Group. As the other pilots made their way back to the Ops Building, they offered an array of jabs and praise. They hung up their flight gear and gathered around the heater. Brian took his usual seat with Karl next to him.

"OK, guys, listen up," Arnie said as he hung up the blue handset. "We're going back to the Ardennes tomorrow. Same timing, same mission." No one uttered even a muffled grumble. They were all tired, but somehow, they all knew how important their work was to the ground-pounders. "Let's get our debriefings done." The Skipper looked at Ellison. "Call the Mess to hold dinner service for the guys."

"Yes Sir." Juli picked up the black handset and dialed.

Although Brian and Karl were complete, they remained until everyone was finished. As pilots trickled in from their debriefings, several volunteered their observations of Hunter's attack on the Tiger and the resultant destruction. Since Hunter and Corn departed the target area early, they also told them the squadron continued their attacks on the *Waffen-SS* armor that was trying to withdraw to the east. They disabled several tanks but achieved no more explosions. The squadron continued into twilight. Several had already reported they were out of ammunition, but Arnie pressed the attack until they had insufficient light to find targets.

They were all tired when they completed their debriefings, were driven to the Mess, and ate a simple dinner. Even though pilots from one of the other squadrons were hootin' it up in the bar, none of the 334FS pilots joined them, opting for bed and sleep.

———

Sunday, 31.December.1944
Standing Oak Farm
Winchester, Hampshire, England
United Kingdom
19:30 hours

New Year's Eve! They were all in the fifth long year of the world war, but somehow, to the ladies of Standing Oak Farm, the final days of the dreadful war were approaching. With Mabel and Edith's encouragement, Charlotte felt the urge to celebrate the new year of peace. Of course, she wished Brian could be with them, but he still had an important job to do.

The BBC reported that the Allies, with the help of their dominant air forces, had stopped the German advance in the Battle of the Bulge in Eastern Belgium. The Allies had begun pushing the Germans back into a fighting retreat. The ladies of Standing Oak Farm also heard the BBC reports that the American Army Air Forces had begun strategic bombing of Japan, which made the distant war in the Pacific seem closer to a conclusion as well. From those dark, foreboding days of 1940, the war situation just inherently seemed brighter. The end did indeed feel near.

The V1 and V2 attacks had diminished to a mere trickle of what they had been in the summer and fall, which was a blessing in itself. Charlotte's recovery was progressing nicely. Her arm cast had finally been removed, and the rehabilitation of her arm, wrist, and fingers continued to advance. People around Charlotte knew she was not fully recovered, but to others, the farm's mistress appeared to be in fine health and excellent shape.

Thanks to her relationship with Countess Selborne, Charlotte arranged for a special barter—a dozen wheels of their premium aged cheddar cheese for a half dozen bottles of Piper-Heidsieck 1938 Champagne. She had to rearrange the refrigerator to make room for the bottles. There was not much room left, but she managed to make everything fit.

The afternoon chores had gone smoothly, as they usually did. Mary had arrived with Malcolm and Charlotte two days before Christmas. Mary had announced that her daughter, Charlotte Mary Spencer, would be called 'CM' henceforth to avoid confusion with the farm's mistress. She also brought Grace, and this time, Harriett Peterman, their cook, who had jumped into her passion for the enjoyment of the farm's employees. The evening's meal was unusually sumptuous even for Harriett with wartime rationing. The entire crew and their families close by had been invited to attend the celebration at the main house.

Seven months pregnant Rosemary arrived after dinner to spend a couple of days. The Selborne's had declined Charlotte's invitation because of their own celebration planned at Temple Manor.

Mary, Rosemary, and Charlotte took advantage of the respite before the festivities began. They sat by the crackling fire. "How often do you hear from him?" Mary asked Charlotte.

"I used to hear from him two or three times a week. Things went totally silent in the months preceding the invasion. Then, I'd hear from him perhaps every other week until this thing in Belgium began. I've not heard since the 10th. I think they must've cut communications again."

"This thing cannot go on much longer," Mary said.

"I pray so every day."

"What do you think Brian is going to do once the war is won?" asked Mary.

Charlotte giggled softly. "I've asked that question every time I've seen him since the invasion. He just wants to fly."

"He's been flying in combat for five years," protested Mary. "I've not heard of anyone else, at least in the R-A-F, and I assume in the American air force. Pretty soon, there will be no fighting."

"He's not keen on getting shot at, Mary."

"Thank goodness," Rosemary interjected. The three ladies laughed.

"We own an airline."

"Wouldn't that mean moving to America?" Mary asked.

"Well, to be honest, that's another common query with Brian. We've not decided. He's uncertain whether he would be able to remain in the Army. He obtained a special waiver that allowed him to remain in the cockpit, but he knows that cannot last indefinitely. What about John?" Charlotte asked, seeking to divert attention.

"I'm afraid he's an R-A-F man to the end, however long that may be. He doesn't get to fly so much anymore."

"Why so?" Rosemary asked.

"He was promoted to air marshal and assigned to the Mediterranean Theater air staff."

"I hadn't heard that," said Rosemary.

"Me either," Charlotte added.

"No one asked," Mary responded. They all laughed again.

Mabel was the first to join them.

"Before we leave the topic," Mary said, "excuse us, Mabel. What is the news of Jonathan?"

"He is still the base commander of R-A-F North Weald," answered Rosemary."

"Linda was here ten days ago with Julia," added Charlotte. "She sees more of her husband in the present assignment than she did when he was commanding a fighter squadron. Do you think Jonathan will stay in the Air Force?"

"He says he's undecided. He also says he'll wait to see how the post-war Air Force plays out."

"You know, I think that perspective is true for all of life. We are approaching the end of the most traumatic, horrific period in human history," Mary stated. "We're all going to have to adjust to a new world once this tragedy passes."

"Oh so true. I'm going to be a mother in a month or two. I'm bringing a child into this mad world."

"Your choice, Rose," Charlotte admonished.

Rosemary smiled. "Yes, it was . . . and I'm extraordinarily grateful, but this war is not over. I worry so much . . . I've done this. We've done this. This is not the world I want for my child."

"This world took my son," Charlotte snarled as she lowered her head into her hands on her knees.

Rosemary jumped to embrace Charlotte, followed by Mary. Rosemary whispered to Charlotte, "I'm so sorry, Sharley." Hearing Todd's affectation of Charlotte's name made them both giggle and break the sour mood. Rosemary kissed Charlotte's forehead. "We love you, Sharley."

The arrival of Edith, Grace, and Harriett instantly lifted Charlotte from the edge of the abyss. June was with her family for a separate celebration. Charlotte felt her duty as mistress of the house. Charlotte waved her hand dismissively as if to signal that she was all right now. Her two friends knew Charlotte's gesture was not authentic, but they were unwilling to challenge her.

The telephone bell ringing startled Charlotte. It was half past ten on the wall clock. She could not recall ever being called so late. Mary was the closest to the telephone, so she answered it. Charlotte could not hear the few words Mary spoke, but she certainly recognized the gesture as Mary looked directly at Charlotte and held out the handset to her.

"This is Charlotte Drummond."

"Happy New Year, my darling."

Tears spontaneously gushed from her eyes and descended her cheeks. "Oh my goodness, Brian, I miss you so much. Are you OK?' Has anything happened?"

"Easy now, my sweet. Everything is fine. We had a very long day and didn't finish until after dark. I also had to wait my turn for the telephones. It seems to be that time of year," Brian said with a slight chuckle.

"It's very late for you."

"Yes, it is, and I need to get off to bed. We've got another early morning tomorrow and probably another long day."

"Well, then, get off the phone and go to bed."

"Sounds like you have a crowd there."

"Yes, we do. Mary, Rose, and Linda with the little ones, who are in bed now, along with most of the farm's crew, are here to celebrate the last New Year of the war."

"I sure hope so."

"I love you, Brian. Now, get along to bed. You need to be fresh and ready for work tomorrow morning."

"I love you so very much, Charlotte."

"As I love you, Brian. Now, get off the phone." She heard an audible kiss that she returned, and then she heard the handset hang up and the connection break.

The whole gathering cheered to acknowledge Charlotte's conversation with her husband as if it was a bright sign of a better future. She smiled and felt the smile.

Charlotte greeted each of the attendees and their families, those that were able to come. Several she had not previously met. Only two were men who were beyond conscription age. To Charlotte's surprise and benefit, the evening was a joyous event that raised her spirits. Grace and Edith took turns going upstairs to check on Todd, who slept soundly despite the laughter and commotion below his bedroom. Not everyone wanted champagne, but those who did enjoy the exceptional sparkling wine.

00:00 hours

"Happy New Year," they all shouted in unison. They hugged and kissed in celebration. Mabel took them into the singing of *Auld Lang Syne*.

They collectively washed up the glasses and the few plates they used before they retired for the night. It was a new year, and they all hoped it would be a far better year.

——

About the Author

Cap Parlier

—

Cap and his wife, Jeanne, live peacefully in the warmth and safety of Arizona—the Grand Canyon state. Their four children have established their families and are raising their children—our grandchildren. Their grandchildren are growing and maturing nice with two college graduates so far and another in her senior year.

Cap is a proud *alumnus* of the U.S. Naval Academy [USNA 1970], an equally proud retired Marine aviator, Vietnam veteran, and experimental test pilot. He finally retired from the corporate world to devote his time to his passion for writing and telling a good story. Cap uses his love of history to color his novels. He has numerous other projects completed and, in the works, including screenplays, historical novels as well as atypical novels at various stages of the creation process.

—

Interested readers may wish to visit Cap's website at <http://www.parlier.com> for his essays and other items or subscribe to his weekly Blog: "*Update from the Sunland*." Cap can be reached at: cap@SaintGaudensPress.com.

—

www.ingramcontent.com/pod-product-compliance
Lightning Source LLC
Chambersburg PA
CBHW020252120726
47904CB00001B/177